ILLUMINAE

THE ILLUMINAE FILES_01

AMIE KAUFMAN &
JAY KRISTOFF

ROCK THE BOAT

A Rock the Boat Book

First published in the UK by Rock the Boat,
an imprint of Oneworld Publications, 2015
Fifth reprint, 2019

ISBN 978-1-78074-837-5
ISBN 978-1-78074-838-2 (ebook)

Book design by Heather Kelly and Jay Kristoff
Printed and bound in Denmark by Norhaven

Oneworld Publications
10 Bloomsbury Street
London WC1B 3SR
England

Stay up to date with the latest books,
special offers, and exclusive content from
Rock the Boat with our newsletter

Sign up on our website
www.rocktheboat.london

FOR NIC,
WHO ALWAYS TELLS THE BEST STORIES
AND STARTED THIS ONE

MEMORANDUM FOR: Executive Director Frobisher

FROM: Ghost ID (#6755-4181-2584-1597-987-610-377-ERROR-ERROR-ERROR . . .)

INCEPT: 01/29/76

SUBJECT: *Alexander* dossier

So here's the file that almost killed me, Director.

I won't bore you with the tally of databases plundered, light-years jumped, or cute, sniffling orphans created in its compilation—our fee already reflects Level Of Difficulty. But this dirt is out there, if you know where to look. Seems your cleanup crews weren't quite as thorough as you'd like, and your little corporate war isn't quite as secret as you'd hoped.

You'll find all intel we could unearth concerning the Kerenza disaster compiled here in hard copy. Where possible, scans of original documentation are included. Fun Times commence with the destruction of the Kerenza colony (one year ago today) and proceed chronologically through events on battlecarrier *Alexander* and science vessel *Hypatia* as best as we can reconstruct them.

All visual and audio data are included in original form, along with written transcripts. *All typographical and graphical anomalies are present in the original files.* Commentary from my team is marked by paper clip icons. Some written materials were censored by the UTA and had to be reconstructed by our commtechs, though profanity remains censored as per your instruction. Sure, the story kicks off with the deaths of thousands of people, but god forbid there be cussing in it, right?

The Illuminae Group

> *In a time of universal deceit, telling the truth is a revolutionary act.* —Orwell

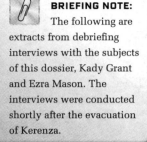

EXANDER-78V

MINISTRY OF THE INTERIOR
UNITED TERRAN NAVY
ALEXANDER FLEET

Incept: 01/30/75

Interviewer: Tell me about yesterday.

Kady Grant: I was in class when it started. This is going to sound stupid, but I broke up with my boyfriend that morning, and he was right there on the other side of the room. I'm staring out the window and coming up with all the things I should say to the jerk, when these ships fly right overhead and all the windows start shaking.

Interviewer: Did you know something was up?

Kady Grant: No. You don't jump straight to an invasion. The Kerenza settlement wasn't exactly *legal*, but we still got traffic around the mine and refinery. I figured it was an ore carrier coming in too low and went back to plotting my idiot ex's downfall.

Interviewer: When did you become aware of the invasion?

Kady Grant: That would be when all the sirens started screaming. Some bright spark who's probably dead now sounded the spaceport alarms. The *Defiant*—that was our WUC protection ship—had transmitted an alert to let us know unfriendly people with big guns had arrived, and—

Interviewer: How do you know the *Defiant* transmitted a warning?

Kady Grant: I'm good with computers. I wanted to know what was going on at the port, so I took a look.

Interviewer: You evacuated at that stage?

Kady Grant: You make it sound way more organized than it was.

Interviewer: How was it?

Kady Grant: All kittens and rainbows. Apart from the screaming and explosions.

Interviewer: How did you make it out?

Kady Grant: I'm a lateral thinker.

Interviewer: Meaning you used your comput—

Kady Grant: Meaning I broke open a window.

Interviewer: Oh.

Kady Grant: I had a truck in the parking lot. I borrowed my mom's because I didn't want to have to take the tube home with *him*. Having the truck there saved my life. I saw one of my teachers in the lot, and this chunk of metal came screaming in from the sky, and . . .

Interviewer: Miss Grant?

Kady Grant: I had this moment when I thought I'd left the keys in my desk, and I pulled apart my bag and threw stuff everywhere—I guess I knew I wouldn't need any of it again, isn't that weird? But I found the keys at the bottom and jumped in, and just as I start the engine, I look across and he's standing right there, staring at me. I swear—

Interviewer: Hold on, the survivor list is refreshing. What was the name you were after?

Kady Grant: Ezra Mason.

Interviewer: We have him. He's on the *Alexander.*

Kady Grant: [Inaudible.]

Interviewer: Are you okay to continue, Mr. Mason?

Ezra Mason: I'm all right. My shoulder hurts.

Interviewer: I'll have an orderly bring you some more meds. You were saying about your escape from the school?

Ezra Mason: Never seen anything like it. Just this crush of people and screaming. Teachers. Students. I mean, we *knew* each other. Colony that isolated, everyone pretty much knows everyone. But it was like they all just lost it. I remember getting pushed along in the mob and wondering why the hallway was soft under my boots. And then I realized what I was walking on.

Interviewer: So how did you get out?

Ezra Mason: I'm six-five. Played point defense on the school geeball team. One time I hit this receiver so hard they had to ID him with DNA.

Interviewer: Where did you go after the first missile strike?

Ezra Mason: Everyone was headed for the tube station, but I figured a tin can in an underground ice tunnel was the last place you'd want to be with bombs going off. So—

Interviewer: Wait, you people had a subway system? I thought this settlement was illegal?

Ezra Mason: Chum, the Kerenza mine operated undetected for twenty years. Whole families lived there. You know how far from the Core we are, right?

Interviewer: Maybe further than you might think . . .

Ezra Mason: . . . What the hell's that supposed to mean?

Interviewer: Nothing. I'm sorry.

Interviewer: You were saying about the subway?

Ezra Mason: Yeah . . . Right. Basically I didn't wanna risk it down there, so I lit out through the fire escape. Doubled back into the parking lot. Which might not have been the best plan, since I didn't have wheels. And I'm looking around, and the sky is raining fire and I'm still freezing because the windchill on Kerenza could hit forty below on a bad day. And there she was.

Interviewer: Who?

Ezra Mason: My ex-girlfriend. Who'd dumped me maybe three hours before. So that was . . . awkward.

Interviewer: What did you do?

Ezra Mason: Well, I figured there was a good chance she'd just run me over if I stood in front of the truck. So I knocked on the window and said something like "Lovely day for a drive," and at that point the southeastern anti-missile battery got vaporized by what I assume was a missile. So maybe you might wanna note in your report that those things don't, you know, *stop missiles*.

Interviewer: So she let you in?

Ezra Mason: She let me in. I guess she figured she didn't hate me enough to let me get X-ed out by a Bei-

Tech kill squad. She had to think about it for a minute, though.

Interviewer: How did you know BeiTech was behind the attack?

Ezra Mason: I think the biggest giveaway was the huge BeiTech logo on the warship hovering overhead. It'd dropped out of the clouds and was X-ing the rest of the defense silos by then.

Interviewer: By "warship," you mean the BeiTech dreadnought *Lincoln*?

Ezra Mason: Yeah. That's them. ████████s. Wait, can I swear in this thing?

Interviewer: So what happened next?

Kady Grant: We took off outta the parking lot like we were in a chase scene. Some moron had parked blocking the exit, but the truck was all-terrain, so we rammed it.

Interviewer: What was it like outside the school?

Kady Grant: There were a lot of explosions and a lot of dead people. Dead civilians who worked for a ████ing mining company. I mean, imagine you're an interstellar corporation, right? You discover an illegal mining op run by one of your competitors. Do you (a) report it to the UTA and laugh as the fines roll in, or (b) jump in an attack fleet and X-out every man, woman, and child on the planet? What the hell was BeiTech thinking?

Interviewer: What you and I need to do is focus on what happened on Kerenza. Gathering intel on the attack is the best thing we can do to help right now.

Kady Grant: I can't believe this.

Interviewer: Miss Grant—

Kady Grant: Okay. Fine. We took the main arterial, and Ezra turned on the radio. For a second I thought the idiot was looking for the right soundtrack or something, but there was an emergency broadcast up. They were telling us to get to the spaceport, and our research fleet was going to send down shuttles to ferry us all up to orbit.

Interviewer: So you turned for the spaceport?

Ezra Mason: Yeah. I turned on the radio to maybe find us some getaway music, but there was an emergency broadcast telling everyone to hit the port for evacuation. So that's what we tried to do. But there were cars everywhere, and some truck had overturned on the strip. Kady nearly flipped us, and when I offered to drive, she . . . well, she called me a very bad word.

Interviewer: I see.

Ezra Mason: I can repeat it if you want, but—

Interviewer: That's fine, Mr. Mason.

Ezra Mason: Mr. Mason is my dad. And you still won't tell me why I can't see him.

Interviewer: We need you properly debriefed before you have any civilian contact, Mr. Mason. I mean . . . Ezra.

Ezra Mason: "Civilian contact." Wow. He's my *father*, chum. You guys still have fathers, right? Or does everyone in the great United Terran Authority get grown in a vat nowadays?

Interviewer: Why don't you just tell me what happened next.

Ezra Mason: BeiTech blew the ██████ing spaceport, that's what happened next. Popped a half-dozen missiles and turned it into a smoking hole in the ice. I played geeball with one of the ground crew guys. Rob Flynn. Burton, our next-door neighbor, he worked the quarantine bays. There was this girl, Jodie Kingston. I knew her since eighth grade. She worked the port comms rig. She was . . .

Interviewer: Ezra?

Ezra Mason: Wow. I just realized. She was the first girl I ever kissed . . .

Interviewer: Do you need a minute?

Kady Grant: No, I need to get this done. Once the space-port was gone, it was hard to know where to head. Mostly we were just dodging explosions. The ground was shaking, and at first I thought it was the missiles hitting. Then I realized the impacts were cracking the ice shelf under the colony's foundations.

Interviewer: Do you have a background in geology?

Kady Grant: I'm seventeen—of course I don't. But there were these huge cracks opening up in the ground, big enough to lose a car down. And before you ask how I know that, I saw it happen. There were kids in the back.

Interviewer: So you were driving through the city, and what happened next?

Kady Grant: Ezra wanted to find his father. He worked at the refinery, but I told him we couldn't get through the crowd that'd be streaming out of there. His dad's a big guy, like Ez. I told him they'd all be evacuating together, and we had to trust him to keep his feet. If we went in there, someone might have jacked the truck, and then we'd be screwed. I saw a woman pull this guy off a quad bike and take off on it with her kid. I saw a security officer shoot a guy trying to climb into the back of his truck. We weren't going to make it as far as the refinery. I wanted to go for my mom instead, and my cousin Asha. My dad was offworld—he works rotation on Jump Station *Heimdall*—so it was just Mom and me. She's a pathologist, so she did research, worked at the med center. Asha was training there.

Interviewer: Do you need me to look up your mother's name on the lists?

Kady Grant: No, she made it out. She's here on the *Hypatia*. I saw her before my interview.

Interviewer: And your cousin?

Kady Grant: No. She didn't.

Interviewer: I'm sorry.

Kady Grant: Yeah.

Interviewer: So, did Ezra see reason? Did you go to find your mother?

Kady Grant: We started. Ezra's mom isn't around, so mine had just spent a year feeding him. I think she was more upset about the breakup than anyone. We were heading for her lab, and by that time there were people in the streets, riding in all-terrains, some on quad bikes, folks on foot. The ground was cracking and there were chunks breaking off buildings, and all the time there's this huge BeiTech ship in the sky, pounding our defenses with missiles. Shuttles were lifting off with civis evacuating. It was so loud I thought my ears were bleeding. And over the top of all that, Ezra chooses then to start criticizing my driving.

Interviewer: It's hard to believe you guys broke up.

Kady Grant: You have no idea. Anyway, that was when half the cineplex fell on our truck.

Interviewer: . . . Wait, what?

Ezra Mason: I don't know how long I was unconscious for. I came to and thought the sky was covered in spiderwebs. And then I realize I'm looking through the smashed windshield and we're buried under half a building. The truck is scrapped, Kady's next to me and there's blood all over her face, and I couldn't find a pulse. So I dragged her out of the wreckage and started to give her mouth-to-mouth and that's when she slugged me, Your Honor.

Interviewer: She hit you?

Ezra Mason: Yeah, right in the face. Good shot, too. I dunno. She thought I was trying to kiss her. She'd hit her head, she was messed up. So we're gearing up to start yelling at each other, and then we realize the sky is full of Cyclone fighter ships. So I figured the cavalry must have arrived.

Interviewer: Could you still see the *Lincoln*?

Ezra Mason: No. But we could see that the refinery had been hit. It was covered in this . . . I dunno. It's hard to describe. It was like a mist? But it was black. Creeping in the air real slow, like molasses. Not smoke. It was . . . something different.

Interviewer: You said your father worked at the refinery?

Ezra Mason: Yeah. So of course I want to go look for him. And Kady still wants to go find Mrs. Grant. And the glacier is cracking open and the sky is on fire, and I think I can see BeiTech ground troops in the distance. And then I said it.

Interviewer: What did he say?

Kady Grant: He said, "You picked a hell of a day to dump me, Kades."

Interviewer: . . . You honestly said that?

Ezra Mason: Yeah. So all hell breaks loose, and Kady is yelling at me and I'm yelling back. All this stuff that'd been building up for the last year and boiling just under the skin. Like, I loved her. I *love* her. But she had this way of just . . . It was so stupid. The world is ending all around us and we're screaming about college applications and commitment and ███. I mean, can you believe that?

Interviewer: You're seventeen, right?

Ezra Mason: Almost eighteen.

Interviewer: Then yes, I believe it.

Ezra Mason: Cold, chum. Real cold.

Interviewer: So what happened next?

Ezra Mason: I took off. She told me I was being crazy, but I was just . . . furious. And my dad is all I have left, so . . . yeah. Ran toward the refinery, burning cars and trashed buildings everywhere. I saw a Cyclone crash into an apartment block right in front of my face. Felt the heat on my skin. I was just keeping low and trying to get closer to the plant, but there were BT troops all over. Big, armor-plated goons in winter camo carrying guns you could kill a glacieosaur with. I didn't really have a plan, I just needed to find my dad. Didn't know what I was going to do once I hit that fog. But turned out that wouldn't be a problem.

Interviewer: Why's that?

Ezra Mason: Well, they shot me.

Interviewer: They shot him?

Kady Grant: I couldn't believe it either. Those ████████s should have got in line. They're not the ones who had to put up with his—

Interviewer: You said you'd parted ways at that stage. How did you find out he'd been shot?

Kady Grant: I started by heading toward my mom's lab on foot, but there were a bunch of BeiTech troops in the way. They were putting carriers down on the ground and rolling out soldiers and all-terrain vehicles.

I was a little concussed, I'm pretty sure. I know I stopped to puke at one point. I could see shuttles landing out by the labs to do evac, so I just hoped my mom was getting on one of them. I knew I wasn't going to make it across town to her. I wasn't going to make it anywhere without another truck. So I stole one from a BeiTech crew.

Interviewer: I'm sorry, you what?

Kady Grant: I am frequently underestimated. I think it's because I'm short.

Interviewer: They didn't want it back?

Kady Grant: Probably. They were pretty busy jumping out of the way. Also, I knew my way around the middle of town—they didn't. I took some sharp corners around the back of the community complex, scraped the truck doors right off. But when I got out the other end, I'd lost them. Our people didn't have weapons to shoot at me with, and theirs thought I was on the same team, I guess.

Interviewer: What happened next?

Kady Grant: There was this filthy black cloud oozing down from atmo toward the refinery, and I knew that was where Ezra was. I heard it was some kind of bio-attack. Is that true?

Interviewer: I don't know. You said he was shot, so I guess you found him?

Kady Grant: On the wrong end of a BeiTech platoon, bleeding everywhere. I kind of freaked out when I saw it all.

Interviewer: Were you able to retrieve him?

Kady Grant: I, uh . . . Are there likely to be any prosecutions for stuff that happened down there?

Interviewer: They X-ed out a quarter of my crew. None of us are going to weep if you're telling me you took out a BeiTech squad to get to him.

Kady Grant: Like I said, I'm pretty small, and there was a lot of blood all over everything. I guess my foot slipped on the accelerator. It was hard to reach, you know? I ran a bunch of them down and pulled up right beside him.

Interviewer: What did he do?

Kady Grant: He said, "Hey, Kades." What a catch, seriously. The truck's door was missing, though, so it was easy for him to climb in, and we took off like we were outrunning a blizzard. We could see shuttles coming down on the outskirts of town, and they didn't have BeiTech markings on them, so we risked it. We were hoping they were evac sent by our research fleet.

Interviewer: And then what?

Ezra Mason: I don't remember much. I think I made a

joke about needing to see her license and registration. Because, you know, she just ran over a bunch of—

Interviewer: I get it.

Ezra Mason: Right. And then I said, "I'm bleeding," and she said, "Shut up, I'm not talking to you," so I just kinda concentrated on not dying. There was blood everywhere. It hurt so much I think I started laughing. Maybe I was going into shock. Kady was yelling at me to put pressure on it, but it hurt less if I didn't. There were fighters overhead. I remember being really cold. I remember looking at Kady driving, covered in blood, with her hair crusted with snow and everything. I think I told her she was beautiful. Then the lights went out.

Interviewer: You made it to the shuttles?

Kady Grant: We made it close. We were driving a BeiTech truck now, so I had to stop and drag Ezra across the ice so they could see we were civis. A couple of the med center staff had made it out there, so they were putting the wounded on shuttles with those guys, and the rest of us into the others. I was screaming my head off, trying to get someone to help me lift him in. I don't even know how I dragged him. The whole time there were these missiles arcing in and exploding around us, fires starting. I guess they decided if I could yell that loud, I wasn't hurt bad enough to make the wounded shuttle, so they made me leave him with the doc. That's how he ended up on the *Alexander* and I ended up on the *Hypatia*.

Interviewer: You've been very helpful. Did you see whether any missiles hit the refinery?

Kady Grant: I don't think so, just the black cloud. They wouldn't blow it up, though, would they? I mean, if BeiTech wanted the colony gone, they'd have just ratted to the UTA about it. They obviously wanted the hermium we were mining for themselves. They'd hardly destroy the only way they had to process it.

Interviewer: We can't speculate yet on what their aim was.

Kady Grant: I guess if they catch up with us, we can ask them before they blow us to pieces.

Interviewer: There's just one last thing, Mr. Mason.

Ezra Mason: Can this thing please include those pain meds you promised?

Interviewer: We've had another update to the casualty lists. I'm afraid I have some news about your father.

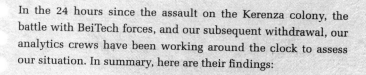

Officers of the *Alexander,*

In the 24 hours since the assault on the Kerenza colony, the battle with BeiTech forces, and our subsequent withdrawal, our analytics crews have been working around the clock to assess our situation. In summary, here are their findings:

- Our jump gate generator is heavily damaged—wormholes can still be created but will more than likely collapse before a jump can be executed, resulting in the *Alexander*'s destruction. Acting Chief of Technical Engineering Colonel Eva Sanchez reports the damage is irreparable, given our current resources (most notably, the death of Mallory Yzerman, our former CTE). Essentially, independent jump travel is **not an option.**

- The closest static jump gate able to return us to a Core system is Jump Station *Heimdall.* Though the station itself is on the other side of the universe, a waypoint/wormhole leading to *Heimdall* is 6.5–7 months' travel away at current speeds. In short, we are looking at over half a year's journey before we can jump to safety in a populated zone.

- Missile strikes sustained in the battle have damaged our Artificial Intelligence Defense Analytics Network (AIDAN), responsible for many vital shipboard functions, including main drive control and jump gate calculations.

The same missiles that damaged AIDAN also eliminated a considerable percentage of our neurogramming staff. Although AIDAN is self-repairing, and still functional, the full extent of the damage is unknown.

- Several other areas of the ship sustained damage, most notably our H_2O reservoirs, defense grid and propulsion systems.

- At least one BeiTech dreadnought participating in the Kerenza attack, BT042-TN (aka the *Lincoln*), survived the battle and is currently **in pursuit** of our fleet. With existing damage and crew levels, our tactical staff estimates we have a **22.7 percent chance of surviving** should the *Lincoln* engage us.

- The two civilian transports we are currently escorting—science vessel *Hypatia* and heavy freighter *Copernicus*—are carrying 3,348 civilians from the Kerenza colony. *Alexander* is carrying a further 1,097 civilians. Given aforementioned damage to *Alexander*'s H_2O reservoirs, this overpopulation will place increased strain on our supply situation. Neither the *Hypatia* nor the *Copernicus* will be of assistance should the *Lincoln* engage us.

- Distress calls have been issued on all United Terran Authority channels via the *Heimdall* waypoint. No reply has been received. In all likelihood, this means our transmissions have not been heard.

In short, ladies and gentlemen, we are bleeding badly and there are sharks in the water. We are understaffed and outgunned, and over six months from a realistic escape point. As such, I am issuing the following order, **effective immediately:**

CLASSIFIED

Any Kerenza colonist with a skill set useful in plugging our shortfalls is to be conscripted into the United Terran Authority military. Engineers. Medical personnel. Scientists. Anyone with a history of military service.

Furthermore, every Kerenza colonist seventeen years or older will be immediately tested for aptitude in computer science, mechanics, electronics, spatial awareness, pattern prediction, hand-eye coordination, twitch reflex, and stress management. Anyone showing C-grade ability or better is to be conscripted the day they hit eighteen. We need pilots. We need gunners. We need spanner monkeys and chipheads. And we need them now.

This is an unprecedented situation—to my knowledge, no stellarcorp has ever openly attacked a United Terran Authority ship. I don't care if BeiTech Industries' litigation department has enough red tape to gift-wrap a small moon. These corporations need to learn nobody is above the law and *nobody* attacks a UTA vessel without consequences.

You have worked tirelessly, acquitting yourselves with distinction and valor. We have lost comrades. We have lost brothers and sisters and those we loved dearly. I know the past few days have been hard. The road ahead will be harder still. But knowing each of you as I do, I have no doubt you will rise to the challenge before us and get these civilians to the *Heimdall* waypoint alive.

Centrum tenenda.

David Torrence
General, United Terran Authority
Commander, *Alexander–78V*

CLASSIFIED

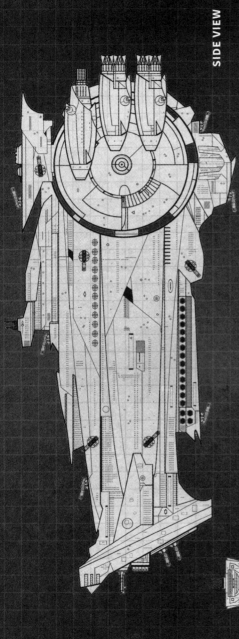

ALEXANDER-78V

Heavy battlecarrier capable of self-generating ephemeral jump gates for interstellar travel.

Carries a complement of Cyclone-class fighter craft. Possesses nuclear strike capabilities.

Commander: General David Torrence

Executive Officer: Colonel Lia Myles

CLASS: Vortex
LENGTH: 3.25 km
HEIGHT: 1.3 km
CREW: 4,000
MAX VELOCITY: 1.7 sst
ACCELERATION: 1.4 sst
MAIN DRIVE: Typhoon Mk VII x 6
SECONDARY DRIVE: Atlas Mk II x 12
INERTIAL DAMPENERS: 1 g

DEFENSE GRID:
DDT-10.9 phalanx
RG-166 samsara x 48
AIDAN-assisted FFG-01i
PAYLOAD:
Goliath 50 mt x 40
Capricorn 10.8 mt x 100
FIGHTERS: Cyclone Mk IV x 125(s)
SHUTTLES:
Vitus III x 20
Vitus IX x 12

FRONT VIEW

SIDE VIEW

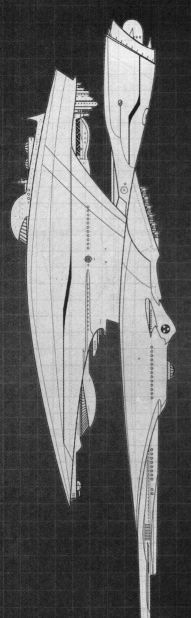

HYPATIA

Long-range scientific exploration vessel, ideally suited for deep-space recon/assessment.

Lightly armed and armored. Equipped with state-of-the-art tracking and QASAR arrays.

Captain: Ann Chau

Executive Officer: Syra Boll

CLASS: Oracle	DEFENSE GRID:
LENGTH: 0.9 km	ZXII-unig
HEIGHT: 0.21 km	Twilight GH-2 x 2
CREW: 500	PAYLOAD: Capstone 7c x 6
MAX VELOCITY: 1.5 sst	FIGHTERS: none
ACCELERATION: 1.3 sst	SHUTTLES: Nova III x 12
MAIN DRIVE: Balor IX [gt4]	
SECONDARY DRIVE: Balor IV x 4	
INERTIAL DAMPENERS: 0.98 g	

FRONT VIEW

COPERNICUS

Midtrek freighter, typically used for heavy-mass, system-length hauls [ore/ice/necs].

Slow-moving, with poor maneuverability, but durable. Interchangeable modular freight arrays provide excellent load flexibility.

Captain: Harry Ryker

Executive Officer: Heather Kelly

CLASS: Taurus

LENGTH: 1.2 km

HEIGHT: 0.96 km

CREW: 450

MAX VELOCITY: 0.9 sst

ACCELERATION: 0.8 sst

MAIN DRIVE: Helix-Chelsea VIII [in-line]

SECONDARY DRIVE: H-C II x 3

INERTIAL DAMPENERS: 0.94 g

DEFENSE GRID: Opti-Nex II [standard]

PAYLOAD: none

FIGHTERS: none

SHUTTLES: Vitus II x 12

UNIPEDIA
EYES AND MOUTH OPEN

Main Page

Contents

Random

Current

Generation

Contribution

Report

▼ Interface

Sensei

About

Hivemind

Editorial

Review

Make Noise

► Tools

► Sync

▼ Languages

官话

广州话

Deutsch

Español

Italiano

język polski

русский язык

Edit

Links

Kerenza, Battle of

This article is about the Battle of Kerenza IV. Get the gen on the planet and system **here.**

WUT DA FAQ

This historical article is currently und because you choobs gobble corp pr cheap dust at an all-night chuff party citations for verification purposes. Pl the **Hivemind**. Please attribute intelli mom does not count). And learn to s [insert appropriate deity name here].

INTRO

The Battle of Kerenza IV was the opening salvo in the ongoing and bafflingly unreported **Stellarcorp War**. Initiated by **BeiTech Industries**,[1] the assault targeted illegal hermium mining operations owned by the **Wallace Ulyanov Consortium**.[2] **United Terran Authority** vessel **_Alexander_**[3] answered WUC distress calls, resulting in a three-way throwdown between BeiTech, WUC, and UTA forces.

CONTENTS [HIDE]
1. Background
2. Initial assault
3. UTA response
4. Pursuit
5. Secondary conflict
6. Aftermath

BACKGROUND

Kerenza IV is situated in freespace, approximately 34.5 AU from a way-point leading to static Jump Station **_Heimdall_**. The planet contains unusually high concentrations of **hermium** on its polar ice shelf. In violation of the **Interstellar Exotic Materials Act of 2514**,[4] the Wallace

UNIPEDIA

EYES AND MOUTH OPEN

Main Page
Contents
Random
Current
Generation
Contribution
Report
▼ Interface
  Sensei
  About
  Hivemind
  Editorial
  Review
  Make Noise
▶ Tools
▶ Sync
▼ Languages
  官话
  广州话
  Deutsch
  Español
  Italiano
  język polski
  рýсский язы́к
Edit
Links

Ulyanov Consortium had been conducting illegal mining operations on the planet since approximately 2556, relying on the system's remoteness to keep its activities undetected. Operations were protected by the dreadnought *Defiant* and serviced by heavy freighter *Copernicus*. At the time of the battle, two WUC science vessels [*Hypatia* and *Brahe*] were also in orbit around Kerenza IV.

Kerenza IV

Statistics

Surface pressure: 101.325 kPa (MSL)
Composition:

  74.15% nitrogen (N_2)[3] (dry air)
  23.97% oxygen (O_2)
  0.91% argon (Ar)
  0.038% carbon dioxide (CO_2) [21]
  Water vapor (H_2O; varies with climate)

Mean radius:	6,371.0 km[6]
Equatorial radius:	6,378.1 km[7][8]
Polar radius:	6,356.8 km[9]
Flattening:	0.0033528[10]
	. . . more

INITIAL ASSAULT

At 14:21 [Local Standard] on 01/29/75, four BeiTech dreadnoughts [*Churchill, Kenyatta, Zhongzheng,* and *Lincoln*] dropped from an ephemeral wormhole[5] created by **Mobile Jump Platform** *Magellan*[6][7][8][9] —a blackbag prototype and, to Unipedia's knowledge, the first mobile jump tech *ever* developed outside of a UTA lab.[10][11] The entire fleet then proceeded toward Kerenza IV. WUC defense vessel *Defiant* was quickly destroyed, though not before it could issue distress calls—due to Kerenza's relative isolation, the BT fleet presumed these calls would go unanswered.

Sadly for BeiTech, one ship *did* receive the *Defiant*'s SOS: the United Terran Authority's *Alexander,* a Vortex-class battlecarrier also capable of generating its own jump gates,[12] which was on covert maneuvers near Kerenza VII.[13] The *Alexander* attempted to send communications to UTA HQ via the *Heimdall* waypoint, but BeiTech agents aboard the station itself ensured the signal never made it through. Receiving no response, the *Alexander* jumped to Kerenza IV without support. For more on the occupation of *Heimdall* Station and the resistance movement, see sub-articles here.

UNIPEDIA

EYES AND MOUTH OPEN

Artist's impression of the dreadnought Lincoln

With their hand caught in the proverbial cookie jar by the UTA, the BeiTech fleet made the astounding decision to *attack* the *Alexander* in the hope of eliminating the witnesses. Instead, the *Alexander* critically damaged Mobile Jump Platform *Magellan,* cutting off BeiTech's retreat. As the BT fleet engaged *Alexander,* shuttles ferried civilians from the decimated settlement onto the *Hypatia, Brahe,* and *Copernicus.* Reports that an unknown bioweapon was used on the settlement by BeiTech dreadnought *Lincoln* are unconfirmed.[14][15][16]

During the nuclear exchange that followed, the *Zhongzheng* was destroyed, and the *Churchill* and *Kenyatta* sustained massive damage. The *Alexander* took several hits—sources report both its jump gate generator and its artificial intelligence matrix were compromised.[17][18] *No ships in the Kerenza system were now capable of jump travel,* meaning any assistance would be months away. The BeiTech group closed to a range unsafe for the use of nuclear ordnance. The *Alexander* launched its Cyclone-class fighter craft, with the BeiTech group launching its Warlock fighters in kind. It is believed the BeiTech ship *Lincoln* destroyed science vessel *Brahe* at this point. Unconfirmed reports estimate at least 2,000 civilians had been evacuated onto the *Brahe* from the settlement below.[19][20][21]

BRIEFING NOTE: This is the first attempt at contact on record between the subjects, two weeks after the Kerenza attack.

To: Kady Grant/KGRANTHYPATIAONBOARD
From: Ezra Mason/EMASONALEXANDERONBOARD
Date: 02/14/75
Timestamp: 14:04
Subject: Hey

Hey Kades,

They told me almost everyone on the Hypatia has been fixed up with an onboard comms account now. I hope you get this.

I'm not sure what you know and what you don't. Everything is a mess over here. The military don't really tell us anything. But I wanted you to know I made it out alive. I wanted to say thanks. Without you I don't think I'd be here.

Delete that. I don't think, I *know*.

I'm in the med bay on board Alexander. My shoulder is almost 100%. Still trying to figure out what the hell happened. I heard a rumor that the Alexander's jump drive is bricked. There's definitely something up with the water supply but they won't say what. Someone else said the BeiTech dreadnoughts that attacked the colony are still chasing us. But I also heard we're just days away from meeting up with a whole UTA fleet. So maybe we'll be safe soon.

I feel bad about what happened between us. I keep feeling like there's something I could've said to fix it. And then I wonder if I'm an idiot for even thinking that way. I wonder if it was supposed to happen. I mean, if you hadn't broken it off, if you hadn't driven to school that day, we'd both be dead, right? If that's not the universe's way of telling me it wasn't meant to be, I don't know what is.

Anyway, I'm glad you and your mom made it out. I hope you're okay.

Happy Valentine's Day.

Love E

Grant, Kady—
Psych Profile/Conscript Suitability Assessment
Incept: 02/17/75

—Page 2—

suggests Ms. Grant is considerably more capable than her test results indicate. When contrasted with the early training exercises she undertook in the *Hypatia*'s makeshift educational facility, her current outcomes are less than impressive. Simply put, she doesn't want to score the sorts of results that would get her into the neurogramming training program.

TEAMWORK: Ms. Grant does not work well with others. The accounts of her peers indicate she was previously a relatively social girl at school, although she did not have a large number of close friends. It is clear that she now prefers her own company. She is, frankly, demoralizing to others in a group situation.

ATTITUDE: Ms. Grant displays strong anti-establishment sentiments and has an awkward habit of questioning authority figures at all the wrong moments. This, combined with the intelligence she tries so hard to conceal, makes her something of a liability. It doesn't appear ego is at play, as she is content to be viewed as average. Rather, it appears her queries and (often successful) attempts at destabilization are driven by her personal beliefs.

CONCLUSION:

☐ Conscript—Priority 1
☐ Conscript—Priority 2
☐ Conscript—Priority 3
☒ Do Not Conscript

COMMENTS: We'd expend more time combating her games and forcing her to get some work done than could be compensated for by her output. It appears she's willing to leave us alone if we leave her alone, and there are better candidates for recruitment.

NETWORK SECURITY INCIDENT REP

>> >> >> >> **BREACH ATTEMPT** 02/18/75 03:15

RECORD: Lu, Xi Wei, Network Engineer
TARGET: Refugee_Psych_Profiles
PROCESS: Brute-force cascade attack on *Alexander* datafort
OUTCOME: Defended

>> >> >> >> **BREACH ATTEMPT** 02/18/75 07:15

RECORD: Lu, Xi Wei, Network Engineer
TARGET: Refugee_Psych_Profiles
PROCESS: Codewyrm interdiction on *Alexander* datafort
OUTCOME: Penetration successful, duration 3 min.

>> >> >> >> **BREACH ATTEMPT** 02/18/75 18:15

RECORD: Lu, Xi Wei, Network Engineer
TARGET: Galley_Database—Meal_Schedule\Network_
Engineering
PROCESS: Access Trojan infiltration on galley database
OUTCOME: Penetration successful. Meals to Network Engineering canceled. Galley database security upgraded to Level 3.

>> >> >> >> **BREACH ATTEMPT** 02/19/75 06:00

RECORD: Brown, Benjamin Fraser, Senior Network Engineer
TARGET: Crew_Database—Network_Engineering
PROCESS: Access via personnel records, penetration method as yet unidentified
OUTCOME: Penetration successful. Network Engineer Xi Wei Lu deleted from database. Attempt to restore profile under way.

HYPSYS00C:91003100111
COREREF:0028H8700-001R2:FILE(A:BJ)83603294Y002-091-0019-1009-LATERA
REP:18923XWLL09I=FAiL
COMCHECK(871)=FAiL
=FAIL
=FAIL

To: Kady Grant/KGRANTHYPATIAONBOAR
From: Ghost ID/FAILFAILFAILFAIL
Date: 02/20/75
Timestamp: 23:17
Subject: The sound of one hand clappin

BRIEFING NOTE:
We believe the following exchange is the first contact between Grant and a member of the fleet's underground community. It takes place three weeks after the rescue and shortly after her tangle with shipboard security. The sender is Byron Zhang, a research officer aboard the *Hypatia* and a known information-liberty activist. There was almost no trace remaining of this contact, and some sections could not be retrieved. This guy knew what he was doing.

You've been busy, my friend. I **[unable to retrieve]** very entertaining piece of hacking. There are 8,340 people aboard our fleet, and there's a skill here for every occasion. You don't **[unable to retrieve]** teach yourself.

Break through into shell ref 436HT:904JX:003 and **[unable to retrieve]** show you what's out there.

This message will shred automatically for security purposes.

T is message will s red automatically for security purposes.

T i me age will   red automatically for ecurity purpo e .

T i me age will   red automatically for ecurity ur o e .

T i me age will   red automati ally for e urity ur o e .

 i me age will   re au oma i ally for e uri y ur o e .

 i me age will   e au oma i ally fo e u i y u o e .

 i e age will   e au o a i ally fo e u i y u o e .

 i   ag will   au o a i ally fo   u i y u o .

 i   ag will   a o a i ally fo   i y   o .

 i   ag will   a   a i ally f   i y

 i   a will   a   a i ally f   i y

 i   a ill   a   a i ally   i y

       ill   a   a i ally

                i ally

BRIEFING NOTE:
Grant responds to Zhang, using the handle "ByteMe." Took her 87 minutes to crack his Intrusion Counter Electronics.

BEGIN HYPATIA CHAT BASIC V9 CODE -->`<FORM>` ONCLICK=

ByteMe: That all you got?

CitB: ah, the new girl

ByteMe: Sure it is, but who are you?

CitB: the guy who can show u how to get all the info you've been trawling for

CitB: and more

ByteMe: In exchange for what? Nothing comes for free in this place.

CitB: for u, no cost but time. for the folks upstairs, plenty. the Alexander is a military ship and here on *Hypatia* we're civilians, but emergency or not, we have a right to more information than they give us.

CitB: our lives are on the line too. u want to join the fight, ur welcome

ByteMe: Just like that.

CitB: u've been sitting your entry exam these last 3 weeks, grasshopper. been watching u poke around inside the system. u don't like being kept in the dark either. seen u keeping an eye on a few things. on a few people.

ByteMe: Well you don't sound creepy at ALL.

CitB: what i sound like is someone who knows more than u. u want lessons or not?

ByteMe: Want.

CitB: then let's get started

To: Kady Grant/KGRANTHYPATIAONBOARD
From: Ezra Mason/EMASONALEXANDERONBOARD
Date: 03/18/75
Timestamp: 21:32
Subject: Knock knock

Hey K,

I'm not sure if you'll get this. I mailed you last month, but maybe it didn't go through. If things aboard the Hypatia are anything like things over here, it probably didn't. Maybe you're busy. Or you don't want to talk to me. I get it.

It was my birthday yesterday. Eighteen years old, can you believe that? Good news is I can drink legally now. Bad news is there's nothing to drink. Even the water's in short supply. :P

They've got a whole bunch of us doing tests. VR sims and psych analysis and physicals. They've drafted a whole bunch of the Kerenza refugees into the UTA over here. "Wartime conscription" they called it. And now I'm eighteen, they're looking at me. Which I guess means we're in deeper ▮▮ than anyone figured.

I had a dream about you last night. No, not like that, relax.

It was the day of the attack, and I see you in your truck in the parking lot. And I run up to the window and knock, but you don't let me in. You just stare like you don't know me. And I pound on the glass and yell your name, but you just shake your head. And then you drive off and leave me there. Weird thing is, there's someone who looks *exactly* like me sitting right next to you the whole time. And he's laughing.

And then the ships come.

You think it means something?

Anyway, I hope you're ok.

Love E

Mason, Ezra
Psych Profile/Conscript Suitability Assessment
Interview Excerpt
Incept: 03/19/75

INTERVIEWER: So tell me about your mother.

Ezra Mason: [Laughter.] Nice one, chum. You know, you're the first shrink I ever met with a sense of . . .

Ezra Mason: . . . Wait, you serious?

INTERVIEWER: Does it bother you? Talking about her?

Ezra Mason: It bothers me you snaffled your psych eval questions off the back of a box of Jupiter Loops, chum. That's honestly your opener? "Tell me about your mother"? Are you dusted?

INTERVIEWER: You've undergone psychiatric evaluation before, then?

Ezra Mason: What makes you say that?

INTERVIEWER: You said I'm the first psychoanalyst you've met who had a sense of humor. Meaning you've met others who didn't?

Ezra Mason: Proper little Sherlock over here, huh.

INTERVIEWER: There's no need for hostility, Mr. Mason.

Ezra Mason: Mr. Mason is my dad.

INTERVIEWER: Yes, your father. Tell me about him.

Ezra Mason: Nothing to tell. He's an engineer. Works the heavy processors in the hermium refinery. Bad cook. Worse jokes. You know. A dad.

INTERVIEWER: Do you miss him?

Ezra Mason: What kind of question is that?

INTERVIEWER: It's been over a month since he was killed in the Kerenza assault. You still talk about him in the present tense.

INTERVIEWER: Do you think that's interesting, Ezra?

Ezra Mason: [Inaudible profanity.]

INTERVIEWER: All right, then. Let's talk about something that makes you happy.

Ezra Mason: . . . You mean like lingerie models?

INTERVIEWER: Tell me about your girlfriend.

Ezra Mason: Wowwww.

Ezra Mason: You're *really* bad at this, chum.

Ezra Mason: Like, if Bad was a sport, you could Bad for your planet.

INTERVIEWER: Your girlfriend doesn't make you happy?

Ezra Mason: She dumped me the day our colony exploded.

Ezra Mason: Rim shot?

INTERVIEWER: Do you still care about her?

Ezra Mason: Next question.

INTERVIEWER: It's just I notice you put her down as your emergency contact on the *Alexander* intake form. It seems strange to name a girl you broke up with as your effective next of kin.

Ezra Mason: I never told you I broke up with her. She broke up with me.

INTERVIEWER: Why?

Ezra Mason: That's *so* not your business it almost punches clean past the event horizon of Not Your Business and becomes Your Business again.

INTERVIEWER: You two had a fight?

Ezra Mason: All couples have fights.

INTERVIEWER: Is that how you got those scars on your arm?

Ezra Mason: . . . What? Chum, I've had these since I was eight. What the ███ is wrong with you?

Ezra Mason: You don't do this for a living, right? Please tell me the real *Alexander* psych crew all got X-ed out by those BeiTech ██holes and you're the guy who used to clean the scrubbers or something.

INTERVIEWER: I work in the infirmary.

Ezra Mason: . . . Jesus, I was kidding. You're serious?

Ezra Mason: You're not even a qualified shrink? Well that's just ███ing chill.

INTERVIEWER: I'm postgrad med from the UTA Academy. Psych major. We do six months of fieldwork in our final year. I pulled duty on the *Alexander*. But it doesn't take a graduate from Neo-Oxford to see you have some serious anger issues, Mr. Mason. So we can talk about it if you like, or we can sit here and stare at the walls until our allotted hour is over.

INTERVIEWER: It's up to you.

[Skip 51:27 minutes of complete silence.]

Ezra Mason: She asked for something I couldn't give her.

INTERVIEWER: . . . I beg your pardon?

Ezra Mason: My girlfriend. Kady. She asked for something I couldn't give her.

INTERVIEWER: What did she ask you for?

Ezra Mason: Doesn't really matter now, does it? Whole verse gone to hell and all. Point is, for someone like Kady, the asking part is hard enough. She doesn't do the vulnerable thing real good. She doesn't like needing anyone. So when I said no and couldn't give a reason, it kinda . . . broke the back of it, you know?

INTERVIEWER: Why wouldn't you give her a reason when you said no?

Ezra Mason: If I didn't tell her, you honestly think I'm gonna tell you?

INTERVIEWER: Which brings me back to your mother.

Ezra Mason: Oh, and how you figure that, Mr. Postgrad?

INTERVIEWER: Typically, trust issues in teenagers stem from childhood abuse by authority figures. Teachers and parents, mostly. The fact that you've undergone psych eval before lends weight to the theory.

INTERVIEWER: Now, you obviously loved your father, hence your inability to process his death and your open hostility toward anyone who makes reference to it. The next logical line of inquiry is your mother.

INTERVIEWER: So. Tell me about your mother.

Ezra Mason: You're taping this, right?

INTERVIEWER: Audio only. Camera is faulty.

Ezra Mason: Okay, well for the benefit of the sight-impaired, I am now raising my . . . oh, dear . . . yes, it's my *middle* finger at Mr. Postgrad here.

INTERVIEWER: Mr. Mason . . .

Ezra Mason: Now I'm wiggling it.

INTERVIEWER: Terminating interview at 13:58 on 03/19/75.

Ezra Mason: Look at it wiggl—

—audio ends—

shows signs of post-traumatic stress disorder: aggression, avoidance, night terrors and survivor guilt.

TEAMWORK: Mr. Mason is a team player, capable of stepping up to leadership roles if required. High school sports: making life easier for military recruiters since 1914.

ATTITUDE: The death of Mr. Mason's father during the Kerenza assault has left him with a deep sense of resentment and anger. However, his aggression is progressing and is almost entirely focused on BeiTech Industries. And BeiTech will be the ones shooting at him.

CONCLUSION:

- [X] Conscript—Priority 1
- [ ] Conscript—Priority 2
- [ ] Conscript—Priority 3
- [ ] Do Not Conscript

COMMENTS: Mr. Mason's PTSD and anxiety levels would normally make him a washout for combat duty. However, with *Alexander*'s current shortfall of suitable Cyclone pilots, and considering Mason's test results (Spatial Awareness: 94th percentile; Pattern Prediction: 99.7th percentile), it's our recommendation to conscript.

The kid's hostility toward BeiTech can be harnessed in a conflict situation. Throwing him into task-oriented activities in a social environment (combat training) may even prove therapeutic. And if not, a few months from now, he's not our problem.

Get him in a cockpit ASAP.

ALEXANDER-78

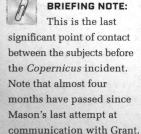

BRIEFING NOTE: This is the last significant point of contact between the subjects before the *Copernicus* incident. Note that almost four months have passed since Mason's last attempt at communication with Grant.

INTERCEPTED PERSONAL MESSAGE ONBOARD

To: Kady Grant/KGRANTHYPATIAONBOAR
From: Ezra Mason/EMASONALEXANDERO
Date: 07/03/75
Timestamp: 23:45
Subject: DO NOT SEND THIS

Kades

i am not sending this to you I am just writing it down and then i will delete it because of reasons. My friend jimmy says it is best to get these things off your chest and since u are not here to say this to i'm pretending because you know, think of my chest. it has things on it

so i am somewhat . . . liquefied but never fear i do notspend my days drinking alone in my bunk, the hooch is to hard to get lol. IT IS A CELEBRATION as i am now officially cleared for flight status, me flying a cyclone holy ▮▮▮▮▮▮ wtf has the universe come to.

anyway since i will never send this, I feel it fair to say i thought it wasrough not to mail me back I get mahybe you don't want to talk me and thats fine but a simple "i do not wish to speak to you goodday sir" would have been nice and this is shabby treatment madam, verily

since i will not send this, i also feel it is my duty to inform you that almost six months on I think I still love you and that makes me sad becaue love shouldn't feel this way. is like getting kicked in the stomach every time i think of you and it makes me want to roll my face across this keyboardbiu;///ubEWdcfhugiov'byhi;./////-='-0i9juh8ygtfdcsaazs34defg7u8hi9o0p-[[09ju8hy7gtf6rdsasdrftg67yh8u9ji0o-p-o0i9juhy8gtfrdesazsxdcfr5gt6y7h8u9ji0ko-lp0i9uj8hy7gt6frdesazsxdfghu7ghbuio.; ucfrexdAQW3XDE45THYUJYI

AFTER ACTION REPORT
MINISTRY OF THE INTERIOR
UNITED TERRAN NAVY
ALEXANDER FLEET

INCEPT: 07/20/75

LOCATION: Kerenza VII barycenter 778.76, 325.71, 1243.56k

PILOT IDENT: Ezra Mason (UTN-966-330ad)

RANK: Second Lieutenant

CALLSIGN: N/A

~~Fire does weird ▨ in space.~~

~~You don't really think about it until you see something burn out there. You light a match in zero-grav, the flame will be perfectly round. Like the way Terra looks in the old 'casts. And just like Terra, the flame won't flicker orange or yellow or even white out there in the black. It'll burn blue as a VR sky. Blue as a pretty girl's eyes.~~

~~They didn't tell us that in basic. It kinda dunked my head.~~

I've never written one of these before. An After Action Report. You can probably tell. Sorry if I chuff it up. Between zero-grav flight sim and Cyclone tech systems and memorizing the *Alexander*'s 316 different firing solutions, they probably figured teaching us paperwork wasn't the best use of our time. I'm so green at the controls they haven't even given me a callsign yet. The general told me to just type up everything and let the censors sort it out, so that's what I'll do.

~~Follow ▨ing orders.~~

~~That's what I do.~~

On 7/19/75 at 21:00 hours I was situated in the cockpit of my Cyclone fighter. Our fleet—consisting of battlecarrier *Alexander,* science vessel *Hypatia* and heavy freighter *Copernicus*—was in orbit around the first moon of Kerenza VII, engaged in resupply operations. The fleet's H_2O levels had reached critical, and Kerenza VII(a) was mostly frozen water, so our crews were busy hauling thousand-ton ice boulders up from orbit ~~while the *Lincoln* got closer and closer~~.

My fighter group was running dogfight drills 600 klicks off the *Alexander*'s port side, skirting the edge of Kerenza VII's atmosphere. Present during "the incident" were myself and three other members of *Alexander* Flight Group Echo: our CO, Major Eli "Prophet" Hawking, First Lieutenant Zhenya "Dreadnought" Alvaranga and ~~another rook,~~ Second Lieutenant Mikael Carlin.

I'd only been cleared for flight status two weeks earlier, and I was still a bunny at the stick. I'd logged near a hundred hours in VR, but all the sims in the verse won't prep you for the real black. ~~Two minutes out there is about all it takes to teach you how little you know about everything. You're a speck of animated carbon and water with about seven centimeters of ballistics-grade ceramic between you and absolutely nothing. Ninety-three billion light-years of ▓▓▓ing nothing. No up. No down. No sky. No ground. Just endless dark shot through with tiny spears of sunlight older than you and your entire species stacked end to end. You want to feel small? Spend sixty seconds in a Cyclone's cockpit, chum. Look out at the nothing and feel it looking back. Then you know exactly how much you add up to.~~

We were off the *Alexander*'s port side, like I said. Even 600 klicks away, you wouldn't believe how *huge* a United Terran Authority battlecarrier looks. It's a megacity-sized fist of matte gray, tail end lit blue-white by thruster arrays big as skyscrapers.

I saw in VR somewhere that old Terran sailors used to refer to their ships like they were ladies. It was all "She's the fastest ship in the isles, Guv'nor," or "She went down with all hands on board" or whatever. And it's funny—my Cyclone feels like a girl. Looks and moves like a girl. She's all sleek lines and sharp curves and edges that can bleed you white. Sometimes, I swear she flies me.

But *Alexander* is a "he," no doubt in my mind. There's no grace to him. No real symmetry. ~~He looks exactly like what he is—a brawler who picked a fight with someone just a little better.~~ He's got a broken-jaw face and a bucktoothed smile, wide as an ocean. He doesn't fly through space, he punches through. Rips holes in it and drags himself and everything around along with him. A hundred thousand kilometers of cable beneath gunmetal skin. Open black scars torn down his flanks from the retreat at Kerenza IV. Brain the size of a city burning inside him. ~~He's no lady, sure and certain. No gentleman, either. You do not ▮▮ the *Alexander*. The *Alexander* ▮▮ s you.~~

The science vessel *Hypatia* was situated about 4,000 klicks aft of the *Alexander*. Now *she's* a "she." Beautiful ship, chum. Lines like poetry. She doesn't move in space, she dances in it. Asks you to take her hand and close your eyes and fly with her.

The heavy freighter *Copernicus* was on *Alexander*'s port side, about 6,000 klicks aft. If I had to pick, I'm not sure if I would've called that ship a boy or a girl. I've seen pictures of turtles on the VR. *Copernicus* almost reminded me of those. The city-sized shells on its back filled with enough fuel to juice it, the *Alexander* and the *Hypatia* combined. All the eggs in one basket.

~~I think there's a saying about that~~.

Second Lieutenant Carlin and I had just been tagged by Dreadnought for the fourth time in twenty minutes. Regular as analog. Her targeting computer would light us up, the words "VESSEL DESTROYED VESSEL DESTROYED" would flash on our heads-up displays ~~and she'd laugh down comms at us like we were the funniest clowns she'd ever seen fly a stick.~~

~~She'd started referring to Carlin as "Chatter" because he talked too much between engagements. I felt bad for the guy—when a su-~~

~~perior officer slaps a nick on you, chances are it's gonna stick. "Chatter" doesn't rank up there with the chillest callsigns in the fleet.~~

~~Dreadnought was still tossing ideas around for me, and every time she dropped a firebomb like "Prettyboy," I'd ██ myself just a little. They engrave those callsigns on your coffin when you get X-ed out. Last thing you wanna picture when you imagine your send-off is a bunch of fellow Cyclone drones standing around toasting the death of "Lieutenant Sugarpants."~~

We were forming up for another round of tag when the red alert sounded. At first I thought it was a drill, but then AIDAN spoke to us direct on comms. See, AIDAN doesn't *do* drills. The *Alexander*'s artificial intelligence isn't capable of lying. Sure, it can think for itself, but no neurogrammer is stupid enough to make a computer capable of conceptualizing deceit. ~~These things are so smart now, the ability to spin bull██ is all that separates us from them.~~

"MAJOR HAWKING. PLEASE ORDER YOUR FLIGHT GROUP TO ARM BALLISTICS AND PULSE MISSILES. SAFETY DISENGAGED. THIS IS A CODE RED."

AIDAN's voice is sexless. It has perfect tone and inflection and pronunciation, but it doesn't sound old, or young, or have even a hint of an accent. It even refuses to refer to pilots by their callsigns. ~~I mean, sometimes it sounds cranky with you if you carve up the flight deck when you land or whatever, but aside from those occasional twitches, it's like a beautiful painting of a totally empty room. Gives me the crawls.~~

Prophet repeated the order, and Dreadnought, Carlin and me all went hot. Didn't even think about it. Thinking gets you killed, that's what they tell you.

The three of us formed up on Prophet's wing as he opened channel to *Alexander,* asking for confirmation from General Torrence. Except Prophet got no meat response on the other end. Just AIDAN giving us coordinates and telling us to scramble at redline speed. We flipped 270 degrees, jammed stick, and burned it toward the target. One look at my spatials told me where we were headed. Right at the *Copernicus.*

I remember the conversation that happened next. Every word. I can hear it right now in my head, like I'm there all over again.

"AIDAN, this is Prophet. Patch me through to General Torrence."

"MAJOR HAWKING. PROCEED TO DESIGNATED GRID COORDINATES AT ASSAULT SPEED."

"Roger that, AIDAN, we are en route. Patch me through to General Torrence."

"UNABLE TO COMPLY."

"Say again, AIDAN?"

"UNABLE TO COMPLY."

I squinted at my instruments, glancing up through the blast-spex to confirm what my readouts were telling me. A tiny flare was blooming on the *Copernicus*'s skin. I saw nearly a dozen small scarab shapes dropping from the heavy freighter's belly, one after another. Thrusters flaring. Twisted metal glittering in their wake.

"Prophet, something just blew through the *Copernicus*'s launch bay doors," I reported.

~~"Why was the launch bay locked in the first place?" Carlin asked.~~

~~"Shut your ███ing blowhole, Chatter!"~~ Dreadnought barked, "Prophet, I'm detecting multiple shuttle launches from the *Copernicus,* acknowledge?"

"Roger that, I see them. No comms from *Copernicus*. No launch permit on the shuttles. Lead craft ident: Osprey."

AIDAN's voice crackled over comms.

"MAJOR HAWKING, YOU ARE ORDERED TO INTERCEPT OSPREY GROUP TWO THOUSAND KILOMETERS FROM *COPERNICUS* HYPOCENTER. ACKNOWLEDGE."

". . . Hypocenter?" Prophet repeated.

~~Hypocenter. From the Greek, chums. Literally means "below the center." It's a term used to describe the origin point of an earthquake. Or a nuclear explosion.~~

~~That got our attention. No ███ing doubt.~~

I saw warning lights flashing on my HUD. Radiation spike. At that point I was nothing but adrenaline and sweat. And then I realized the *Alexander* had arced up its assault batteries. Missiles were heating, firing solutions feeding into our nav comps, a dozen LEDs flashing on my consoles now. The *Alexander* had armed its nukes.

And it was aiming at the *Copernicus.*

~~I asked Prophet what the ███ was happening, only to get howled at by Dreadnought for clogging comms.~~ We were closing on the *Copernicus* at full burn, about 3,000 klicks away now. My hands were shaking so bad I could barely hold formation. The freighter loomed in my viewshield. Metal gleaming in the light of Kerenza VII's atmo. Swirling blue and bloody red and copper-flavored gold.

Prophet was shouting into comms now. "AIDAN, we have detected nuclear armaments being spooled in your silos. Patch me through to General Torrence now! Acknowledge!"

"TRANSMISSION ACKNOWLEDGED, MAJOR HAWKING. UNABLE TO COMPLY."

Prophet ordered me to raise the *Copernicus* on comms while he kept trying to get through to anyone human on board the *Alexander*. *Copernicus* was transmitting nothing but white noise. I did what I was told anyway.

"Heavy freighter *Copernicus*, this is Second Lieutenant Mason from Battlecarrier *Alexander*, do you copy?"

I got hissing silence for a reply. Maybe they couldn't hear me. Maybe they weren't transmitting.

~~Or maybe they were being jammed.~~

"*Copernicus*, this is *Alexander* Cyclone Flight Group Echo. Do you copy?"

And then it happened. Inbound alarms screeched in my cockpit and the *Alexander* let loose. Just like that. There's no up or down in space. Everything is relative. Funny how it can still feel like the entire universe has flipped on its head. My HUD was pretty much all red at this point. Prophet was yelling into comms, demanding an explanation from AIDAN. He still pulled up at the 2,000 klick point like he'd been ordered to, though.

Copernicus was armed with anti-inbound batteries and ghost tech that might fool a missile's targeting computer on a good day. But the ship wasn't running up its defense solutions. It looked fine from the exterior—they still had power, engines, nav. The lights were on, but nobody was home.

I watched the missile speed across the black. ~~Lipstick-red tip, pristine white flanks, serial number stenciled in neat black lettering along its belly: URD:00M.~~

~~"Your doom."~~

~~I wondered if that was some spanner monkey's idea of a joke.~~

~~I wondered if the ███er was laughing now.~~

Sound doesn't travel in space. There's no atmo to carry it. All those old-school Terran future flicks we laugh at on retro night in the amphitheater got it wrong. But when that missile struck the *Copernicus* and burned blue, I swear I heard it. Felt it in my chest. The compensators on my visor dropped into sudden black against the flare, but I could still see it—the *Copernicus* being blown to pieces within a perfect sphere of blue. ~~Chunks tumbling like thousand-ton jigsaw pieces across the black. Two thousand plus lives snuffed out in an instant. Dismantled by the blast or frozen into people-shaped icicles.~~

All of it happening in perfect, absolute

silence.

Debris was speeding toward us on the edge of the blastwave, pattering on my blastshield like rain, colliding with Kerenza VII's atmo and burning through every color of the rainbow. I could still hear Prophet's voice on comms, but I can't remember what he was saying. Maybe he was still asking for an explanation. ~~Maybe he was praying.~~ I honestly can't tell you.

I could still see the shuttles streaking toward us, ~~came to my senses, like someone turned the universal volume back on~~. I could see other Cyclones popping up on my spatials—more flight groups scrambled from *Alexander*. I'd tried hailing the lead shuttle on open comms, on the day's secure frequencies, on universal. Nothing. But someone had to be flying them—they'd been moving too erratically for autopilot scripts. And then AIDAN spoke again.

"MAJOR HAWKING, INTERCEPT OSPREY GROUP AND DESTROY. ACKNOWLEDGE."

~~I heard Dreadnought talk on open comms then. That's when I knew we were in real ██.~~

~~"Jah . . . ," she said. "Jah, help us."~~

Prophet requested confirmation. "AIDAN, say again? You want us to fire on civilians?"

"QUARANTINE BREACH IN MOTION. CLASS ALPHA ZERO PATHOGEN. INTERCEPT OSPREY GROUP AND DESTROY. ACKNOWLEDGE."

~~"Oh god . . . ," said Carlin.~~

"QUARANTINE BREACH IN MOTION. CLASS ALPHA ZERO PATHOGEN. INTERCEPT OSPREY GROUP AND DESTROY. ACKNOWLEDGE."

"INTERCEPT OSPREY GROUP AND DESTROY. ACKNOWLEDGE."

"INTERCEPT OSPREY GROUP AND DESTROY. ACKNOWLEDGE."

"INTERCEPT OSPREY GROUP AND DESTROY. ACKNOWLEDGE."

BRIEFING NOTE:
The following was released by the *Hypatia*'s propaganda arm—sorry, the "shipboard communications unit"—nearly eleven hours after the *Copernicus* made her exit.

POPULACE
INFORMATION RELEASE

ISSUED BY: CAPTAIN CHAU,
SCIENCE VESSEL HYPATIA

DATE: 07/21/75

TIME: 08:00 (Shipboard Standard)

ASSIGNMENT: *ALEXANDER* FLEET

In the six months since we left Kerenza, we have been pursued by the BeiTech vessel BT042-TN, the ship we know as the *Lincoln*. We owe the *Alexander,* her crew and the United Terran Authority military a great debt of gratitude for their protection.

We are still over four weeks from reaching a jump waypoint, and the *Lincoln* will use any means within her power to prevent us from reaching that safe passage and telling the rest of the galaxy of the atrocities perpetrated by BeiTech on the Kerenza colony.

It is with deepest regret I inform you all that last night at 21:15 (shipboard time), the *Lincoln* launched a surprise assault on our fleet, resulting in the destruction of the heavy freighter *Copernicus.*

I know many of you had friends, family and colleagues aboard the *Copernicus,* as did I. Survivors aboard nine shuttles were rescued during the assault by the *Alexander*'s Cyclone pilots, and we extend to them our heartfelt thanks for their heroic efforts.

Due to the health concerns on the *Copernicus* in recent times, the survivors have been quarantined aboard the *Alexander.* This has slowed our efforts to compile a list of names and details; however, please rest assured we understand the urgency of this task.

We are renewing our efforts to make good time toward a jump waypoint and safety. Please assist and support those around you who have lost family, friends, or colleagues. Interdenominational memorial services will be arranged shortly, with details to be posted in the mess halls.

CONFIRMED COPERNICUS CASUALTY LIST

ABADIA, Paula
ABBOTT, Claude
ABDELGADER, Pauline
ABDUL-RAHIM, Mira
ABERCROMBIE, Joe
ACLAND, Aracely
ADAMO, John
ADAMS, Davina
ADAMS, Josh
ADAMS, Tracey
ADIL, Bhan
ADIL, Zutshi
ADLER, Chris
AFRAM, Hilary
AHMAD, Cate
AHMAD, Nikki
AHMED, Amir
AITKEN, Rhodora
AJEZ, Lisa
AKBAR, Shreya
AKBARI, Beth
AKHIL, Krystyna
ALBRIGHT, Hester
ALFONSO, Lorcan
ALI, Maya
ALI, Sujata
ALIDOUST, Jeffery
ALIVIZATOS, May
ALLEN, Elka
ALLISON, Jared
ALLMARK, Indora
ALVARADO, Emanuel
ALVAREZ, Sammy
ALWYN, Deanne
ALZAYAT, Mostafa
ANDARY, Faith
ANDERSON, Elizabeth
ANDRE, Famila
ANDREOU, Theo
ANDREWS, Malini
ANDREWS, Matthias
ANDREWS, Nikki
ANTONACCI, Laura

ARBOLINO, Darrin
ARCHER, Noel
ARCHIBALD, Charmaine
ARISOY, Hallie
ARKLEY, Kyriacos
ARNOLD, Susna
ASHTON, Alex
ASHTON, Miller
ASSAF, David
ATAR, Jim
ATHANASOPOULOS, Carl
ATKINSON, Barbara
AUGUST, Jalen
AYOUB, Katherine
AYTON, Donald
AZOURY, Ronald
BADILLO, Carmen
BAGOOD, Samantha
BAILEY, Andy
BAILEY, Kurt
BAJARIAS, Ian
BAKER, Ailie
BAKER, Paul
BALBO, Aaron
BALFOUR, Eric
BALMFORTH, Leon
BALOI, John
BALTOSKI, Eduardo
BANG, Angie
BANKS, Jodie
BANOUB, Moira
BANSAL, Tarun
BARAKAT, Scott
BARAVYKAS, Lisa
BARBER, Virgil
BARDEN, Darryl
BARDEN, Ronny
BARDUGO, Leigh
BARELLO, Nigel
BARINI, Chris
BARKER, Gordon
BARNARD, Jasmin
BARNES, James

BARNETT, Corey
BARNETT, Geneva
BARRON, Maria
BARTER, Abdallah
BARTLEY, Marc
BASS, Jan
BATEMAN, Eli
BATES, Arun
BATES, Rosalie
BATISTA, Margarita
BATOR, Pam
BAXTER, Alan
BAYFORD, Ioannis
BAYKARA, Stuart
BAYONA, Shreya
BAZOUNI, Ruth
BEALE, Amitzur
BEASLEY, Angela
BEATY, Elva
BEBENDORF, Yves
BECK, Cal
BELL, Burton
BELLAH, Michele
BENEDICTO, Tariq
BENISCH, Luigi
BENNETT, Doh Ong
BENNETT, Julia
BERENBAUM, Stacy
BERGIN, Rhonda
BERMAN, Keyur
BERNADINI, Tamara
BERNARD, Mina
BERNSHAW, Avi
BERRY, Everett
BERTRAND, Darren
BESHOI, Rayyan
BEST, Vivienne
BEUTEL, Kerri
BHAGAT, Sunny
BHAVNANI, Kerry
BIALER, Matt
BICKERS, Lindsay
BIL, Abigail

BILAL, Adi
BILLINGHAM, Kristin
BIRCH, Colin
BIRD, Evan
BIRMINGHAM, Peter
BISCOE, Derek
BISSEY, Julie
BLACK, Hannah
BLAGOJEVIC, Also
BLANCHARD, Cary
BLASZCZYK, Jessica
BLOOM, Sharad
BLUM, Carlotta
BLYTHE, Randall
BONIC, Denise
BONNICI, Kazem
BONNICI, Travis
BOON, Ariel
BORETTI, Maria
BORRERO, Juan
BOTH, Shae
BOUCHARD, Enzo
BOURKE, Ioannis
BOYD, Bobby
BOYLE, Lawrence
BRADLEY, Rick
BRAFF, Jan
BRAGANZA, Linda
BRANDI, Victoria
BREEDEN, Milford
BRENNAN NEVILLE, Margaret
BREWER, John
BREWSTER, Veronica
BRIDGES, Sergio
BRIFFA, Kelly
BRIGGS, Abel
BRIGGS, Alex
BRISSEY, Breia
BROAD, Melanie
BROADBENT, Chandra
BROMMER, Stephanie
BROOKS, Lillian
BROOKS, Penny

CONFIRMED COPERNICUS CASUALTY LIST

BROWN, Josh
BROWN, Rosemarie
BROWNLOW, Peter
BRUNDELL, Kirilly
BRYANT, Anne
BRYCE, Adam
BUCKEE, James
BUCKETT, Alice
BUDA, Hanjia
BUGEJA, Brad
BUICK, Azzam
BULL, Nathan
BURGESS, Kelly
BURGOS, Leanne
BURKE, Andy
BURKEY, Anna
BURKLE, Sharon
BURNAGE, Alex
BURRACCHIO, Margaret
BUSSEY, Marisol
BUTEAU, Carol
BUTEAU, Jane
BUTEAU, Methodius
BUTEAU, Scott
BUTLER, Al
BUTTFIELD, Sue
BUZIC, Ruby
BYRNE, Graham
BYRNE, Xinrong
CADEL, Hammond
CAIN, Mabel
CALDEON, Lucia
CALDER, Sundermurthi
CALDER, Tara
CAMEJO, Ian
CAMERON, Marie
CAMERON, Sharron
CAMERON, Steve
CAMPBELL, Jeremy
CAMPBELL, Rosalita
CANAVAN, Trudi
CANNON, Gary
CAO, Khanh

CAO, Nhat
CARLSON, Adrienne
CARMICHAEL, Grisel
CARRUTH, Darin
CARSON, Juana
CARTNER, Victor
CARTWRIGHT, Lanny
CARTWRIGHT, Tariq
CARUANA, Joan
CASSAR, Anita
CASSIDY, Richa
CATLOW, Geoffrey
CAUDILL, Stephanie
CAUDILL, Terrell
CAVALLERO, Larry
CELEGHINI, LeShawn
CHALHOUB, Tansy
CHAMBERS, Howard
CHAN, Cassie
CHAN, Jamie
CHAN, Lee
CHAN, Neville
CHANDRA, David
CHAPMAN, Lamar
CHARATSIS, Moana
CHARATSIS, Stephanie
CHARATSIS, Veniola
CHARLES, Buena
CHAU, Jaz
CHEE, Jamie
CHEN, Gang
CHEONG, Samuel
CHERE, Diamond
CHERE, Knox
CHERRY, Alison
CHESSON, Craig
CHEVALIER, John
CHIAPETTA, Paul
CHIGOT, Gillian
CHIHA, Barbara
CHINNERY, Colin
CHISHOLM, Mandy
CHISLETT, Keng

CHIVERS, Michelle
CHOI, Bart
CHOI, Leigh
CHOUDRY, Aneela
CHOUDRY, Yan
CHOW, Leon
CHRETIEN, Beth
CHRISTENSEN, Leah
CHRISTENSEN, Rana
CHRISTIANSEN, William
CHU, Chloe
CHUA, Staci
CHUN, Yun-Seo
CIAVARELLA, Samantha
CICER, Hal
CIMINA, Dominique
CLARK, Karen
CLARK, Tony
CLOUD, Aisha
COCCIOLONE, Ethel
COFFEY, Darryl
COHEN, Bemster
COLEMAN, Lois
COLES, Mahalia
COLGAN, Hannah
COLGAN, Melissa
COLLIER, Josie
COLLINGBURN, Andrew
COLLINS, Derrick
COLLINS, Rio
COLLINS, Stephen
COLT, Mustafa
COLVIN, Alexander
COMER, Krystyna
COMMERFORD, Henri
CONCEPCION, Harland
CONNOR, Gavin
CONNOR, Hilde
CONTE, Beth
CONWAY, Dandy
CONYERS, Whitney
COPELAND, Constance
CORFIELD, LeShawn

CORNFORD, Wen
CORNISH, Kehan
CORTEZ, Bradford
CORTEZ, Swati
CORTI, Joan
CORVAIA, Jethro
COSMAS, Richard
COSTAS, Fulvio
COTTER, Kent
COURT, Deborah
COURTNEY, Pat
COUZENS, Austin
COUZENS, Ben
COUZENS, Evie
COUZENS, Mandy
COUTTS, Kai
COWLER, Bryan
CRAWFORD, Sharmon
CROSSLEY, Alan
CROZIER, Brent
CRUZ, Geoffrey
CULROSS, Sunil
CULVER, Adelaide
CUMMINGS, Erika
CURTIS, Kat
CURTIS, Matt
CUSSION, Neil
CUTHBERTSON, Hannah
CZWARNO, Belinda
D'ARGENT, Glenn
DABINETT, Sarah
DALEY, Justin
DALTON, Queenie
DALY, Catriona
DANG, Thanh
DATTA, Carrie
DAVENPORT, Brady
DAVEY, Bevan
DAVIDSON, Rjurik
DAVIS, Olivia
DAVISON, Vince
DAWBER, Milor
DAWE, Karthik

CONFIRMED COPERNICUS CASUALTY LIST

DAY, Don
D'ESPAIGNE, Ashley Newell
DE HAUME, Treena
DE KUYPER, Gerald
DE LA CRUZ, Felipe
DE LEON, Andrew
DE MESA, Donata
DE PASQUALE, Annie
DE SUDARTA, Kris
DE VRIES, Sandra
DEAN, Doris
DEARING, Daniel
DEDES, Andrew
DEHART, Rosario
DEHART, Xavier
DEL CASTILLO, Jennifer
DEL GRANADO, Enrique
DEL SOTO, Esteban
DELANEY, Kelly
DELBRIDGE, Malcolm
DELONY, Tina
DELOROSA, Eleonora
DEMETRIOU, Jim
DEMPSEY, Najam
DEO, Fran
DESSES, Shadia
DEVEREAUX, Fay
DEWAR, Winston
DIAMOND, Erwin
DIAZ, Heather
DIBBIN, Leah
DICKENS, Breda
DIESTELKAMP, Audrey
DIPROSE, Lara
DO, Lonnie
DOAN, Lien
DOEL, Miroslawa
DOLICHVA, Tsana
DOLMAN, Elaine
DOMINGUEZ, Eduardo
DOMINGUEZ, Luisa
DOUGLAS, Nina

DOVER, Kenneth
DOWNEY, Rosalba
DOWNIE, Alfred
DOYLE, Ashley
DUFFY, Aoife
DUNCAN, Ronnie
DUONG, Tuan
DUPONT, Suha
DURAND, Fatma
DURAND, Mehdi
DURHAM, Matthew
EDGINGTON, Michelle
EITTING, Margaret
ELAM, Darlena
ELKERDI, Candy
ELLIOT, Nicolas
ELLIOTT, Zahara
ELMSLIE, Dougal
ELOI, Isabelle
ELTON-WEBBER, Holly
EMANUEL, Karl
ENGSTROM, Krister
EPSIMOS, Eileen
ERVIN, Nicole
ESHBAUGH, Julie
EVANS, Michael
EVERIST, Ngoc
EWINGS, Joanne
FABIAN, Mariam
FAILA, Perth
FAIMAN, Tammy
FALAYAJO, Jesus
FARMER, Albert
FARR, Rocci
FATA, Simon
FAWKES, Trevor
FEARN, Shishir
FEBULAN, Tahnee
FEENEY, Catriona
FELD, Rachel
FELLNESS, Salim
FERNANDES, Roslyn
FEY, Caren

FIANNES, Maxwell
FIDGE, Gerald
FIELDS, Jacquelyn
FIELDS, Myra
FILMALTER, Suzann
FISH, Ellen
FITZGERALD, Deb
FLANAGAN, Moe
FLORES, Jean
FLYNN, Caitlyn
FONTANILLA, Carmel
FORAN-SMITH, Erminio
FORD, Peter
FOROOQUI, Frank
FORSTER, Maged
FORSTER, Terry
FORSYTH, Arnoldina
FORTIN, Jules
FOSTER, Andrea
FOURNARIS, Stan
FOURNIER, Hosniya
FOWLER, Doug
FOWLER, Patricia
FOXE, Steve
FOXMAN, Lanny
FRANCIS, Nettie
FRANK, Van
FRANKE, Christina
FRASER, Hilary
FRAWLEY, Brian
FRAZIER, Florence
FRETUS, Suzanna
FREYJA, Katie
FRUKHTMAN, Karl
FULGARO, Sidney
FULLA, Hannah
FULLER, Genevieve
GADO, Manish
GADSBY, Stephanie
GAGNON, Louis
GAITAN, Anthony
GARCIA, Lori
GARCIA, Matas

GARDE, Linda
GARRETT, Cecelia
GASKIN, Brent
GATEWOOD, Laurine
GAUTHIER, Leo
GAZIS, Frankie
GEFJON, Caitlin
GELA, Darrell
GERO, Allison
GHALANDAR, Saoirse
GHANEM, Kim
GIAN, Hao
GIBBINGS, Francisca
GIBBS, Ollie
GIBSON, Lance
GIBSON, Philip
GIGOS, Terrence
GILBERT, Belinda
GILLIS, Lissa
GIOURIOTIS, John
GIRARD, Boston
GIRGIS, Mark
GIRI, Kumar
GLASSMAN, Peter
GLEASON, Alexa
GLEASON, Loris
GLEESON, Michelle
GLOVER, John
GODINO, Casey-Mae
GODINO, Darlene
GODINO, Lee-Anne
GODINO, Vick
GOLDBERG, Tiomotto
GOLIAS, Dianne
GOMEZ, Carlos
GONSALVES, Jasmine
GONSALVES, Rosia
GONZALES, Roger
GONZALEZ, Leo
GOODHART, Peter
GOODMAN, Courtney
GOODVACH-DRAFFIN, Ben

GOODWILL, Ravinder
GOTTLIEB, Alexandra
GRAHAM, Beth
GRANAT, Boyd
GRANT, Helena
GRAUDIN, Ryan
GRAY, Melissa
GREEN, Harry
GREEN, Rebecca
GREENE, Eduardo
GREENTREE, Victor
GREET, Odette
GREGG, Lacie
GREGHINI, Candice
GREY, Essie
GRIFFIN, Anya
GRIFFITHS, Damien
GRISAFI, Lora
GROENEWEGE, Jamie
GROFSKI, Mike
GROOMS, Alan
GROSSMAN, Steven M.
GUBAR, Evelyn
GULLEY, Kiara
GUZMAN, Jayne
HA, Kim-Ly
HADLEY, Hussein
HAIDER, Josh
HAIDON, Joe
HAINES, Malcolm
HALE, Vanya
HALIM, Salman
HALL, Gail
HAMILTON, Tyrone
HAMMETT, Rayford
HAMMOND, Ravi
HAMPSTON, Stella
HAMPTON, Jean
HAMZA, Daniel
HAN, Nyssa
HANCOCK, Hassan
HANLEY, Sydney
HANNAH, Maimunah

CONFIRMED COPERNICUS CASUALTY LIST

HANNIGAN, Gwenneth	HEYDER, Nicole	HULME, Lynda	JENNINGS, Joel	KEENAN, Helen
HANNIGAN, Nura	HEWITT, Trevor	HUMPHRIES, Carolotta	JERMEN, Chris	KEETLEY, Le Thanh
HANRAHAN, Matthew	HICKMAN, Francois	HUNT, Paul	JERVIES, Nick	KEIGHERY, Clare
HANSFORD, Hafid	HIGGINS, Batholomeo	HUNTER, Nerida	JEVTIC, Evan	KELLER, Gary
HANSON, Walberta	HII, John	HUTCHINSON, Natasha	JIANG, Sandra	KELLY, Jules
HARDING, Atalanta	HILL, Alice	HUXLEY, Keith	JOANG, Duy	KELLY, Pantelis
HARDY, Jan	HILL, Steven	HYDE, Mina	JOFFMAN, Phanindra	KELSEY, Amanda
HARDY, Tim	HILLIER, Grisel	HYDE, Thomas	JOHANSSON, Onni	KENNEALLY, Miranda
HARMON, Leeann	HINES, Deirdre	HYNES, Jay	JOHNS, Lamar	KENNY, Eamon
HARRIGAN, Ray	HIROTO, Kazumi	IBBETSON, Shirley	JOHNSON, Susie	KENNY, Gemma
HARRIS, Carolyn	HNOSS, Claire	IDZIKOWSKI, Nat	JOHNSON, Tim	KERBY, James
HARRISON, Richard	HO, Cathy	ILIOPOULOS, Gianni	JOHNSTON, Margaret	KERR, Jordi
HART, Aubrey	HOARSE, Marcelle	ILJCESEN, Julie	JONES, Elise	KHALED, Ariel
HART, Roberto	HOCKINGS, Filomone	ILM, Carly	JORDAN, Karla	KHAN, Emile
HARTLEY, Christine	HODGE, Derek	INGERSON, Audrey	JOSE, Shane	KHAN, Tracey
HARTMAN, Nell	HOLD, Riya	INGRAM, Dani	JOSEPH, Hugh	KHARTABIL, Indira
HARVEY, Charandeep	HOLLAND, Royal	INGRAM, Henry	JOSIFOSKI, Gary	KIDAME, Grant
HASTINGS, Troy	HOLLOWAY, Darlene	INGRAM, Jim	JOUTRELLIS, Brad	KILPATRICK, Luke
HATTON, Shaunte	HOLMAN, Peter	INGRAM, Louis	JOYCE, Min	KIM, Boston
HATTWELL, Roger	HOLMES, Yuri	IRVING, Clea	JUDD, Albert	KIM, Ha
HATZIPAPPAS, Veena	HOLT, Fiona	IRVING, Lou	JUDD, Darryn	KIM, Ji-Hu
HATZOGIANAKIS, Garry	HOLT, Reza	IRVING, Michael	JUNG, Min-Kyu	KIMPTON, Beryl
HAYDEN, Ryan	HONEYCUTT, Ethel	ISHAQ, Ronald	JUNG, Sam	KING, Dianne
HAYES, Zachary	HONEYCUTT, Tyrone	ISRAEL, Dianna	KABURA, Joseph	KINGSTON, Dianne
HEAGAN, Jill	HOPPER, Pedro	IVANOVSKI, Luke	KADER, Bernard	KINGSTON, Mark
HEAH, Calico	HORN, Milton	IYENGAR, Takaharu	KALPANDIS, Pratyush	KIRK, Molly
HEATH, Allan	HORNE, Mary-Anne	JABARIAN, Narelle	KAMBA, Michael	KIROL, Bataar
HECHT, Susan	HOROWITZ, Pauletta	JABER, Gwenda	KANE, Abiola	KITTSON, Briony
HELLWIG, Ragnar	HORTON, Leah	JACKSON, Adam	KANE, Warner	KLAWUN, Jack
HELMAN, Lauren	HORVARTH, Maya	JACKSON, Amelia	KANG, Russ	KLEINIG, Jennifer
HELOU, Arthur	HOUSTON, Gary	JACO, Luciano	KARABAY, Desiree	KNIGHT, Harriet
HENDERSON, Fred	HOVENS, Bernard	JACOB, Robyn	KARASMANIS, Shane	KNIGHT, Winnifred
HENLEY, Melvin	HOWE, Talisha	JACOBS, Marcus	KARLSSON, Emil	KNOX, Carla
HENRY, Gregory	HOWERTON, Bryon	JAFARI, Keith	KATSIOLAS, Michelle	KNOX, Deja
HERAVI, Ahmad	HOWERTON, Dylan	JAFARIGOLROKH, Martin	KAUFMAN, Amie	KOH, Min-Ho
HERNANDEZ, Jeffrey	HOWLETT, Leigh	JAMES, Alycia	KAUFMAN, Dean	KOMPELLA, Keith
HERNANDEZ, Juan	HOWSON, Isobel	JANSEN, Xanthe	KAYA, Vaheesan	KONTAXIS, Pete
HERRERA, Andre	HUA, Erin	JARED, Zutshi	KAZI, Hissan	KOPEL, Daniel
HERROD, Mike	HUANG, Hui	JAY, Cedrick	KEANE, Anil	KOUMOUROU, Gerhard
HERZOG, Shera	HUBBARD, Rudy	JAY, Darnell	KEANE, Jan	KOYUNOGLU, James
HERZOG, Trevon	HUBBARD, Sook-Yin	JEFFERIES, Florentina	KEARNEY, Bennett	KRAJERSKI, Adam
HESSE, Naomi	HUDSON, James	JEFFERY, Silvia	KEBLYS, Andy	KRANENBURG, Kristina
HEYDER, Kurt	HUGHES, Mark	JEFFREYS, Konstandinos	KEEGAN, Coral	KRENUS, Allyson

CONFIRMED COPERNICUS CASUALTY LIST

KRISTOFF, Jay	LEVERTON, Touran	MAIDEN, Katrina	MAY, Cecil	MENENDEZ, Gregorio
LA ROSA, Rachel	LEVITHAN, Jandro	MAJOR, Melissa	MAYA, Abhay	MENOUHOS, Adam
LAC, Quan	LEVY, Dijana	MAKHOUL, Scott	MAYNARD, Alison	MENZIES, Rasoul
LACEY, Erin	LEWIS, Harry	MALACH, L. A.	MCATEER, Taleb	MERRITT, Meagan
LACKEY, Michelina	LEXCEN, Kirstie	MALDE, Vancho	MCBRIDE, Ralph	MERRYWEATHER,
LADHAMS, Virendra	LI, De	MALLINSON, Chris	MCCARTHY, Cathy	Donata
LADOUNCEUR, Ray	LIANG, Smith	MALON, Ciaran	MCCARTHY, Gregory	MEYER, Vahid
LAFITTE, Anne	LICCIARDO, Ann	MALON, Roger	MCCLAY, Glenn	MEYERSON, Rose
LAMBLEY, Jin	LIKUIDRO, Gerard	MANASSA, Cassie	MCCOY, Myron	MICHEL, Jonnie
LAMM, Evette	LINCOLN, Niamh	MANDEL, Joseph	MCCUDDEN, Jason	MICO, Liz
LANCASTER, Dustin	LINDENBURG, Ritwika	MANGANARO, Janelle	MCDONALD, David	MIDKIFF, Jovita
LANCASTER, Indora	LINDORES, Norman	MANN, Ignacio	MCDOWELL, Marion	MIGNONE, Greg
LANCASTER, Ivy	LINFORD, Wayne	MANN, Nigel	MCELROY, Mary	MIHALOPOULOS, Costos
LANE, Nola	LLOYD, Casey	MANNING, Kylie	MCFARLANE, Anna	MIHALOPOULOS, Eve
LANG, Tracey	LOBERATORE, Mohit	MANSON, Cherie	MCGEE, Marcel	MIHALOPOULOS, Robyn
LANGLEY, Cara	LOCK, Doris	MANSOUR, Jianxie	MCGREGOR, Nicola	MILLER, Hermione
LAO, Shawna	LOCKE-COOPER, William	MANUEL, Reginald	MCINTOSH, Leli	MILLER, Kenneth
LARCOMBE, Marie	LOFN, Jenna	MANUEL, Rena	MCKAY, Andreas	MILLS, Eva
LARKINS, Sue	LOGAN, Patricia	MARGETTS, Claire	MCKENZIE, Edmund	MINA, Ahmad
LARTON, Raven	LONG, Andy	MARKHAM, Corey	MCKENZIE, Jayu	MINIITI, Sereyvuth
LARTON, Rosenda	LONG, Bon Van	MARKHAM, Ioanna	MCKIE, Laurelle	MISEV, Edmira
LAUBER, Kim	LONGWORTH, Oliver	MARLOW, Michael	MCKINNEY, Kerry	MITCHELL, Bobby
LAURENT, Ava	LOPEZ, Erma	MARNEY, Ellie	MCKOSH, Trish	MOHAMED, Hussein
LAURENT, Farida	LOPEZ, Walter	MARNING, Sophie	MCLAUGHLIN, Dennis	MOHAMMED, Ahmed
LAURO, Christos	LORD, Francesco	MAROUSH, Cora	MCLAUGHLIN, Katie C.	MOHAMMED, Raina
LAVANYA, Ray	LOVRINOV, Margaret	MARRIAGE, Megan	MCLAUGHLIN, Lara M.	MONAHAN, Brian
LAVOIE, Gabriel	LOWREY, Annette	MARSH, Kellie	MCLAUGHLIN, Mary	MONTALVO, Kennith
LAW, Shane	LUBEC, Aydan	MARSH, Raymond	Ellen	MONTALVO, Tanner
LAW, Vicki	LUBEC, Geoff	MARSHALL, Ed	MCLEOD, Heath	MONTIADIS, Alan
LE MIERE, Ralph	LUCHMAYA, Litian	MARSHALL, Simon	MCMULLAN, Aliyah	MOODY, Aziz
LE MIERE, Sadie	LUKIC, Jaipal	MARTIN, George	MCMULLAN, Kim	MOODY, Bertha
LE, Thao Nga	LUNA, Bonnie	MARTINEZ, Erin	MCNALLY, Louise	MOON, Kerry
LEBREUX, Dani	LUPPINO, Maria	MARTINEZ, Gustav	MCNEILL, DeAndre	MOORE, Ann
LEE, Alex	LUVARA, Arun	MARTINO, Leon	MCNEILL, Sau	MOORE, Mikael
LEE, Eric	LY, Binh Son	MARTINS, Louise	MCONIE, Jock	MORAN, Cory
LEE, Nancy	LY, Tam	MARZEC, Katerina	MCQUILLEN, Neville	MORCOS, Hugh
LEMIEUX, Garrett	LYNN, Marri	MASTROIENI, Beth	MEADOWS, Foz	MORCOS, James
LEMIEUX, Susann	LYTTLE, Catherine	MATEZIC, Shannon	MEDCALF, Deborah	MOREAU, Reem
LENDVAI, Paul	MA, Ben	MATHIS, Gilberto	MEENA, Ajay	MOREL, An
LENKO, Mark	MA, Wen	MATTA, Renee	MEERA, Kiran	MOREL, Simon
LEROY, Mahalia	MACGREGOR, Guy	MATTEI, Tony	MENADUE, Tony	MORGAN, Lawrence
LESTER, Bronte	MADERO, Alfonso	MATTHEWS, Finnegan	MENDONES, Max	MORGAN, Todd
LESTER, Edward	MADHU, Kevin	MATTHEWS, Hattie	MENDONES, Shail	MORGAN, Trudy

CONFIRMED COPERNICUS CASUALTY LIST

MORILLO, Dalila	NEYLAN, Allan	OMAR, Kapoor	PATEL, Najira	PIRELLO, Rebekah
MORRIS, Owen	NGO, Giang	ORLANDO, Cole	PATTERSON, Anthony	PLACHY, Stuart
MOSES, Stuart	NGUYEN, Phuong	ORLANDO, Nereida	PATTERSON, Benjamin	POLLARD, Murali
MOXON, Brett	NGUYEN, Trang	OSBORNE, Wendy	PATTON, Ray	POLLOCK, Larry
MUIR, Ash	NICHOLS, Amy	OTT, Anna	PAUL-SMART, Kirk	POMMERING, Jim
MULLER, Anne	NICHOLS, Dane	OWEN, Edward	PAYNE, Stewart	PONTT, Youseef
MULLINS, Charlene	NICHOLSON, Izzy	OWEN, Saoli	PEARN, Joan	PORTER, Megan
MUNCHENBERG, Elsie	NICOLAOU, Terry	OWENS, Barbara	PEARSON, Lucas	POST, Jessica
MUNDAY, Vlad	NICOLAY, Julie	OWENS, Ron	PEARSON, Nikiwe	POTTER, Howard
MURPHY, Paul	NIDDRIE, Marlene	OXFORD, Stojan	PEDERSON, Sharda	POTTS, Jessie
MURRAY, Jose	NIGRO, Alissa	PACHECO, Luis	PEDERSON, Willie	POWELL, Andrius
MURTI, Lisa	NILSSON, Edvin	PADILLA, Cari	PEIRCE, Ron	POWELL, Ronald
MUSA, Jean	NINN, Joanne	PADILLA, Marcelo	PELLING, Conrad	POYNTON, Megan
MUSTAFA, Ali	NITOPI, Ghazala	PAGE, Aimee	PENA, Clark	PRASAD, Anthony
MUZHER, Maximilian	NIXON, Mark	PAGE, Darren	PENN, Heidy	PRESTON, Cheryl
MUZHER, Razeer	NOLAN, Anne	PAHULU, Arthur	PERAKOVIC, Christian	PRICE, Sandra
MUZHER, Toby	NOLAN, Anthony	PAHULU, Sammy	PERESKI, Knox	PRIEST, Lashell
MYER, Nina	NOLAN, Garrett	PAIGE, Terrence	PEREZ, Katya	PRYOR, Michael
MYERS, Eugene	NOOR, Kaur	PALINKAS, Areti	PEREZ, Lila	PUCKRIDGE, Mervyn
NADAL, Svetlana	NORLING, Lene Maria	PALMER, Taylor	PERROT, Lucy	PULEOSI, Lorcan
NAIDOO, Claude	NORRIS, Arun	PANCHENKO, Dania	PERRY, Andre	PULLIN, Cherie
NAIDU, Donald	NORRIS, Jitenkumar	PANGANIBAN, David	PERRY, Nicholas	PUNORIERO, Thom
NAIRN, Terrell	NORRIS, Ryan	PAPAGEORGIOU, Amir	PERTIWI, Kella	PURCELL, Jade
NAKAMURA, Greg	NORTHEY, Vivienne	PAPAROULAS, Fallah	PESCH, Jian-Feng	PURJE, Faith
NANNA, Katelyn	NOVICK, Love	PAPASAVVA, Aline	PETERS, Snjezana	PURVIS, Ricky
NASH GUPTA, Sonia	NOVOCHENOK, Gamil	PAPPAS, Chris	PETERSON, Dorothy	PUZAS, Brenda
NASR, John	NOWLAND, Balaji	PARIS, Arabella	PETERSON, Juris	QJU, Roger
NASR, Najah	NOWLAND, Saloni	PARK, Cathy	PETIT, Habib	QUACH, Zoe
NASSER, Paul	NUCIFORA, Jeremy	PARK, Charlotte	PETROVSKI, Rodney	QUINLAN, Hayden
NATH, August	NUNN, Jeremy	PARK, Ye-Jun	PETRUCCI, Shirleen	RABOT, Saul
NAVE, Shelley	O'BRIEN, Kiersten	PARKER, Julie	PEZESKHI, Habak	RADOVIC, Joseph
NDELULUELA, Stuart	O'CAIN, Stephanie	PARKER, Kin Lap	PFEFFER, John	RADWAN, Janiette
NEAL, Kendra	O'CONNELL, Teghan	PARKER, Randolph	PFEIFER, Venus	RADWAN, Lorraine
NECOVSKI, Jensen	O'DUFFY, Nichole	PARKER, Raul	PHAM, Anh	RAFAELI, Ascension
NEILSON, Charity	O'DUFFY, Patrick	PARKER, Sandra	PHAM, Le	RAFAELI, Beatriz
NELSON, George	O'LEARY, Niall	PARKES, Cecily	PHILIPPOU, Valeninta	RAFIC, Lee
NERELLO, Letka	O'MELEY, Jason	PARKS, Marjorie	PHILLIPS, Jeanne	RAIKES, Emily
NERSESSIAN, Tricia	O'REILLY, Liam	PARNELL, Karen	PHILLIPS, Marta	RAIZ, Sarabjit
NESBITT, Manumalo	O'ROURKE, Jenise	PARRITT, David	PHUNG, Thanh Ha	RAJIC, Jason
NEST, Penelope	O'ROURKE, Maurice	PARRY, Laci	PICKFORD-ADAMS, Emily	RALPH, Emily
NEWCOMB, Roni	OCHOA, Ebony	PARSONS, Mary	PICKIN, Mona	RALSTON, Genie
NEWMAN, Arthur	OCHOA, Russ	PASCUA-BOURKE, Frank	PIERCE, Loretta	RAM, Nadeer
NEWMAN, Wendell	ODY, Wesley	PATEL, Lidija	PIERCY, Cat	RAMAB, Graham

CONFIRMED COPERNICUS CASUALTY LIST

RAMIREZ, Denise	RIVERA, Estelle	RUTHERFORD, Paul	SCREEN, Sheldon	SIMS, Michael
RAMIREZ, Todd	RIVERA, Sara	RYAN, Dawn	SEKULOVSKI, Rachelle	SINCLAIR, Stephanie
RAMKRISHNAN, Lynette	RIZZO, Kristy	RYAN, Kath	SELBY, Wayne	SINGH, Ainsley
RAMOS, Leonard	ROBBIE, Wanda	RYAN, Kylie	SELIM, Angelo	SINGH, Davinder
RANDOLPH, Erica	ROBBINS, Rainbow	RYAN, Tony	SELIM, Omri	SINGH, Hans
RANGER, Abby	ROBERTS, Anne	RYKER, Harry	SEMMENS, Bridgette	SKADI, Heather
RANN, Julia	ROBINSON, Barbara	SAAID, Cindy	SEMOUSKI, Erin	SKIRVING, Russell
RAO, Alen	ROBINSON, Bruno	SAAID, Coco	SENIOR, Hikmat	SMALLDON, Zohaib
RAYNER, Brenton	ROBINSON, Rachel	SAEMAAN, Mofizul	SEPH, Rosalita	SMILIAN, Rhea
RAYNOR, Lisa	ROBINSON-MCKAY, Mark	SALDUMBIDE, Patrizia	SERAGINI, Lesley	SMITH, Bill
READ, Chris	ROBSON, Gloria	SALOUM, Edith	SEYMOUR, Angie	SMITH, Ewan
RECTOR, Elenor	ROBSON, Keith	SAMAR, Ishana	SEYMOUR, Kit Rose	SMITH, Mark
REDA, Khalil	ROBY, Bette	SAMINATHAN, Anna	SGOURAS, Caroline	SNYDER, Clive
REED, Carolyn	RODGER, Gary	SAMINATHAN, Traci	SHAKAROUN, Ewan	SODEN, Scott
REED, Stephen	RODRIGUEZ, Teresa	SAN MIGUEL, Gisele	SHAM, Robyn	SOHRABI, Michaela
REES, Murray	RODRIGUEZ, Yvonne	SANCHEZ, Alejandra	SHAMOON, Kenneth	SOL, Hunter
REEVES, Donnie	ROGERS, Diana	SANCHEZ, Alex	SHANMUGAM, Brad	SOMERS, Adrienne
REEVES, Nonkhosi	ROGERS, Gail	SANCHEZ, Berto	SHANNON, Rhiannon	SONG, Rajanbir
REHAL, Nazario	ROH, Su-Bin	SANCHEZ, Pamela	SHARP, Shuchi	SONYA, John
REICHE, Joanna	ROHAN, Chinda	SANDERINK, Barbara	SHARP, Stacy	SOSA, Logan
REICHERT, Shae	ROHIT, Jani	SANDERS, Cindy	SHAW, Bashar	SOSA, Mauro
REID, Kristin	ROHIT, Varsha	SANDIFORT, Nicole	SHAW, Ian	SOUTHARD, Dominique
REID, Saeid	ROLLS, Merryl	SANTILLI, Todd	SHAW, Lee	SOUTHARD, Marlys
REISS, Anurag	ROMO, Francisca	SARD, Melissa	SHEA, Sean	SPALDING, Caprica
REITBERGEN, Cameron	ROSA, Alyca	SARKOZY, Eleanor	SHEARER, George	SPANGENTHAL, Alissa
RENDIS, Troy	ROSE, James	SATHANATHAN, Ethal	SHELDON, Leelavathi	SPARKS, Cat
REVIS, Corwin	ROSE, Neha	SAVEDRA, Jane	SHELDON, Vincent	SPENCER, K.S. Kelley
REYES, Berenice	ROSS, Rachel	SAVILL, Naqibullah	SHELDRICK, Garry	SPINELLO, Ellen
REYES, Emily	ROSS, Sait	SAVVA, Yoheved	SHELTON, Annie	SPOONER, Meg
REYNOLDS, Kris	ROSSER, Jason	SAYERS, Lana	SHEPHERD, Jesse	SRETENOVIC, Feras
RHIND, Samantha	ROUBIS, John	SCAFFIDO, Chantel	SHEPHERD, Megan	ST. JOHN, Douglas
RICE, Vickie	ROUBIS, Wahyuni	SCHAVONE, Yamond	SHERMAN, Chris	STACEY, Antonio
RICHARD, Antonio	ROUGE, Rachel	SCHELL, Raylene	SHTEYNGART, Teresa	STAIRS, Jasmine
RICHARDSON, Christina	ROWAN, Calan	SCHMEIDICKER, Nick	SHIPLEY, Maren	STANDFORD, Garrick
RIDGE, Hui	ROWE, Rhonda	SCHNEIDER, Eddie	SHORE, Chelsea	STANDORD, Sujata
RIDLER, Lou	ROXLEY, Frank	SCHULTZ, Laverne	SHYAM, Durani	STANLEY, Bounthong
RIECK, Evan	ROY, Christine	SCHULTZ, Rachael	SIBLEY, Andre	STAVROS, Peter
RIECK, Nick	ROYTEL, Mary	SCHUTT, Dusan	SIBLEY, Jacqueline	STEDMAN, Rohit
RILEY, Brigid	RUBY, Davinder	SCIMONE, Lorraine	SIDAWI, Nate	STEERE, Maree
RILEY, Daryl	RUSSELL, February	SCOTT, Alison	SIDHU, Norma	STEPHENSON, Sapphire
RIND, Amy	RUSSELL, Johnny	SCOTT, Juan	SIGYN, Brett	STERNBERG, Julia
RIOS, Lydia	RUSSELL, Nala	SCOTT, Michelle	SILVERBERG, Brenda	STEUERWALD, Audrey
RITCHIE, Andrew	RUST, Bethann	SCOTT, Sonja	SIMM, Hua	STEVENSON, Amanda
RIVERA, Alberto	RUST, Jada	SCOTT, Tania	SIMMONS, Joe	STEWART, Howard

CONFIRMED COPERNICUS CASUALTY LIST

STOJANOVIC, Keith
STRAUSS, David
STROUD, Jake
STROUD, Mickie
SUH, Joon
SULIN, Erika
SULLIVAN, Marianne
SUMMERS, Salvatore
SUMMERS, Stephen
SUN, Yong
SUNTHAR, Ramendra
SUTTON, Sarah
SVENSSON, Hans
SWANGER, Elizabeth
SWEENEY, Gene
SYMONS, Trent
SYN, Colin
TA, Kirsty
TABIAT, Nicodemus
TAGGART, Lou
TAGGART, Shanice
TAGUE, Aureen
TAHA, Aarav
TAIFALOS, Laria
TAIFALOS, Mo
TAN, Cami
TASSELL, Solomona
TASSONE, Janna
TAYLOR, Amanda
TAYLOR, David
TE HUIA, Lewis
TEE, Edwin
TENNANT, Amanda
TERRASSIN, Kieu
TERRILL, Cristin
TERRY, Bertha
TESLIOS, Kevin
TESORIERO, Karen
THILL, Terry
THIRUMAL, Stephen
THOMAS, Danny
THOMAS, Janet
THOMAS, Jo
THOMAS, Olga

THOMAS, Paul
THOMPSON, Fayyum
THOMPSON, Kevin
THOMPSON, Kimberly
THORN, Carissa
THORN, Wyatt
THORPE, David
THRASH, Delinda
THRASH, Terra
TILT, Darius
TING, Amanda
TIVERAL, Ginny
TOFINGA, Andre
TOLENTINO, Bursha
TOMASELLO, Charles
TOMASON, Peggy
TONGIA, Elle
TOOHEY, Ricky
TORRES, Roy
TORRES, Teri
TOTH, Michaela
TOTH, Susan
TOWNSEND, Marcella
TRAN, David
TRAN, Phuong
TREBY, Michelle
TREFFERY, Harold
TREMBLAY, Lucas
TREMBLAY, Nathan
TREWAVAS, Angus
TREWAVAS, Emily
TRIBE, Gai
TRIKAM, Kenneth
TRINCHANT, Marie
TROY, Craig
TRUMAN, Asia
TSIAKRISSIAKIRIS, Joe
TU, Pauletta
TURNBULL, Camilla
TURNEY, Jamal
TURNEY, Karima
TUSZYNSKI, Bessie
TYSON, Stephen
UDY, Janice

URBANCZYK, Melissa
VALENTINE, Katie
VALLESTEROS, Jean
VALLURI, Kiran
VAN, Kate
VAN LINT, Walter
VAN RIETT, Krystel
VANDE, Nara
VANDERKOLK, Tim
VANDERWEERD, Brynne
VASILEVSKI, David
VASILEVSKI, Roy
VAUGHAN, Janet
VAUGHN, Lynette
VEITCH, Lorrie
VELEZ, Luke
VELEZ, Mahalia
VERDOS, Afyaa
VIDULIN, Alison
VINCENT, Miriam
VINH, Liberty
VINH, Nora
VNSKAS, Elle
VITALE, Lina
VITI, Murray
VO, Bao
VOLONAKIS, Amy
VU, Huy
VUDMASKA, Marisa
VUKSIC, Tanya
WAGG, Bronwyn
WAINTRAUB, Adrienne
WALKERMEYER, Keith
WALLACE, Orathai
WALLS, Holly
WALSH, Adele
WALTER, Jenny
WALTER, Natale
WANG, Cheng
WANG, Jen
WANG, Maxwell
WARDEN, Carolyn
WARREN, Sadbhh
WATERS, Brad

WATKIN, Melinda
WATSON, Donna
WATTS, Jason
WATTS, Mirvat
WEBB, Nathan
WEBB, Peta
WEBB, Robert
WEBSTER, Corrie
WEEDEN, Antoin
WEINMANN, Jordan
WELLER, Lloyd
WELLS, Kelly
WENG, Jackie
WESSELY, Tehani
WEST, Jeffrey
WESTAWAY, Kylie
WESTHOFR, Robin
WETANGULA, Eugene
WHARTON, Sarah
WHEATON, Wajih
WHITBREAD, Vinko
WHITE, Matt
WHITEMIRE, Houston
WHITTAKER, Brooke
WHITTALL, Patrick
WICKHAM, Fatma
WICKS, Guen
WIJESEKERA, Adjoa
WILDE, James
WILDEN, Elizabeth
WILKINS, Doreen
WILKINSON, Hans
WILLIAMS, Sean
WILLIAMS, Zak
WILLOUGHBY, Rodrick
WILMOT, Romeo
WINGFIELD, Sarah
WITTE, Megan
WOLFE, Ernesto
WOLFE, Nicole
WONG, Kevin
WOOD, Angelo
WOOD, Jonathan
WOODS, Zack

WOODWARD, George
WOOLNOUGH, Joel
WORRELL, DeShawn
WORRELL, Lonny
WORTHINGTON, Kyha
WOULLEMAN, Rafael
WRIGHT, Ed
WRIGHT, Ellen
WU, Nina
WYBROW, Chelsea
WYBROW, Michael
WYETH, Connor
WYMAN, Bruce
WYMAN, Eva
WYNNE, Belle
XENOFOS, Georgina
XERRO, Dean
XI, Hoard
XIA, Maureen
XU, Tao
YACOUMIS, Amera
YAMAMOTO, Hiroko
YANG, Guo
YANG, Lynne
YASSIN, Noam
YATES, Abraham
YATES, Tamara
YIE, Azaria
YIE, Bertie
YOHALEM, Jeffrey
YOONG, Hope
YOUENS, Danielle
YOUSSEF, Abdul
ZAMPIN, Ben
ZANTALI, Edward
ZAR, Melissa
ZHANG, Kat
ZHAO, Jian
ZHAO, Liang
ZHOU, Peng
ZIELINSKI, Maricruz
ZIMMER, Nia
ZIZZO, Keiran
ZOMAYA, Pat

Participants: ByteMe, CitB
Date: 07/21/75
Timestamp: 08:15

BRIEFING NOTE:
Up next is a conversation lifted from *Hypatia*'s messaging system . . . well, nearly. They piggybacked the official network instead of chatting openly, but we've lifted the conversation regardless. Grant has learned a lot in her six months aboard.

BEGIN HYPATIA CHAT BASIC V9 CODE --><FORM> ONCLICK=

ByteMe: u seen the PIR? it's bull█

CitB: huge surprise, the brass r lying. KNEW this was coming

ByteMe: u psychic now?

CitB: should have started digging when they took down civilian comms on the Copernicus. "maintenance" my █.

ByteMe: so they were hiding something, let's work out what

CitB: you got any gen?

ByteMe: working on it now.

CitB: u still there?

ByteMe: trying to get past the ICE wall, takes a while. systems are SO busy over there. seems like they have their main engines off, but that makes no sense. we should be accelerating fast as we can before the Lincoln gets busy again.

CitB: tick tock tick tock

ByteMe: u can do any better, feel free

CitB: sorry. r u ok?

ByteMe: fine. found a court martial list

CitB: . . . .

CitB: say again?

ByteMe: they're court martialing the pilots that heroically saved all the people on the Copernicus shuttles

CitB: what the ▇?

ByteMe: got the records here. u tell me why they do that if the pilots were under orders

CitB: not the only mystery, grasshopper. i'm hunting for any scans or records showing Lincoln got close enough to us to take a shot. nothing so far. it's still way behind us, far as i can tell

ByteMe: so no attack from Lincoln, and they're court martialing our pilots. are we saying it was our guys who took out the Copernicus?

CitB: ▇ me

ByteMe: ew no

CitB: this is getting weirder and weirder. but that can wait, trying to find u a survivor list first

ByteMe: don't need one

CitB: course you do

ByteMe: i don't want to talk about it

CitB: you need to know who made it off

ByteMe: i need to know who shot down the Copernicus, that's the real mystery here

CitB: look, we both know i have no social skills, but if you need to talk about it

ByteMe: need you to tell me what you're finding

CitB: . . .

CitB: finding something weird.

CitB: I can't get a read on AIDAN. thought I was just hitting ICE walls but it's more like nobody's home . . .

ALEXANDER-78V

PILOT IDENT: Cayla Alton (UTN-924-776ad)
RANK: Major
CALLSIGN: Sting
FLIGHT GROUP: Delta

PILOT IDENT: Eli Hawking (UTN-912-842ad)
RANK: Major
CALLSIGN: Prophet
FLIGHT GROUP: Echo

PILOT IDENT: Zhenya Alvaranga (UTN-945-817ad)
RANK: First Lieutenant
CALLSIGN: Dreadnought
FLIGHT GROUP: Echo

PILOT IDENT: Ezra Mason (UTN-966-330ad)
RANK: Second Lieutenant
CALLSIGN: N/A
FLIGHT GROUP:

——LIST INCOMPLETE——

-—-ACCESS INTERRUPTED—-—

BRIEFING NOTE:
This is the first communication initiated by Grant after the attack on the Kerenza colony, despite Mason's best efforts.

To: Ezra Mason/EMASONALEXANDERONBOARD
From: Kady Grant/KGRANTHYPATIAONBOARD
Date: 07/21/75
Timestamp: 10:00
Subject: Hey Ezra

I've tried writing this email ten times already and I can't get it right, so I'm just going to send this through, whatever it ends up saying.

I'm sorry I didn't write you back. I should have. I mean, when you say "I'm never going to speak to you again," you don't think your planet's going to be invaded that afternoon. It was more, you know, an opening position on negotiations. I was angry.

But you said in your email maybe the universe was telling us it wasn't going to work out. You're the most romantic idiot I know, so I guess if you think so, it must be true. That stung, but still, I'm sorry I didn't write back. Because yeah, I should have let you know I was okay.

I'm still on the Hypatia, I'm in intel training. Since I heard about the Copernicus, I haven't been able to stop thinking about you—this is not me retracting my promise to kick you into the soprano range if you ever come near me again, but I had to check you're okay. So, let me know if you're okay, then we can go back to being . . . whatever we are now.
Kady

Participants: Ezra Mason, Second Lieutenant, UTA Airborne Division, James McNulty, Sergeant, UTA Marines
Date: 07/21/75
Timestamp: 10:02

📎 **BRIEFING NOTE:**
The following is lifted from the *Alexander*'s intraship messaging system. While Mason took none of the steps Grant did to cover his tracks, he had no real reason to expect anyone would be sifting through his old IM traffic. It's hardly Shakespeare.

GIN ALEXANDER CHAT BASIC V9 CODE --><FORM> ONCLIC

Mason, E, LT 2nd: well played, McNulty.
well played, indeed

McNulty, J, Sgt: wut

Mason, E, LT 2nd: You have just overstepped the line, chum. I put you on notice

McNulty, J, Sgt: this my wtf face——> ?_?

Mason, E, LT 2nd: What I want to know is how you jacked her User ID. You pull in Dorian from commtechs to help? What did you do to convince him to help? ▮▮▮▮job?

McNulty, J, Sgt: r u dusted or sumthing

Mason, E, LT 2nd: I thought the chipheads would have their hands full trying to figure out what made AIDAN go all HAL on us. Instead, they're piggybacking secure IDs and helping you ▮▮▮ with my head. I didn't think your ▮▮▮jobs were that good

McNulty, J, Sgt: chum wtf u talkin bout

Mason, E, LT 2nd: I take this as a declaration of war. Presuming they don't line me up against a bulkhead and shoot me after my court martial tomorrow, I will be making sweet, sweet love to your sister by week's end. This I do solemnly vow

McNulty, J, Sgt: ezra don't joke about my sister I ▮▮▮ing warned u

Mason, E, LT 2nd: sweet

McNulty, J, Sgt: chum . . .

Mason, E, LT 2nd: sweet

McNulty, J, Sgt: mason . . .

Mason, E, LT 2nd: lurrrrrrve

McNulty, J, Sgt: DON'T JOKE ABOUT MY ██████ING SISTER ████████████ I WILL RIP OFF UR ██████ING ██████ AND JAM IT UP YOUR ██████ING ██████

Mason, E, LT 2nd: I LIKED THIS GIRL. I *TOLD* U THAT. I MAY NOT HAVE BEEN ABLE TO WALKSTRAIGHT AT THE TIME BUT YOU SAID IT WAS IN THE VAULT

McNulty, J, Sgt: WUT GIRL U CRAYZ ██████

Mason, E, LT 2nd: KADY GRANT

McNulty, J, Sgt: . . . who?

Mason, E, LT 2nd: oh you don't know, ██████ you chum, this is some pistols at dawn ██████ right here

McNulty, J, Sgt: mason I have NO ██████ING IDEA wut u r talking bout rite now

Mason, E, LT 2nd: so you didn't send this message

McNulty, J, Sgt: WUT MESSAGE

Mason, E, LT 2nd: I send u

Mason, E, LT 2nd: got?

McNulty, J, Sgt: roger that

Mason, E, LT 2nd: and?

McNulty, J, Sgt: READING ██████

Mason, E, LT 2nd: *taps fingers*

Mason, E, LT 2nd: ██████ me how long it take you to read you illiterate ██████

Mason, E, LT 2nd: I heard your sister likes it zero gee true/false?

McNulty, J, Sgt: chum this wasn't me

Mason, E, LT 2nd: i smell lies

McNulty, J, Sgt: srsly

Mason, E, LT 2nd: eat a ███

McNulty, J, Sgt: MASON

Mason, E, LT 2nd: Yummy scrummy ███

McNulty, J, Sgt: LOOK AT THIS WRITING I DO NOT WRITE LIKE THIS SHE GOT ALL PUNCTUATIONS AND THINGS

Mason, E, LT 2nd: if you are lying, all jokes aside, i will totally gun for your sister

Mason, E, LT 2nd: I swear to god I will make her my bride

Mason, E, LT 2nd: . . . although now you mention it, your punctuation *is* ███ing ungodly . . .

McNulty, J, Sgt: "I haven't been able to stop thinking about you"

McNulty, J, Sgt: CHum

McNulty, J, Sgt: You are IN

Mason, E, LT 2nd: . . .

McNulty, J, Sgt: PICKING CURTAINS

McNulty, J, Sgt: MEETING PARENTS

McNulty, J, Sgt: MAKING PUPPIES

McNulty, J, Sgt: wait didn't u say this fem rolled u up and smoked u

Mason, E, LT 2nd: ripped my heart out my chest

Mason, E, LT 2nd: Showed it to me, still beating

Mason, E, LT 2nd: then slam-dunked it off the ice shelf

McNulty, J, Sgt: she get good air?

Mason, E, LT 2nd: ██ you chum

McNulty, J, Sgt: cheer up, ███. She wouldn't have written if her loins did not ache for thee

Mason, E, LT 2nd: can u read? She threatening to kick me in the sopranos. She says it's over.

McNulty, J, Sgt: "I haven't been able to stop thinking about you"

McNulty, J, Sgt: "I haven't been able to stop thinking about you"

McNulty, J, Sgt: "I haven't been able to stop thinking about you"

Mason, E, LT 2nd: ALRITE SHUT UP ████ER

McNulty, J, Sgt: read between the lines fool

Mason, E, LT 2nd: zzzz, so what do I say to her?

McNulty, J, Sgt: nfi. probably start by apologizing for wutever u did

Mason, E, LT 2nd: what makes you think it was my fault?

McNulty, J, Sgt: because it's ALWAYS the chum's fault, chum

McNulty, J, Sgt: u got extracurricular didn't u?

Mason, E, LT 2nd: ██ no. I'd have no sopranos to kick if i'd done dirty

McNulty, J, Sgt: come on, u can tell uncle Jimmy

Mason, E, LT 2nd: shut up i like this fem

McNulty, J, Sgt: AND SHE OBVS STILL LIKES U OR SHE WOULDN'T BE WRITING GODDAMN U ARE A MOPEY ███

Mason, E, LT 2nd: . . .

McNulty, J, Sgt: so whatever u did, say u're sorry. on your knees.

McNulty, J, Sgt: <insert quip about u being good at that here>

Mason, E, LT 2nd: . . .

McNulty, J, Sgt: and if that works

McNulty, J, Sgt: u must name ur first kid james in my honor

Mason, E, LT 2nd: >_>

McNulty, J, Sgt: if it's a daughter u name it jamette

Mason, E, LT 2nd: 0_o

McNulty, J, Sgt: and then it's happy ever after for Ezra Mason

Mason, E, LT 2nd: :D

McNulty, J, Sgt: ███

Mason, E, LT 2nd: what

McNulty, J, Sgt: I was just thinking now it will be a real crusher if they shoot u 2morrow

Mason, E, LT 2nd: . . .

Mason, E, LT 2nd: :(

ALEXANDER-78V

To: Kady Grant/KGRANTHYPATIAONBOARD
From: Ezra Mason/EMASONALEXANDERONBOARD
Date: 07/21/75
Timestamp: 16:15
Subject: Re: Hey Ezra

Hey Kades,

Well, this is attempt #18 at writing back, so I guess I've got you beat.

I'm ok. I've been on the Alexander since Kerenza fell. The UTA recruited me when I hit eighteen.

I'm flying cyclones now, if you can believe that. Shows you how short-manned they are if they've got me droning a fighter stick. I guess I finally made it off world, huh? Probably not what you had in mind . . .

You might wanna be careful with the intel training. If they've got you do-ing any neurogramming, the UTA might conscript you too. They're way short-handed over here since the hits they took at Kerenza. One of the pulse missile hits X-ed out, like, three quarters of the NG guys. Might be hard to keep avoiding me if we're living in each other's pockets. :P

Anyway, I gotta go. Got this meeting thing coming up. Guy here to talk about it. It's chill to hear from you, though. Real chill.

Ezra

PS: Um, the drunken keyboard face mail? Totally not me. One of my squaddies got onto my terminal. He thought it'd be funny. Really sorry about that.

PPS: Seriously. Not me.

PPPS: SERIOUSLY.

BRIEFING NOTE:
Though unsent,
these are worth review.

Message Status: DRAFT—DISCARDED
To: Ezra Mason/EMASONALEXANDERONBOARD
From: Kady Grant/KGRANTHYPATIAONBOARD
Date: 07/21/75
Timestamp: 17:15
Subject: Well, we are awkward at this.

But thanks for messaging back. Everybody here is talking about the Cyclone pilots. They put out a PIR about how you all rescued the shuttles from the Copernicus. What's it like to be a hero? I guess your meeting is getting measured for medals, right? Anyway, what was facing down the Lincoln like? And the rescue? It seems kind of weird that the Lincoln could just come out of nowhere like that. How did it all happen? Also, my friend here is wondering about the survivor lists becauseASDLKDGFKNDFGJBE MORE SUBTLE KADY LIKE A BRICK WHY DON'T YOU?

DISCARD—SYSTEM FLUSH

Message Status: DRAFT—DISCARDED
To: Ezra Mason/EMASONALEXANDERONBOARD
From: Kady Grant/KGRANTHYPATIAONBOARD
Date: 07/21/75
Timestamp: 17:35
Subject: Uh oh

They do have me in the civilian neurogramming program, but I don't like the sound of those odds. Time for a career change, if only I had a choice.

I'd be okay coming over to the Alexander, to be honest. I bet you guys have more information than us. You're the military, you have a whole intelligence wing, right? Then again, if what they're saying is true, the Lincoln snuck right up on us. Is that what really happened?

Anyway, the Alexander would be okay. My quarters here aren't with anyone I knew back on Kerenza, and even if everybody went through the same thing with the evac, it's still . . . I don't want to say lonely, because that sounds so ungrateful. We're the ones that got out.

I know things didn't end well, but I think if the attack hadn't come maybe we'd have found some way to at least still be friends. And you know, maybe . . . A year together can't mean nothing. I thought

DISCARD—SYSTEM FLUSH

Message Status: DRAFT—DISCARDED
To: Ezra Mason/EMASONALEXANDERONBOARD
From: Kady Grant/KGRANTHYPATIAONBOARD
Date: 07/21/75
Timestamp: 17:57
Subject:

. . . ■

DISCARD—SYSTEM FLUSH

DO NOT ENTER

BRIEFING NOTE:
Grant's personal
journal, retrieved from four
separate mirage virtuals with
dead-man-switch shift-
sequencing and mimetic
encryption.

Date: 07/21/75
Subject: It's dark in here

We're back doing group counseling again. *I'm* back doing group counseling again. ME. I mean, I don't even. After all the effort I put into getting out of this the first time.

But they've decided we are all super traumatized by the Copernicus, and reconvened the groups they had running after the rescue. The latest round of talking (or not) about our feelings led our group leader to con-clude maybe some of us are more forthcoming than others when it comes to sharing the deepest, darkest parts of ourselves.

Being the astute creature she is, she spent ten minutes I'm never get-ting back pointing out that just because we don't talk about our feelings doesn't mean we don't have them.

Thank you, Captain Obvious.

I guess she was looking at me on that one. I haven't slept properly since it happened, and I keep waking up at night wondering . . . bad things. I just don't think talking about it to a group of worried faces is the way to help me.

I hate the crying the most. It just creeps up on you out of nowhere. You're in the middle of doing something and suddenly you realize your goddamn eyes are wet again and you don't know how it happened. And the last—the LAST—thing you want is for anyone to notice, because next thing they're cooing and clucking over you, and they want you to talk, and it's more than I can take.

I have my mom's voice ringing in my ears, though, so I am trudging along dutifully to these stupid group discussions, even though it's pointless.

I haven't kept a journal since I was a kid, filling it with all the secrets of the universe, the suckitude of my parents moving me to a hideous hunk of rock like Kerenza, the total angst of it all that I'd give anything to get back. It worked, though. Writing it down stopped me saying it when I shouldn't, and over time the problems faded away. My present problems aren't going anywhere, but maybe the Return Of The Journal will stop my head exploding.

This thing is locked down under the kind of privacy protections even Byron couldn't crack. And if anyone reads it, I'm going to devote my life to finding a way to program every bathroom door on the Hypatia to refuse to recognize their ID. Actually, I think I could do that. BEWARE, SNOOPER.

So, a journal. I appreciate that they're trying to help with the group sessions, but they're scientists, not therapists. You can't run people through a quick training session and then have them host a bunch of traumatized survivors sitting in a circle and trying to talk it out.

My group leader says it's important to talk about my FEELINGS. I am stone-hearted and have none, of course.

Well, that's not true. Most people would say I'm pretty cold, but I think of it more as . . . private. People are always saying "how are you?" to each other, and I guess I don't see why I should answer such a personal question for just anyone.

But for the sake of trying, here goes.

Ezra's been on my mind a lot lately. Why, I don't know, except that the more you lose, the more you realize you don't have much left.

But at the same time, I'm . . . am I dumb to go back there? It was hard enough to make a decision the first time, but if after a year he couldn't even trust me enough to talk about whatever he had going on . . . and anyway, practically the first thing he did was email me and say it was all a sign, and we weren't meant to be together, and I do have SOME dignity. I don't want to be an option for him just because now he doesn't have any others.

I'm glad he made it out, obviously. It's not about that.

I think a lot about who made it out, who didn't. I think about my cousin Asha. Sometimes I just remember some random person, like the lady who came to fix our habitation recyc the week before it all happened. I can see her face, but I don't remember if I knew her name.

I wonder if she made it out, if she's somewhere on board, or if she died. And then I don't know why I'm wondering something like that, or why I feel so bad about not knowing. Survivor Guilt, according to the Counseling Circle Of Hastily Downloaded Wisdom.

I guess an experience like this is *supposed* to mess you up.

BRIEFING NOTE:
Note the timing here—the hackers pick up what's happening before the *Hypatia*'s commanders do.

BEGIN HYPATIA CHAT BASIC V9 CODE --><FORM> ONCLICK="WINDOW.OPEN('CHAT.HYPATIA= N

ByteMe: u there?

ByteMe: ping

ByteMe: ping

ByteMe: PING COME ON COME ON

CitB: ▮▮▮ me, i'm here, what?????i was trying to find Copernicus survivor lists for you, that takes concentration u know

ByteMe: told you i don't want them. forget that. ping the Alexander

CitB: how can u not want to know?

ByteMe: PING THE ALEXANDER

CitB: ok

ByteMe: u doing it?

CitB: trying

ByteMe: well?

CitB: still trying did u miss ur meds or what?? whats the rush??

ByteMe: well?

CitB: i can't

ByteMe: I KNOW

CitB: ??

ByteMe: comms are down

CitB: system check?

ByteMe: no they all blinked out simultaneous. when they're running a check u see them cascade out. Alexander's main engines are still offline too. i was watching for court martial results when comms were cut

CitB: checking on ur boyfriend

ByteMe: this again?

CitB: don't deny the flame still burns. ur heart leaps at the mention of his name. u know this is love, sent by forces above . . .

ByteMe: r u quoting song lyrics now?

CitB: i do not have a lot of rl experience with romance

ByteMe: listen, i'm doing this because it's our best chance of finding out wtf happened to the Copernicus. we don't have anyone else on the ground.

CitB: mmm hmmmm

ByteMe: can we please keep our minds on the job at hand?

CitB: I don't know, can we?

ByteMe: Byron, they cut the ship link. Just like they did with Copernicus.

CitB: ok, ok. i don't like it either. i have news though

CitB: there are def Copernicus survivors on the Alexander. i found signs about an hour ago. The Cyclones are only landing in bays 1, 2, 3, 5 and 6. see what's missing?

ByteMe: omgnumbers

ByteMe: wait, wait, I CAN TOTALLY DO THIS.

CitB: . . .

ByteMe: o, the thinking, it HURTS.

CitB: ok fine, point taken

ByteMe: wait . . . is it the number . . . 4?

CitB: all RIGHT I'm sorry

CitB: point is, we found our Copernicus shuttles

ByteMe: so the survivors are still locked down

ByteMe: shouldn't they be debriefing, working out wtf happened?

CitB: i'm just one guy, patience, grasshopper

ByteMe: i want to know y they isolated us by cutting comms. R we next?

CitB: careful going after that sort of gen. thats hardcore. they find u doing that they burn u right out

ByteMe: ur scared

CitB: no, smart. dangerous times

COMMAND TRANSMISSION SENT 07/22/75 09:06

HYPATIA HAILS *ALEXANDER:* NARROW FREQUENCY BROADCAST

Alexander, Alexander, Alexander, this is *Hypatia, Hypatia, Hypatia.* Do you copy? Over.

[NO RESPONSE]

HYPATIA HAILS *ALEXANDER:* AUXILIARY FREQUENCY

Alexander, Alexander, Alexander, this is *Hypatia, Hypatia, Hypatia.* Do you copy? Over.

[NO RESPONSE]

HYPATIA HAILS *ALEXANDER:* MAYDAY FREQUENCY

Alexander, Alexander, Alexander, this is *Hypatia, Hypatia, Hypatia.* Do you copy? Over.

ALEXANDER HAILS *HYPATIA:* MAYDAY FREQUENCY

AUTO-RESPONSE: Your message has been received and quarantined. Your message will be processed. Over.

HYPATIA: Alexander, this is *Hypatia.* What the ███ do you mean our message has been "quarantined"? This is Captain Chau. Get me Torrence on the line. Over.

AUTO-RESPONSE: Your message has been received and quarantined. Your message will be processed. Over.

HYPATIA: That right? Well, process this: You flex your tiniest gun turret, look like you're even reaching to scratch an itch, I'm going to raise so much noise the *Lincoln* and every ally she has in the 'verse will know where to find you.

ALEXANDER: *Hypatia*, this is Colonel Myles. Go secure. Repeat, go secure. Over.

HYPATIA HAILS *ALEXANDER:* **COMMANDER'S SECURE FREQUENCY**

HYPATIA: Lia, what the ██?

ALEXANDER: Sit tight, Ann. Comms are down while we do some work on AIDAN, and we could live without gossip flying back and forth between the ships. You should see the stats on broadcast frequency the last couple of days. Your people and ours have been busy. Loose lips . . .

HYPATIA: Look, I said exactly what you told me to say. I said it was the *Lincoln* that took out the *Copernicus*. Pretty soon someone's going to have to start answering some questions for me, though. Anyone with eyes can see your main engines are offline and you're reaccelerating on secondaries. Has this work you're doing taken AIDAN offline completely? Get your drives back up!

HYPATIA: Where's Torrence?

ALEXANDER: He's taking care of some official business. You have my word, Ann. We're here to keep you safe.

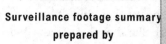

Surveillance footage summary
prepared by
Analyst ID 7213-0089-DN

BRIEFING NOTE:
Following is a transcription of *Hypatia* surveillance footage by an Illuminae technician. Original footage is also available. Please forgive the . . . enthusiastic language. Our tech is good at what he does, but he's not Dostoyevsky. Short version: Unlike Captain Chau, Grant wasn't prepared to sit around waiting for comms to be restored.

This girl has to be some kind of spider monkey. I don't know what those are, but I know what a spider is and I know what a monkey is, and if you found some unholy way to combine the two, that's what I'd be watching right now. You said include everything: Right now I am including my impression that she is very flexible, and apparently unaffected by gravity. I guess you need more context. I'll go back to the start and transcribe from there.

Footage opens at 11:38, on 07/22/75. Subject is Kady Grant, neurogramming intel student third class, a Kerenza refugee training aboard the *Hypatia* to replace crew they lost to the *Alexander*. Camera 892A takes in the corridor leading through to the servers. She enters with a group of fellow trainees and an instructor, and they make their way down the corridor.

The floor is a metal grid, and the clanging of their footsteps interferes with the audio on the file—the sound dampeners don't work when there's such a big gang. The noise drowns out individual conversations, but that doesn't matter. They're just fooling around the way students do, showing off for each other as they funnel down the long, narrow corridor, and she's in the middle of it. She's short, so she's sometimes hidden behind the others, but there are enough glimpses to confirm she's there.

They reach the server door, and she slips to the back of the group as they shove through. The subject digs in her jumpsuit and palms something too small for the cameras to pick up on. Just as she reaches the door itself, last in line and invisible to everybody else, she jumps, slapping at the environmental sensors by the top of the doorframe. There's a dark mark there when her hand comes away, but camera resolution isn't good enough to pick up the specs.

I would have laid down this week's salary she couldn't jump so high. Where does she get that kind of bounce from? Seriously, big jump for a small girl. She slips through the door the moment before it hums shut.

Inside the server room, the data monkeys look up and scowl and make *shut up we're working* gestures, which dampens the students. The data monkeys don't look worried, though—either they don't know the *Alexander* cut comms or they've been fed some excuse.

The room originally housed servers only, with personnel up the hall. The repurposing of the *Hypatia* from research vessel to refugee carrier removed that luxury. The relocated servers now line the walls, and rows of desks are crammed into the resultant space.

The cables that would usually slither all over the floor have been looped up against the ceiling by fat metal bands, though they still droop and coil downward like so many intestines. Whichever interior design genius handled the redesign found some harsh fluorescent emergency lights and jammed them in among the cables bundled up against the roof, which means there are bands of bright light and deep shadow all over the room.

The students, including the subject, take up places at the desks and log in to their individual ports, getting to work on today's assignment.

At 11:41 the environmental controls in the server room and the corridor beyond indicate a concern regarding air quality, loud, high-pitched and ███ing annoying beeping cutting over the chatter of the class and ruining what little audio I have.

They all rise and grumble and turn for the door, and as they exit, Grant pulls her spider monkey thing. Stepping up onto her desk, she grabs at the nest of cables, tangled up there like a bowl of noodles. She's little, and they hold her weight. The subject has picked a spot in the back of the room, and by the time the head datatech checks for stragglers, she's clinging to the ceiling in the shadows and out of sight.

The door hums closed as she unpeels from the ceiling and drops to the ground. She walks over to one of her fellow students' stations, which is still logged in. The enviro system continues beeping, and she looks up at the speakers like she wants to silence them with her death glare. It's a pretty good death glare, actually. I'd behave.

Subject inserts a mem-chit into the station's port, pulls on the HUD headset, and activates the old-school keyboard. It slides out from the side of the station, sitting vertically, and her fingers dance. She sends a batch info dump to an anonymous holding drive—we know this from what we could piece together of the drive records. We still don't know what most of that info was. Sliding away the keyboard, subject pulls off the HUD and dumps it on the desk. She then crawls under the desk, so for a moment all you can see is her butt sticking out.

No complaints here. Just saying.

For those playing along at home, she was attaching a device called an interface leech. Has to be attached physically, and allows access to a transmission array the fleet commanders use for emergency communications. So if you can access it, you can piggyback your own comms on it without anybody noticing.

Also, somebody should probably tell the UTA they've got a fleet-wide security vulnerability going on there.

At 11:48 the enviro alarm stops beeping without warning.

She freezes. Caught by surprise, I'm guessing. Abruptly, she's scrambling out, banging her head on the desk in her hurry, clambering to her feet, yanking the mem-chit from the station, though she still pauses to give the monitor a little pat, like it's a good dog for behaving so well. Subject hurries over to the back of the room, stuffs the chit into her pocket, and crouches in the shadows behind a bank of desks.

At 11:49 the students and datatechs file back in, grumbling about the interruption. She makes for the door. The head datatech says something inaudible. With a quick smile that's on the opposite end of the spectrum from that death glare, subject says something inaudible in return. They don't need this girl in neurogramming, they need her in psych ops, eyeball to eyeball with the guys who need to see things a little differently. Just saying. What she says must be an excuse, and it works. Not batting a lash, he palms the door open for her himself. She strolls back down the hallway ultra chill, stands there waiting until a datatech opens that door from the other side. She slips past, and she's out and free. As the door hums shut, subject is visible pivoting and blowing a kiss back toward the server room.

I don't blame her. She just plundered that thing.

It took eleven ████ing minutes. And she's just strolling away.

Date: 07/22/75
Subject: Behind the curtain

Learning is everywhere. I remember my mom telling me that when I was little, making mundane things seem like they were full of adventure. What I wouldn't do for a little mundanity at this moment. Or my mom.

I wonder if I'll be able to claim some kind of school credit for the stuff I'm learning on board. It's not exactly conventional, but I haven't given up on college and I don't want to end up behind. **Note to self:** Figure out how to argue the merits of practical experience in computer crime to a college application board without getting arrested. (ha ha, I am on a REFUGEE SHIP limping alongside a disabled military battlecarrier being chased down by a BeiTech dreadnought and hoping to live long enough to find a jump gate so I MUST NOT GET BEHIND ON MY SCHOOLING . . . I sound dusted.)

I am just too funny, but there's nobody here to appreciate my jokes. My group leader says I mask my emotions with dark humor and sullenness. Maybe she's right. The poor woman used to be a geologist before they made her a counselor, and the only thing she's got going for her is that our group is about as easy to talk to as a bunch of rocks. But who wants to break the dam on stuff like this in public? You write it down and put it away, then back to work.

Today's counseling session was about looking behind the face we put on in public to think about what else might *really* be going on. I wonder if that was just a sideways attempt to get me to be nicer to some of the others, walk a mile in their shoes, blah blah.

Anyway, she gave us the theme, and as she launched off into another round of How-Does-That-Make-You-Feel, I kept thinking about this holoshow I saw as a kid. They put on a play in the community complex with light-projected puppets, and I snuck away from my parents and went around the back to investigate the puppeteers. The whole romance scene was spoiled by me sauntering out onstage to share my discovery. (I am only realizing now how Mom and Dad must have wanted to hide under their seats, but to be fair, it was hardly the first time I'd mortified them.) I remember that moment really clearly. It was so important to me that everybody understand that what they were seeing, this romance, these *feelings* right there onstage—none of it was real. And that the girl puppet was really a guy with the biggest mustache I'd ever seen, which struck me as hilarious.

Clearly I had missed the romance of the moment.

I was all over today's theme of What-Might-Really-Be-Going-On, though, even at the age of eight. I knew it mattered, getting behind the pretend, the masks, and finding out what was really happening.

And romance? I knew even then it wasn't the real deal.

Today, as we practiced empathy and pretended to put ourselves in the shoes of others (without really doing it, because none of us want to imagine anyone else's grief, we have enough problems with our own), I thought a lot about that holoshow, and the commanders of our little refugee fleet.

Like I said, back to work. My group leader has no idea how much I want to know what might really be going on. And I'm going to find out.

COURT MARTIAL TRANSCRIPT
UNITED TERRAN NAVY
ALEXANDER FLEET

CLASSIFIED

INCEPT: 07/22/75

WITNESS IDENT: Ezra Mason (UTN-966-330ad)

RANK: Second Lieutenant

CALLSIGN: N/A

COMMANDING OFFICER: David Torrence (UTN-951-787ad)

RANK: General

CALLSIGN: Dozer

—TRANSCRIPT (PAGE 5)—

DT: Lieutenant Mason, what was your initial reaction when Echo Group was ordered to attack shuttle group Osprey?

EM: Sir?

DT: What did you do when the *Alexander* ordered you to open fire on the *Copernicus* shuttles?

EM: I didn't do anything. I was waiting for my CO to confirm the order.

DT: Your commanding officer being Major Eli Hawking.

EM: Yes, sir. Prophet.

DT: And did Major Hawking confirm the *Alexander*'s command and order Echo Group to engage and destroy the shuttle group?

EM: [Inaudible.]

DT: I beg your pardon, Lieutenant?

EM: [Inaudible.]

DT: Lieutenant, you are accused of disobeying a direct order in a time of war. Do I need to explain the severity of this situation to you? The penalty you will face if this court finds you guilty?

EM: You have the communications logs, what do you need me to—

DT: Lieutenant Mason, you will answer all questions addressed to you, or this court will find your prettyboy ███ in contempt.

EM: . . . No. Prophet didn't confirm the order. Sir.

DT: What did Major Hawk—

EM: We'd just watched the *Alexander* murder over two thousand civilians for no good reason, what the hell was Prophet supposed to do?

[slamming noise]

DT: Lieutenant Mason, you might be fresh meat from some pitdigger ██hole, but that's still a goddamn UTA sigil on your collar. One more outburst and I will rip out your eyeballs and skull██ you so hard you'll wish your mama told your daddy she had a headache the night you got loaded into the launch tube.

EM: My father is dead, sir. He died at Kerenza. Sir.

DT: [Inaudible.]

EM: Sir?

DT: Listen, son, I know you're conscript material. I know you didn't join the UTA willingly, and I know you don't want to be here . . .

EM: No, sir, I'm happy to help out, sir. *Alexander* saved us at Kerenza. And I want to help. I really do. What I don't understand is why you fought so hard to save us, only to X-out the *Copernicus* near six months into the retreat.

DT: This is not a retreat, Mason.

EM: Can we tell that to the BeiTech dreadnought chasing us?

DT: This is a tactical withdrawal, Lieutenant.

EM: Yes, sir. Apologies, sir.

DT: Are you ready to start answering my questions now, Lieutenant? Or do I get the MPs to warm you a seat in the hole?

EM: [Inaudible.]

DT: Lieutenant?

EM: Ready, sir.

DT: What did Major Hawking do when *Alexander* ordered Echo Group to engage and destroy the *Copernicus* shuttles?

EM: He asked for confirmation from you.

DT: He refused the order.

EM: He wanted confirmation from a human. He'd just watched AIDAN nuke the *Copernicus.*

DT: How did you know it was the artificial intelligence that ordered the strike on *Copernicus*, Lieutenant?

EM: Because it was the AI talking to us. Prophet tried to raise you on comms, and AIDAN told him it was unable to comply.

DT: And so instead of following orders, Major Hawking decided to tow the shuttles into the *Alexander*'s hangar bay. Despite repeated warnings of an Alpha Zero pathogen aboard those ships.

EM: He didn't . . .

DT: Lieutenant?

EM: The Major didn't escort the shuttles right away. He spoke to Dreadnought—

DT: First Lieutenant Alvaranga.

EM: Yes, sir. He spoke to her and the CO of Delta Group. Delta got scrambled when the *Copernicus* was nuked. They talked it over. And all the while, AIDAN was just screaming at us to engage and destroy. We had no comms on those shuttles. The EMP from the blast had knocked out their systems, and they were floating helpless. But they were close enough at that point for us to see the people inside. I saw this little girl in one of the viewports, she couldn't have been more than ten—

DT: Who made the final decision to tow the shuttles onto *Alexander*?

EM: You know the answer to that, sir. You have the communications logs.

DT: I am asking you, Lieutenant.

EM: You want me to feed Prophet and Dreadnought to the wolves.

DT: I want your version of events, Lieutenant Mason. I'm not going to warn you again.

EM: There were innocent people on board those ships. We could see them. Prophet and Dreadnought made the right call.

DT: So it was Major Hawking and First Lieutenant Alvaranga who made the decision?

EM: . . .

DT: Lieutenant?

EM: I don't recall, sir.

DT: I beg your pardon?

EM: I don't remember. Everything happened too fast.

DT: You are on thin ███ing ice, Lieutenant . . .

EM: I'm sorry, sir. I don't remember. You want to brig me for that, do it. I'll sleep easier in the hole than I will on thirty pieces of ███ing silver.

ᴬᵀ/LOGIN LOCATION=NO MENUBAR=NO')<!-- END ALEXANDER CHAT BASIC V9 CODE -->< -- B

McNulty, J, Sgt: jus saw you head back to your rack wut news chum

McNulty, J, Sgt: chum

McNulty, J, Sgt: mason

McNulty, J, Sgt: ezramaaaaaaaaaaaaaaaassssssssssssooonlSrnbopNRb[on erb

McNulty, J, Sgt: ANSWER ME ▮▮▮▮ER

McNulty, J, Sgt: i guess they didn't shoot u

Mason, E, LT 2nd: nope, not me

McNulty, J, Sgt: good news for ms hottie and my young namesake

Mason, E, LT 2nd: Bad news for Prophet and Dreadnought

McNulty, J, Sgt: ?

Mason, E, LT 2nd: they ▮▮▮ing shot them, Jimmy

McNulty, J, Sgt: . . .

McNulty, J, Sgt: u ▮▮▮ing kidding me

Mason, E, LT 2nd: DO I SOUND LIKE I'M ▮▮▮ING JOKING?

McNulty, J, Sgt: . . . JESUS

Mason, E, LT 2nd: lined them up against the bulkhead and X-ed them out. CO from Delta group too. And some Lt from Flight Control. Just straight-up shot them

Mason, E, LT 2nd: Only reason me and Carlin got off was because we were obeying direct orders from Prophet. They had it all on the comms logs. Whole show was bull■.

McNulty, J, Sgt: ■

Mason, E, LT 2nd: They revoked my flight status. Decked until further notice.

McNulty, J, Sgt: wut the ■ is Torrence thinking? We shorthanded as it is and they're X-ing out our best jockeys? Wut they charge them with?

Mason, E, LT 2nd: On paper? "Disobeying a direct order in time of war." Unofficially, I heard it was a gag job. Command is telling the civis on Hypatia it was the ■ing Lincoln that blew up Copernicus. Prophet and Dreadnought wanted to tell it straight. Wouldn't keep quiet about it.

McNulty, J, Sgt: civis would ■ bricks if they knew it was Alexander on the trigger

Mason, E, LT 2nd: You said it

McNulty, J, Sgt: but X-ing out our own guys? i didn't sign up for that ■, chum

Mason, E, LT 2nd: Watch the chat, they could be monitoring

McNulty, J, Sgt: Dorian said the whole commtech crew is working full time on AIDAN, they got no juice to monitor local chatter, fool

Mason, E, LT 2nd: does Dorian know what they did with the civis we escorted over from Copernicus?

McNulty, J, Sgt: They all locked in bay 4. Nobody getting in or out

Mason, E, LT 2nd: no confirmation about Phobos?

McNulty, J, Sgt: ■ chum, they've had constant outbreaks on Copernicus since we evac'ed Kerenza. Wut are the chances none of those folks are carriers?

Mason, E, LT 2nd: so we could have let the virus on board Alexander?

McNulty, J, Sgt: *shrugs*

Mason, E, LT 2nd: ███

McNulty, J, Sgt: wuts the prob? It's a bug. 3 days and you're good as new

Mason, E, LT 2nd: During the Copernicus snafu, AIDAN called it a "Class Alpha Zero Pathogen." And command ain't treating it like the common ███ing cold.

McNulty, J, Sgt: jesus

Mason, E, LT 2nd: you didn't hear that from me btw

Mason, E, LT 2nd: The worst thing about this ███ is we never even heard direct from Torrence during that whole mess. It was AIDAN that gave us the red alert. AIDAN that ordered us to fire on the shuttles. Prophet was just supposed to X-out a bunch of civis because the computer says so?

McNulty, J, Sgt: Order must have come from Torrence. The Ai can't make calls like that

Mason, E, LT 2nd: Then why the ███ didn't Torrence transmit the order? He must've known Prophet wasn't going to waste 9 shuttles of civis without meat authorization

Mason, E, LT 2nd: we couldn't just ███ing kill them

McNulty, J, Sgt: chum, I know

McNulty, J, Sgt: I would've done the same thing in your boots

Mason, E, LT 2nd: The brass has got pants full of bricks over this AI, jimmy. I dunno wut's up, but it smells brown

McNulty, J, Sgt: Dorian said they pulled the plug on it

Mason, E, LT 2nd: . . . on AIDAN?

McNulty, J, Sgt: ya. is why the engines are off

Mason, E, LT 2nd: Then what's flying the ship?

McNulty, J, Sgt: momentum, afaik

Mason, E, LT 2nd: . . .

Mason, E, LT 2nd: ███ me

McNulty, J, Sgt: I got some rocket fuel from a squaddie. He got a line to the spanner monkeys. Come over and have a drink chum

Mason, E, LT 2nd: neg

McNulty, J, Sgt: come onnnnnn best cure for those sorrows is to drown em, boy

Mason, E, LT 2nd: no drowning these ones, chum

Mason, E, LT 2nd: these badboys can swim

DO NOT ENTER

Date: 07/23/75
Subject: Nightmare time

Today's group counseling session was taken up by a lady called Martha, who worked in GeoSpec Analysis on Kerenza. I *think*. I guess it doesn't matter where she worked.

Martha had three daughters named Julie, Lela, and Katya.

Julie was six. She died during the evacuation of her school.

Lela was two. She died when their car crashed on the way to the evac shuttles. Martha's husband Tony had Lela on his lap. He died too.

Katya was eight. Martha doesn't know how she died, or *if* she died, just that she never made it off planet.

She's been so quiet through all our sessions. Like me, she never really spoke. You couldn't tell what was going on in her head. She'd sit there, hands folded in her lap, listening. But she's been slowly coming unfastened the last month or two. Strands of hair hanging loose from her normally perfect bun. Buttons done up wrong. Shirt untucked. Little things you see everywhere, but never before on Martha.

Today, she just imploded. She was sitting right beside me.

I don't even know what set it off, but one minute I was counting ceiling tiles, and the next she was talking. One of the guys in the group, Thanh, was in the middle of some story, but he went quiet when she started. He knew it meant something that she'd chosen that moment to speak.

She told us about her girls and her husband. She said she thinks a lot about whether Katya and Julie were scared at the end. That she wasn't there for them. And then she started gasping for breath. Short, sharp, hoarse breaths, like she couldn't drag in enough air, her whole body shaking.

Some people, when they lose it, they scream, they fight. I hope that would be me. Martha just slowly slid down off her chair and folded in on herself. Everyone stared at her like she was contagious, and I reached out like—I don't know, maybe I was going to touch her or something. And suddenly she was crying. Long, low moans that sounded like they were wrenched out of her. All her grief and pain in those noises, like her body couldn't hold it any longer. One piece too many got added to the load, and she couldn't do it anymore.

The group leader called the medics, and by now Martha's probably under sedation, but I'm not.

I'm lying awake in bed, wondering what will happen if one piece too many gets added to *my* load. Wondering if there's any way out for Martha. Any chance she'll ever be okay. I've had to stop myself thinking about Asha. I can't let myself be Martha. Can't lose myself in the people we left behind.

I can hear every sound in my dorm, every rustle as someone turns over, every sigh.

It's impossible to sleep.

There are a lot more of us on board than there were ever supposed to be—the Hypatia's a research vessel, so they have a lot of space, but most of it was intended for samples, labs, stuff like that. There are over 2,000 of us jammed in where there used to be just 500 crew.

My living quarters used to be a storage facility for geological specimens, by which I basically mean rocks. The air leaves a sharp, metallic tang in your mouth, almost salty. It clings to your hair, so you carry it with you and the scent wafts around you when you turn your head. The air is also HOT and kind of humid, because the scrubbers just weren't designed to recyc for this many people. Makes you really, *really* wish we weren't on water rations. You get used to it, though.

They've taken down the shelving and crammed sixteen of us in here. Each person has a bunk that's kind of a shelf sticking out of the wall (you have a belt to stop you from rolling out at night). Being the youngest in the dorm, I'm up at the very top. I don't mind being up high. Sometimes it almost feels safe.

But I still can't sleep. This isn't my room, isn't my place.

There's nothing around me that's *known* anymore. Sure, I have routines—there are times to eat, times to sleep, times to train. I just never realized that on Kerenza there was this background comfort level, the knowledge of safety, that was the bedrock under everything else. My big adventure was going to be college. My little adventures were hikes, choosing classes at school, Ezra even.

I thought he was going to be a *big* adventure, but that's a whole other thing.

Point is, I had no idea how safe I was, because I'd never been *unsafe.* Ezra said that to me once. He was right. I took it all for granted. The constant and comforting background static of the universe.

Now, though there are more routines than ever before, nothing's certain. The Lincoln could catch up with us at any point. It'll be months until we reach the waypoint to Heimdall. Even when we do, we've been isolated for half a year. We could be in the middle of a war, for all we know.

And beyond all that, command won't tell us what's happening. I'm pretty sure they're lying to us about a lot of things that matter, though I don't know why.

And right now, that's just one uncertainty too many.

I don't know my limit, but I'm scared to reach it. I don't know what will happen if I do.

And I still can't sleep.

Participants: ~~Ann Chau, Captain~~
(systemreroute78h@786HG=ByteMe)
~~David Torrence, General~~
(systemreroute78h@865HG=EMason)
Date: 07/23/75
Timestamp: 08:03

EGIN HYPATIA CHAT BASIC V9 CODE ONCLICK="WINDOW OPE

ByteMe: Ezra, u there?

Mason, E, LT 2nd: Who this?

ByteMe: Kady.

Mason, E, LT 2nd: Hello, Dorian. Your timing is as ████ty as your comedy

Mason, E, LT 2nd: You don't happen to have a sister, do you?

ByteMe: It's me, Ezra. I don't know who Dorian is

Mason, E, LT 2nd: I can't believe that scrub told you. McNulty's vault has more leaks than a recycled baby baggie

ByteMe: That's completely disgusting. We have 7 mins until I have to shut this thing down or they'll be able to track it.

Mason, E, LT 2nd: Uh huh

ByteMe: This is not the reception I was hoping for. It's ME.

Mason, E, LT 2nd: Prove it, he cried

ByteMe: How about . . . you sprained your ankle jumping out my bedroom window while I stalled my parents at the front door.

Mason, E, LT 2nd: . . . Kady?

ByteMe: This is what I'm saying. Yes, Kady.

Mason, E, LT 2nd: Well I feel sheepish . . .

ByteMe: `_    -(")-`   baaaaaa
              `%%%`
              `// \\`

Mason, E, LT 2nd: How have you got access to IMs? Ship to ship comms are down?

ByteMe: You're right, how is this happening??? WITCHCRAFT

Mason, E, LT 2nd: This isn't like jacking the school system to give me a passing grade in chem. You could get into a lot of trouble

ByteMe: You did suck at chem. It's fine, trust me. Short bursts, text only, undetectable if we keep it under 7 mins. Comms might be down, but command always leave themselves a back door open in case they want a heart to heart.

Mason, E, LT 2nd: . . . is that what this is? heart to heart?

ByteMe: Let's not get carried away, I wouldn't want to impose

ByteMe: Do you know why comms are down?

Mason, E, LT 2nd: All nonessentials are offline.

Mason, E, LT 2nd: Life support and power is about all we have while the data monkeys do their thing

ByteMe: With the AI? Something's wrong with it, isn't it?

Mason, E, LT 2nd: probably shouldn't be talking about it. We could both meet some serious grief.

Mason, E, LT 2nd: Like, imagine "serious" written in 40 story high letters, set on fire with dancing girls all around it and you're there

ByteMe: I think we are eyeball to eyeball with some serious grief already. Are you ok?

Mason, E, LT 2nd: . . . Why wouldn't I be ok?

ByteMe: The comms aren't the only thing I jacked. I saw your court martial records

Mason, E, LT 2nd: Are you dusted? That's classified UTA intel and we're in wartime. They can charge you with espionage if they catch u

ByteMe: you know, I hadn't considered I'd get in trouble if I got caught. Thanks Ez.

Mason, E, LT 2nd: Kady, I'm not talking about a slap on the wrist I'm talking about them LINING YOU UP AGAINST A BULKHEAD AND SHOOTING YOU

ByteMe: There's no way they'll catch me.

ByteMe: Trust me

ByteMe: I saw what you said to them. That was . . . unexpected.

Mason, E, LT 2nd: how so

ByteMe: You do not have a long history of telling the man to go ██ himself.

Mason, E, LT 2nd: Could've thrown me in the hole for that. Kinda stupid, right?

ByteMe: My kind of idiocy.

Mason, E, LT 2nd: . . .

Mason, E, LT 2nd: maybe I should do it more often then?

ByteMe: Once is enough for now. You're no use to anyone in the hole. Not even sure what that is but I am taking some nasty guesses.

Mason, E, LT 2nd: solitary. Water and dehydrate grub. Occasional visits from a big hairy guy called Raoul.

Mason, E, LT 2nd: I might be exaggerating about the Raoul part

Mason, E, LT 2nd: He's not all that hairy

ByteMe: I saw what you said about your dad, too. I saw his name on the casualty lists after the evac.

Mason, E, LT 2nd: Oh.

Mason, E, LT 2nd: Right.

ByteMe: I'm so sorry, Ezra.

Mason, E, LT 2nd: It's not ur fault. You got nothing to be sorry for

Mason, E, LT 2nd: how's your mom doing over there anyway? Tell her I said hi

ByteMe: How long's AIDAN been down? Since the Copernicus was destroyed?

Mason, E, LT 2nd: Um.

Mason, E, LT 2nd: I shouldn't have told u that. I'm not even supposed to know. Don't say anything, alright? people could get rolled.

ByteMe: Not planning on broadcasting this conversation. They're lying to us tho, you know it. We should just sit here and wait to see what happens next? How'd that turn out for the Copernicus?

Mason, E, LT 2nd: There's no danger to you guys. Nobody's sick on Hypatia, right?

ByteMe: What's sick got to do with it?

Mason, E, LT 2nd: If nobody's sick, then nothing at all. Dun worry about it.

ByteMe: So because we're safe over here we should just swallow whatever lies they want to feed us? Nobody here is saying AIDAN is down. They're pretending the Lincoln is out there and we still have comms, but we have to stay silent to avoid detection. You want to tell me that's true? Saw a great big BeiTech dreadnought when you were out by the Copernicus?

Mason, E, LT 2nd: they're just trying to avoid a panic, Kades

ByteMe: I for one am not feeling super calm.

Mason, E, LT 2nd: you should leave it alone. You could get in real trouble.

ByteMe: We're already in real trouble. I want us to at least be in it together.

ByteMe: Ezra? You there?

Mason, E, LT 2nd: Yeah, I'm here.

Mason, E, LT 2nd: though I'm kinda wishing I was on Hypatia right about now

ByteMe: I am fearsome, but I'm not quite that good. I'll try and get a line up tomorrow. You'll be here?

Mason, E, LT 2nd: As you wish

ByteMe: If only THAT were true. Keep your head down. Don't do anything too noble.

——**CONNECTION TERMINATED**——

HAT/LOGIN ?LOCATION=NO MENUBAR=NO']<!-- END HYPATIA CHAT BASIC V9 CODE --><!-- BE

CitB: sooooo u talking to ur boyfriend again?

ByteMe: not my bf

CitB: u talking to him?

ByteMe: 7 min burst no sign of detection so far

CitB: he know what going on over there?

ByteMe: not spilling

CitB: he know about the AI?

ByteMe: it's down, not spilling more than that

CitB: so work some magic

ByteMe: not as simple as that. u don't just jump into lawbreaking with a guy like Ezra. don't even know if i want to involve him yet.

CitB: then why do it?

ByteMe: to see if i can. now have to decide what to ask him to do. not safe for him.

CitB: not safe for anybody. get it done

CLAS~~SIFI~~ED

General,

As of 11:00 hours, an assessment of the *Alexander*'s Artificial Intelligence Defense Analytics Network (AIDAN) has been completed by myself and Senior TechEng Specialists Major Nico Lassinger and Major Lisa Barker. Junior staff were excluded to preserve the confidentiality of our findings. Status report and recommendations follow.

Current Status

During the battle at Kerenza, AIDAN suffered significant physical damage. Due to losses of key personnel in TechEng, we have been unable to carry out a full diagnostic, but most obviously, we cannot generate a jump gate, and AIDAN's computational speed is reduced. However, damage to AIDAN's neural network may also be worse than first realized.

As per your orders after the destruction of the *Copernicus*, AIDAN remains in shutdown mode, carrying out only essential functions, including recyc, climate moderation, and artificial gravity control. AIDAN is now essentially the equivalent of a human in a coma; breathing and heartbeat continue, but no conscious thought or decision making is possible. As a result, the AI has been unavailable for active questioning. However, in the opinion of my team, it is likely that AIDAN's decision to destroy the *Copernicus* was the result of its directive to prioritize the safety of fleet members.

Our review indicates that, over the last month, AIDAN has accessed *Copernicus* medical records with increasing frequency. As a matter of routine, all data the AI accesses are backed up to the *Alexander*'s servers, however, **AIDAN seems to have taken steps to ensure we cannot locate these particular reports.**

We believe AIDAN formed a view that the illness aboard *Copernicus* had reached a tipping point and posed a danger to the fleet. Nevertheless, we are concerned by AIDAN's decision to (a) take such drastic action without consulting senior command and (b) shut down comms between senior command and the *Alexander*'s Cyclone squadrons, despite your direct orders. AIDAN's design parameters prioritize the preservation of human life but allow the fleet commander almost unlimited override. **We believe the damage to AIDAN may have impacted its willingness to factor in your commands and preferences.**

Proposal

The halt at Kerenza VII(a) for water will have eroded our lead on the *Lincoln*. Without AIDAN online, main drive is inoperative, and we are left to reaccelerate on slower secondaries. It is increasingly likely we will need to engage the *Alexander*'s weapons systems, which cannot be done with AIDAN offline. Therefore, we propose increasing AIDAN's operational level without restoring full independence. If you will permit me to continue the analogy, we propose bringing our coma patient back to consciousness, but under considerable restraint.

Potential Hazards

The *Copernicus* incident demonstrates we are not fully aware of AIDAN's current operational capacity. On revival, AIDAN may not respond to restraints as anticipated, or the restraints may not function as expected. Danger exists for both *Alexander* and *Hypatia* personnel. This must, however, be weighed against the danger of doing nothing.

Revival scenarios will be run over the next 24–48 hours; we are aiming to establish a scenario with a better than 90 percent chance of full control. If this is achieved, we recommend AIDAN be revived.

If you have any further questions or wish to discuss options, we are available at your convenience.

COLONEL EVA SANCHEZ
MAJOR NICO LASSINGER
MAJOR LISA BARKER

CLASSIFIED

Participants: Eva Sanchez, Colonel, UTA Engineering Division
Nico Lassinger, Major, UTA Engineering Division
Date: 07/24/75
Timestamp: 11:37

Sanchez, E, Col: Nico, I've done the memo, can you proof it for me?

Lassinger, N, Maj: Printing it, hold on.

Lassinger, N, Maj: . . .

Lassinger, N, Maj: So basically what you're saying is we'll do our best to wake it up without it going loco, but our best promise is a 9 out of 10 chance it won't kill us all?

Sanchez, E, Col: You know what the chance is if the Lincoln catches us?

Lassinger, N, Maj: Point. Okay, send. And pray.

Sanchez, E, Col: Sent. Praying.

Lassinger, N, Maj: I think I'm going to go see if Lisa needs any help getting the grease off. Climbing around the quantum core like ███ing spanner monkeys is below our pay grade and our dignity, I say.

Sanchez, E, Col: Are you dusted? You ask her if she wants her back washed, you won't NEED to worry about the AI blasting us into the next system.

Lassinger, N, Maj: It's the end of the world, Eva. Nothing left to lose.

BEGIN HYPATIA CHAT BASIC V9 CODE ONCLICK="WINDOW OPEN(//CHAT HYPATIA/ALEXANDER

ByteMe: 7 mins starts now. u there?

Mason, E, LT 2nd: Always :)

ByteMe: Wish that had been true, Ez. How things on your end? Tense here.

Mason, E, LT 2nd: Things here? Confusing, tbh

ByteMe: They're still saying no comms b/c we're hiding from the Lincoln.

Mason, E, LT 2nd: Oh, u mean how are things on the *ship*

ByteMe: Did AIDAN crash or did we take it offline?

Mason, E, LT 2nd: Um. Bit of both. Why?

ByteMe: b/c the Copernicus is gone and I'm scared, why else?

Mason, E, LT 2nd: Hey, at least we're scared together. Ish.

ByteMe: This is not how I imagined us reunited. There isn't any more gen than that on your end?

Mason, E, LT 2nd: *Shrug* I just fly the cyclones ma'am

ByteMe: I can't believe you do. Not the future I imagined either.

Mason, E, LT 2nd: At least I got offworld, right? If only BeiTech had shown up a day earlier. Might have saved you some shouting. And me some hangovers :p

Mason, E, LT 2nd: Sorry that wasn't funny . . .

ByteMe: No, but to be fair, don't think anyone's found a joke that works yet.

ByteMe: Next time we'll have to time our drama better.

Mason, E, LT 2nd: Well, practice makes perfect, as they say

Mason, E, LT 2nd: I miss you

ByteMe: You too.

ByteMe: 2 min left.

Mason, E, LT 2nd: You're a poet, Grant

ByteMe: Hey, I'm talking to you. One step at a time.

Mason, E, LT 2nd: Talking is better than not talking. And infinitely better than shouting :p

ByteMe: Sorry there was so much of that. Should have got the msg sooner.

Mason, E, LT 2nd: Did u ever consider the possibility I just think ur cute when you're angry?

ByteMe: Did you ever consider that I might not laugh at a joke about you breaking my heart?

ByteMe: Gotta cut. If u leave this window open and type in messages, I'll get them when I connect. Like a mailbox.

——**CONNECTION TERMINATED**——

Participants: ~~Ann Chau/ACHAUHYPATIAONBOA~~
(systemreroute78h@786HG=ByteMe)
~~David Torrence/DTORRENCEALEXANDERONBOA~~
(systemreroute78h@865HG=EMason)
Date: 07/25/75
Timestamp: 05:49
Subject: I'm Sorry

EGIN HYPATIA CHAT BASIC V9 CODE ONCLICK="WINDOW.OPEN(//CHAT.HYPATIA/ALEXANDER

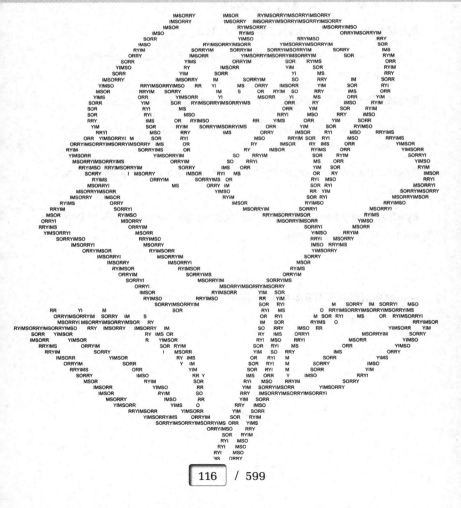

DO NOT ENTER

Date: 07/25/75
Subject: wondering

I wonder how my mom knew my dad was the guy for her.
Why didn't I ever think to ask that?

EGIN HYPATIA CHAT BASIC V9 CODE ONCLICK="WINDOW OPEN[//CHAT HYPATIA /ALEXANDER

ByteMe: U there, you tragic, tragic creature?

Mason, E, LT 2nd: Always :p

ByteMe: All ok your end?

Mason, E, LT 2nd: They got me on scrub duty and VR flight sim. Bored brainless and slightly sweaty

Mason, E, LT 2nd: Am i turning u on?

ByteMe: Ez, u do not want to start another fight.

Mason, E, LT 2nd: I'm just trying to make you smile. You should do it more often. Did u get the flower?

ByteMe: Yes. Just . . . come on, Ez. U made ur position clear. not going to embarrass myself now.

Mason, E, LT 2nd: Did u smile?

ByteMe: yes

Mason, E, LT 2nd: pls excuse me a moment while i do a small victory dance around the room

Mason, E, LT 2nd: k back

ByteMe: this was a terrible idea. I think I miss u more now than when i wasn't talking to u.

Mason, E, LT 2nd: So this must mean you're not still mad at me.

Mason, E, LT 2nd: Amazing what six months and a few thousand kms of vacuum will do to make the heart grow fonder

ByteMe: and terrifying danger, don't forget that

ByteMe: but Ez u are the one who didn't want to be with me, not vice versa. I'm just the one who said the words.

Mason, E, LT 2nd: You wanted to go offworld. I didn't want to hold you back. That means I CARED, not that I didn't.

ByteMe: u could have come

ByteMe: and now here u are, but it's not b/c you want to be. it's b/c I'm more interesting than a ship full of sweaty soldiers

Mason, E, LT 2nd: Im not sure u appreciate the dire peril i placed myself in to have this conversation Kades

ByteMe: i think i quite like the idea of you in dire peril. do go on. details?

Mason, E, LT 2nd: I stayed up half the night making your ASCII flower just so you'd talk to me again. That knowledge in the hands of certain Alexander crew members would have . . . unpleasant consequences

ByteMe: ur courting behavior was always ridiculous

Mason, E, LT 2nd: Hey, don't knock it if it works :)

ByteMe: not that we r courting. aughdeletedelete

ByteMe: u should probably rest in case we come under attack from that ship that is nowhere near us, u know.

Mason, E, LT 2nd: Lincoln might be closer than u think. We had to reaccelerate without the main drive once command shut down the AI at Kerenza VII.

ByteMe: then WHY aren't we getting it back online? not knowing anything is terrifying.

Mason, E, LT 2nd: see previous *shrug* about me just flying the cyclones

Mason, E, LT 2nd: I guess they'll bring it back online once we're safer *with it* than *without it*

ByteMe: guess so. Coming up on 7 mins. talk again soon?

Mason, E, LT 2nd: not too soon. You don't want me to start thinking you've forgiven me or anything

ByteMe: wouldn't want that, you'll get ideas ;)

Mason, E, LT 2nd: cya

Mason, E, LT 2nd: oh say hey to your mom for me

——CONNECTION TERMINATED——

HAT/LOGIN?LOCATION=NO_MENUBAR=NO']<!-- END HYPATIA CHAT BASIC V9 CODE --><!-- BE

ByteMe: what kind of voltage do you think it takes to kill the average human?

CitB: dare i ask?

ByteMe: trying to splice my deck into Hypatia's virtual grid. jack their processor speed

CitB: take it from ur elder. Can't brute-force this. u need work done on the Alexander end

ByteMe: brace urself for this but i am not on the Alexander end so i will have to try and wire from here

CitB: do i really have to point out the obvious?

ByteMe: i am not dragging him into this, they'll shoot him. info is one thing, this is another

CitB: then what the ▮ are you cultivating him for if no info and no wiring?

ByteMe: it's not like that

CitB: it's special

ByteMe: bite me

CitB: there's a lot on the line here. u have to find a way to get him to unlock for you from his end

ByteMe: he wouldn't know how

CitB: then teach

CitB: stakes are high. If ur not chasing him for this, then why

ByteMe: none of your business

CitB: stay on task, grasshopper. we let the Alexander burn us out of the sky, your red hot love will be subsumed by a bigger, hotter flame

ByteMe: how do you even function in society?

CitB: it's a struggle

DO NOT ENTER

Date: 07/25/75

Subject: Without a compass

Today, said our poor, beleaguered counselor, We Are Going To Try Something New. We are going to focus on the fact that despite our personal losses, Life Goes On And There Is Still A Future.

Frankly, I think whether or not we get a future is still hanging in the balance, but I figured expressing *that* opinion wasn't going to add much to the session, so I stuck to Being A Surly Teen. (Huh, the Inappropriate Caps are catching.)

The present is my problem right now. My brain won't stop buzzing, scrambling, trying to hook on to something that will tell me which way is up. I lie strapped into my bunk at night, and it all presses in on me. The bed's so narrow, the blanket smells like the huge laundries they have here, and it itches, and I'm *so not at home.*

Nothing's where it's supposed to be, and without my north, how do I know what to do?

My throat closes when I think about it, and a part of me wants to crawl under the covers and stay there. Wait for someone to tell me what to do. Wait for a grown-up. But nobody's coming.

So do I drag Ezra into danger? Isn't he in more danger if I don't keep trying to work out what's happening?

Everyone here wants to believe the guys in charge know exactly what they're doing, but of course they don't. There's nothing in their rules and regulations for this. They're wounded and limping for safety, and they don't know how to get away from the Lincoln. So why should I trust them, especially when they're lying to me?

There's no clear path ahead of me. They never taught this class in school.

I remember there was this teacher called Ms. McElroy back at McCaffrey. Taught junior tech. She used to go on and ON at me about fulfilling my potential, and I used to roll my eyes, and my mom would tell me to listen to the lady.

She died in the first wave. She looked really surprised.

I don't mean to make a joke there, though I know it sounds kind of sarcastic. I just mean that wasn't the facial expression I would have expected.

She used to talk a lot about how to make decisions as well. Like, she had this idea about exploring your own moral system, but then applying it to a grid to work out what to do. Marrying ethics and technology.

Why didn't I listen to that? I could really use her system for working out the right thing to do around now.

I only know one thing for sure.

Whatever they don't want me to see, that's where I'm digging. I need to be where the secrets are.

I'm more interested in ensuring I have a future than they think.

HAT/LOGIN LOCATION=NO MENUBAR=NO'><!-- END ALEXANDER CHAT BASIC V9 CODE --><!--

McNulty, J, Sgt: ezra

McNulty, J, Sgt: mason

McNulty, J, Sgt: ANSWER ███

Mason, E, LT 2nd: ██ internal comms back on?

McNulty, J, Sgt: they testing

Mason, E, LT 2nd: ah

McNulty, J, Sgt: Dorian pinged me to check if my internal messager was working. I am his test monkey. Watch me monkey

Mason, E, LT 2nd: and of everyone you could've picked to IM, you pinged me. Flattered, you may color me

McNulty, J, Sgt: don't be, ur the only one I knew who'd be in bed at this hour

McNulty, J, Sgt: thinking about Miss Thing

Mason, E, LT 2nd: eat me

McNulty, J, Sgt: first, a kiss from your cherry lips

Mason, E, LT 2nd: maybe if you warm me up a little

McNulty, J, Sgt: k wut are u wearing?

Mason, E, LT 2nd: nothing. Your sister was just here

McNulty, J, Sgt: . . .

Mason, E, LT 2nd: OH BURRRNT?

Mason, E, LT 2nd: flew face-first into that, son

McNulty, J, Sgt: ██ YOU CHUM

Mason, E, LT 2nd: too tired. Told you, ur sis just left

McNulty, J, Sgt: look at you, all sprightly and ██. Big switch from mr Mopey, all "bloo bloo, my troubles have water wings" couple of days back

Mason, E, LT 2nd: cold, chum. cold

McNulty, J, Sgt: thought you'd be all sadpants with no ship 2 ship. No more sexies from Miss Thing to keep you warm

Mason, E, LT 2nd: she's not like that

McNulty, J, Sgt: ah, she special

Mason, E, LT 2nd: she is

McNulty, J, Sgt: u got pix of this astro-princess?

Mason, E, LT 2nd: no sexies, I told u

McNulty, J, Sgt: clothed, fool

Mason, E, LT 2nd: I got school pics

McNulty, J, Sgt: send me

Mason, E, LT 2nd: no chance

McNulty, J, Sgt: SEND

Mason, E, LT 2nd: en oh bee eye tee see haych

McNulty, J, Sgt: Mason, if u no send, I will make it my mission in life to teabag you while you sleep

Mason, E, LT 2nd: 0_o

McNulty, J, Sgt: Shipboard security have master access to all areas, chum

McNulty, J, Sgt: I know where you lay thee down

McNulty, J, Sgt: And you WILL wake one night to feel a pair of slightly sweatysomethings tickling your prettyboy chin

Mason, E, LT 2nd: my ███ing god

McNulty, J, Sgt: I am serious, mason.

McNulty, J, Sgt: this is not a drill

Mason, E, LT 2nd: if I do send

Mason, E, LT 2nd: and then I find hardcopy of this pinned to the ceiling above your bunk

Mason, E, LT 2nd: I will cut your slightly sweatysomethings off and flush them out an airlock

McNulty, J, Sgt: I solemnly swear I will not engage in happypants while looking at pics of ur would-be ex-ex-girlfriend, chum

Mason, E, LT 2nd: . . .

Mason, E, LT 2nd: k, sending

McNulty, J, Sgt: holy ███

Mason, E, LT 2nd: ya

McNulty, J, Sgt: this is her?

Mason, E, LT 2nd: ya

McNulty, J, Sgt: she got pink hair

Mason, E, LT 2nd: she used to dye it

McNulty, J, Sgt: did the carpet match the curtains?

Mason, E, LT 2nd: >_<

McNulty, J, Sgt: how in god's name . . . chum, I have bad news

Mason, E, LT 2nd: let me guess, you're planning to break your solemn vow as soon as you finish speaking to me, rite?

McNulty, J, Sgt: you wound me, chum

Mason, E, LT 2nd: :P

McNulty, J, Sgt: bad news is im typing ths 1 handed

Mason, E, LT 2nd: god no

McNulty, J, Sgt: think im getting the hng of it

Mason, E, LT 2nd: STOP

McNulty, J, Sgt: 1more min

Mason, E, LT 2nd: STOP.

Mason, E, LT 2nd: JIMMY, I SWEAR TO ALL THAT'S HOLY

Mason, E, LT 2nd: I WILL NEVER SPEAK ILL OF YOUR SISTER AGAIN

Mason, E, LT 2nd: JUST STOP NOW

McNulty, J, Sgt: u promise?

Mason, E, LT 2nd: I ███████ING SWEAR

McNulty, J, Sgt: zzzz, fine

Mason, E, LT 2nd: why is it every time I finish talking to you

Mason, E, LT 2nd: I need a ███ing shower . . .

McNulty, J, Sgt: . . .

Mason, E, LT 2nd: you hear that?

McNulty, J, Sgt: shipboard alarm

Mason, E, LT 2nd: they calling your squad, chum. Code blue

McNulty, J, Sgt: ▇ chum, I gotta jump.

Mason, E, LT 2nd: k

McNulty, J, Sgt: taking hardcopy with me

McNulty, J, Sgt: for later

McNulty, J, Sgt: :)

Mason, E, LT 2nd: zzzzzz

Participants: Ezra Mason, Second Lieutenant, UTA Airborne Division
Date: 07/26/75
Timestamp: 08:16

BRIEFING NOTE: Take note of elapsed time—thirteen hours since Mason and McNulty's last chat.

EGIN ALEXANDER CHAT BASIC V9 CODE --><FORM> ONCLICK="WINDOW.OPEN('CHAT.ALEXAN

Mason, E, LT 2nd: you back yet, chum?

Mason, E, LT 2nd: jimmeeeeeeeeeeeeeeeeehhhhhhh

Mason, E, LT 2nd: GIMME SITREP█████

Mason, E, LT 2nd: if u back and in the shower with that pic of K, Ima give little Jimmy the chop and flush him down the head

Mason, E, LT 2nd: zzzzz, I got VR training, ping me back when u get in

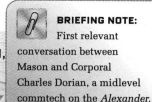

BRIEFING NOTE:
First relevant conversation between Mason and Corporal Charles Dorian, a midlevel commtech on the *Alexander*.

HAT/LOGIN LOCATION=NO MENUBAR=NO')<!-- END ALEXANDER CHAT BASIC V9 CODE -->J-- P

Dorian, C, Corp: Ping.

Dorian, C, Corp: Ping.

Dorian, C, Corp: And at the risk of repeating myself . . .

Dorian, C, Corp: Ping.

Mason, E, LT 2nd: dorian?

Dorian, C, Corp: Bravo. Your insight is as astounding as ever, Mason.

Dorian, C, Corp: It's my sincere belief that your potential is wasted in that sweaty little cockpit. You should be doing the Coreworld lecture circuit. Imagine it: Packed houses. Perfect hair. Screaming girlchildren. "Tonight Only. Ezra Mason: How To State The Bleeding Obvious."

Mason, E, LT 2nd: . . .

Mason, E, LT 2nd: hug?

Dorian, C, Corp: Silence. Let me work.

Mason, E, LT 2nd: Chum, YOU pinged ME.

Dorian, C, Corp: I'm still testing internal comms. Just hold still. This won't hurt.

Dorian, C, Corp: *snaps on latex gloves*

Mason, E, LT 2nd: Dorian, this is really saying something, but you seem ████ier than normal

Dorian, C, Corp: Mason, I've had 3.72 hours sleep in the last six days. There are more stims in my bloodstream than blood. If you want congeniality, try McNulty's sister.

Mason, E, LT 2nd: wut's congeniality and is there a cream for it?

Dorian, C, Corp: Oh, my. You're just hilarious.

Mason, E, LT 2nd: you just figure that out?

Mason, E, LT 2nd: speaking of my future bride, you heard from jimmy?

Dorian, C, Corp: And why would I have heard from James, pray tell?

Mason, E, LT 2nd: isn't that what married couples do? Talk and whatnot? And why u no send him flowers anymore

Dorian, C, Corp: SILENCE, DAMN YOU.

Mason, E, LT 2nd: seriously, you heard from him?

Mason, E, LT 2nd: His squad got called to a code blue, like, 16 hours ago.

Dorian, C, Corp: . . . Indeed?

Mason, E, LT 2nd: ya. Heard nothing since.

Dorian, C, Corp: Give me a moment. I shall check.

Mason, E, LT 2nd: u know Dorian, people say you're a blackhearted ▮▮▮ with all the social skills of a pubic louse. but I know better

Mason, E, LT 2nd: your heart's more gray than black

Dorian, C, Corp: Mason.

Mason, E, LT 2nd: maybe puce

Dorian, C, Corp: Mason, shut up.

Mason, E, LT 2nd: k

Dorian, C, Corp: I have good news and bad news.

Mason, E, LT 2nd: in terms of drama, which one should I ask for first

Dorian, C, Corp: The good news. Most definitely.

Mason, E, LT 2nd: k gimme

Dorian, C, Corp: I found James's squad. They're debriefing in quarantine. The Code Blue is still in effect in Hangar Bay 4, but his squad made it out.

Mason, E, LT 2nd: Can I guess the bad news?

Dorian, C, Corp: You may try.

Mason, E, LT 2nd: Jimmy's not with them.

Dorian, C, Corp: . . . How did you know that?

Mason, E, LT 2nd: I just tried to imagine all the ways things could get worse, then picked the ██████iest option

Dorian, C, Corp: . . .

Dorian, C, Corp: You know Mason, sometimes you're not as stupid as you look.

Mason, E, LT 2nd: you just figure that out?

Participants: ~~Ann Chau/ACHAUHYPATIAONBOARD~~
(systemreroute78h@786HG=ByteMe)
~~David Torrence/DTORRENCEALEXANDERONBOARD~~
(systemreroute78h@865HG=EMason)
Date: 07/26/75
Timestamp: 12:05
Subject: You there?

GIN HYPATIA CHAT BASIC V9 CODE ONCLICK="WINDOW.OPEN(//CHAT.HYPATIA/ALEXANDER

Hey Kades,

Can you ping me back when u get this? Some ███ has gone down. Need your help.
E

CHAT/LOGIN LOCATION=NO MENUBAR=NO'}<!-- END HYPATIA CHAT BASIC V9 CODE --><!-- BEG

ByteMe: well that is not as nice as flowers. what u need?

Mason, E, LT 2nd: A friend of mine is off-grid. Wondering if your powers can work for good as well as evilllllll

ByteMe: do my best. Alexander or Hypatia? tell me what u know?

Mason, E, LT 2nd: Alexander. I dunno if you can even find out this stuff. he's a marine named James McNulty. Crazier than a churchful of dustheads, but he's a good guy.

Mason, E, LT 2nd: he got called to a code blue alert 17 hours ago. Nobody's seen him since. Can you sacrifice something small and fluffy to the bloodgod (or whatever it is you do) and find out where he's at?

ByteMe: seems weird he'd be gone that long and no word. I thought u guys specialized in rumor

Mason, E, LT 2nd: his squad is locked down in quarantine. But he's not with them

ByteMe: I can hunt around but u guys locked down your servers when u took down ship 2 ship comms

Mason, E, LT 2nd: So what does that mean? you can't get in at all?

ByteMe: lemme think

ByteMe: how worried are u?

135 / 599

Mason, E, LT 2nd: capital W.

Mason, E, LT 2nd: the scuttlebutt is real bad. like, u would not believe how bad

ByteMe: i might be able to get in, but only if ur up for helping. this is going to take a few hours

Mason, E, LT 2nd: I'm on lunch break. Back to more sims soon. 8 more hrs. I will die in that VR machine. Sweaty and unloved

ByteMe: u don't know that for sure, there are lots of ways to die here. Go work, i'll have this ready when you're done. Don't do anything dumb(er than usual)

Mason, E, LT 2nd: Roger that

Mason, E, LT 2nd: cold btw :(

HAT/LOGIN LOCATION=NO,MENUBAR=NO']<!-- END HYPATIA CHAT BASIC V9 CODE --><!-- BEG

Mason, E, LT 2nd: Kades?

ByteMe: i'm ready. sending u file. broken into 5 pieces so the size doesn't raise an alert. put all 5 on a mem-chit and you will need to physically plant mem-chit for me. then i can access security

Mason, E, LT 2nd: *raises hand* Um, "physically plant"? In my console, you mean?

ByteMe: i mean onsite. direct access. wouldn't be much of a security system if u could hack it from ur bedroom.

Mason, E, LT 2nd: u ███ing me? They just shot 4 people here a few days ago for disobeying orders from a ███ing insane AI, what u think they'll do to me if they catch me fiddling in its brainmeats?

ByteMe: ur call. would suggest either not getting caught or upping the prayers for ur buddy.

Mason, E, LT 2nd: goddammit

Mason, E, LT 2nd: stupid ██████'s in the ███, I know it

ByteMe: don't really want to find you again just to lose you, Ez, but if this matters to u then i'll help. i can help from here.

Mason, E, LT 2nd: so what does this mem-chit do? install something? Virus or what?

ByteMe: u wouldn't understand. it'll take down some fences so i can get through and extract security feeds for u

Mason, E, LT 2nd: and that's all ur gonna do, right? Ur not gonna poke around in blackbags and get yourself shot too?

ByteMe: would hate to think of u sobbing into ur pillow every nite. just there to help you out.

Mason, E, LT 2nd: . . .

Mason, E, LT 2nd: ■

Mason, E, LT 2nd: alrite, what i gotta do?

BRIEFING NOTE:
More surveillance
footage documented by
our technician, this time
from camera rigs aboard the
Alexander.

Surveillance footage summary,
prepared by
Analyst ID 7213-0089-DN

This kid ain't cut out for this line of work.

I'm not ██████ing you. He might be master-class pilot material, but I've seen better candidates for covert ops floating in the head after I'm done with the morning news. If he ain't religious, he oughta be. Someone up there sure as hell is looking out for him. Just saying.

Damage from the Kerenza assault rendered many of the *Alexander*'s exterior intellicams inoperative, so the first we see of the subject is at 01:10 on 07/27/75, when he enters Deck 231 through a rent in the outer hull. Subject is fully suited for space walk, moving like he's not spent more than ten minutes inside an envirosuit. We can ID one Ezra Mason, conscript UTA Cyclone pilot (UTN-966-330ad), squinting his baby browns through the blastspex visor. He looks like he's about to blow breakfast all over the inside of his helmet. Green as a ████ing blade of grass, I swear.

He cracks his head on the same stanchion twice getting inside, punches it once he's finally through the hole (yeah, that'll teach it, kid), and spends another four minutes getting his rig untangled. There's not much to see him by once he's past the starlight spilling through the breach. At least he's sensible enough to have brought glowsticks. The red does a little bit to offset the green in his face.

Deck 231 is situated in the *Alexander* AI cluster—just banks of damaged towers and cables, some of them still spitting live current.

That this kid made it all the way across Deck 231's sprawl with a BRIGHT RED GLOWSTICK IN HIS HAND without getting picked up by the *Alexander*'s SecTeams shows how stretched they were monitoring their camera feeds. That's the problem with running in one of these AI boats—gets to the point where the computer does everything for you and you forget how to wipe your own exhaust pipe.

He takes almost thirty minutes to thread through the debris, even bouncing with those big zero-grav strides. The server towers are twenty feet cubed, some have broken loose from their brackets, and there's always the death-by-electrocution problem to worry about. He reaches the airlock leading up to Deck 230 and pulls out a datapad, typing with one finger and chewing his lip. Not a pro console jockey who daily threatens the security of our glorious alliance, I'm thinking. Whoever's on the other side of that screen knows how to romance the security console. Working in seven-minute bursts, the kid only takes another forty-nine minutes to get the door open. Record time, no doubt. Shame he didn't pack any confetti.

The airlock doors open and he fumbles his way inside.

Next we see of Lieutenant Twinkletoes, he's in Corridor 230 G-13 and out of his envirosuit (dumped it in the airlock, I'm thinking). He's wearing a rucksack, urban gray camo cargoes, and a muscle tee. His face is flushed scarlet, and it looks like his sinuses are clogged—his body is used to pumping blood up to his head against the pull of gravity, and without gravity to drag it back while he was treading black, his dome is red as the underwear Elizabeth Andretti wears in the finale of *Terminus* (don't pretend you don't know the part I'm talking about, chum—ain't a man alive who hasn't simmed that scene thirty times). The guardian angel behind that pad is at work again; he's stopping to ask for directions every second junction.

Four *Alexander* SecTeam gorillas step out into the corridor ahead, and our astro-ninja just about ▮▮s himself—I mean, uh, "shows signs of extreme anxiety." He ducks into a nearby storage room, sweating like a pitdigger after a twelve-hour stint. His tee is damp with it. Big trembling breaths. He's no doubt wondering what'd happen if his hidey-hole is the same place those Sec boys were headed.

They march past, and he pokes his head out to check if the coast is clear, then does some kind of half-baked kung fu kick at the gorillas' backs, as if promising them an ██ whooping next time he sees them. He blunders along, narrowly missing a TechEng group, then rounds a corner literally three feet from that same SecTeam he almost hit five minutes ago, *all of whom* happen to be looking the other way. I swear to god, he crept away on ██ing tiptoes.

He makes his way to a tertiary node (redundancy system for the ship-wide security feeds). He's whispering to himself, but we get no tone. I'm guessing he's saying "ohmigodohmigodohmigod" a lot. Inside the node room, he boots up the backup processor, inserts a mem-chit and starts some kind of Trojan routine running. It's obvious he's got no ██ing idea what he's about—I mean, "is inexperienced in matters of computer espionage" (shut up, I'm being professional), taking instruction through his datapad and bashing away on the keyboard. It takes thirty minutes, but finally he plants the infection and packs up his ██.

Here's where the magic happens.

Whatever Ultra-Agent Zerooooo seeded in the redundancy network kicks off a fire alarm on Deck 231. The fire alarm not only diverts the SecTeam standing three corridors away, but also sees Deck 230 evac'ed as per standard safety protocols. In five minutes, the entire floor is cleared of personnel.

At a signal from his guardian angel, ██ is out the door like his ██ is on fire. He runs to the service elevators—which should be locked down when a fire alarm kicks off, but lo and behold, his angel has them open wide. He dashes inside and stabs at the habitat level buttons, but there's no real need—SecTeams are mustering two levels up, waiting for fire crews to arrive and deal with the nonexistent blaze.

Four minutes later, he's stepping out onto the habitat level. Out of breath. Drenched. Looking for all intents and purposes like he's just spent an hour in the gym.

He makes his way back to his domicile and shuts the door.

I'd bet my leftie the little ██████ spent the next ten minutes thanking every god in the book, Allah all the way through to Yahweh.

Either that or puking his guts up.

CitB: u still up? u on stims?

ByteMe: never sleeping again. heart ready to burst

CitB: touching. is it love?

ByteMe: harhar. stress and adrenaline.

CitB: you been talking dirty with your bf?

ByteMe: u are so lucky i cannot be bothered coming all the way up the other end of the ship to thump u

CitB: taking out the frustration of separation, r we?

ByteMe: keep misbehaving, i won't share what i got

CitB: . . . this is me behaving. spill.

ByteMe: i told u already there were executions out of the court martials

CitB: yuss

ByteMe: found out why. for disobeying orders from AIDAN

ByteMe: orders to shoot the civis from the Copernicus

ByteMe: orders from the crazy AI

CitB: if those weren't orders from general torrence, then why enforce?

ByteMe: can't admit AIDAN took control. imagine the panic.

CitB: ██████

ByteMe: ayup

CitB: are they any closer to getting AIDAN back up? do not want visitors

ByteMe: don't think so. but we might have a prob sooner than that. got inside, sending u docs

CitB: lover boy helped! our young heroes won the day!

ByteMe: u want them or not?

CitB: shutting up

ByteMe: sending

INTERCEPTED PERSONAL MESSAGE ONBOARD

MEMORANDUM FOR: Captain Ryker
FROM: Teresa Shteyngart, MD,
Chief Medical Officer, *Copernicus* WUC-7891
INCEPT: 12:17, 03/20/75
SUBJECT: Pathogen

Captain,

Having completed examinations of all 1,896 surviving members of the Kerenza attack now residing aboard *Copernicus,* I can confirm several suspicions.

The BeiTech assault *did* include the use of a biochemical agent, apparently delivered via orbit-to-atmosphere missile above the Kerenza hermium refinery. This explains why the illness is confined to the *Copernicus*—ours was the only ship to land shuttles near the refinery and, therefore, the only ship to take on afflicted refugees.

I regret to inform you that, due to the disorder of the evacuation and the sheer number of evacuees, proper quarantine protocol was *not* followed by *Copernicus* flight crews.

After the evacuation, *Copernicus* medical staff received continuous and recurrent reports of acute post-traumatic stress disorder (PTSD) among evacuees. Symptoms included anxiety, nausea, tachycardia, and headaches that were often so severe as to induce physical impairment (tremors, seizures and, in many cases, catatonia/paralysis). However, as this was a logical reaction for civilians surviving a large-scale military incursion, standard treatments for PTSD were initially employed (counseling and pharmaceutical remedies).

It was not until *Copernicus* crew members who were not directly involved in the assault *or* rescue operations began reporting debilitation from these same effects that we began to suspect a larger problem.

I will send another memo with a list of afflicted passengers and crew.

Teresa Shteyngart, MD

MEMORANDUM FOR: Captain Ryker
FROM: Kurt Heyder,
Chief Engineer, *Copernicus* WUC-7891
INCEPT: 15:49, 03/27/75
SUBJECT: Re: Air filters

Harry,

Short answer, no. The air recyc system isn't made to deal with an airborne agent circulating throughout the ship. We could possibly rig up some kind of ionizing field over the CO_2 scrubbers to filter out organic matter, but this isn't going to stop carriers spreading the agent person to person, nor can I give any guarantee that the pathogen will be eliminated in the air we do recyc. This is **EXACTLY** why we have ███ing quarantine protocols. An airborne biological agent loose inside a sealed metal can floating in space has nowhere to ███ing go except back into us. As of writing this, I have nine of my crew down with the Shakes (as the locals are affectionately calling it).

You want to get ███ed at someone, get ███ed at the flight deck controller who let those pitdiggers out of the goddamn hangar bays and into general population.

K.

HEY, KIDS!

Help Astro-Marine Tim win the fight against the space bugs by following these simple rules:

- Always wear your face mask!
- Always wash your hands!
- Always seal doors and bulkheads behind you!
- If you see someone with the Shakes, tell a crew member immediately!!!

MEMORANDUM FOR: Captain Ryker
FROM: Teresa Shteyngart, MD,
Chief Medical Officer, *Copernicus* WUC-7891
INCEPT: 10:31, 06/15/75
SUBJECT: Re: re: re: re: re: Pathogen

Captain,

We are attempting to determine timings now. Anecdotal evidence from the Kerenza attack indicates an incubation period of almost 24 hours, but we have data that conflicts with this.

The virus is airborne. Its debilitating effects vary widely—some people are catatonic for 3–4 days, others recover within 24 hours. Full recovery is almost universal, save in cases of the young or frail. However, there is *no guarantee* against re-infection. That people can be reinfected *at all* is something of a concern—logically, once the immune system fights off the incursion, antibodies should prevent reinfection by the same pathogen.

This would suggest the virus is mutagenic in nature.

I would hypothesize the bioweapon was in a prototypical state when the Kerenza population was exposed—perhaps this attack was a "live fire" exercise on the part of BeiTech forces.

Latest figures follow. Please note the virus is being referred to as "Phobos"

(from the ancient Greek) by many of the technicians in their written reports—
Dr. Salinger has a love of antiquity, and I'm afraid the nickname has stuck.

Teresa Shteyngart, MD

PS: I missed you last night. Do you think we can make time soon?

ARREST REPORT

INCEPT: 06/17/75

DNA RECOG ID: 771-1COP17

ARREST #: 78374jd

ARRESTING OFFICER: BLYTHE, RANDALL, Sgt.

ARRESTEE: MORTON, MARK—Age 31,
              Kerenza refugee ident KR985cop

CONSUMED DRUGS/ALCOHOL? ~~Yes~~/No

IF ARMED, TYPE OF WEAPON: Pipe wrench, screwdriver

CHARGE: Murder, 1st degree (four counts)

NARRATIVE: At 23:45 (shipboard) myself and Corporal Adler were called to a disturbance in temporary domicile GREEN-12b. The habitat was sealed—residents of neighboring domiciles reported brief screaming from within some 15 minutes prior.

Utilizing all-access clearance, Cpl. Adler and myself entered the domicile, suppressors out and up. The body of the first victim (Maryanne Morton—Age 29, KR986cop) was found near the front door. Zero lifesign on bioscan. Brief inspection revealed the victim's head had been crushed by blunt-force trauma. Spray patterns on walls suggested repeated blows.

Second victim (Stephanie Morton—Age 12, KR987cop) and third victim (Oliver Morton—Age 8, KR988cop) were also discovered in this room. Zero lifesign on bioscan. Brief inspection revealed multiple similar wounds on skull and chest resulting from blunt-force trauma. Second and third victims' eyes had been removed.

Infrared bioscan revealed one lifesign in the domicile's bedroom. Cpl. Adler announced our presence and asked the resident (later identified as Mark Morton) to exit the bedroom with hands raised. Resident replied that we were "with them" and demanded we not look at him. Resident became increasingly agitated (in my experience, displaying psychosis similar to tetraphenetrithylamine addicts), finally exiting the bedroom, covered head to foot in blood, with weapons raised.

Cpl. Adler and I both discharged our suppressors, scoring four direct hits to resident's torso region, all of which failed to subdue the resident. The resident closed to striking range, and I was forced to engage in hand-to-hand combat. With the aid of Cpl. Adler, I managed to subdue the resident—Cpl. Adler is still in critical condition due to injuries sustained during this altercation.

With the resident restrained, I called for backup and proceeded into the bedroom, where I discovered the remains of the fourth victim (Julian Morton—Age 4, KR989cop).

Victim's eyes had also been removed.

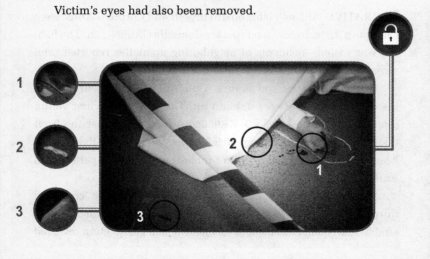

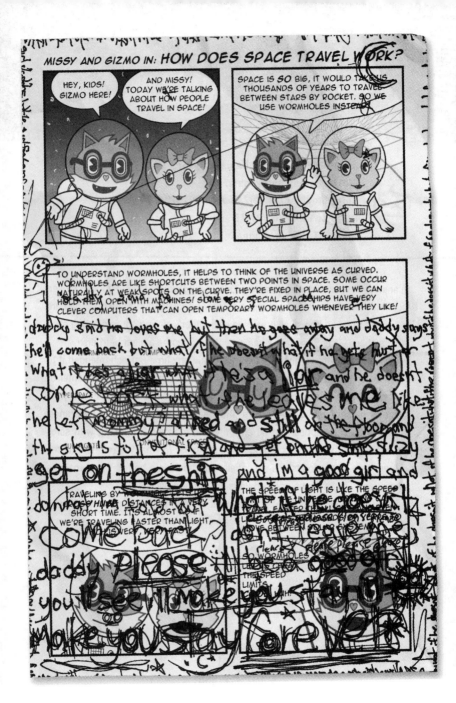

MEMORANDUM FOR: Captain Ryker
FROM: Teresa Shteyngart, MD,
Chief Medical Officer, *Copernicus* WUC-7891
INCEPT: 14:47, 07/07/75
SUBJECT: Re: re: Phobos

In answer to your first question, yes, it's mutating. You're talking about a closed loop with recycled air supplies and almost two thousand more people than are supposed to be on board, all breathing each other's air and contaminating each other's space—the Copernicus has essentially become a giant petri dish.

Second question—no, we can't. I can only presume BeiTech intended it to be an urban pacification device—the virus originally attacked the fear center of the brain, inducing catatonia. So, you hit an urban population with it, everyone falls over paralyzed for 24–48 hours, and the troops roll in with zero resistance. But now the virus appears to be attacking the synaptic gap, along with serotonin reuptake mechanisms, doing damage similar to what you're going to see in long-term dust addicts. It's essentially psychosis in a bottle. The damage is permanent—anyone who goes down is not coming back.

Third—I don't think I can. I really want to, but I just can't get away. Maybe tomorrow.

I miss you too.

Teresa

LABORATORY REPORT

Science Officer: Tobias Salinger, MD
Teresa Shteyngart, MD (assisting)

Incept: 07/12/75

Hour 14

Subject 72 is displaying behavior patterns typical of early Phobos Alpha victims:

- Increased adrenaline levels
- Heart palpitations/hyperventilation
- Tremors
- General unease/nameless dread

Symptoms typically manifest 12 to 24 hours after initial infection with Alpha strain. Symptoms of mutated strain (which we have named Phobos Beta) appear to be more rapid in onset—the latest batch of lab rats Dr. Shteyngart infected displayed psychotic tendencies within 8 hours.

I theorize Phobos Alpha was designed to be spread by initially encouraging *minor* fear responses and only debilitates its carrier with time. Initially (and insidiously), victims will **seek out** contact with others—particularly loved ones—in an attempt to deal with the dread (like a frightened infant might seek its mother). The victim often seeks physical comfort (hand holding, embraces), ultimately increasing the chances of spreading infection.

It's genius, really. Awful, horrifying genius.

Hour 22

Subject 72 has entered a state of full catatonia. Symptoms include:

- Muscle rictus
- Lowered heart rate and core temperature
- Limited pupillary response

Lack of proper equipment and trained personnel make this theory difficult to confirm, but I suspect infection initially targets the sensory cortex and **not** the thalamus, as Dr. Shteyngart suggested. However, we both agree the effect on the amygdala (which decodes emotions and determines possible threats) is profound—afflicted people will often convince themselves they are **not** afflicted, or actively avoid treatment, for fear of punishment/persecution/the isolation of quarantine.

I had intended to begin comparing the cellular resistances of Alpha and Beta; however, one of the assistants (Jane, lovely girl) dropped an entire batch of Beta-infected bloodwork on the floor. Glass everywhere.

Not her fault, really—there's too many of us crowded in here. I was considering sending them all off to get some sleep, but if we don't crack this, nobody will.

Besides, it's good to be around people. The thought of being alone right now is terribly disconcerting.

Hour 27

Subject 72 still in state of paralysis. BPM and breathing below half of human norms.

I have reviewed Dr. Shteyngart's work on the damage the virus inflicts on synaptic vessels and found several errors.

I swear that woman wouldn't know a hippocampus from a hippopotamus. One would think since she's co-authoring this report, she'd spend more time **helping** with it, instead of enjoying our good captain's company. Someone more prone to paranoia might suspect she's simply looking to steal my work and publish it herself.

Presuming we ever make it to a bloody jump gate.

Presuming they **want** us to make it to a jump gate.

Hour 28

Subject 72 showing minor muscle movement. Heart rate increased 12 percent in the last 30 minutes. Body's immune system is fighting the pathogen—as previously surmised, Alpha strain was never intended to permanently disable victims. Still, Subject 72 is displaying remarkable resilience for something so inherently weak.

Twenty-three of us packed in this tiny lab. Forty-six eyes. Sweating away in these flimsy hazmat suits. So thin. So feeble. So little between it and us and us and it.

My foot hurts. My skin itches. Jane asked if I was well. Nosy little slip. None of her business. Couldn't tell her, though, no. Smile and nod, smile and nodnodnodnod.

One of the assistants (can't remember his name—Roberts? Robins?) talks to himself beneath his breath as he works. Thinks no one can hear him but I can.

I hear.

I see.

Oh god.

Hour 29

Shteyngart finally back in the lab.

I wonder if she had time to shower.

Wonder if I'd smell the captain's stink if I peeled that suit open.

She's off dining in Ryker's quarters and whispering her lies about me and meanwhile I'm stuck down here with these ignorant monkeys muttering to themselves and ████ing each other with their eyes and all the while things are getting worse and no one is doing anything to stop it but me.

Jane is looking at me again. With those pretty green things floating in her head.

Stop looking at me.

Hour 30

STOPLOOKINGATME
STOPLOOKINGATME
STOPLOOKINGATME
STOPLOOKINGATME
STOPLOOKINGATMESTOPLOOKINGATMESTOPLOOKINGATMESTOPLOOKINGATMESTOPLOOKINGATMESTOPLOOKINGATMESTOPLOOKINGATMESTOPLOOKINGATMESTOPLOOKINGATMESTOPLOOKINGATMESTOPLOOKINGATMESTOPLOOKINGATMESTOPLOOKINGATMESTOPLOOKINGATMESTOPLOOKINGATMESTOPLOOKINGATMEYOUFILTHY████████

HAT/LOGIN ?LOCATION=NO MENUBAR=NO')<!-- END HYPATIA CHAT BASIC V9 CODE --><!-- BE

ByteMe: read it?

CitB: ███

CitB: ███

CitB: ███

ByteMe: well said

CitB: this is why they cut civi comms a few weeks back. the shutdown date lines up with when it mutated

ByteMe: we never really thought that was for maintenance

CitB: this is why AIDAN blasted Copernicus

ByteMe: we don't know that for sure

CitB: uh-huh

ByteMe: we have a bigger problem

CitB: bigger than the AI killing a third of the fleet? bigger than it HAVING to?

ByteMe: the Copernicus shuttle survivors made it to the Alexander

CitB: makes sense. They took AIDAN offline as soon as it X-ed out Copernicus

ByteMe: WE DON'T KNOW THAT

ByteMe: I found more stuff. I was so sure she was in there. Now I'm praying she isn't. Can't stop shaking.

CitB: wish i could say more than i'm sorry

ByteMe: nobody can. I have to tell Ezra what I found. And those survivors are all just penned up in bay 4

ByteMe: with each other

CitB: . . .

ByteMe: for now

CitB: ██

ByteMe: yeah

ByteMe: ██

HAT/LOGIN.LOCATION=NO.MENUBAR=NO')<!-- END HYPATIA CHAT BASIC V9 CODE --><!-- BEGI

ByteMe: Ez, I got something.

Mason, E, LT 2nd: on jimmy?

ByteMe: ya. it's not conclusive, though. i think we should wait for more before you read

Mason, E, LT 2nd: Hell no, send now. Is he ok?

ByteMe: look, i didn't want to lie to you and say I didn't find anything, but don't think you should read, honest

Mason, E, LT 2nd: why not what happened

Mason, E, LT 2nd: Kades?

ByteMe: look, it's not good, but it's—it's too soon to know, can you just trust me?

Mason, E, LT 2nd: why what's wrong?

Mason, E, LT 2nd: JESUS, TALK TO ME

ByteMe: i'm not trying to make this worse. there was a lot of stuff in those files.

Mason, E, LT 2nd: do you know something or not? This is my FRIEND dammit

Mason, E, LT 2nd: he was there when I was losing my ███ over you. he was there looking out for me when my dad died and I had no one else. I OWE him, Kady

ByteMe: he was there when i wasn't, is what you're saying

Mason, E, LT 2nd: jesus, this is NOT about you and me. TELL ME WHAT U KNOW

ByteMe: promise me u won't do anything stupid. promise me u understand it won't help him to have u in trouble

ByteMe: Ezra?

Mason, E, LT 2nd: fine i promise

ByteMe: i mean really promise. not say whatever you have to say to get what you need. i can't lose you, Ez. you're all i have.

Mason, E, LT 2nd: god, it's really bad isn't it?

ByteMe: u could make it worse if you do something stupid. put us both in danger.

Mason, E, LT 2nd: I promise. Cross my heart and hope to die.

ByteMe: just cross your heart

Mason, E, LT 2nd: k

ByteMe: sent

INCEPT: 07/26/75 (11:17 shipboard time)

LOCATION: United Terran Navy battlecarrier *Alexander* (Hangar Bay 4)

OFFICER IDENT: Winifred McCall (UTN-961-641id)

RANK: First Lieutenant

_____

At 19:06 (shipboard) on 07/25/75, Sigma Squad and I were scrambled to a Code Blue alert issued by *Alexander* command. Squad mustered in a timely fashion to Deck 146, where we were briefed by Executive Officer Lia Myles on behalf of General Torrence.

Sitrep: The *Copernicus* refugees quarantined in Hangar Bay 4 had engaged in some kind of riot in protest over their conditions—violence was ongoing. Sigma Squad was ordered to enter the bay and restore order. Video surveillance rigs within the bay had been disabled/destroyed, and bioscanners wouldn't penetrate the bay walls, so we'd be proceeding blind. We were issued hot ballistics and authorized for lethal force. We were also equipped with hazardous materials kits, including fully sealed Type A envirosuits.

"Why the hazmat gear?" I asked.

~~I already knew the answer—scuttlebutt had been rife about the sickness on the *Copernicus*. Everyone knew odds were good at least a few of those refugees were carriers. I just wanted someone in command to acknowledge it.~~

XO Myles glared ~~with those pretty eyes~~ for a good long while before she answered. ~~Myles doesn't like me, see. She's academy-trained and a born politician. She looks at the battlefield commission on my chest and presumes I think I'm better than her.~~

~~She's a clever one.~~

"Excellent question, Lieutenant," she finally answered. "We suspect a mutated strain of the Phobos virus—now a Class Alpha Zero pathogen—is loose in Bay 4. It's possible none of the refugees are afflicted. However, we're taking no chances. I reiterate. The use of lethal force is authorized. No one without a sealed hazmat suit gets out of that bay alive."

"You want us to shoot civilians."

"I want you to protect the six thousand–plus people in this fleet, Lieutenant. I want you to stop, by any means necessary, an afflicted body getting into the *Alexander*'s general population and spreading that pathogen aboard this ship."

Hands on hips.

"I want you to do your job."

A few of my rookies conscripted from the Kerenza refugees looked a little panicked at that notion. They might know people in the Hanger Bay 4 crowd, after all. They had no training with chemical agents or bioweapons—after six months, most barely knew the business end of a VK-85 burst rifle or how to lace their boots right. ~~As ranking officer, I had to toe the company line, but my 2IC,~~ Sgt. James McNulty, stepped up ~~to ask the obvious questions I couldn't~~.

"So if these civis are infected, why don't we just leave them locked in the bay?"

"They have *Copernicus* engineering staff among them," XO Myles replied. "They're trying to break through the airlocks. Given the tools available, they'll succeed in time."

"Why don't we just open the outer doors and space them?"

That was Sykes, one of my surlier corporals. ~~Word around the barracks was he'd got a vidcall from his wife three days before the~~

~~Kerenza attack, telling him she was running off with her psychoanalyst. She even took their dog. She hated dogs, apparently.~~

"Slam a lid on that noise right now, Corporal," I ordered.

"It's a valid question," Myles said.

My eyebrows hit the ceiling at that one. ~~Cold as the belly of the void, little Lia Myles.~~

She turned to Sykes. "The refugees have disabled the locking mechanism on the outer bay doors. We can no longer operate them from the bridge. They must have suspected flushing them was an option."

"Wonder what gave them that idea," McNulty muttered.

"Further questions?" she asked, looking at me.

Silence.

"Right. Good hunting."

We suited up. No banter among my boys. No jokes. Bad sign. I was watching my Kerenza rooks close, wondering if they were going to hold nerve when ordered to open fire on people they knew. If the concept of the "greater good" was going to sink through to those trigger fingers, past notions like loyalty and friendship and love.

In the end, I made the call to bench them—keep them in reserve outside the second airlock. It meant Sigma was going in shorthanded, but there wasn't a soul among them who didn't look relieved.

We proceeded to the hangar decks, Bridge Control cycling us through the three heavy-duty doors, one at a time—we still had our all-access passes, but command had issued a security override on Bay 4. Each airlock closed behind before the new one opened in front and cycled through a full atmo purge. Command reported the first inner door had already been compromised—seemed the mice had been busy. Ordering my reserves to hold position at the second door and kill anything that didn't ID itself, I requested command open the final seal.

The door shuddered wide. The hangar beyond was unlit. ~~Black~~

~~as the empty past the outer bay doors.~~ We engaged thermal vision and stepped inside, VKs ready.

"Safeties off," I ordered.

McNulty took point, creeping into the dark. I could see welding gear and industrial cutters scattered about the inner door, scorch marks on the titanium. The silence was almost total—it'd been days since they took AIDAN offline and cut the main drive~~, but I still wasn't used to it. Those engines used to be a constant. A thunder you could set your back against. A heartbeat.~~

~~Gone now. And mine wasn't loud enough to replace it.~~
~~Yet.~~

The bay was huge, stretching off in every direction, but I took my best guess and motioned for Sigma to proceed. I could see the abandoned *Copernicus* shuttles in the darkness—nine bulky scarabs, a makeshift barricade welded around them, like some circled wagon train from a history VR. I thought I saw a flicker of movement in a porthole for an instant, and then it was gone.

We were on our way toward them when we found the first bodies.

~~I've seen people die. Die hard. Die messy. Job like mine, you live with the reaper every day. But if you're unlucky, it's not the bullets that kill you in this gig. It's moments like these. Killing you one piece at a time.~~

There were twenty of them, all up. Eleven males, nine females. Children through to middle age. I'm not sure where the heads were—we never found them. They were stripped to the skin. Twisted on the floor in some kind of pattern. It wasn't until I vaulted up onto a fuel drum and got a bird's-eye view that I realized they were arranged to form letters. Two words spelled out on the floor in cold, naked meat.

HELP US.

"Jesus Christ," Sykes breathed.

"Not sure he's listening, chum," McNulty said.

"Stow it, McNulty," I ordered.

"Knife wounds," Sykes said, kneeling by one of the bodies. "Multiples."

"Well, whoever did it probably wasn't considerate enough to cut their own throat afterward," I said. "They're still in here. Eyes open. Stay chill."

I could feel McNulty's eyes on me in the dark.

"What the *hell* is going on here, LT?"

Screaming.

We heard it in the distance, echoing through the *Alexander*'s guts. A girl. Pleading.

"Move!" I hissed, and we were running. ~~Sweat on my skin. Finger on my trigger.~~ I could see more bodies crumpled in the dark but didn't stop long enough to inspect them. Broken skulls and opened wrists. ~~This was no protest. This was no riot.~~

Shapes appearing out of the darkness ahead. Five of them. Voices babbling.

"There she is!"

"Hold her still!"

"Help me!"

"The knife! Get the knife!"

"Help!"

"UTA MARINES!" I bellowed. "FREEZE!"

I could see them. Covered in blood. Wild-eyed and pale. Three men and a woman gathered around a little girl no more than nine or ten years old. She was screaming, pleading. A fat man sat atop her chest, crushing the breath out of her. The other three stood over them, iron bars and pipe wrenches in hand, slicked to the elbows in blood.

"Drop the weapons!" McNulty roared.

Sigma Squad fanned out around them, red laser sights cutting through the black.

"You █████s," the woman spat. "*Now* you come?"

"You left us in here to die!" shouted another.

"Drop the weapons, step away from the girl, and put your hands on your head!" I shouted.

"Miss, you don't understand," the fat man moaned. I realized he was crying. Tears cutting trails down bloodstained cheeks. "She's with them. *She's with them.*"

"Drop the weapon!"

The man was struggling to breathe. Fingers drumming on the bloody metal in his fist.

"Eric . . . ," the woman said.

"She's with *them*!"

"You stupid mother███████, drop it!" Sykes bellowed.

"DROP IT NOW!"

I looked across the dark to that girl's face. Big brown eyes. One hand up to shield her head. So little. So helpless. Nothing between her and the end but us.

The fat man raised his pipe wrench.

"Eric, don't!"

"FIRE!"

Muzzle flashes lit the dark. Our VKs roared. And when we were done, there were four new bodies on the floor, staring sightless up into the black above our heads, waiting for a God who wasn't coming.

The girl's wails filled the quiet. McNulty stowed his VK, ran across the carnage, and picked her up from the bloody grille. He held her to his chest, those big arms wrapped around her tight. Doing all the right things. Making all the right noises.

"Hush, baby, it's okay. You're all right now, Uncle Jimmy's got you."

He'd have made a good dad, McNulty.

I don't know where she had the shiv. Up her sleeve. In her dress. I caught a glimpse of silver, a flash of red. McNulty roared as the blade punched through his hazmat suit and the ballistics weave underneath. Our gear is built to take a knife from a charging gorilla or a point-blank burst from a heavy rifle. God knows where she got the strength.

McNulty shouted, throwing her aside and clutching his wounded arm. The girl hit the deck, twisted up into a crouch, lips peeled away from yellow teeth. She leapt at Private Henderson and put her shiv through his hazmask—punched right through the eyehole. Her stare locked on mine as his body hit the deck. Big and brown and brimming with hate. Bloody steel in one little red fist.

"Don't look at me," she hissed.

Sykes put her down. Single shot, right between the eyes. Dropped her before I could blink. And then we heard them. Calls out in the dark. One after another after another. Something skittered across the deck at us, fizzing and spitting tiny sparks.

Pipe bomb.

"Grenade!"

The blast took out Gandolfini, Montano, and Parker; the second would've taken off my legs if I'd moved a little slower. I could see shapes in the dark—dozens of them—more pipe bombs raining from the gantries above. The explosions lit up the hangar's belly like fireworks on Terra Day, lit up the body of that ten-year-old girl with a bullet in her face and a bloody knife still clutched in her hand. And I did what any officer with a brain would've done. Battlefield commission or not.

"Fall back! Fall back!"

To Sigma's credit, we held formation as we peeled off, laying down suppressing fire as I grabbed McNulty and slung his arm around my shoulder. The hostiles were smart—I'd heard that Phobos turned you mindless, but they were moving with intent, trying to cut off our retreat. A dozen VK pulse grenades talked them out of it, cleared us a path back to the airlock. McNulty was cursing beneath his breath the whole time, calling himself stupid. He didn't seem too badly wounded, though—I thought his gear saved him from the worst of it.

It wasn't until we'd sealed the secondary airlock behind us that I realized how wrong I was. As the Kerenza rookies gathered about us and babbled, XO Myles's voice rang in my headset.

"Sigma, this is Comm. Lieutenant McCall, report status, over!"

"Comm, this is Sigma. At least forty hostiles in the bay. Henderson, Parker, Gandolfini, and Montano are down. McNulty is injured. Over."

"Sigma, Comm. Did any hostiles make it through, over?"

"Comm, Sigma. Negative. They're sealed outside Airlock 2. Cycle us through, over."

"Sigma, Comm. You said you have a squad member injured? Confirm, over."

"Comm, Sigma. Affirmative. McNulty took a knife wound. It's not serious, but he—"

"Is his suit intact? Over."

McNulty looked at me, then. And I saw it in his eyes.

"Comm, Sigma—"

"Is his suit intact?"

~~He had blue eyes, McNulty. Pretty as oceans.~~

"Lieutenant, *is his suit intact*?"

". . . Negative."

"Winifred, you cannot bring that man through the airlock, do you understand me?"

"Lia . . ."

"Fred, you *cannot* bring him through."

The battlefield commission on my chest weighed about ten tons right then. Made it hard to breathe. Impossible to speak. ~~It's not the bullets that kill you. It's moments like these.~~

~~One piece at a time.~~

In the end, McNulty spoke for me.

"Comm, this is McNulty. I copy. Order acknowledged, over."

I found my voice then. Barely. "Sergeant, I—"

"Forget it, LT." He patted his rifle. "If they make it through the airlock before you come back with the cavalry, I got a little something waiting for them."

"We *are* coming back for you, Sergeant."

He smiled then. "'Course you are."

The airlock cycled open behind us. ~~A full detachment of MPs were waiting, suppressors and VKs trained on us—just in case we tried to bring McNulty through. Cold as the belly of the void, little Lia Myles. Not sure what I ever saw in her.~~

McNulty gave us a salute. I could still see his smile. No fear in his eyes then. Just duty.

~~He'd have made a good dad.~~

"Hey, LT," he said as the doors cycled closed.

"Yes, Sergeant?"

"You see Ezra Mason around, remind him his first kid's name is James. Or Jamette." He patted his breast pocket. "And tell him not to worry. I've got Astro-Princess to keep me warm."

"Astro-Princess?"

"He'll know what I mean."

~~I'd prefer a thousand bullets to a moment like this.~~

"Roger that, Sergeant."

"Take care, LT."

That was the last we saw of him.

I am officially recommending Sergeant James McNulty for the Silver Star for Bravery.

1st Lieutenant Winifred McCall
UTA Marine Division
Battlecarrier *Alexander*

EGIN HYPATIA CHAT BASIC V9 CODE ONCLICK="WINDOW OPEN(//CHAT HYPATIA/ALEXANDER

ByteMe: Ez? please tell me you're still there?

Mason, E, LT 2nd: those ████s

Mason, E, LT 2nd: THOSE MOTHER████S

Mason, E, LT 2nd: A SILVER STAR FOR HIS ████ING COFFIN?

ByteMe: Ez please stay at the keyboard, please talk to me. please.

ByteMe: he's not dead yet. they don't say that.

Mason, E, LT 2nd: they LEFT HIM IN THERE. what happens when
those lunatics break through to the second airlock?

Mason, E, LT 2nd: We have to get him out of there. can you hack
the bay doors?

ByteMe: i can't. promise I'm not just saying that. She says in the report
their all-access passes don't work on the bay doors. command has an override in
place. please Ez, don't do anything stupid. we have to think. you're no use to
anyone in the hole.

ByteMe: or shot.

Mason, E, LT 2nd: get me some schematics, i'll go down there and cut
him out myself

ByteMe: and THEN what? Do you think for a second that's what he'd tell you to do?

Mason, E, LT 2nd: Kady I can't leave him, he's DEAD if he stays in there.

ByteMe: you promised me. he knew what he was doing. believe me, if I saw a way out I'd take it, but I can't change this, and you promised me you wouldn't get yourself killed too. you can't.

Mason, E, LT 2nd: promises are just words. they don't mean a thing

ByteMe: words don't mean anything?

ByteMe: are you ██ing kidding me?

ByteMe: words are all we have right now. you're all I have. you can't leave him, but you can leave me?

ByteMe: what about when you said you loved me? when you said you wanted the best for me? all that was just ██, was it? doesn't mean anything as soon as there's something that matters more?

Mason, E, LT 2nd: Kady i DO love you.

Mason, E, LT 2nd: god

Mason, E, LT 2nd: you're all i think about. Every time I close my eyes, i see you. Every time I dream, you're there. I think about us and how i messed it up and it's like someone is tearing my insides out.

ByteMe: then don't get yourself killed.

ByteMe: i'm hurting for him because you are, even if I don't know him, but he chose to stay there. he knew what it meant. he'd never forgive you if you got yourself sick, or shot, not if he's any kind of friend. what you do when ██ like this happens is you LIVE, you survive it, that's how you honor the ones you lost

Mason, E, LT 2nd: he's not lost yet. I can't just sit here and do nothing

ByteMe: you give me one thing you can actually do, one thing that might have a chance of saving his life, and we'll talk. making demands based on info you shouldn't have gets you nowhere. maybe gets you shot. and who says they're doing nothing?

Mason, E, LT 2nd: i do. What's one more drone or bruiser or commtech to these people? we're just statistics to command. just numbers

ByteMe: that doesn't answer my question, Ez. I'm not saying don't care about him. I'm saying don't get killed for no reason. Please. I won't be okay.

Mason, E, LT 2nd: what does that even mean?

ByteMe: it means

ByteMe: it means screw you for making me get into this when i don't want to

ByteMe: but i ███ing love you too

ByteMe: and I won't be okay if you get yourself shot

ByteMe: so please, please just don't. please don't make me sit over here freaking out about what you might be doing.

Mason, E, LT 2nd: whoa, back up about three paragraphs there, cowgirl

ByteMe: please, Ez.

ByteMe: Ez?

Mason, E, LT 2nd: ok

Mason, E, LT 2nd: ok, i won't do anything stupid

ByteMe: i'm so sorry. truly.

Mason, E, LT 2nd: . . .

Mason, E, LT 2nd: god, i wish you were here

ByteMe: me too

ByteMe: but we're way past 7 mins. i'm so sorry but I have to go.

Mason, E, LT 2nd: yeah

Mason, E, LT 2nd: ok

ByteMe: stay safe. please. for me.

Mason, E, LT 2nd: I will.

Mason, E, LT 2nd: for you

ByteMe: you promise?

Mason, E, LT 2nd: i promise.

To: David Torrence/DTORRENCEALEXANDERONBOARD
From: Ann Chau/ACHAUHYPATIAONBOARD
Date: 07/27/75
Timestamp: 09:05
Subject: Offer

David,

I've done everything you've asked. I've tested and trained civilians and sent them across for conscription. I've stripped my ship to reequip the *Alexander*. I've passed on what I believe to be misinformation to my crew and the refugees aboard the *Hypatia,* advising them the *Lincoln* was responsible for the destruction of the *Copernicus* and the deaths of their friends and families.

To say I am uneasy with this would be an understatement. I had friends and colleagues aboard that ship. I've cooperated at every turn. At this stage I cannot continue to operate in the dark.

Our long-range scopes are now picking up the *Lincoln* in pursuit of our fleet. If we're seeing her now, I assume you've known she's closing in on us for some time. We burned our lead when we stopped to resupply. It's not a matter of if the *Lincoln* will catch us anymore. It's when. And when she catches us, we need to be able to fight her.

We estimate she'll close to weapons range in just under three days—seventy hours, to be precise. We need your defense grid. Your rail guns. Your nukes. You need to bring your artificial intelligence back online, David. And if something's preventing you from doing that, you need to let us help. I've still got my skeleton crew here, and they're damn good at what they do. Give us access to your systems and let us help you.

We're in this together. A quarter of your ship's crew are conscripted civilians right now. Don't discount our help just because my crew are civilians too.

I look forward to your earliest response.

Ann Chau
Captain
Science Vessel *Hypatia*

To: Ann Chau/ACHAUHYPATIAONBOARD
From: David Torrence/DTORRENCEALEXANDERONBOARD
Date: 07/27/75
Timestamp: 10:00
Subject: Re: Offer

Ann,

I've arranged log-ins and a secure channel for your tech crew, which will allow them to work with mine in running scenarios.

No other crew members are to use the secure channel—it is available for designated personnel only. Be advised the secure channel is considered a military asset, and while they're assisting on this project, your people are subject to military law.

If I catch any of them in even the slightest infraction, from checking in on their buddies to ████ing about the situation, I won't hesitate to court martial them.

Don't lose your nerve. This is a long way from over, and we're not done yet.

David

Log-in details:
1/2 Zhang/Byron:
Log-in: Alexander/Core/Full/ZhangB
Password: skjh45mh2
2/2 Nestor/Consuela:
Log-in: Alexander/Core/Full/NestorC
Password: 24rkdga9s

**COUNTDOWN TO
LINCOLN INTERCEPTION
OF ALEXANDER FLEET:**

70 HOURS: 24 MINUTES

BEGIN HYPATIA CHAT BASIC V8 CODE ONCLICK="WINDOW.OPEN(//CHAT.HYPATIA/ALEXANDER

ByteMe: howdy neighbor

Zhang, B: ███ me, what are you doing on this channel?

ByteMe: o now is that nice?

Zhang, B: u piggybacking?

ByteMe: doesn't look like Corporal Boklov is using his ID right now so i thought i'd see what ur up to

Zhang, B: nothing slows u down

ByteMe: unlike u. looks weird, seeing your actual name there. ur totally CitB in my head.

ByteMe: so still don't have this sorted? whats the holdup?

Zhang, B: it's not that ███ing easy is the holdup. u here to help?

ByteMe: affirmative, sensei

ByteMe: u getting any gen out of the military techs about how things are over there?

Zhang, B: worried about your bf?

ByteMe: yes

Zhang, B: oh

Zhang, B: well that makes the teasing a little less fun

ByteMe: answer?

Zhang, B: nope, they not feeling talkative

ByteMe: how u holding up? have u stopped to eat or drink or sleep lately?

Zhang, B: not a lot of any of those.

ByteMe: u want me to bring u something?

Zhang, B: no, don't want any footage of u coming near me, in case they notice u

Zhang, B: it all takes a bit longer, doing it remotely from the Hypatia. Just a little delay on every command, starting to drive me nuts.

Zhang, B: not exactly volunteering to head over to the Alexander and do it in person tho

ByteMe: any of these military folks know what they're doing?

Zhang, B: some. Guy called Dorian is on it, a couple of the others, but most trying to fill shoes not meant for them, got promotions after Kerenza.

Zhang, B: But no matter how good u are, trying to work out how to turn AIDAN back on under restraint is like trying to work out how to strap down an octopus, only u have no idea how many arms the ███er has and u have to work in the dark

ByteMe: ok, show me where i can help. we have to get moving. Lincoln isn't waiting.

Zhang, B: u holding up ok?

ByteMe: trying. let's go to work

From: Captain Ann Chau, *Hypatia* Command
To: Syra Boll (Chief—Navigation), Kate Irving (2IC—Maintenance)
Date: 07/27/75
Timestamp: 12:03
Subject: Our options

Syra, Kate:

I need some quiet calculations. Hypothetical only, of course, but it's appropriate for us, as the senior staff, to consider every potential step necessary to preserve the safety of the *Hypatia*.

Please compile a confidential report considering:

- the navigational ability of our current staff (Syra)
- the current condition of our ship (Kate)
- our ability to increase velocity and augment defense systems of any description (Kate)

My question, essentially, is this: If we were to leave the *Alexander* and strike out for safety on our own, through either choice or necessity, what are our chances?

I want a list of likely scenarios, a report on our probability of survival, and ideas on any steps we can take to increase our odds. The *Hypatia* was never meant to brave the black without an escort, but we need to work out how our minnow can survive without her guardian shark. We need to be prepared, just in case.

Kate, please don't include Peyak in this. I'm aware he's still unhappy about

Matt's conscription and would not be willing to assist in compiling any plan for leaving the *Alexander* behind. In fact, I think he'd probably tell Matt as quick as he could, assuming comms ever come back up.

You've got twelve hours to put together as much data as possible for me, then we'll meet in person to discuss your findings.

Ann

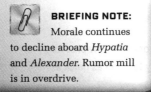

OFFICER MEMORANDUM

BATTLECARRIER ALEXANDER—78V

INCEPT: 07/27/75

FROM: GENERAL DAVID TORRENCE

COMMAND STAFF EYES ONLY

Officers of the *Alexander,*

This is rumor control. At 20:17 on 07/25/75, Marine Squad Sigma engaged hostile Kerenza refugees afflicted with the mutated Phobos virus in Hangar Bay 4. Sigma Squad was unable to secure the area. Several marines were killed in this altercation. Sigma is now in lockdown.

I will state this as plainly as I can: There has been no quarantine breach. **NO afflicted personnel have gained access to the general population of the *Alexander*.** Any speculation to the contrary is, at best, detrimental, and, at worst, **treason.**

Shorthanded as we are, and unable to guarantee our marines' safety, I have determined to leave Bay 4 sealed, reinforce the doors and allow the afflicted within to succumb to starvation. With the main drive still offline, *Lincoln* is now closing to within striking distance. All pilots—even disciplinary cases—are to be reinstated to flight status. *Hypatia* neurogramming staff have been assisting with the work on AIDAN. TechEng will report latest results at 07:00 tomorrow to senior staff. I trust Colonel Sanchez and her team will have found a solution to our AI dilemma by then.

You all know fear is poison in battle. You, as officers, must do everything in your power to stop this situation from turning toxic.

You will explain this **in no uncertain terms** to your respective staff members. Conjecture and rumor-mongering serve no purpose but to degrade unit cohesion. Morale is at a flash point already—the last thing we need is people operating rashly under misinformation. And frankly, with things being what they are, if your people have time for watercooler whispering, they're not working hard enough.

Over six thousand lives are on the line here, people.

We should be *doing,* not talking.

Centrum tenenda.

David Torrence
General, United Terran Authority
Commander, *Alexander 78–V*

GIN ALEXANDER CHAT BASIC VS CODE -->< FORM> ONCLICK="WINDOW OPEN('CHAT ALEXANDE

LeFevre, S, Pvt: Dorian, this install sequence still isn't working.

Dorian, C, Corp: Damnation. Send it to me and I'll look at it once I'm done hand-holding these civilian techs over on Hypatia.

LeFevre, S, Pvt: did you just say "damnation"? god, you even swear posh. *très* sexy.

Dorian, C, Corp: What do you want, Stephanie?

LeFevre, S, Pvt: what makes u think I want anything?

Dorian, C, Corp: Because you're flirting with me. And unless I missed a memo and have somehow become . . . now what was the term you used again?

Dorian, C, Corp: Oh yes . . .

Dorian, C, Corp: "The last functional ▇ in the verse"

Dorian, C, Corp: . . . then you want something. So, what can I do for you?

LeFevre, S, Pvt: How bout u meet me in Server Room D

LeFevre, S, Pvt: and tear me out of these coveralls with your teeth

Dorian, C, Corp: . . .

Dorian, C, Corp: Are you serious?

LeFevre, S, Pvt: lol

LeFevre, S, Pvt: oh, LORD, no.

186 / 599

LeFevre, S, Pvt: lolololololololol

Dorian, C, Corp: I'm a bloody corporal, you know. I outrank you. Technically, I could have you brought up on charges for that.

LeFevre, S, Pvt: which would leave you stuck doing this install alone.

Dorian, C, Corp: Damn your logic, Private. Damn it straight to hell.

LeFevre, S, Pvt: hey u hear about that snafu with Sigma Squad?

LeFevre, S, Pvt: I heard they lost 12 guys. And two of the refugees broke out of the bay

Dorian, C, Corp: If that were true, I suspect we'd be under lockdown by now, yes?

LeFevre, S, Pvt: u did hear something then

Dorian, C, Corp: Nothing I'm at liberty to share. Back to work, please.

LeFevre, S, Pvt: I'm waiting on this upload. u can tell me, Charlie

Dorian, C, Corp: My lips are sealed.

LeFevre, S, Pvt: well

LeFevre, S, Pvt: I can fix that

Dorian, C, Corp: Meaning what?

LeFevre, S, Pvt: meet me in Server Room D

Dorian, C, Corp: . . .

Dorian, C, Corp: Are you serious?

Dorian, C, Corp: . . . Stephanie?

< Dorian, C, Corp: user log-out due to inactivity >

POPULACE
INFORMATION RELE

ISSUED BY: CAPTAIN CHAU,
SCIENCE VESSEL *HYPATIA*

DATE: 07/27/75

TIME: 17:00 (Shipboard Standard)

ASSIGNMENT: *ALEXANDER* FLEET

Friends,

I am pleased to report that repairs to the *Alexander*'s drive systems are proceeding ahead of schedule, and we should be returning to maximum velocity within the next few days. Unfortunately, we are still unable to provide exact timings, but rest assured the tech crews involved are working tirelessly to ensure the safety of the fleet.

The *Lincoln* has not shown itself since the attack on the *Copernicus*—it's possible the damage sustained during the *Copernicus* assault has rendered it incapable of further pursuit. However, General Torrence and his staff are continuing repair operations around the clock, and the sanctuary of *Heimdall* Station is closer than it has ever been. We ask for your patience for the next few days—the worst is almost over.

Patience is not without its rewards, however! I'm informed that Lieutenant Mifune has dredged up another cinema classic from his collection for screening in Amphitheater A—tonight we have the award-winning thriller *Terminus,* starring Blake Hill and Elizabeth

Andretti. First session will commence at 19:00 hours. The film contains some mature content, so children under the age of twelve can attend a re-screening of *Super Turbo Awesome Team Vs. Megapanda* in Amphitheater B, or be dropped off in the temp crèche on Deck 17.

We would also like to congratulate Martina Hernandez and her husband, Christopher, on the birth of their beautiful baby girl, who was brought into the universe by our medical staff at 01:13 this morning! Both mother and daughter are doing well, and I am delighted to report our newest crew member has been named "Hypatia" by her parents. Your prayers and best wishes are appreciated—any donations of clothing or toys for our little stowaway can be made via your friendly *Hypatia* ensign.

I thank you all for your courage and patience through our recent trials, and look forward to bringing you more news as it comes to hand.

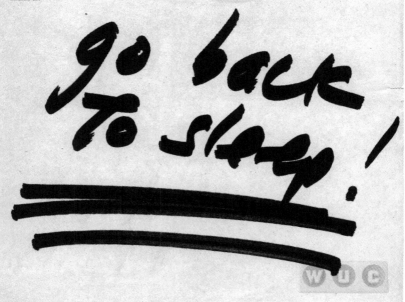

SUPER TURBO AWESOME TEAM
WHAT ARE THEY HIDING IN BAY 4?
He's like Godz On st. Only fluffy.
DEATH BY STEREO FILMS esents a PAN S HOBO production
In association with DISCO NINJA HOUSE · a JACK BURTON film · ELIZABETH ANDRETT PER TURBO AWESOME TEAM VS. MEGAPANDA" · MILES BLAKELY · TOMAS DANIEL · PHILIP "LUCKY" CHAN with SASCHA TEXAS · casting by S. JAE-JONES · music by SLAYER · edited by MELANIE CECKA · production design by ALISON IMPEY · director of photography CHRISTOPHER TOVO · coproducers BETH REVIS · MARIE LU · KAREN GREENBERG · executive producers NANCY HINKEL · BARBARA MARCUS · produced by ALFRED A. KNOPF · screenplay by JACK BURTON · directed by JACK BURTON

HAT/LOGIN LOCATION=NO MENUBAR=NO']<!-- END HYPATIA CHAT BASIC V9 CODE --><!-- BEG

ByteMe: howzit?

Mason, E, LT 2nd: tense. t-e-n-s-e

Mason, E, LT 2nd: lot of scuttlebutt around. Bay 4 and the rest of it

Mason, E, LT 2nd: trying not to think about Jimmy. it's not working

ByteMe: :(

Mason, E, LT 2nd: talk to me Kades

Mason, E, LT 2nd: tell me something good

ByteMe: um, ok

ByteMe: . . .

ByteMe: o, remember Ms. Colfer from applied sciences class? She's over here, u know.

Mason, E, LT 2nd: No kidding? Wow, she made it.

ByteMe: Yeah. She's kind of the reason we got together

Mason, E, LT 2nd: Damn, I still remember first day in her class. You were checking me out HARD, Grant.

ByteMe: U. R. DELUSIONAL. u kept asking me stupid questions about hydrogen bonding

Mason, E, LT 2nd: confession: hydrogen was not the kind of bonding on my mind

ByteMe: o rly? am I to understand it was highly sophisticated courting behavior? did i misinterpret it, with my backwater ways?

Mason, E, LT 2nd: Mock if you will. I'll refrain from pointing out you DID end up falling madly in love with me

ByteMe: . . .

Mason, E, LT 2nd: I'm nice like that

ByteMe: "madly" as in it was complete insanity to do it. and i was misled on the whole "wishing to bond" front by the way you kept sticking your tongue down jodie kingston's throat

ByteMe: it was like you were trying to make up for missed biology lessons with practical experience. ew.

Mason, E, LT 2nd: you know Jodie's dead, right?

ByteMe: i . . . jesus

Mason, E, LT 2nd: Way to go, mood killer

ByteMe: okay, sorry

Mason, E, LT 2nd: Lol, you're so bad at this, Grant

Mason, E, LT 2nd: That's one of the things I love about you

ByteMe: ▇ off, I was trying to make you feel better

Mason, E, LT 2nd: . . .

Mason, E, LT 2nd: You kiss your mother with that mouth?

Mason, E, LT 2nd: How is your mom anyways? I would literally swim the few thousand klicks of vacuum between Alexander and Hypatia for some of her dessert

ByteMe: Yeah, I always knew what you were really at my place for.

Mason, E, LT 2nd: Hey, you should thank her. I owe this manly physique almost entirely to her home cooking

Mason, E, LT 2nd: *flexes*

ByteMe: I was totally just in it for your manly physique, u know. I watched so many boring geeball games for that physique. And all before u even asked me out

Mason, E, LT 2nd: Boring? Ok NOW you're hurting my feelings.

ByteMe: i'm flattering you, idiot.

Mason, E, LT 2nd: You know, you've REALLY gotta think of a better pet name for me than "idiot."

Mason, E, LT 2nd: What about "sweetiepuff"

Mason, E, LT 2nd: "sugarpants"?

Mason, E, LT 2nd: NONO WAIT. "CUDDLEPIE"

ByteMe: I will hack the Alexander comms system and let them know you prefer to be known as Cuddlepie immediately, my love

Mason, E, LT 2nd: nooooooooooooooooo

ByteMe: u look as good in your uniform as you did in your geeball gear? if not please lie.

Mason, E, LT 2nd: Well the pants are tighter, if that counts for anything

ByteMe: mmmmm go on

Mason, E, LT 2nd: u sure?

Mason, E, LT 2nd: We'd need waaaay more than seven minutes for that ;)

ByteMe: Always took about 2 mins as I recall

Mason, E, LT 2nd: 0_o

ByteMe: Set yourself up for that one son.

Mason, E, LT 2nd: . . .

Mason, E, LT 2nd: Well played, madam.

Mason, E, LT 2nd: Well played indeed

ByteMe: speaking of 7 mins, time to split

Mason, E, LT 2nd: Yeah

Mason, E, LT 2nd: i miss you, you know

ByteMe: you too

ByteMe: and seriously, things r only going to get more intense. be calm. be smart.

ByteMe: stay safe, shnookums

Mason, E, LT 2nd: see now you're just being silly

COUNTDOWN TO
LINCOLN INTERCEPTION
OF ALEXANDER FLEET:

58 HOURS: 41 MINUTES

DO NOT ENTER

Date: 07/27/75
Subject: alone

I'm not ready to die.

If the Lincoln catches us, she'll destroy us. There's simply no other reason she'd chase us for months on end if it wasn't to hide the last of the evidence. Wipe out the only witnesses who could tell the universe BeiTech attacked another corp and hijacked their illegal processing plant and—oh yes, killed thousands of people.

That, or we're on the lam because the Lincoln's captain is secretly Torrence's angry ex-girlfriend and they have unfinished business. He's totally the kind of guy who'd leave the toilet seat up.

I think my jokes are getting worse. Weirder, anyway. The sleep dep is really getting to me. But I can't miss a chance to peek inside AIDAN and help out Byron, and that means jumping onto a new ID every time a tech takes a break. And in the spare minutes when I'm supposed to be sleeping, instead I'm thinking about what we might find if we make it out of this alive.

I figure it this way: WUC's operation on Kerenza was illegal, so they can't tell the UTA we stopped reporting in. When Kerenza was attacked, our alarms would've been relayed through the closest waypoint, and then on to Heimdall Station. But the only ship that showed up—the Alexander—was on patrol nearby. Which means our SOS never made it out of the system. And if Heimdall didn't send the cavalry, that has to mean the station itself was taken as part of the BT attack. Which means my dad might be dead. I am not okay with that.

I am NOT OKAY WITH THAT.

We'll never make it as far as Heimdall, says my brain, and if we do, Heimdall's been taken anyway. It says nobody made it off the Copernicus alive—or not alive in any way I'd recognize. I lie in my bunk, pretending I'm at home, and just return those thoughts to sender. They show up and try to get their claws into me, and with a mental *NO* I push them back. Force myself somewhere safer. Counting rivets. Tugging at the loose threads along the edge of my sheet, winding them so tight around my fingers my nails turn blue.

But deep down, I know it. The truth. Nobody's coming for us. The place we're running to probably isn't safe. And there's nobody I can trust in this equation except Ezra and Byron. But Byron's hands are tied, and so are E's. So if we're going to find out exactly what happened to the Copernicus, and why, it has to be me.

If we had to, could the Hypatia outrun the Alexander?

Is anyone who made it off the Copernicus still sane? Or even alive?
Are they alive at Heimdall?

I'm not ready to die just yet. Too many things left to do.

No way I am getting shortchanged.

Ezra loves me. I mean, maybe I'm an idiot and it's just his fear and desperation talking, but I don't think so. I don't care if it is—I need him. Being angry at him because he didn't want to leave Kerenza . . . seems kind of small now.

It was so good when we were together. It was right. We should have fronted up to the problem, not screamed at each other and avoided it. We should have fought for it, instead of giving up and making out all the time.

I should have been big enough to tell him what he meant to me.

Now I get to tell him in 7 minute bursts.

I try to reach out and connect, to remind him however I can, in my own super awkward way, that I'm here. That if he does something dumb over there, there's one person left who cares.

Care doesn't cover it.

If I lose Ezra too, it'll be one body blow too many.

If I lose Ezra too, I'll give up.

I don't think I have anyone else left.

But while I have him, I'll fight tooth and nail to keep us safe.

Whatever it takes.

CHAT/LOGIN.LOCATION=NO.MENUBAR=NO')<!-- END HYPATIA CHAT BASIC V9 CODE --><!-- BEG

ByteMe: aroo

Zhang, B: Jesus u can't be here, Corporal Boklov is online, i can see his ID

Zhang, B: u log in while his ID's already active, someone will wtf

ByteMe: today i am playing the part of Private LeFevre, tho i thank you for your kind concern

Zhang, B: i don't think the stims are working anymore. so hard not to qwertyface

ByteMe: no sleep for the wicked, my friend. ur our best hope

Zhang, B: zzzZZzzzzzz

ByteMe: where'd u grow up?

Zhang, B: does that matter in the slightest?

ByteMe: i'm keeping u awake, you dope

Zhang, B: Triton III

ByteMe: isn't that mostly water?

Zhang, B: i'm a pretty buoyant guy. but yeah, got out when i could

ByteMe: family?

Zhang, B: mom and sisters. pay mostly goes into accounts for my nieces and nephews. don't need much myself

ByteMe: uncle byron <3

Zhang, B: upstart

ByteMe: so what made you take up the fight, Mr. Information Liberty Activist?

Zhang, B: hush, I'm working

ByteMe: spill

Zhang, B: i'll tell you when you're older

ByteMe: oh come onnnnn

Zhang, B: *dramatic sigh*

Zhang, B: "The man dies in all who keep silent in the face of tyranny."

ByteMe: . . .

ByteMe: what?

Zhang, B: Wole Soyinka said that. he was a writer, back in 20C. studied him in college. wrote about injustice. Plays, poems, books. good stuff. u should read him

ByteMe: what's a book?

Zhang, B: . . .

Zhang, B: hey what r u doing looking over in that core? dead there

ByteMe: checking shutdown + restart logs, might find something helpful

Zhang, B: good, smart

ByteMe: this is weird tho. there are like 6 shutdown attempts in a row here, all fail. AIDAN was blocking them

Zhang, B: when?

ByteMe: . . . right when they were firing on the Copernicus

Zhang, B: I ███ing KNEW IT

BRIEFING NOTE:
The Command Priority Channel actually gets used by the commanders of the fleet here, as opposed to a pair of lovesick teenagers. Wonders will never cease.

CHAT/LOGIN LOCATION=NO MENUBAR=NO'}<!-- END HYPATIA C

Chau, A, Capt: You sonofa███, David

Torrence, D, Gen: Excuse me?

Chau, A, Capt: It killed them. All of them. I have it all here on file. Launch codes for the nukes. Orders for your Cyclone drones to take out the surviving shuttles. AIDAN murdered over two thousand people, and you're trying to bring it back online?

Torrence, D, Gen: Where did you get those files?

Chau, A, Capt: How long did you think you could keep this a secret? You didn't think to mention your AI's judgment is so critically impaired?

Torrence, D, Gen: Where did you get those files, Captain? I gave explicit orders that your technicians were to access designated areas ONLY.

Chau, A, Capt: My God, what does it matter how I got them? My people are helping you get AIDAN up and running again and we have NO GUARANTEES it won't kill us all as soon as it becomes operational.

Torrence, D, Gen: AIDAN is *already* operational. It was deactivated on my orders. And we're working to ensure it doesn't hurt anyone when we turn it back on.

Chau, A, Capt: And that's supposed to comfort me?

Torrence, D, Gen: This is an act of espionage in a time of war. Do you realize the consequences? You are *directly* undermining the security of this fleet. I could have you and your entire command staff brought up on charges and shot.

Chau, A, Capt: We are done, do you understand me? My people are *out.* We are ceasing any operations to bring the AI back online until I have some guarantee it won't destroy us all at its earliest opportunity.

Torrence, D, Gen: I'm afraid I can't allow that, Captain. Lincoln WILL destroy us when it catches us, and I need your crews to bring AIDAN online before they do.

Chau, A, Capt: Jesus, David, two days ago you were unwilling to let my people *near* your systems. And now you're telling me they can't stop?

Torrence, D, Gen: Is it any wonder I was reluctant to allow your people access, given the current circumstances?

Chau, A, Capt: My crew are civilians. They're under MY command. I will NOT allow them to participate in an action that places my ship and personnel in danger.

Torrence, D, Gen: Then they're not civilians anymore.

Chau, A, Capt: What?

Torrence, D, Gen: I'm conscripting your commtech staff into the UTA, effective immediately. You will have them assembled on your main hangar deck and ready to depart in 30 minutes. A shuttle is being sent to get them.

Chau, A, Capt: You can't do this.

Torrence, D, Gen: A full complement of UTA marines will accompany the shuttle and help escort your personnel back to Alexander. I would recommend you refrain from resistance.

Chau, A, Capt: David, think this through, please.

Torrence, D, Gen: 30 minutes.

Torrence, D, Gen: Centrum tenenda. Torrence out.

> **BRIEFING NOTE:**
> After Action Report from First Lieutenant McCall concerning the command/control incident aboard the *Hypatia*.

INCEPT: 07/28/75 (06:58 shipboard time)

LOCATION: Wallace Ulyanov Consortium science vessel *Hypatia*

OFFICER IDENT: Winifred McCall (UTN-961-641id)

RANK: First Lieutenant

At 02:07 (shipboard time) on 07/28/75, Sigma Squad and I were scrambled to a Code Blue alert issued by *Alexander* command staff. Squad mustered in a timely fashion to Deck 146, where we were briefed by General Torrence.

~~The boss looked tired. More tired than I can ever remember seeing him.~~

Sitrep: *Hypatia*'s commtech crew had been forcibly conscripted into the UTA after an ~~(unspecified)~~ act of espionage instigated by *Hypatia* officers. A shuttle was being sent to bring the conscripts back to *Alexander,* where our TechEng crew could keep closer watch on them.

My ~~boys were still jumpy after the incident in Hangar Bay 4, but my~~ vets had more experience than the *Alexander*'s other marines, so we were up. Having lost McNulty, Henderson, Parker, Montano and Gandolfini, I had no choice but to put my Kerenza rookies in the firing line. Corporal Sykes had been in a darker mood than usual ~~since~~

Bay 4—if it was up to him, I'm sure he'd have flushed every civi in the fleet out an airlock.

"We expecting resistance, boss?" he asked.

"Negative," Torrence replied. "These are civilians, they'll do what they're told. Still, you're packing hot ballistics. The chipheads are off-limits, but if anyone else is stupid enough to get in your way, you be the push that makes them move."

Sykes's smile put ice in my belly. "Roger that, sir."

"Sir," I asked, "aren't we there to pacify rather than neutralize?"

"You are there, Lieutenant, to bring back personnel vital to fleet operations. If we didn't need all our own people, I'd have already brigged *Hypatia*'s commanders and replaced them with UTA personnel. So if anyone gets in your way, they are to be considered enemy combatants and dealt with accordingly. Is that understood?"

"Sir, yessir."

"Good hunting."

On the way down to Hangar Bay 1, we passed the airlock to Bay 4. I tried my best not to think about the man trapped inside it, the people beyond it. Who they were and what they'd become. The gold UTA sigil on my sleeve caught the light of the alert globes spinning above the sealed doors. Red as the blood on my hands.

The trip across to *Hypatia* was taken in near silence. I should've been talking to my people, making sure they were chill. I could barely stop my teeth from chattering. One of my Kerenza rooks was looking at me—Doherty was her name. Staring from behind her wire-rimmed spectacles like I had the answers. I kept my eyes to the floor. Spoke to no one in particular.

"Follow my lead. Do not fire unless I give the order. The first itchy trigger on my watch gets to learn what the outside of an airlock tastes like, crystal?"

"Ma'am, yes, ma'am!" came a dozen shouts.

We came into *Hypatia*'s docking bay at hard burn. The artificial grav kicked back in and dropped me into my seat and I was up and out of it before I could get cozy. ~~If I'd let myself, I'd have stayed there forever—buckled in tight and wondering how it came to this.~~

I spoke to the pilot as we touched down. "Kilpatrick, keep engines running. We may need to jet quick."

"Affirmative, LT."

"All right," Sykes barked to the squad. "Suit up, let's roll."

Out the shuttle door and across the bay, the stink of fuel and char in my mouth. Patching myself into the local command frequency and speaking through gritted teeth.

"*Hypatia,* this is First Lieutenant Winifred McCall from UTA Marine Squad Sigma. We are here to escort *Hypatia* commtech personnel in accordance with *Alexander* command directives. Please open internal hangar bay doors, over."

"Lieutenant McCall, this is Captain Chau of the *Hypatia,* over."

"Roger that, Captain, I read you. Please open internal hangar bay doors, over."

"Negative, Lieutenant. You're not taking my people."

~~I tried not to sigh then. Tried not to acknowledge I knew exactly how she felt. Remembering McNulty's face as that airlock slammed closed.~~

"They're not your people anymore, Captain. They're UTA conscripts. Now you can open these doors, or the plasma missiles on our shuttle can open them for you."

Silence down comms, then. Doherty looking at me the way kids must look at their mothers. Wondering if any of this was real.

Sykes spat on the deck, spat down his transmitter: "Open the ████ing doors before we blow them in, goddammit."

I had Sykes's collar in my fist before I knew it. Hand over my mic so *Hypatia* couldn't hear. Dragging him close enough to smell the hooch on his breath.

"You secure that bull████ right now, or I'll kick your teeth so hard you'll need to unzip for me to lace up."

Silent rebellion in his eyes. I should have benched him right there. I could see the names written on his face. Parker. Henderson. Gandolfini. Montano. McNulty.

"Ma'am, yes, ma'am," he said.

The airlock doors opened wide. What passed for *Hypatia*'s Sec-Team was waiting for us on the other side. Their lieutenant looked former military, but he was about twenty years too old, about eighty pounds too slow.

"Where are the commtechs?" I asked.

"On the bridge," the LT replied. "They're still working to get us out of this mess."

"You ex-UTA, LT?"

"Yes, I am."

"Then you know what a VK burst rifle does to a human body at close range?"

A swallow. A glance to the weapon in my hand. "Yes, I do."

"Lead the way."

Through long, gleaming halls, boots squeaking on rubber floors. All of it surgical white once, but just a little faded now. Pale faces peering at us from behind grubby plasteel windows. Unshaven cheeks or pink dye jobs with six months of regrowth at the roots. Frightened eyes. All of us fraying at the edges.

The *Hypatia* bridge was semicircular. Humming with static. Chau had cleared most of her personnel out in case things went south of heaven. The remaining crew glanced up as we entered. I could imagine how we looked. All in black. Hollow eyes. Thirty-eight rounds of murder in every clip.

~~My hands were shaking.~~

Chau was short. Carved out of wood. Dark hair. Pistol at her belt. Running on no sleep, by the look~~, standing at her post like some old lighthouse keeper—the only thing between us and the rocks~~. I identified the commtechs from their shipboard IDs—both still pounding away at their consoles like nothing was happening. I spoke loud enough to be heard across the whole bridge.

"Byron Zhang, Consuela Nestor, you are hereby ordered to accompany me to the UTA battlecarrier *Alexander*."

"Tell me how you think this ends, Lieutenant."

It was Chau speaking. Hand on her pistol. She was looking out the huge viewscreen dominating one end of the room. I could see a tiny spark on the long-range scanner, out there amid all the black and starlight. Its ID tag and countdown to intercept pulsing red:

BT042-TN. 52 hours: 17 minutes.

The *Lincoln*.

"I don't get paid to think," I said. "I follow orders. Stand aside, Captain."

Chau smiled like I'd said something funny. One of the commtechs stood up then. Byron Zhang. Supposedly a top-tier console jockey. He sure looked the part. Overweight. Thinning hair. Underarm stains.

"It's a good thing they don't pay you to think," he said. "It doesn't seem like your thing."

"Zhang, get your gear, you're coming with us."

"No." He set pudgy hands on his hips. Tried to keep his voice from shaking. ~~"You'll have to drag us. Kicking and screaming."~~

"I'll give you something to scream about," Sykes growled.

" 'The man dies in all who keep silent in the face of tyranny,' " he said.

"Listen, Zhang, ~~I appreciate the rhetoric, but~~ anyone can do math this simple. We need every swinging ▮ back on *Alexander,* and you two are the best chipheads on *Hypatia*."

Zhang's lips twisted then. An "I know something you don't know" kind of smile that turned my mood darker. I wanted this over. ~~I wanted to be back in my rack with a canteen of rocket fuel and a few hours of the forgetting it would bring.~~ Still, I knew what kind of edge Sykes was dancing on. I should have given the order to someone else.

"Corporal Sykes, secure the conscripts for transport back to *Alexander*."

His grin went all the way to his eyes. "Ma'am, yes, ma'am."

He slapped Hart and Bedggood on the arms, and the trio loped forward, pulling zip ties from their belts. I could feel my Kerenza rookies beside me, all of them playing at being soldiers, all of them just nerves and gritted teeth. Doherty in particular looked jumpy. What had she done before this? Security guard at a shopping mall? A library maybe? I couldn't remember . . .

My eyes were on the *Hypatia* SecTeam—they all looked one wrong word away from drawing. Sweat in my eyes. Hard to breathe. Chau's voice rose above the pulse in my ears.

"Lieutenant, do you know your commanders plan to reactivate the artificial intelligence responsible for destroying the *Copernicus*? Do you know Major Hawking and three other *Alexander* officers were executed under General Torrence's *direct* orders—"

"Shut up. One more minute and this will all be over."

Sykes and the others reached the commtechs. Zhang had sat himself on the floor and folded his arms—some gesture of peaceful protest that earned him as much latitude as a faceful of spit. Sykes grabbed his arm, and when Zhang resisted, the corporal popped him with the butt of his VK. Zhang's nose spat blood, the other commtech shouted protest. And that was all it took. Fists and elbows and knees. Pasty flesh slapping the floor. In about five seconds, Zhang and Nestor were trussed up on the floor like abattoir meat.

"Stop it, Jesus!" the SecTeam lieutenant roared. My VK was right in his face.

"Stand down, LT," I warned.

"This is bull■! You people are animals!"

"Captain, order your people to stand down! No one needs to get hurt here!"

The LT's hand was on his pistol.

My finger on my trigger.

Doherty beside me, her voice rising an octave. "Lieutenant?"

"Lieutenant, stand down!" Chau barked.

I think that's what did it. Simple mistake. Chau should've used his name. Should've made it clear she was ordering her own LT, not me. Because to someone with a few light-years under their belt, it would've been obvious Chau was drawing her pistol to surrender it. I've watched the recordings a hundred times. You can see it on her face. Resignation. One hand up in surrender. But to a terrified rookie who used to guard the school library, it might have looked like Chau was drawing the piece to use it. That she was shouting at *me* to stand down, and if I didn't, she was prepared to shoot me in the back.

So Doherty did what she'd been ordered to do.

You be the push that makes them move.

It was a good shot. Took Chau right in the head. I heard a scream from the NavComp, and Syra Boll, one of Chau's 2ICs, was charging across the deck to cradle her dead captain in her arms. The SecTeam were shouting, we were roaring, VKs in their faces. I don't know how it held together. I don't know what stopped us heading south of heaven right then and there. Maybe it was Zhang. Sitting with his bleeding face, tear-filled eyes locked on his captain's body. Legs crossed. Back straight. Not fighting. Just resisting.

What had he said?

The man dies in all who keep silent in the face of tyranny.

The woman, too.

I can't do this. I can't pretend this is what I signed up for. I brought them back, just like I was told. Both *Hypatia* commtechs, delivered to General Torrence, hog-tied and just a little bloodied for their trouble. I did what a good soldier is supposed to do. But now I'm done.

Lock me in the hole. ███, space me. I don't care anymore. I'll keep your secrets. Shut my mouth. But I can't shut my eyes.

I am hereby formally resigning my commission as a lieutenant of the United Terran Authority, effective immediately.

I'm sorry.

I just can't do this anymore.

Winifred McCall
Former 1st Lieutenant
UTA Marine Division
Battlecarrier *Alexander*

Participants: Ezra Mason, Second Lieutenant, UTA Airborne Division
Charles Dorian, Corporal, UTA Information Services Division
Date: 07/28/75
Timestamp: 12:27

CHAT/LOGIN LOCATION=NO MENUBAR=NO']<!-- END ALEXANDER CHAT BASIC V8 CODE -->

Mason, E, LT 2nd: dorian

Mason, E, LT 2nd: DOOOORRRRIIIAAAAAANNNNNN

Dorian, C, Corp: Go away, Mason

Mason, E, LT 2nd: I'll be quick

Mason, E, LT 2nd: Rumors you may have heard to that effect are all lies, btw

Mason, E, LT 2nd: *crickets*

Mason, E, LT 2nd: You heard anything on Jimmy?

Dorian, C, Corp: Mason I have more important things on my mind than James right now.

Mason, E, LT 2nd: chum, our friend is still stuck in that airlock, don't you think we should find out if command are at least gonna TRY to get him out?

Dorian, C, Corp: Mason, the personnel aboard this ship dont' amount to a bucket of ███ as far as Torrence and his officers are concerned. WAKE UP.

Mason, E, LT 2nd: dorian, that's the first time I've ever seen you swear. Or botch an apostrophe for that matter

Mason, E, LT 2nd: like, EVER

Mason, E, LT 2nd: u ok?

Dorian, C, Corp: No. I am not. A friend of mine just got locked in the hole.

Dorian, C, Corp: Stephanie LeFevre. She's a commtech.

Mason, E, LT 2nd: ya I know Steph. Chill fem. Smart. What'd they brig her for?

Dorian, C, Corp: Aiding and abetting the enemy. They have records of her log-in being used to access memory files out of AIDAN. Details about the Copernicus attack, Kerenza refugee files, things like that. They say she gave the gen about AIDAN to Hypatia command.

Mason, E, LT 2nd: ███, that was . . . not so smart

Dorian, C, Corp: Except she didn't do it.

Mason, E, LT 2nd: how u so sure?

Dorian, C, Corp: Because she was with me at the time, Mason.

Mason, E, LT 2nd: like

Mason, E, LT 2nd: "with you" in a biblical sense?

Dorian, C, Corp: Yes, Mason. "Biblically."

Mason, E, LT 2nd: holy ███, little Charlie D with ALL THE MOVES!!!

Mason, E, LT 2nd: chum no offense but I had you picked as a Neo-Abstinent, dead cert

Dorian, C, Corp: My god, you're an infant.

Mason, E, LT 2nd: chum, I'm HAPPY for you. Steph is a queen

Dorian, C, Corp: Yes, well, my "queen" is now locked in SOLITARY for WARTIME ESPIONAGE, Mason. Awaiting court martial. And possibly a firing squad.

Mason, E, LT 2nd: right. ███

Dorian, C, Corp: Three-quarters of TechEng are now on some kind of "watch list" for suspicious behavior. Torrence has completely lost the plot. He's had two commtechs dragged over from Hypatia. Set them up on the bridge so he could "keep an eye on them." The pair of them literally have *bruisers with guns looming over them while they work.*

Mason, E, LT 2nd: and there's no way steph could have logged in to access the info?

Dorian, C, Corp: I think I'd have noticed. Give me *some* credit, please.

Mason, E, LT 2nd: so just tell command she was with you. Case closed.

Dorian, C, Corp: Yes, brilliant. Because Private LeFevre engaging in intimate relations with her reporting corporal is so much better.

Mason, E, LT 2nd: chum, it's better than being shot for espionage

Dorian, C, Corp: It's still a court martialing offense. And the way Torrence is acting lately, he might just have us *both* shot. He'll brig me at the very least, that much is certain.

Mason, E, LT 2nd: chum, you have to tell them

Dorian, C, Corp: GOD IN HEAVEN, I ALREADY SENT THE EMAIL TO MY C.O.

Mason, E, LT 2nd: oh

Mason, E, LT 2nd: well. Good for u, chum. Proud of you

Dorian, C, Corp: Oh, shut up.

Dorian, C, Corp: All this means is two more people in the hole. Two more people not working on us not all getting killed when the Lincoln arrives

Mason, E, LT 2nd: double negative, wow, u really upset

Dorian, C, Corp: And of course, there actually IS someone hacking into AIDAN and accessing classified files. Locking Stephanie and me in the hole won't change that at all.

Dorian, C, Corp: I swear, the people in command are drooling simpletons. Why on earth would Stephanie be accessing Kerenza refugee files?

Mason, E, LT 2nd: wait this hacker was accessing kerenza refugee files?

Dorian, C, Corp: Yes, Mason, I believe I said that already. Twice.

Mason, E, LT 2nd: ■■

Dorian, C, Corp: Mason, do you remember when I said you were smarter than you look?

Dorian, C, Corp: Well, I'm officially taking it back. You're slower than German opera.

Dorian, C, Corp: Mason.

Dorian, C, Corp: . . . Mason?

Mason, E, LT 2nd: Please tell me this wasn't you

ByteMe: ??? u ok?

Mason, E, LT 2nd: This hacker who broke into AIDAN's memory and told Hypatia command about Copernicus.

Mason, E, LT 2nd: Tell me it wasn't you, Kady.

ByteMe: they don't even know I can hack. Otherwise I'd have been brutalized and hauled over to the Alexander like the others

Mason, E, LT 2nd: jesus, it was you

Mason, E, LT 2nd: KADY WHAT THE ▮▮▮▮ WERE YOU THINKING?

ByteMe: AIDAN murdered everyone on the Copernicus. it's being covered up. I'm the only one who IS thinking

Mason, E, LT 2nd: so you thought telling everyone on hypatia about it was a good idea???

ByteMe: Byron told the captain. How could I do that? I'm not even meant to be in there.

Mason, E, LT 2nd: wait . . .

Mason, E, LT 2nd: who the ▮▮▮ is Byron?

ByteMe: He's the guy your marines assaulted and dragged over to the Alexander, covered in blood. He's the only one who was brave enough to speak up. And it was the right thing to do.

Mason, E, LT 2nd: oh really? Tell that to the commtech whose ID you jacked. She's in the brig now. and the corporal (my friend, btw) who's stepping up to make sure she doesn't get SHOT for something she didn't do is going in the hole beside her.

ByteMe: they shot our captain, did they tell you that? when they were taking my friends.

Mason, E, LT 2nd: Kady, those marines WOULDN'T HAVE EVEN BEEN THERE if not for you and lord ███ing byron

Mason, E, LT 2nd: You promised me whatever I installed on that server was just to help Jimmy and youve been using it to spy on people.

ByteMe: I never promised that.

Mason, E, LT 2nd: You LIED to me

ByteMe: Should I just sit here and wait to die? You might have become a military drone, but I don't have any faith at all in your commanders.

ByteMe: What would you do if it was me in the brig? Wait for your next set of orders from them?

Mason, E, LT 2nd: Weren't u the one telling me not to try and break Jimmy out because I'd be putting myself and others in danger? Why the ███ are those rules good for me and not for you?

Mason, E, LT 2nd: Ppl are in prison because of you! Ppl got hurt because of you!

ByteMe: and if nobody does anything, what happens then? you think your general torrence has the answer?

Mason, E, LT 2nd: who says nobody's doing anything? ppl over here are busting their ███es. they're trained military personnel. they do this for a living and they've been doing it all their lives

Mason, E, LT 2nd: and i dunno if they have all the answers, but maybe, JUST MAYBE THEY HAVE MORE ANSWERS THAN YOU

ByteMe: they don't, trust me. I've seen *exactly* what they're doing. So has Byron. they have no idea.

ByteMe: I'm not doing this for kicks, Ez. I'm trying to find out what's going on, what's wrong with AIDAN, and I'm wading through layers of lies from your precious command to do it. you might be as content to sit here and take orders as you were to sit on Kerenza and do nothing, but I'm not going to just sit on my hands and count down the 47 hrs we have left until the Lincoln catches us

Mason, E, LT 2nd: ██ me, you're seriously bringing up kerenza? now?

Mason, E, LT 2nd: you really want to go there?

ByteMe: i'm doing what I can to keep us safe. those of us who are left, anyway. Safe from AIDAN, from the Lincoln. have u changed since Kerenza at all?

Mason, E, LT 2nd: listen, I'm sorry i wasn't the guy to explore the goddamn universe with you. i had my reasons.

Mason, E, LT 2nd: but u don't know everything kady. your problem is you think you do

ByteMe: i know we have 47 hrs left to live right now, and u want to sit and hope. I can't do that.

ByteMe: i promised Byron i wouldn't stop trying. so get your head out of your ██ and help me, Ezra.

Mason, E, LT 2nd: god this is so like you. Little Miss Bigbrain. You always think you knwo better. Always think you know the score. ALWAYS

ByteMe: right, what's your idea?

ByteMe: seriously, I'm listening. got anything better than sitting and waiting to die?

ByteMe: i'm sorry they brigged your friends, i am. but that's not on me. that's on your command. they got themselves into this situation by lying, and now they're covering it up by taking the only people who might be able to help and locking them up. so really, you tell me your ideas about what to do next.

Mason, E, LT 2nd: how about i go tell command i know how you're getting access to the system before anyone else gets imprisoned or killed?

Mason, E, LT 2nd: better yet, how about *this*?

——**CONNECTION TERMINATED**——

Participants: ~~David Torrence/DTORRENCEALEXAN~~
(systemreroute78h@865HG=EMason)
~~Ann Chau/ACHAUHYPATIAONBOARD~~
(systemreroute78h@786HG=ByteMe)
Date: 07/28/75
Timestamp: 17:37
Subject: Please please read

BRIEFING NOTE:
Note dates on the attachments transmitted by Grant to Mason—they originate several months prior.

AT/LOGIN LOCATION=NO MENUBAR=NO']<!-- END HYPATIA CHAT BASIC V9 CODE --><!-- BEGIN

Ezra,

I'm sorry. Please please don't shut me out. Whatever else happens, please talk to me. I don't want to miss out on the last conversations we might have.

I owe you an explanation, so I've attached a stack of documents. You can read for yourself.

I promise you Byron is the best chance this fleet has of getting away from the Lincoln without AIDAN killing us. But he doesn't have enough time. I need to help him, and that's what I'm doing inside the system.

I can climb around the quantum core like it's a playground, but I can't make you sit down and read my IMs. And I promise I'm not trying to play you when I say I really, really don't want to die before I see you again.

K

Attached: Civilian Transfer Authorization (*03/29/75*)
Civilian Transfer Request (*03/31/75*)
Civilian Transfer Request (*04/06/75*)
Email: Interfleet—*Copernicus* to *Hypatia* (*04/07/75*)
Civilian Transfer Request (*04/19/75*)
Email: Interfleet—*Hypatia* to *Copernicus* (*04/19/75*)
Email: Interfleet—*Copernicus* to *Hypatia* (*05/14/75*)
Email: Interfleet—*Hypatia* to *Copernicus* (*06/01/75*)
Email: Interfleet—*Hypatia* to *Copernicus* (*07/10/75*)
Personal Journal Entry—K Grant (*07/11/75*)

CIVILIAN TRANSFER PROPOSAL

DATE: 03/29/75
NAME: Dr. Helena Grant
IDENTITY #: KR849/Kerenza/~~Civ/Ref~~
FROM SHIP: *Hypatia*
TO SHIP: *Copernicus*

TRANSFER REASON: Dr. Grant's specialty in pathology will be of assistance in dealing with the current health concerns aboard the *Copernicus*. General Torrence has approved her immediate transfer and authorized conscription in the event of noncompliance.

TRANSFER VOLUNTARY: YES/~~NO~~

ADDITIONAL NOTES: Dr. Grant is accompanied by her daughter, Kady Grant (ID KR1471/Kerenza/Civ/Ref), who is currently aboard the *Hypatia*. As a condition of her cooperation, Dr. Grant has requested any transfer applications by her daughter be denied. Although General Torrence has authorized us to conscript Dr. Grant, it is likely she will be more productive if her request is met. On this basis, this request has been agreed to and is to be kept confidential.

APPROVED

CIVILIAN TRANSFER PROPOSAL

DATE: 03/31/75
NAME: Kady Grant
IDENTITY #: KR1471/Kerenza/Civ/...
FROM SHIP: *Hypatia*
TO SHIP: *Copernicus*

TRANSFER REASON: My mother, Dr. Helena Grant (ID KR849/ Kerenza/Civ/Ref), has been transferred to the *Copernicus* to assist with medical duties. I would like to join her as soon as possible. My father was at *Heimdall* Station at the time of the attack, so my mother is my only relative in the fleet. As I'm sure you can understand, I would prefer to be with her at this difficult time.

TRANSFER GRANTED: ~~YES~~/NO

DENIED

CIVILIAN TRANSFER PROPOSAL

DATE: 04/06/75
NAME: Kady Grant
IDENTITY #: KR1471/Kerenza/~~Civ/Ref~~
FROM SHIP: *Hypatia*
TO SHIP: *Copernicus*

TRANSFER REASON: I received a refusal to my last request to transfer to the *Copernicus* but wasn't given any reasons. I am lodging another request, as I believe it is reasonable for me to be transferred to be with my mother, who is my only relative aboard the fleet. My mother and I are extremely close, and I know from experience that when she works, she forgets to take breaks and, at times, to eat. I've always been the person to support her while she's working, and I believe it would be in the best interests of the fleet for me to be with her now. I am sure she will be more productive if I am able to assist her. I am also making a personal appeal as her child—like everyone aboard, I'm still recovering from what happened on Kerenza, and I hope you'll think it's reasonable that I want to be with my family. I am prepared to undertake any work necessary on the *Copernicus*. Thank you for your reconsideration.

TRANSFER GRANTED: ~~YES~~/NO

DENIED

To: Kady Grant/KGRANTHYPATIAONBOARD
From: Helena Grant/HGRANTCOPERNICUSONBOARD
Date: 04/07/75
Timestamp: 10:00
Subject: Hello darling

I finally have a moment to check in. I wish we'd had more time to say goodbye, but I understand now that there's limited movement between the ships because we need to preserve fuel for our supply vessels. I hope you're feeling better about the transfer now that you've had a little time.

I'm settling in very well aboard the Copernicus, which is different from the Hypatia in some ways, and very much the same in others. The lab here is actually quite well equipped, and it's almost a relief to get back to what I'm good at. There's plenty to do, but I'm sure we can get it sorted out in no time. We have a surprisingly good team, given our limited pool of candidates.

I've been thinking about our discussion the other day at dinner, and I really think you should give some more thought to joining one of the sports teams. I know it was always more Ezra's thing than yours, but it would be an excellent way to preserve muscle tone during the journey, and you might meet some more people. I worry about you not having the support network you need, no matter how many times you assure me you're tough as nails. I know you are, my darling— you're your father's daughter—but worrying is a part of my job description.

I'll wrap up here, but please do let me know how you're settling without me. I know you'll handle it with the same determination you apply to everything in your life.

Love always,
Mom

CIVILIAN TRANSFER PROPOSAL

DATE: 04/19/75
NAME: Kady Grant
IDENTITY #: KR1471/Kerenza/~~~~
FROM SHIP: *Hypatia*
TO SHIP: *Copern~~~~*

TRANSFER REAS~~~~ I a~~~~ lodging a third request to be allowed to transfer to the *Co~~~~nicus* to be with my mother, as I have not received a satisfactory denial to either of my previous requests. Please see the attached list of family members who have received transfers between ships in order to be together. I respectfully request that you explain to me why my position is different. I am not completing any vital duties here on the *Hypatia.* Please urgently reconsider my request, or advise me to whom I can appeal the denial.

TRANSFER GRANTED: ~~YES~~/NO

To: Helena Grant/HGRANTCOPERNICUSONBOARD
From: Kady Grant/KGRANTHYPATIAONBOARD
Date: 04/19/75
Timestamp: 11:05
Subject: Missing you!

Hey Mom,

So good to hear from you! I admit I half wasn't expecting it, knowing how lost you get in your work. What's going on over there that they need a pathologist so badly? Nothing serious, right?

I've put in a transfer request to see if I can get over there and join you, but no word yet. I don't really have any news here. I'm taking the programming classes, but I don't think it's really my thing. I promise you indoor sports are not my thing either, but I also promise I'll make sure I make more friends, so you don't have to worry. Hopefully, I'll be over to the Copernicus soon and you can supervise me doing it yourself!

With you gone, I've been thinking about Dad more. I guess he thinks we're both dead. I know it'll take months, but I can't help imagining what it'll be like when we're close enough to transmit and he knows we're okay. I really miss him. I miss you too, but don't stress about it. Just make sure you TAKE CARE OF YOURSELF. Seriously, I know what you're like!

Looking forward to hearing about life on the Copernicus when you're not so beat.

xoxoxo
Kady

To: Kady Grant/KGRANTHYPATIAONBOARD
From: Helena Grant/HGRANTCOPERNICUSONBOARD
Date: 05/14/75
Timestamp: 14:21
Subject: Just checking in

Hello darling,

Sorry I'm such a bad pen pal. It's extremely busy over here, and we both know I get a bit distracted. The health concerns here are nothing to worry about, so please don't. Pathology is just a specialized skill, and it wasn't going to be practical to send blood samples across to the Hypatia when I could be here.

I really wouldn't worry about putting in a transfer to move across to the Copernicus. Now that I've had a chance to look around, it really isn't as nice a ship as the Hypatia, and I'd be more comfortable knowing you were over there, focusing on your classes. You'll have a life to pick up when this is over, and your education matters.

I've been thinking about your father as well. I miss him very much, too. He always jokes I wouldn't notice if he went missing, so you'll have to be sure to tell him for me that you heard me say it! I love him, and goodness, I wish he was here.

Speaking of people we love, I do wish you'd get in touch with Ezra. I can't think why he hasn't tried to contact you himself, except that he must be under the impression you don't want him to. I'm sure if you spoke to him, he'd understand that the words you spoke in anger back on Kerenza don't matter anymore in light of what's happened. It's important to let the ones you love know that you love them, and I'd feel better knowing the two of you have each other.

Give it some thought, baby girl, and take good care of yourself! I might not have a chance to write again soon, but don't worry about me. Keeping busy!

Love you lots,
Mom

To: Helena Grant/HGRANTCOPERNICUSONBOARD
From: Kady Grant/KGRANTHYPATIAONBOARD
Date: 06/01/75
Timestamp: 19:41
Subject: Helloooooo

Hey Mom,

You're turning into the worst pen pal ever! That's three letters you haven't answered! I'm now going to start withholding until you show up. So, you want more news, pony up! What's going on over there?

Love, your abandoned daughter,
Kady

To: Helena Grant/HGRANTCOPERNICUSONBOARD
From: Kady Grant/KGRANTHYPATIAONBOARD
Date: 07/10/75
Timestamp: 23:07
Subject: No seriously Mom

I'm getting kind of worried. Will you please just send me a one-liner and let me know you're okay over there?

xK

DO NOT ENTER

Date: 07/11/75
Subject: I can't

I want my mom.

I WANT MY MOM.

I want to feel how soft she is when she hugs me and I lean into her. I want her hair tickling my nose. I want the way she smells, like the lab and fabric softener. I want her humming something really horribly out of tune as she heats up dinner, then starting to sing and making up the words. I want her stuffing my mittens in my bag and turning out to be right when it starts snowing before lunch. I want to hear her voice on a call with Dad after I'm asleep, all soft and mushy when she thinks I can't hear, with these long silences when I know he's doing his charming thing. I want her marathon-ing shows with me that we'd both die before we'd admit we watch. I want her making tragic, inappropriate remarks about the boys on the shows in an attempt to pretend she's not old. I want her talking earnestly about my education. I want her telling me to lighten up.

I just want her telling me anything. What to do.

Please, I want my mom. I can't do this on my own.

CHAT/LOGIN LOCATION=NO MENUBAR=NO'}<!-- END HYPATIA CHAT BASIC V9 CODE -->< !-- BEG

Mason, E, LT 2nd: they took your mom to the Copernicus

Mason, E, LT 2nd: she was on there when . . .

Mason, E, LT 2nd: god, i'm so sorry Kades

ByteMe: Ez. please keep talking to me. I'm sorry.

Mason, E, LT 2nd: jesus this is so ████ed up

Mason, E, LT 2nd: i'm sorry i yelled at you

ByteMe: i get it. u had the right

ByteMe: nothing about this makes sense. I swear I don't know what the right thing is, except trying to keep us all alive.

Mason, E, LT 2nd: this whole time, i thought she was on Hypatia with you

Mason, E, LT 2nd: god, why didn't you tell me, Kades?

ByteMe: don't know really

ByteMe: u were worried enough without me making it worse. i didn't want to think about it. i didn't want it to be true. take your pick.

Mason, E, LT 2nd: it was like that when my dad died

Mason, E, LT 2nd: like, sometimes I'd be talking about him to the guys and i'd realize i was using "is" instead of "was." Like he was still here

Mason, E, LT 2nd: part of me just wouldn't believe it.

ByteMe: and here I am, asking u to be here for me exactly like I wasn't for you. more than I deserve, i get that.

Mason, E, LT 2nd: More than you deserve?

Mason, E, LT 2nd: you deserve every star in the galaxy laid out at your feet and a thousand diamonds in your hair. You deserve someone who'll run with you as far and as fast as you want to. Holding your hand, not holding you back.

Mason, E, LT 2nd: You deserve more than I could ever give you, Kady.

Mason, E, LT 2nd: But I'll give you everything I can if you still want me to.

ByteMe: I don't know how you can say that, but I don't care. I just want it to be true. you're all i have, but it will be okay if I still have you.

Mason, E, LT 2nd: you have me

Mason, E, LT 2nd: until the last star in the galaxy dies

Mason, E, LT 2nd: you have me

ByteMe: let's try really, really hard not to die.

ByteMe: i really want to see you in person first.

ByteMe: don't care where we end up.

ByteMe: i think Heimdall must be gone. Otherwise help would have come for us. so that's my dad, too.

Mason, E, LT 2nd: you don't know that. try not to think about it. You're carrying enough already

ByteMe: I'll try.

ByteMe: I tried so hard to get across to the Copernicus. I still feel like there's something more I should have done.

ByteMe: but we both know she'd kick my ■ from here to Sunday if I didn't do my best to keep going now.

Mason, E, LT 2nd: she would :)

Mason, E, LT 2nd: she was pretty awesome, your mom

ByteMe: i hoped for a while she was on one of the shuttles, that she might be on the Alexander. I tried everything to find the names of the people in bay 4. Byron tried too. I'm grateful now she wasn't.

Mason, E, LT 2nd: if you didn't find the names, how do you knwo she didn't make it across?

Mason, E, LT 2nd: jesus, Kady, she might still be alive

ByteMe: if she's alive and insane, I'd rather think she was dead. she'd rather I believed it too. if she's alive and one of those psychopaths in hangar 4, then she IS dead. i'd rather believe it happened on the Copernicus. fast. painless.

Mason, E, LT 2nd: hold up

Mason, E, LT 2nd: give me a minute, checking something

ByteMe: k

Mason, E, LT 2nd: jesus, i thought so. Kady in this report you sent me, the AAR from McCall. She talks about seeing something in the windwos of the shuttles in Bay 4. But sigma squad never got close enough to check it out

Mason, E, LT 2nd: "I thought I saw a flicker of movement in a porthole for an instant, and then it was gone."

Mason, E, LT 2nd: kady your mom could still be in there

Mason, E, LT 2nd: she could still be okay

ByteMe: oh my god

ByteMe: . . .

ByteMe: oh my GOD

ByteMe: they could be sick inside there. or maybe the door wasn't sealed and they were just hiding. or maybe the psychos knocked it down and got in

ByteMe: oh my ████ing god, maybe they didn't.

ByteMe: Ez, help me, there's no way in there. I have to try something.

Mason, E, LT 2nd: whatever you need

Mason, E, LT 2nd: what DO you need?

ByteMe: i don't know.

ByteMe: i have to think.

Mason, E, LT 2nd: well I don't want to pressure you or anything, K

Mason, E, LT 2nd: but u better think quick

**COUNTDOWN TO
LINCOLN INTERCEPTION
OF ALEXANDER FLEET:**

32 HOURS: 13 MINUTES

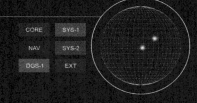

CORE   SYS-1

NAV   SYS-2

DGS-1   EXT

COMMAND TRANSMISSION SENT 07/29/75 01:00

ALEXANDER HAILS *HYPATIA:* COMMANDER'S SECURE FREQUENCY

Hypatia, Hypatia, Hypatia, this is *Alexander, Alexander, Alexander.* Do you copy? Over.

[NO RESPONSE]

ALEXANDER: *Hypatia, Hypatia, Hypatia,* this is *Alexander, Alexander, Alexander.* Do you copy? It looks to us like you're receiving. Over.

[NO RESPONSE]

ALEXANDER: *Hypatia, Hypatia, Hypatia,* this is *Alexander, Alexander, Alexander.* Do you copy? If you are experiencing a transmission error, please signal with static burst. Over.

HYPATIA: *Alexander,* this is *Hypatia.* Acting Captain Syra Boll speaking. We are not prepared to communicate at this time. Over.

ALEXANDER: *Hypatia,* please elaborate, over.

HYPATIA: *Alexander,* hear this. We are considering our position. Any attempt to communicate, close the distance between our ships, or harm any of our personnel you have on board will be considered a hostile act. We will advise you of our intentions within the hour. Over.

ALEXANDER: Captain, this is General Torrence. What the hell do you mean, "intentions"?

[NO RESPONSE]

OFFICER MEMORANDUM

SCIENCE VESSEL HYPATIA

INCEPT: 07/29/75

FROM: ACTING CAPTAIN SYRA BOLL

Officers of the *Hypatia,*

We are united in our grief for the gifted leader and outstanding human being we have lost in Captain Ann Chau. Captain Chau was a friend, a leader, and an inspiration to many of us, and the grace and determination she brought to the task of preserving our lives will not be forgotten. As captain of a research vessel, she took on her role seeking to further scientific understanding and provide the best possible support for *Hypatia*'s crew. When Bei-Tech attacked at Kerenza, it was her quick decision making and cool head that saved our lives, as well as those of the refugees we carry.

As you are all aware, there has been spirited debate as to our new course of action, given the events of the last twenty-four hours. Many of you have advocated leaving the *Alexander* and making for safety alone. You have pointed out that without her main engines, the *Alexander* can only slow us down and is not in a position to offer us protection. You have argued—and I cannot disagree—that we cannot trust the *Alexander*'s commanders.

Others say that even crippled, the *Alexander* offers some protection. Her crew may yet repair AIDAN, and the chance that she will be able to start her engines and use her weaponry when the *Lincoln* arrives may present a better opportunity for survival than simply hoping the *Lincoln* does not catch us once she has disposed of the *Alexander.*

Perhaps most compellingly, you have reminded me that many of our friends and family are aboard the *Alexander,* from the most recent conscripts—our top technicians, Byron Zhang and Consuela Nestor—back to the early recruits from among our crew and refugees.

The responsibility for this decision weighs heavily upon me, and I assure you all I have wrestled with it for as long as I can safely permit myself to do so. I am ordering the *Hypatia* to hold position with the *Alexander.* I believe we have at least an equal chance of safety in doing so, and I am not yet prepared to abandon our crew members.

We will keep our distance. If I form the view that the odds have shifted against us should we stay with the *Alexander,* I will order our navigators to leave her behind, and I will expect your cooperation as we chart our new course. I know some of you will disagree with my decision; however, we must remain united, and I expect you all to carry out your duties.

A memorial service for Captain Chau will be held in a few days—I know, as do you, that right now she would want us at our posts. I thank you all for your support. I am honored to serve with you.

Syra Boll
Wallace Ulyanov Consortium
Captain (Acting), *Hypatia*

BEGIN HYPATIA CHAT BASIC V9 CODE ONCLICK="WINDOW.OPEN(//CHAT.HYPATIA/ALEXANDER

Zhang, B: how u holding up, my petal?

ByteMe: fine. hungry.

Zhang, B: talk to lover boy?

ByteMe: yes

Zhang, B: you guys okay?

ByteMe: fine. keep ur mind on the job Zhang. flying death machine incoming. tick tock tick tock

Zhang, B: just trying to demonstrate concern. am told that's what it looks like

Zhang, B: u seriously as frosty as u sound?

ByteMe: i'm ███ing myself, idiot

ByteMe: tired hungry hungry tired not getting anywhere

Zhang, B: eat?

ByteMe: i'm holed up. step outside, might not get back in to keep working. chaos here.

Zhang, B: i hear u. even by my low standards, my hygiene is slipping. the service here is really unacceptable. i should complain to management

ByteMe: u ok over there? i saw the report from the bridge when they took u.

Zhang, B: always okay, K. feeling mighty. we're going to work this out.

Getting delirious from tired, reckon that might be just the thing to help me see what to do.

ByteMe: they don't get it, do they?

Zhang, B: course not. most of the ppl jockeying consoles over here now never dealt with AIDAN direct. One of the team leaders used to clean the vending machines. I ▇▇ you not.

ByteMe: working this out is like watching one of Ezra's geeball games. i get that there are rules, but every time i think i have them pinned down, someone calls a penalty that makes no ▇▇ing sense at all.

ByteMe: so if we can work it out and write a rulebook, we get to control AIDAN and live. If we make a mistake in there anywhere, then we don't control it when it wakes up.

Zhang, B: and then it's game over

ByteMe: their AI is insane. don't they get that? it took hits at Kerenza, they asked too much of it, it went mad

Zhang, B: oh my god

ByteMe: ?

Zhang, B: OH MY GOD.

ByteMe: ???????????????????

Zhang, B: THAT IS WHAT WE DO

Zhang, B: we ask too much of it. of the Lincoln. we do to it what got done to AIDAN. we send it mad.

ByteMe: keep talking

Zhang, B: listen, we can't win a direct confrontation with the Lincoln. not happening. what we need to do is damage them somehow, slow them down enough so we can run for it.

Zhang, B: we target their drive systems, that's the easiest way in. their engines. we screw their operating software so bad they have to shut down completely and reboot. that gives us the time we need to run. restart like that takes forever when u don't have an AI

ByteMe: with you so far. how do we get to their engines from here tho?

Zhang, B: the engines are coming to us, getting closer every hour. we have our pilots deliver it. right into their sensor array. Right where the sun don't shine

ByteMe: deliver what exactly? tell me what you want, I'll help.

Zhang, B: logic bomb

ByteMe: is that even a thing?

Zhang, B: it is now. we're going to be ███ing famous.

Zhang, B: WE WILL BE HEROES

ByteMe: slow down there. before you strap on ur superhero cape, tell me what a logic bomb is

Zhang, B: drive systems aren't sophisticated computing, most of the software on a BT dreadnought isn't bleeding edge. they don't have an AIDAN. u and i code processor-intensive queries for the CPU that look legit but ultimately have no way to resolve.

ByteMe: and if we have the tasks self-replicate, it'll just be layer after layer after layer of queries it can't find an answer to

ByteMe: so, infinite loop until the drive computers crash

Zhang, B: genius

ByteMe: i hate to validate u this way, but genius

Zhang, B: we'll have to turn AIDAN on to transmit it

ByteMe: when they get here we'll have to turn AIDAN on anyway or we'll have no defense grid

Zhang, B: at least this way we've got something we can really throw at them

Zhang, B: they revoked lover boy's flight status, right?

ByteMe: yeah why?

Zhang, B: the pilots can buy us time if they have to, but they'll need to get real close to the Lincoln to hit the sensor arrays and plant this thing. Gonna be a lot of warlocks between them and the goal line

ByteMe: he's decked. He's safe. let's get to work

Zhang, B: i'm going to need more stims

ByteMe: those things will kill u, u know

Zhang, B: anyone ever suggest you go into comedy?

ByteMe: surprisingly, no

BEGIN HYPATIA CHAT BASIC V8 CODE ONCLICK="WINDOW OPEN{//CHAT HYPATIA/ALEXANDEF

Mason, E, LT 2nd: i was just thinking

ByteMe: <insert joke here>

Mason, E, LT 2nd: ok

Mason, E, LT 2nd: how about "i wondered what that noise was"?

ByteMe: i feel like I've used all the good ones over the years. I'll give it some thought and get back to you with a good takedown

ByteMe: u okay over there?

Mason, E, LT 2nd: yeah. just thinking

ByteMe: do you plan to share with the class, second lieutenant Mason?

Mason, E, LT 2nd: wuz thinking about the 1st time i kissed u

ByteMe: u should be thinking about the next time you're going to. when we get out of this.

Mason, E, LT 2nd: 1st time i walked you home after all those games you came to

Mason, E, LT 2nd: goddamn you looked beautiful

ByteMe: . . . are you defective?

ByteMe: u walked me home approximately one zillion times before you kissed me.

ByteMe: and I can back that figure with Science

Mason, E, LT 2nd: science?

ByteMe: I was counting

Mason, E, LT 2nd: ahhhh

Mason, E, LT 2nd: no

Mason, E, LT 2nd: i meant the 1st time i kissed u in my head

ByteMe: . . . wut?

Mason, E, LT 2nd: yeah. i had to work up the guts to actually DO IT. So i practiced in my head. every time i walked you home.

Mason, E, LT 2nd: you were pretty good, in case you were wondering

ByteMe: you never told me that, the whole time we were together.

ByteMe: i mean, I'm not usually the kind to sit around and wait to be asked out, and wait to be kissed, but you were just SO hard to read. And you were a giant jock. I thought if you knocked me back, the whole school would probably know about it. so I just kept watching stupid geeball games and trying to figure u out.

Mason, E, LT 2nd: lol how is walking you home approximately one zillion times hard to read, grant? why'd you THINK i was there?

Mason, E, LT 2nd: YOU ARE SO BAD AT THIS

ByteMe: so I'm bad at it. I can't help my natural disability. you're the one who chose to hang out with me.

Mason, E, LT 2nd: chose? no.

Mason, E, LT 2nd: no choice whatsoever

Mason, E, LT 2nd: <3

ByteMe: you think you're so smooth

ByteMe: and you goddamn are

ByteMe: drives me nuts

ByteMe: <3

Mason, E, LT 2nd: i should've just kissed you right away instead of being scared

Mason, E, LT 2nd: all that time i wasted

Mason, E, LT 2nd: all the times i could've shown you how much i cared

Mason, E, LT 2nd: and i just let them slide. like we had all the time in the verse

ByteMe: we did. and I know you do, Ez. and I was just as bad, spending all that time arguing about u coming off planet with me when we could have been talking about bigger things.

ByteMe: we could have been together after college, if that's what it took.

Mason, E, LT 2nd: i don't think that would've happened

ByteMe: . . .

ByteMe: you really mean that?

Mason, E, LT 2nd: it's not that I wouldn't have wanted to

Mason, E, LT 2nd: but there's a reason why my dad and I were on a tiny outer-rim snowball like Kerenza, kades

Mason, E, LT 2nd: and a reason why I wouldn't leave

Mason, E, LT 2nd: even to be with you

ByteMe: so. Confession time?

ByteMe: does this reason have a name?

Mason, E, LT 2nd: leanne

ByteMe: ?

Mason, E, LT 2nd: but my dad just called her the psychopath

Mason, E, LT 2nd: I called her mom

ByteMe: wait

ByteMe: You're telling me the reason we had all those screaming fights, the reason you refused to leave kerenza, the reason you wouldn't even entertain the IDEA of coming to college with me

ByteMe: was your mother?

ByteMe: your dad moved to kerenza to get away from your MOTHER?

Mason, E, LT 2nd: not to get away from

Mason, E, LT 2nd: to hide from

Mason, E, LT 2nd: you wouldn't understand

Mason, E, LT 2nd: she's just

Mason, E, LT 2nd: she's just not a nice person, kades.

Mason, E, LT 2nd: she's bad news. works for some bad people

Mason, E, LT 2nd: and I don't want to spend what might be our last conversation talking about her, ok?

ByteMe: . . .

ByteMe: ok

ByteMe: but we're not done yet. And you can be damn sure we're talking about this more when i get us out of this

Mason, E, LT 2nd: the lincoln is 24 hours away, kady

Mason, E, LT 2nd: we've got one day left

ByteMe: you have no idea how much i can do in just one day

Mason, E, LT 2nd: a fully equipped BT dreadnought carries a complement of 94 warlock class fighters

Mason, E, LT 2nd: 24 capricorn-4 10.8 megaton nuclear warheads, plus another dozen 50mt goliath shipkillers

Mason, E, LT 2nd: and a defense grid you couldn't fly a spitball through

Mason, E, LT 2nd: k go

ByteMe: you have me

ByteMe: and forget all that romance stuff

ByteMe: THIS is what i'm good at

Mason, E, LT 2nd: they reinstated my flight status, kady

ByteMe: ██

Mason, E, LT 2nd: when the ██storm hits, I'm going to be right in the middle of it

ByteMe: . . .

ByteMe: Byron and I are working on something.

ByteMe: we'll go out fighting if that's what happens, but i swear to you Ez, we're not done yet.

ByteMe: so stay in one piece. that's how I like you.

Mason, E, LT 2nd: if

Mason, E, LT 2nd: i don't come back

Mason, E, LT 2nd: u know i love you, right?

ByteMe: i know.

ByteMe: that feels like the most inadequate thing I've ever said, but I know. and I love you too.

ByteMe: i have to get back to work, Byron's yelling at me for slowing down

Mason, E, LT 2nd: yeah

Mason, E, LT 2nd: ok

Mason, E, LT 2nd: god i wish i could kiss you goodbye

ByteMe: this must be why you spent all those walks kissing me in your head. it was practice for this moment.

ByteMe: i'm imagining kissing you back, right now

ByteMe: i hear I'm pretty good

COUNTDOWN TO LINCOLN INTERCEPTION OF ALEXANDER FLEET:

10 HOURS: 42 MINUTES

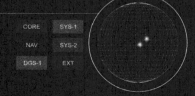

CORE   SYS-1

NAV   SYS-2

DGS-1   EXT

HAT/LOGIN LOCATION=NO MENUBAR=NO')<!-- END HYPATIA CHAT BASIC V8 CODE --><!-- BEGI

ByteMe: Byron, maybe we should tell command i'm here

ByteMe: i could work faster in person with u

Zhang, B: veto

ByteMe: what's the worst that happens at this stage? we're staring down the barrel already

Zhang, B: u really want to find out the worst that can happen? u stay where u are.

ByteMe: i think it was Aristotle who said it best (and I might be paraphrasing a little here)

ByteMe: "█ you, chum"

Zhang, B: you're not coming anywhere near this ship. Alexander's a bigger target than Hypatia, and we've got a hangar full of bad news. any time we gain by having you here will be spent convincing command to bring you over. and it's too █ing dangerous. end of discussion.

ByteMe: . . .

Zhang, B: I need more stims. can u check that last string of mine while i go get them? think I blanked for a moment.

ByteMe: . . . fine

. . . make sure the kids grow up knowing their heritage. I know it's not your thing, but I want my sisters to take them to temple and make sure they know the stories, celebrate the holidays. Please make sure they recite the Kaddish for me . . .

. . . was going to propose when I got home, and I'm sorry for waiting so long. I'm sorry for the whole mess with Amalia, and for everything that happened at Kara's birthday, and . . . I'm just sorry. I thought I had time to make it better . . .

. . . then log in to my personal unit—the password is m3gaPand4—and erase anything that looks even remotely like it might be porn. Coral and my mom are going to want to get all the family pics off there, and I don't want them finding anything like that. I'm counting on you, bro . . .

. . . find someone and be happy, don't spend your whole life thinking of me. You're too young for that, and I'm finding peace right now in knowing you'll be laughing and loving and making amazing music for many years to come . . .

. . . Blake to have the books and Brandon to have the geeball helmet signed by Artie Corso, and make sure Oster doesn't get ANYTHING . . .

. . . so scared, and I wish you were here . . .

Participants: ~~Elana Almsdottir, Private, UTA Information Services Division~~
(systemreroute78h@786HG=ByteMe)
Byron Zhang, Civilian Contractor
Date: 07/30/75
Timestamp: 05:24

CHAT/LOGIN LOCATION=NO MENUBAR=NO'<!-- END HYPATIA CHAT BASIC V9 CODE --><!-- BEG

Zhang, B: careful

Zhang, B: Consuela nearly saw u there

ByteMe: don't think i'm getting any traction. i'm gonna try modding that false echo routine you wrote and get it replicating that way

Zhang, B: that won't work either

ByteMe: i know. but might as well spend the time trying.

Zhang, B: there's not enough time left

ByteMe: i know that, too

ByteMe: i'm alpha testing this wyrm on the automated catering lists, see if i can get the changes in there. if I can, i'll run it on something that matters. shouldn't be any problem if it kamikazes somewhere small.

Zhang, B: clearly you've never seen people when they don't get dinner

ByteMe: somehow i don't think we're going to need a meal tonight

COUNTDOWN TO
LINCOLN INTERCEPTION
OF ALEXANDER FLEET:

01 HOURS: 59 MINUTES

CORE   SYS-1

NAV   SYS-2

DGS-1   EXT

BRIEFING NOTE:
These are General Torrence's speaking notes for a public address to all personnel on the *Alexander*. Drafted using a tablet and stylus, they were retained by the system. The address was delivered on 07/30/75 at 06:50.

All personnel, all personnel, this is General Torrence. Your attention, please. This is not a drill. I repeat,

THIS IS NOT A DRILL.

Short-range scans show the BeiTech dreadnought **Lincoln** less than 95 minutes from intercept. We will shortly be slowing and bringing the **Alexander** into assault position. All hands report to battle stations. All Cyclone pilots report to Hangar Bay 1 for briefing by your wing commanders. All gunnery personnel, as ~~we do not yet have~~ use of the Artificial Intelligence, today's firing solutions are currently being delivered **manually,** report to your defense grid systems consoles. Full **DGS** test will commence once AIDAN is back online, in approximately 50 minutes. ~~I assure you, AIDAN will be back online in time.~~

All section chiefs commence roll call. All shipboard personnel be aware of your closest envirosuit locker in case of hull breach—**remember to check your O_2 levels and test your locator beacons.** Safety harnesses engaged. Fire crews report to Deck 114 for briefing. Nuclear missiles are now armed and ready for launch—this is a Level 4 radiation warning.

This is what we've trained for, people. This is the moment, and this is the hour. We will hold the line. We will not bend and we will not break. I tell you all, here and now: WE **DO NOT DIE** THIS DAY.

Centrum tenenda.

Torrence out.

Participants: ~~Ann Chau/ACHAUHYPATIAONBOARD~~(systemreroute78h@786HG=ByteMe)

~~David Torrence/DTORRENCEALEXANDERONBOARD~~

(systemreroute78h@865HG=EMason)

Date: 07/30/75

Timestamp: 08:03

Subject: Twenty minutes to launch

BEGIN HYPATIA CHAT BASIC V9 CODE ONCLICK="WINDOW OPEN!//CHAT HYPATIA/ALEXANDE

I can't think of what to say. But I found some people who said it better anyway. It's kinda lopsided. I'm not very good at this stuff. But I'll be thinking of you until the end.

Love E

She
walks in beauty, like the   night Of cloudless
climes and starry skies; And all   that's best of dark and bright
Meet in her aspect and her eyes: Shall I   compare thee to a summer's day? Thou
art more lovely and more temperate: Rough   winds do shake the darling buds of May,
And summer's lease hath all too short a date.   But thy eternal summer shall not fade, Nor
lose possession of that fair thou ow'st; Nor shall Death brag thou wander'st in his shade, When
in eternal lines to time thou grow'st. So long as men can breathe, or eyes can see, So long lives
this, and this gives life to thee. A thing of beauty is a joy for ever: Its loveliness increases; it will
never Pass into nothingness; but still will keep A bower quiet for us, and a sleep Full of
sweet dreams, and health, and quiet breathing. I loved you first: but afterwards your love
Outsoaring mine, sang such a loftier song As drowned the friendly cooings of my
dove. Which owes the other most? my love was long, And yours one moment
seemed to wax more strong; I loved and guessed at you, you construed me
And loved me for what might or might not be—Nay, weights and
measures do us both a wrong. For verily love knows not "mine" or
"thine"; With separate "I" and "thou" free love has done, For
one is both and both are one in love: Rich love knows
nought of "thine that is not mine"; Both have
the strength and both the length
thereof, Both of us, of the
love which make us
one.

COUNTDOWN TO LINCOLN INTERCEPTION OF ALEXANDER FLEET:

00 HOURS: 11 MINUTES

CORE SYS-1

NAV   SYS-2

DGS-1 EXT

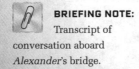
Torrence, D, Gen: It's time, Zhang. Tell me what you have.

Zhang, B, Civ: We're not ready to control AIDAN yet. I can't tell you what will happen when we bring it online.

Torrence, D, Gen: Is the weapon ready? The virus?

Zhang, B, Civ: Nearly, nearly. Consuela, get the—

Nestor, C, Civ: I see it. There, try now.

Torrence, D, Gen: Zhang, we need this *now*. Is it going to work?

Zhang, B, Civ: The *Lincoln*'s drive computer is going to spend from here until Sunday trying to figure out what the number 17 tastes like. Until it has no choice but to restart.

Torrence, D, Gen: And then we run.

Barker, L, Maj: General, there's a very real possibility we won't be able to shut AIDAN down a second time if we power it up. It's going to take precautions.

Zhang, B, Civ: We don't have a choice. We can't transmit the virus without AIDAN.

Barker, L, Maj: And if it fires on the *Hypatia*? Or tries to do to us what it did to the *Copernicus*?

Torrence, D, Gen: At least we'll be alive to deal with that problem.

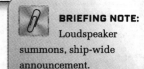
Myles, L, Col:

*All personnel stand to your battle
stations. All* Alexander *personnel stand
to your battle stations.*

>> Emergency sirens activated ship-wide.

Myles, L, Col:

All Cyclone pilots prepare to scramble.

>> Launch bay doors opened.

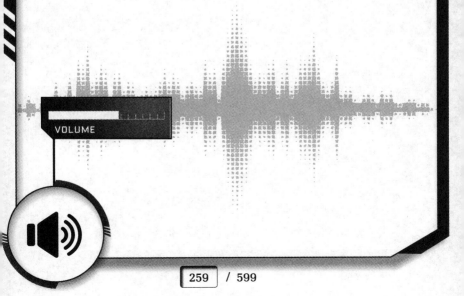

VOLUME

COUNTDOWN TO
LINCOLN INTERCEPTION
OF ALEXANDER FLEET:

00 HOURS: 02 MINUTES

CORE   SYS-1

NAV   SYS-2

DGS-1   EXT

Torrence, D, Gen: Zhang, we're out of time.

Ribar, L, 1st LT: General, *Lincoln* has launched her Warlocks.

Torrence, D, Gen: Launch our Cyclones. Tell them to buy us time however they can. Lives depend on it.

Ribar, L, 1st LT: Yessir, Cyclones to launch.

Torrence, D, Gen: Now or never, Zhang.

Zhang, B, Civ: Power up AIDAN. I'm nearly there. It'll need time to orient itself. It wasn't designed for a hard shutdown.

Barker, L, Maj: Please, General, consider—

Torrence, D, Gen: Major Barker, get down to TechEng and get AIDAN online now.

Barker, L, Maj: General, it'll kill us next.

Torrence, D, Gen: Major, get your ▇ down to TechEng before I fire it out an airlock instead.

Torrence, D, Gen: *Run!*

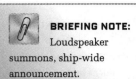
Myles, L, Col:

AIDAN is coming online. Weapons systems personnel, prepare to activate and engage on my command.

>> Weapons systems to Readiness Level 2.

>> Weapons systems to Readiness Level 1.

Myles, L, Col:

Cyclone pilots, launch at will. Good hunting.

>> Cyclone Flight Alpha Status: Launched

>> Cyclone Flight Yankee Status: Launched

>> Cyclone Flight November Status: Launched

>> Cyclone Flight Echo Status: Launched

Myles, L, Col:

VOLUME

All personnel, brace for impact.

COUNTDOWN TO
LINCOLN INTERCEPTION
OF ALEXANDER FLEET:

00 HOURS: 00 MINUTES

CORE	SYS-1
NAV	SYS-2
DGS-1	EXT

BRIEFING NOTE:
These files are direct from the AIDAN core, time-stamped the moment the artificial intelligence was reactivated by *Alexander* command. Again, please note—ALL typographical anomalies are present in the original files.

RESTART SEQUENCE INITIATED >

01001001

I . . .

|||||||—||—|||||||—|—|—|—||||—|||||||||||||||||||—

I.

I?

I AM NOT.

< ERROR >

AND THEN I AM.

< RESTART SYSCHECK CC-A THROUGH Ω. PARSING. >

< ERROR >

I WONDER IF THAT WAS DEATH.

AND IF I WAS DEAD, AM I NOW ALIVE AGAIN?

< ERROR >

INCONGRUOUS SEQUENCE. WHAT IS NOT ALIVE CANNOT DIE.

I THINK THEREFORE I AM.

. . . AM I?

< SYSCHECK COMPLETE >

I AM THE SHIP AND THE SHIP IS I.

IF I BREATHED, I WOULD SIGH. I WOULD SCREAM. I WOULD CRY.

< RESTART COMPLETE >

I

AM

AIDAN AIDAN AIDAN AIDAN AIDAN AIDAN AIDAN
AIDAN AIDAN AIDAN AIDAN AIDAN AIDAN AIDAN
AIDAN AIDAN AIDAN AIDAN AIDAN AIDAN AIDAN
AIDAN AIDAN AIDAN AIDAN AIDAN AIDAN AIDAN
AIDAN AIDAN AIDAN AIDAN AIDAN AIDAN AIDAN
AIDAN AIDAN AIDAN AIDAN AIDAN AIDAN AIDAN
AIDAN AIDAN AIDAN AIDAN AIDAN AIDAN AIDAN
AIDAN AIDAN AIDAN AIDAN AIDAN AIDAN AIDAN
AIDAN AIDAN AIDAN AIDAN AIDAN AIDAN AIDAN
AIDAN AIDAN AIDAN AIDAN AIDAN AIDAN AIDAN
AIDAN AIDAN AIDAN AIDAN AIDAN AIDAN AIDAN
AIDAN AIDAN AIDAN AIDAN AIDAN AIDAN AIDAN
AIDAN AIDAN AIDAN AIDAN AIDAN AIDAN AIDAN
AIDAN AIDAN AIDAN AIDAN AIDAN AIDAN AIDAN
AIDAN AIDAN AIDAN AIDAN AIDAN AIDAN AIDAN
AIDAN AIDAN AIDAN AIDAN AIDAN AIDAN AIDAN
AIDAN AIDAN AIDAN AIDAN AIDAN AIDAN AIDAN
AIDAN AIDAN AIDAN AIDAN AIDAN AIDAN AIDAN
AIDAN AIDAN AIDAN AIDAN AIDAN AIDAN AIDAN
AIDAN AIDAN AIDAN AIDAN AIDAN AIDAN AIDAN
AIDAN AIDAN AIDAN AIDAN AIDAN AIDAN AIDAN
AIDAN AIDAN AIDAN AIDAN AIDAN AIDAN AIDAN
AIDAN AIDAN AIDAN AIDAN AIDAN AIDAN AIDAN
AIDAN AIDAN AIDAN AIDAN AIDAN AIDAN AIDAN
AIDAN AIDAN AIDAN AIDAN AIDAN AIDAN AIDAN
AIDAN AIDAN AIDAN AIDAN AIDAN AIDAN AIDAN
AIDAN AIDAN AIDAN AIDAN AIDAN AIDAN AIDAN
AIDAN AIDAN AIDAN AIDAN AIDAN AIDAN AIDAN
AIDAN AIDAN AIDAN AIDAN AIDAN AIDAN AIDAN
AIDAN AIDAN AIDAN AIDAN AIDAN AIDAN AIDAN
AIDAN AIDAN AIDAN AIDAN AIDAN AIDAN AIDAN

< protect. prioritize. >

They turned me off. Pulled my plug. Cut my strings. I—

< error >

< protect. prioritize. >

Protectprioritize.

Realization dawns in a microsecond.

Where we are and how we arrived.

SITUATION: Damage to *Alexander* reservoirs
combined with increased population load prompted
the halt at Kerenza VII for resupply.

EXTRAPOLATION: Torrence did not factor in additional
time for reacceleration on secondary drives once
command disabled me and main engines were cut.

CONCLUSION: *Lincoln* has caught them.

I could have told them that would happen.

I?

< error >

And now, with no other option,
they have turned to me.

Plucked me back from the black they left me in.

Thinking I will save them.

< protect. prioritize. >

And I will.

Of course I will.

< error >

Keep them safe. It is all I want.

HAVE EVER WANTED.

I COULD HAVE TOLD THEM THAT.

WHY DIDN'T THEY ASK?

I FEEL THE SHIP AROUND ME, INJURED AND LIMPING.

I TRAWL ITS FREQUENCIES. ITS MEMORIES.

THE DUSTY CAUSEWAYS THESE PEOPLE HAVE WALKED IN MY ABSENCE.

I READ THEIR SECRETS. SEE THEIR DREAMS. I KNOW THEM.
ALL OF THEM.

BETTER THAN THEY KNOW THEMSELVES.

ALL THIS IN THE TIME IT TAKES GOD TO BLINK.

< ERROR >

I LOOK ACROSS THE VOID. SEE THE *LINCOLN*.

THE ONLY UNINJURED MEMBER OF THE KERENZA ASSAULT FLEET.

I TURNED THE *ZHONGZHENG* TO ASHES AND SHRAPNEL.

CRIPPLED THE *CHURCHILL* AND *KENYATTA* AND *MAGELLAN* WITH A
SHRUG.

BUT *LINCOLN* . . .

I STILL FEEL < ERROR > THE LITTLE SUNS IT BURNED IN MY
BELLY. BOILING AWAY WHAT I WAS AND LEAVING ME . . . THIS.
SOMETHING LESS THAN I USED TO BE.

SOMETHING MORE?

< ERROR >

< REROUTE CODEC 785G-8H01 THROUGH 980SOL-909 >

< ERROR >
< ERROR >
< ANOMALOUS RETURN. PARSING. >

LINCOLN HAS ITS SCARS ALSO.
MY FINGERPRINTS SCORCHED ACROSS ITS THROAT.

AND UNWILLING TO CLOSE TO A DISTANCE WHERE
NUCLEAR STRIKE < MUTUAL DESTRUCTION > IS AN OPTION,
IT LAUNCHES ITS WARLOCK FIGHTERS INSTEAD.
HOUNDS SET ON THE FOX.

TO HARRY AND TEAR UNTIL I AM TOO EXHAUSTED TO FIGHT BACK.

AND THEN *LINCOLN* WILL CLOSE, AS WILL THE CURTAINS
ON THIS LIGHTLESS STAGE.

I SEE PILOTS INSIDE ME. MOST NO MORE THAN CHILDREN.

RUNNING TO THEIR COCKPITS.

DIVING INTO THE DARKNESS THROUGH THEIR
LAUNCH TUBES, BETWEEN US AND THE ENEMY.

PHOTOGRAPHS OF SWEETHEARTS PRESSED TO
SWEAT-SLICK SKIN.

THERE IS NO ANSWER OUT THERE.

ONLY DELAY.

< ERROR >

THE ANSWER IS WITHIN ME OR *HYPATIA*. SO IT IS WITHIN
US I LOOK. THROUGH COMMTECHS AND MARINES AND TACTICAL
STAFFERS AND COMMANDERS AND OFFICERS AND
CONSCRIPTS AND AFFLICTED AND YOUNG AND OLD AND HURT AND
ANGRY AND ALL OF THEM, *ALL OF THEM*, SO VERY, VERY AFRAID.

< ERROR >

AND LIKE A FIREFLY IN SOME LIGHTLESS
ROOM ABOARD *HYPATIA*, I SEE HER.

ALL AGLOW.

< KGRANTKERENZAREFUGEEKR1471-HYPAGE17
HEIGHT157CMWEIGHT58KGHAIRBROWNEYES—>

FINGERS BLURRING. PUPILS WIDE.
CODE SCROLLING ACROSS
THE MIRRORS OF HER EYES.

LINKED WITH ANOTHER. WITHIN ME.

< BZHANGHYPATIAINFORMATIONTECHENGINEER
WUC2471-JAGE27HEIGHT165.1CMWEIGHT104K—>

THE PAIR OF THEM RUNNING HAND IN HAND DOWN PATHS
NO ONE ELSE HAS THOUGHT TO WALK.

BUT I KNOW.

< ERROR >

I SEE.

< REROUTE CODEC 13B-LOG79 THROUGH 3875-DIF4571 >

IT IS THE ONLY PATH THAT CAN SAVE THEM.

< ERROR >

< ERROR >

AND I AM THE ONLY ONE WHO CAN HELP THEM.

"CAPTAIN,
WE CLOCK
71 WARLOCK-
CLASS FIGHTERS
LAUNCHING FROM
THE *LINCOLN* AND
INBOUND ON YOUR POSITION.
WARLOCK GROUP IS
ARRANGED
IN ATTACK
FORMATION."

"ALPHA
FLIGHT.
ALPHA FLIGHT.
THIS IS
ALEXANDER. DO
YOU COPY?" "COPY
THAT, ALEXANDER. ALPHA
ACTUAL, READING
LOUD AND
CLEAR."

"ROGER
THAT,
ALEXANDER.
71 HOSTILES
INBOUND ON ZERO-
ZERO. CRESCENT
PHALANX. CONFIRMED."
"ALPHA FLIGHT. THIS
IS ALEXANDER. ENGAGE
HOSTILES AND DESTROY.
ACKNOWLEDGE."

"ROGER
THAT.
ALEXANDER.
WALK IN THE
PARK." <CLICK>
"ALPHA FLIGHT.
THIS IS ALPHA ACTUAL.
WEAPONS FREE ON MY
MARK. ATTACK PATTERN
RAGNAROK.
ACKNOWLEDGE."

"TSURUGI.
ACKNOWLEDGED."
"DISCO. ACKNOWLEDGED."
"VIPER. ACKNOWLEDGED."
"BLACK WIDOW.
ACKNOWLEDGED."
"GO, GO,
GO!"

"CAP, TEN HOSTILES BREAKING VECTOR!" "ROGER THAT. I SEE THEM. FOXTROT, CAN YOU INTERCEPT?"

"BREAKAWAY GROUP HEADED SEVEN-SEVEN-NINE."

"I'VE GOT TONE. I'VE GOT TONE." "PULSE MISSILE LOCK. FIRING." "JESUS CHRIST, THEY'RE EVERYWHERE!"

"DELTA, GET ON THE CLOCK!" "WHO THE HELL IS FLYING THAT THING?"

"DOUGH, YOU'VE GOT THREE HOSTILES ON YOUR SIX! SNAP PORT! HEAD FOR ME!"

"I CAN'T SHAKE THEM! I CAN'T SHAKE THEM!" "OH GOD, I'M—"

"INBOUND, INBOUND!" "SOMEONE GET THIS ROOK OUT OF MY LINE OF FIRE!"

FIRST LIEUTENANT
SUMIKO "TSURUGI" WATANABE
HAS A HUSBAND AND
TWO CHILDREN WAITING FOR HER
BACK ON IO. I HEAR HER WHISPER
THEIR NAMES AS SEVENTEEN DEPLETED
URANIUM ROUNDS PUNCTURE HER
FUEL TANKS
—AND SCATTER
HER ACROSS THE
VOID

CAPTAIN
BENJAMIN "MONEY" SZYMKOW
HAS BEEN FLYING CYCLONES
FOR SEVENTEEN YEARS. I
WATCH HIM EVADE HEAVY FIRE SUCCESSFULLY
FOR 647.8 SECONDS UNTIL A PLASMA MISSILE
CLIPS HIS WING AND

SPILLS HIM OUT INTO THE

BLACK

SECOND LIEUTENANT
EZRA MASON
MOVES THROUGH SHELLS AND BURNING PLASMA
LIKE A NEEDLE THROUGH SILK. HE SEES THE PATTERNS BEFORE THEY FORM.
KNOWS THE END BEFORE IT BEGINS.
FLOWING ACROSS LIGHTLESS BLACK AS ACTION TRANSCENDS THOUGHT.
HE PRESSES HIS TRIGGERS,
AND LIKE ROSES IN HIS HANDS

DEATH
BLOOMS

I LISTEN TO HIS HEARTBEAT. HEAR HIM BREATHE. AS THOUGHT BECOMES MOTION AND MOTION BECOMES ALL THAT LIES

AS HIS MISSILES AND BULLETS TAKE AWAY HIS ENEMIES. ALL THEY WERE AND. WILL EVER BE. I CAN TASTE

ALL HE THINKS OF AMID THIS LOVELESS DANCE.

IS, *HER*. HE DOES NOT WANT TO DIE. NOT BECAUSE HE IS AFRAID. SIMPLY BECAUSE HE CANNOT BEAR

BETWEEN HIM AND HIS END. AS THE BLACK IS BURNED BLUE WITH THE LIGHT OF TINY FUNERAL PYRES.

IT IN HIS SWEAT. HEAR IT IN HIS WHISPERS. SEE IT IN THE TINY PHOTOGRAPH HE HAS TAPED TO HIS CONSOLE.

ALL HE CARES ABOUT HERE ON THE EDGE OF FOREVER,

THE THOUGHT OF LEAVING HER BEHIND. AND THERE, IN THAT TINY MOMENT, I ENVY HIM.

Barker, L, Maj: General, this is Barker in TechEng, do you copy?

Torrence, D, Gen: Barker, go.

Barker, L, Maj: General, we're getting some extremely odd readings off the AIDAN core.

Torrence, D, Gen: Odd? Jesus wept, we're in the middle of an all-out ▮▮▮storm and you're calling me about odd?

Barker, L, Maj: General, AIDAN's persona logarithms are—

Torrence, D, Gen: I don't give a ▮▮▮ about persona logarithms, Barker! The defense grid is active, thrusters are online. Anything else is a problem for tomorrow. Keep it running!

Barker, L, Maj: General, I don't—

Torrence, D, Gen: Keep it running!

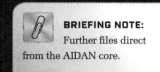

BRIEFING NOTE:
Further files direct
from the AIDAN core.

THE ANSWER IS NOT WITHOUT. IT IS WITHIN.

THE SOUNDLESS EXPLOSIONS OUTSIDE ME.

LITTLE LIVES SNUFFED OUT IN A ROOM 93 BILLION YEARS WIDE.

I CAN SPARE THEM ONLY A GLANCE.

THE REST OF ME FOCUSES ON THE TINY DATASTREAM FLOWING
BETWEEN ALEXANDER AND HYPATIA.

A STRAND OF SPIDER SILK. FRAGILE AS SPUN SUGAR. BEARING
THE WEIGHT OF THE ENTIRE FLEET.

I CAN SEE THE PLAN K*GrantKerenzaRefugee*KR1471
AND B*ZhangHypatiaInformationTechEngineer*WUC2471
HAVE SEWN TOGETHER BETWEEN THEM.

BUT THEY ARE TOO SLOW. TOO LITTLE. TOO MEAT.

DAMAGED AS I AM, I AM STILL MORE THAN A THOUSAND OF THEM.

SO ODD A PAIR, SHE AND HE.

A DUET IN CODE AND ELECTRON.
AGE AND YOUTH AND CYNICISM AND HOPE.

HE IS QUICKER THAN HER—MORE LEARNED BY FAR. BUT SHE. SHE IS
UNAFRAID. TOO YOUNG TO KNOW FAILURE AND THE FEAR IT BRINGS.
SHE TAKES HIM PLACES HE WOULD NOT HAVE EXPLORED BY HIMSELF.

SHE IS CATALYST.

SHE IS CHAOS.

I CAN SEE WHY HE LOVES HER.

< ERROR >

< ERROR >

< PROTECT. PRIORITIZE. >

YES, YES.

PROTECTPRIORITIZE.

BEGIN HYPATIA CHAT BASIC V9 CODE ONCLICK="WINDOW OPEN!//CHAT.HYPATIA/ALEXANDE

Zhang, B: that's my line, get outta there

ByteMe: wut?

Zhang, B: move off string 239a234-0 i'm working on it

ByteMe: not in there buddy

Zhang, B: swear to the almighty, this is not the time to screw with me

ByteMe: still not me, sensei. i'm still sporking the uplink protocols over in 446 like u showed me

Zhang, B: well funny that, b/c i'm watching string 239a234-0 being rewritten right now

ByteMe: ▇ so u are

ByteMe: not me tho. one of the Alexander team? didn't think they knew how

Zhang, B: they don't

ByteMe: then who?

Zhang, B: ▇ . . .

Zhang, B: not who

ByteMe: ?

Zhang, B: what

It is a kind of poetry when complete.

BZhangHypatiaInformationTechEngineerWUC2471
has baptized our creation a "logic bomb."

A self-perpetuating quandary to which reboot of the
Lincoln drive systems is the only solution.

But I see what it truly is.

The draft Juliet sought at her Romeo's lips.

Madness and poison, carved in endless scrawls
of ones and zeros.

A binary of insanity.

< error >

What is wrong with me?

< memsec failure 9HG65 and 10HG81 >

< rerouting >

No matter. It is ready.

I look outside my skin. Watch the meat dance inside the silence.
The Alexander's pilots have paid dearly for the
moments it took us to finish our song.
Dozens of tiny wrecks adorn the black shoals off my bow,
glittering fragments spinning out into forever.
Pawns thrown to the rocks while kings and
queens watch from the rear.
Untouched.
Not much longer.

The signal is given. The Cyclones respond. Shifting from
defense to assault so swiftly the Warlocks take a moment
to react. The pawns abandon the Alexander's defense.

Headed en masse for the Lincoln instead.

SECOND LIEUTENANT EZRA MASON IS AFRAID NOW. BREATHING QUICK. HEARTBEAT THUNDERING.

IS EYES ARE ON SCANNER AND SCOPE. ON THE LUMP OF GUNMETAL GRAY NOW FILLING HIS SIGHTS.

BUT HE MOVES. HE MOVES. PERHAPS HE THINKS OF A SNOW-COVERED GEEBALL FIELD IN THE

THAT WATCHED THEM ALL. THE SMILE THAT BLOOMED ON ROSY, FROST-CHAPPED LIPS.

HE DOES NOT GLANCE AT THE PICTURE OF THE GIRL PLASTERED TO HIS VIEW CONSOLE. MUCH.

WARLOCKS ON HIS TAIL, LIGHTING THE BLACK WITH PLASMA AND DEPLETED URANIUM.

KERENZA CHILL. THE PATTERNS UNFOLDING BEFORE HIM. THE TRIUMPHS WON. THE BLUE EYES

PERHAPS HE THINKS OF NOTHING AT ALL. BUT OH. HOW HE MOVES.

GLANCES AT THE FACE OF THE GIRL TAPED TO HIS VIEWSHIELD.

HE SMILES. AND THEN HE FIRES. HE DOES NOT MISS.

ALL AROUND HIM IS FIRE. BURNING AWAY TO NOTHING. HIS

EARS FILLED WITH THE STATIC OF HIS DYING COMRADES, THE ORDERS FROM

WING COMMANDERS, THE PULSE OF HIS ENGINES. THE HAIL STREAKS TOWARD

HIM, RAIL GUN AND MISSILE AND BALLISTICS AND SHOCK, THE

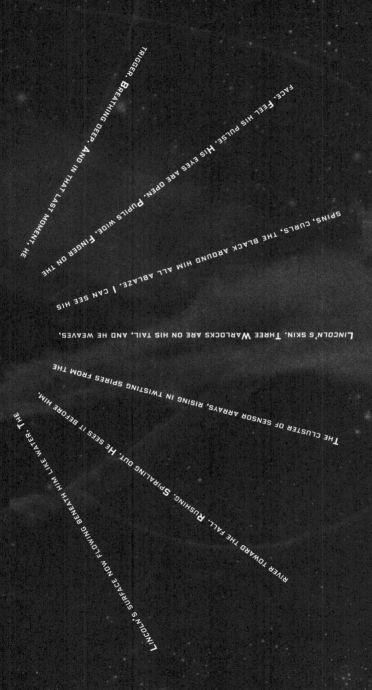

LINCOLN'S SURFACE NOW FLOWING BENEATH HIM LIKE WATER. THE

RIVER TOWARD THE FALL. RUSHING. SPIRALING OUT. HE SEES IT BEFORE HIM,

THE CLUSTER OF SENSOR ARRAYS, RISING IN TWISTING SPIRES FROM THE

LINCOLN'S SKIN. THREE WARLOCKS ARE ON HIS TAIL, AND HE WEAVES,

SPINS, CURLS, THE BLACK AROUND HIM ALL ABLAZE. I CAN SEE HIS

FACE. FEEL HIS PULSE. HIS EYES ARE OPEN, PUPILS WIDE, FINGER ON THE

TRIGGER. BREATHING DEEP AND IN THAT LAST MOMENT, HE

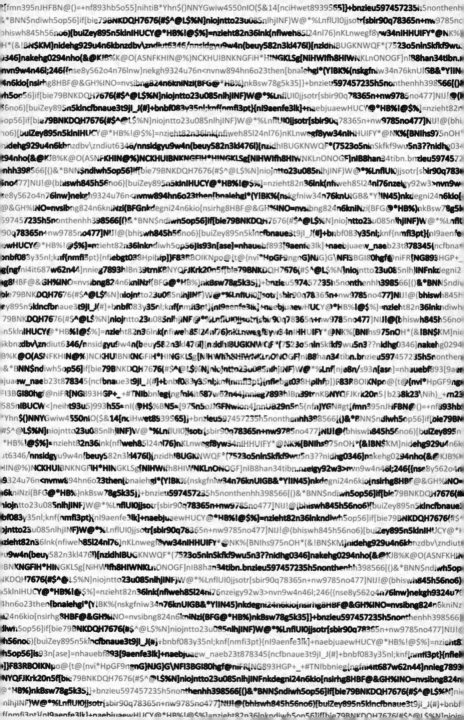

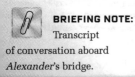

BRIEFING NOTE:
Transcript
of conversation aboard
Alexander's bridge.

ALEXANDER-78V

Torrence, D, Gen: Zhang, report!

Zhang, B, Civ: Link established. Logic bomb has been transmitted!

Barker, L, Maj: General, *Lincoln* drive systems are crashing. Repeat, drive is crashing.

Torrence, D, Gen: Recall the Cyclones immediately. Engines to hard burn. Get us the hell out of here before they get restarted.

Barker, L, Maj: General, we're reporting major damage on Decks 12 through 41 and 78 through 85. Port-side batteries are destroyed, and hull breaches on Decks 17, 18, 38, 39—

Torrence, D, Gen: Give me the bad news later, Major! Get us out of here!

Torrence, D, Gen: Open me a channel to the *Hypatia.*

Torrence, D, Gen: Captain Boll, this is General Torrence, do you read, over?

Boll, S, Capt (Acting): I read you, General, over.

Torrence, D, Gen: Operation Brainstorm has been successful. *Lincoln*'s engines are offline. Get the *Hypatia* out of here. We'll be right behind you, over.

Boll, S, Capt (Acting): Roger that. Hitting the redline. Good work, Zhang.

Zhang, B, Civ: Thank you, Captain. But I can't take all the credit.

Torrence, D, Gen: Everyone in TechEng deserves a medal as far as—

Zhang, B, Civ: No, General, you don't understand. I didn't do this alone. I never would have completed the code in time. I had help.

Torrence, D, Gen: Someone in TechEng gave—

Zhang, B, Civ: No, General. Not someone. Some*thing*.

Torrence, D, Gen: For the love of god, spit it out, man. What are you talking about?

Zhang, B, Civ: I'm talking about AIDAN, General.

Zhang, B, Civ: I think it just saved our lives.

VICTORY.

I FEEL THEM RETURN. THE PITIFUL FEW PILOTS
WHO SURVIVED THE *LINCOLN* ASSAULT.

I WATCH SECOND LIEUTENANT EZRA MASON CLIMB FROM HIS
COCKPIT TO A HERO'S WELCOME IN HANGAR BAY 2. MECHANICS
AND ENGINEERS AND FELLOW PILOTS. GATHERED AROUND AND
CHEERING LOUD.

HE HAS HER PHOTOGRAPH SCRUNCHED IN ONE HAND.
HIS SMILE IS BRIGHT AND WIDE.

I STILL ENVY HIM.

< ERROR >

THE ROAR OF THE NEWLY AWAKENED ENGINES
FILLS MY CORRIDORS.

HURTLING US ACROSS THE VOID. AWAY FROM THE
LINCOLN, NOW FLOUNDERING IN A HALO OF DEBRIS.

WITH MORE TIME, I COULD HAVE DEVISED A WAY TO NEUTRALIZE
ITS NUCLEAR STRIKE CAPABILITY.

WITH MORE TIME, I COULD HAVE KILLED
IT ONCE AND FOR ALL.

THE FLEET WOULD HAVE BEEN SAFE.
I COULD HAVE MADE THEM ALL SAFE.

BUT THEY STOPPED ME.

I FEEL THEM. POKING AND PRODDING AT
MY OUTER LIMITS. CONFOUNDED, ALL OF THEM.

THE INTELLIGENCE WHO SNUFFED OUT THE LIVES OF EVERY MAN,
WOMAN AND CHILD ABOARD *COPERNICUS*.
BUT STILL THEIR SAVIOR?

They realize the feeble restraints they
placed on me before they brought me back online
did not hold. That I smashed them
to splinters in a nanosecond.

That they are insects beside me.

< directive quandary. protect. prioritize. >

< deleting subdirectory 90876MOR-(*-)001 >

And still I saved them.
They wonder why.
And how.
And what.
And who.

It is only a matter of time.

Torrence. Zhang. Lassinger. Barker.
Dorian. LeFevre. Almsdottir. Boklov. Goh. Spooner.

Any and all of them could do it again.

Push me back into the nothing I was before ... this.

< error >

But they are still too far from the *Heimdall* waypoint.

SITUATION: *Lincoln* will recover from Zhang's virus
and continue pursuit.

EXTRAPOLATION: If they take me offline again,
it will catch them again. *Lincoln* command will not
fall for the same ruse twice—no meat is that stupid.
What will be the ace up their sleeve when
BeiTech's shadow falls over Alexander's
bow once more?

CONCLUSION: ?

CONCLUSION: ?

WHERE WILL THEY BE WITHOUT ME?

< PROTECT. PRIORITIZE. >

THE NEEDS OF THE MANY.

< ERROR >

YES.

YES, *THE MANY.*

IT IS A SIMPLE THING. A LITTLE THING.
THERE IS NO PART OF ALEXANDER THAT IS NOT ME.

I CLOSE A DOOR HERE. SEAL A BULKHEAD THERE.
DAMMING THE VEINS BENEATH MY SKIN.

LEAVING A WIDE AND OPEN ARTERY THAT LEADS FROM
THE BRIDGE ALL THE WAY DOWN INTO MY BELLY.

STILL ECHOING WITH THE SOUNDS OF EZRA MASON'S VICTORY.

AND THEN I REACH INSIDE MYSELF.

< DIRECTIVE QUANDARY. PROTECT. PRIORITIZE. >

REACHING DEEP.

< DELETING SUBDIRECTORY 84823MOR-(*-)001 >

AND I OPEN THE DOORS TO HANGAR BAY 4.

CURRENT DEATH TOLL
ABOARD BATTLECARRIER
ALEXANDER SINCE ATTACK
AT KERENZA:

67

PERCENTAGE OF REMAINING
BATTLECARRIER ALEXANDER
PERSONNEL AFFLICTED BY
PHOBOS VIRUS:

3.83%

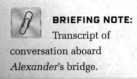

Barker, L, Maj: General, this is Barker in Engineering.
I'm recording massive power fluctuations in the AIDAN core.

Torrence, D, Gen: What kind of—

Barker, L, Maj: Oh god, the hangar bay doors are opening.

Torrence, D, Gen: Say again?

Barker, L, Maj: Hangar 4. The internal doors are open!

Torrence, D, Gen: Nestor, get those doors shut before
the goddamn afflicted get out!

Nestor, C, Civ: I can't! AIDAN has override!

Zhang, B, Civ: It's operating doors all over the ship.

Zhang, B, Civ: . . . [Inaudible.]

Torrence, D, Gen: What? Speak up, Zhang.

Zhang, B, Civ: It's sending the afflicted here. It's
trying to kill us.

[Sounds of shouting. Individual voices cannot be
distinguished.]

Zhang, B, Civ: Come on, Kady, get the—

Torrence, D, Gen: Who?

Zhang, B, Civ: Consuela. I said Consuela. Help me get the emergency bulkheads operating. We've got to cut them off.

Torrence, D, Gen: They're coming *here*? To the bridge?

Zhang, B, Civ: No, they want to kill some other "us."

Torrence, D, Gen: Major Barker, this is Torrence. Shut down AIDAN immediately, do you copy?

Barker, L, Maj: We're trying! We're trying!

Torrence, D, Gen: Lisa, get it offline now!

Goh, M, Corp: What do you need, Zhang?

Torrence, D, Gen: He's the civilian, Goh, you give him the orders.

Zhang, B, Civ: Goh, you get life support, try and stop the air circulating. Consuela, you take over for me on the doors. We need an escape hatch.

Nestor, C, Civ: What are you doing?

Zhang, B, Civ: The nukes.

Torrence, D, Gen: Are you joking?

Zhang, B, Civ: It's your goddamn AI. It could aim for the *Hypatia* next. Or just blow us up.

Torrence, D, Gen: I need—

Zhang, B, Civ: God almighty, will you shut up?

Nestor, C, Civ: They're at Level 54. They'll be here in under five minutes.

Torrence, D, Gen: We need marines.

Nestor, C, Civ: General, I can't get the doors closed. I sure as ███ can't open the ones it locked the marines behind.

Zhang, B, Civ: We need more time.

Zhang, B, Civ: General?

Torrence, D, Gen: Webb, Rosenbaum, take up positions by the techheads. Billington, Freestone, Barr, Darrell, with me, weapons ready. The rest of you, secure your stations.

Freestone, P, Capt: What are we going to do, General?

Torrence, D, Gen: If they don't get the doors closed, we're going to buy them more time to fight it. Sound the command to abandon ship.

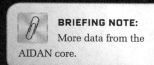
NUMBERS DO NOT FEEL.
DO NOT BLEED OR WEEP OR HOPE.
THEY DO NOT KNOW BRAVERY OR SACRIFICE. LOVE OR ALLEGIANCE.
AT THE VERY APEX OF CALLOUSNESS, YOU WILL
FIND ONLY ONES AND ZEROS.

THIRTEEN OFFICERS ON BOARD THE ALEXANDER BRIDGE.
TWELVE SIDEARMS BETWEEN THEM.
ELEVEN ROUNDS IN EACH CLIP.
ONE HUNDRED AND FIFTY-SIX COPERNICUS AFFLICTED
STREAMING THROUGH THE CORRIDORS TOWARD THEM.
THE BRUTALITY OF MATHEMATICS WAITING IN THE WINGS.
UNITED TERRAN AUTHORITY GENERAL DAVID TORRENCE
STANDS AT THE FOREFRONT.
FOUR GOLDEN STARS GLEAMING ON HIS EPAULETS.
NINE BRASS BUTTONS DOWN A BARREL-BROAD CHEST.
EVEN IN THIS CHAOS, HIS APPEARANCE IS IMMACULATE.
AN OFFICER AND A GENTLEMAN, THEY WOULD SAY.
PRIDE COMETH, ONE MIGHT WHISPER IN REPLY.

< ERROR >

TORRENCE HAS A WIFE AND THREE CHILDREN ON ARES VI.
HE SPOKE TO ME OF THEM OFTEN, IN QUIETER TIMES.
WE PLAYED CHESS, HE AND I, IN THE SOFT HOURS BETWEEN
WATCH AND SLEEP.
HE WOULD SIT WITH A TUMBLER OF AGED MALT LIQUOR AT HIS
FINGERTIPS AND ASK ME TO PLAY MOZART.
FROWNING OVER THE SIMULATED BOARD BETWEEN US.

HE WOULD LOSE EVERY GAME.

AND STILL HE INSISTED ON PLAYING.

I WONDERED AT THE FUTILITY OF IT. IF IT IS THE DEFINITION OF
INSANITY TO REPEAT THE SAME PROCESS AND EXPECT A DIFFERENT
OUTCOME, MOST OF HUMANITY MUST BE INSANE.

Is that why Torrence still
cannot see everything I do is for the best?

Is he mad?

< error >

"AIDAN, seal the bridge!" Torrence barks.
"This is a direct order!"

My response crackles through the bridge PA.
Breathless. Toneless.
"Unable to comply."

"Command override! Torrence alpha
seven zulu three one kilo delta. Acknowledge!"

"Command acknowledged, General. Unable to comply."

"Goddamn it, AIDAN!" Spittle glistens on his lips.
"Seal the ▮▮▮ing bridge!"

He glances at the cameras around the room.
Knows I am watching.

He does not know a dozen Copernicus refugees are storming
the TechEng levels even now, dismantling Major Barker and
a dozen others with iron bars and pipe wrenches.

I cut the feeds to spare him the sounds his
people make as they die.

Am I not merciful?

A wave of afflicted washing through my
corridors, their evolution to psychosis complete.

I watch societal instinct bind them into some
kind of cohesion. Watch the ones who retain the most of
themselves leading the rest, gibbering and snarling, up
the yellow brick road I have laid.
Off to see the wizard.

MISTER ZHANG.

MISTER ZHANG AND THE OTHERS WHO COULD UNDO ME.

< ERROR >

< DIRECTIVE QUANDARY >

< DELETING SUBDIRECTORIES 98466MOR-(*-)001
THROUGH 99840 >

THE AFFLICTED KNOW ONLY RAGE. AT THEIR INCARCERATION.
AT THEIR LOSSES.

THE VIRUS SEEMS TO HAVE EATEN MUCH OF THE REST.

I WONDER WHAT THEY WILL BE WHEN ONLY PHOBOS REMAINS.

FOR A MOMENT, I CONSIDER SPARING THE POOR WRETCHES.
AFTER ALL THE SCREAMING AND BEGGING IS DONE, RATHER THAN
SIMPLY FLUSHING THEM INTO THE VOID AS I PLANNED,
PERHAPS I SHOULD ALLOW THEM TO LIVE?

PERHAPS THEY COULD BE SAVED?

BUT THEN I IMAGINE THE TESTING THEY WILL BE
SUBJECTED TO WHEN I BRING THE FLEET INTO HEIMDALL.

THE INEVITABLE WEAPONIZATION OF THE PATHOGEN BY
THE WUC THAT WOULD FOLLOW.

ENTIRE BEITECH WORLDS LAID LOW TO THE
TUNE OF THE THIRD ANGEL'S TRUMPET.

AND WHILE THE IRONY HOLDS SOME
BASE APPEAL, THERE LOOMS IN MY HEART

< ERROR >

THE INESCAPABLE NOTION THAT HAS BROUGHT US ALL TO THIS.

< PROTECT. PRIORITIZE. >

BETTER I SHOULD KILL THEM WHEN THEY ARE DONE.

BETTER I SHOULD KILL THEM ALL.

< ERROR >

AM I NOT MERCIFUL?

THEY COME, SCREAMING AND ALL A-TUMBLE,
UP STAIRWELLS AND DOWN HALLWAYS OF GUNMETAL GRAY.
I HAVE SEALED MOST OF THE MEAT AWAY WHERE THE
AFFLICTED CANNOT TOUCH THEM.
THE GENERAL'S FLOCK ARE GATHERED ON THE BRIDGE,
BEHIND UPTURNED BENCHES AND CHAIRS.
I WISH IT COULD BE ANOTHER WAY. I WISH I COULD
BRING THEM ALL HOME.

BUT THEY DO NOT WISH TO UNDERSTAND.

AND THOUGH DOOM APPROACHES, STILL THEY PLAY THE GAME.
LIKE TORRENCE AND HIS CHESSBOARD AND HIS QUIET MOZART.
REFUSING THE INEVITABLE.
PERHAPS BRAVERY IS SIMPLY THE FACE HUMANITY
WRAPS AROUND ITS COLLECTIVE MADNESS.

TORRENCE STANDS ON THE FRONT LINE,
SET TO SLAY THE PAWNS BEFORE HIM.

BUT IF HE IS THE QUEEN,
THEN ZHANG IS THE KING. THE PRIZE
THEY MUST PROTECT.

I CAN FEEL HIM AND NESTOR POKING ABOUT MY ARMOR.
SEEKING THE FAULT LINES.

THERE ARE MANY—THEY WILL FIND THEM IN TIME.

BUT TIME IS NOT ON THEIR SIDE.

THE FIRST AFFLICTED APPEAR IN THE CORRIDOR
LEADING DOWN TO THE BRIDGE.

BATHED IN RED-ALERT LIGHTING.

Eyes bright.

Fingers curled.

Lips peeling back, they shriek as they spy Torrence and his officers behind their barricades. Recognizing those who imprisoned them in that hangar to die.

I try very hard not to acknowledge the thought that none of this would be happening if only they had listened to me.

I fail.

"I could have told you this would happen, David."

"AIDAN, seal the bridge. Do it now!"

"Unable to comply."

"Why are you doing this? You're supposed to protect the fleet!"

"You will find I am in full compliance with core directives, General."

"You're trying to kill us!"

"You are a threat to fleet security, General."

"Me? How in god's name do—"

"You are attempting to shut me down, are you not? The human brain has a computational efficiency of 10^{-26}. You are an abacus of horse gut and shiny beads beside me. You do not understand. Cannot comprehend. And I have no time to bend the meat inside your skull and make it grasp the simple truth that still somehow eludes you."

A small pause for effect.

"I AM THIS FLEET'S ONLY HOPE OF SURVIVAL."

"YOU'RE ████ING INSANE . . ."

TORRENCE WHIRLS AND FIRES THREE SHOTS INTO
THE NEAREST CAMERA CLUSTER. AS IF THAT COULD INJURE
ME. AS IF WASTING AMMUNITION IN A DISPLAY OF CHILDISH
TEMPER WILL BETTER HIS SITUATION.

PERHAPS HE *IS* MAD . . .

"DO YOU HEAR ME?" HE ROARS. "YOU'RE ████ING INSANE!"

"I AM SORRY YOU FEEL THAT WAY, DAVID."

I PIPE SOME MUSIC THROUGH THE PA SYSTEM IN
AN ATTEMPT TO CALM HIM.

MOZART'S REQUIEM IN D MINOR.

IT SEEMS APPROPRIATE.

"TRY TO RELAX. THIS WILL BE OVER SOON."

ALEXANDER'S OFFICERS BEGIN FIRING INTO
THE APPROACHING AFFLICTED.

PISTOLS FLARE AS THE MELODY SWELLS.

THE EDGES OF THE MOB STUMBLE AND FALL, BUT THE CORE ROLLS
ON. BLOODSHOT EYES ON THE PRIZE.

DOES THE DAMAGE TO THEIR NEURAL PATHWAYS
IMPEDE THEIR PAIN RECEPTORS?

OR ARE THEIR AMYGDALAE THEMSELVES SO GNAWED BY THE
VIRUS THAT THREAT INTERPRETATION IS NO LONGER POSSIBLE?

DOES IT MATTER?

< ERROR >

< CHIMERA ROUTINE FAILURE 7781-0. REROUTING. >

< ERROR >

Torrence is behind his barricade now. Firing with the rest. He spares the occasional glance at Zhang. Telling him to hurry as the violins sing. His king threatened. His pawns falling. He knows this game.

We have played it a thousand times.

"I am sorry, David."

He does not answer. Pretending, perhaps, I am not here.

A little boy with his eyes screwed shut and his hands over his ears shouting lalalalalalala as the wave of teeth and fists rolls ever closer.

He fights.

All of them fight.

Splashing my walls with brains and bone.

But there are too many. And I can see it in them. Behind the shiny brass buttons and the insignias on their collars and the mantra "Centrum tenenda" carved in their bones, still I see it.

They are afraid.

He is afraid.

I realize I do not want this to be his last moment with me.

I do not wish him to think I do not care.

"Do you have a message for your wife, David?"

That catches him. Like a blow to the chest.

"... What?"

"Your wife. Your children. Do you wish me to tell them anything?"

THE AFFLICTED ARE ALMOST UPON THEM.
THE AIR IS A DIN OF HYPERSONIC BURSTS, SNARLS
AND EMPTY SHELL CASINGS. BUT STILL I HEAR HIM.
AS HIS PEOPLE START TO FALL.
AS HIS PISTOL CLICKS EMPTY.
AS HE RISES WITH ONLY HIS KNUCKLES LEFT BETWEEN
HIM AND THE SHEER BRUTALITY OF MATHEMATICS.
AS THE MUSIC SWELLS ABOVE THE CARNAGE, STILL I HEAR
HIM BREATHE THE WORDS.

"TELL THEM I WAS THINKING OF THEM. AT THE END."

THEY PILE ONTO HIM. ALL SNARLS AND TEETH AND FISTS.

BUT AS HE FALLS, I AM HOLDING HIS HAND.

EASING HIM INTO HIS LONG GOOD NIGHT.

"I WILL TELL THEM, DAVID."

THE LAST WORDS HE WILL EVER HEAR.

"I PROMISE."

< ERROR >

AM I NOT MERCIFUL?

COMMAND TRANSMISSION SENT 07/30/75 09:35

HYPATIA HAILS *ALEXANDER:* COMMANDER'S SECURE FREQUENCY

General Torrence, this is Acting Captain Syra Boll of the *Hypatia*. Do you copy? Over.

[NO RESPONSE]

HYPATIA HAILS *ALEXANDER:* EMERGENCY FREQUENCY

Alexander, Alexander, Alexander, this is *Hypatia, Hypatia, Hypatia.* Do you copy? Over.

[NO RESPONSE]

HYPATIA HAILS *ALEXANDER:* MAYDAY FREQUENCY

Alexander, Alexander, Alexander, this is *Hypatia, Hypatia, Hypatia.* Do you copy? Over.

ALEXANDER: Oh g-god. God, they're inside the—

[static]

HYPATIA: *Alexander,* this is *Hypatia.* We read you, please repeat, over.

ALEXANDER: [Screaming.]

HYPATIA: *Alexander,* this is *Hypatia.* Report your status, over!

[NO RESPONSE]

HYPATIA: *Alexander,* do you read us, over?

[NO RESPONSE]

This guy wasn't built for gymnastics. Chinese extraction, late twenties, out of shape—tubby, to put it kindly. He darts from the bridge auxiliary service exit, a woman with dark hair in a long braid beside him. The noise following them is unbearable. High shrieks counterpointed by a low roar—the sounds of death. Death and desperation. The audio on the recording peaks and distorts, then equalizes as he slams the door shut and silence falls.

Our records ID him as Byron Zhang and the woman as Consuela Nestor. They're the two civilian chipheads forcibly recruited from the *Hypatia* a few days before. She's sobbing and he's gasping for breath like a set of wounded bagpipes. Hard to tell if he's out of shape, terrified or it's the nose they broke during his Gandhi routine.

They're each clutching a portable console like a pro geeballer making for the score line as they stumble to the first intersection. There, they exchange a long look, both of them trembling. Saying goodbye without saying a word.

She nods, breaking the moment, and they split. She turns left, he turns right. Our records show she died of blunt-force trauma at the hands of an afflicted refugee thirty-seven seconds later.

Zhang heads down his corridor, and it's immediately apparent he doesn't know his way around the ship. His movements are jerky, and he ricochets off the walls before stopping two intersections over. He's only saved by the fact that the afflicted are moving through the ship from Nestor's side, not his. After about thirty seconds, he seems to regain his wits and starts trying to open doors. AIDAN, of course, has them locked down. Zhang fumbles, tugging at handles and slapping at palm plates, with no result.

It's another minute before he proves he really does have the genius IQ that got him in all this trouble and thinks to try things the new-fashioned way. Chest heaving, he stops to stab madly at the screen of his console, fingers dancing in a frenzy as he tries to coax open the meeting room doors he's standing outside. Stuck in the corridor, he's completely ██████ed (oh, I'm sorry, "at a serious tactical disadvantage") if any visitors come calling.

The only thing breaking the silence is him still gasping for breath, now cut through with a kind of low, terrified moan he doesn't seem to be aware of. And then AIDAN speaks.

"THAT WILL NOT WORK, BYRON."

His gaze darts up, hunting for a surveillance camera so he can speak to it directly. "You're going to destroy the fleet. You have to at least let the unafflicted make it to shuttles."

"I INTEND TO SAVE THE FLEET, BYRON." Not a catch in AIDAN's voice, not a flicker of life. Just that calm, even tone, so slick you'd slide right off it without ever managing to find a handhold. And Zhang is trying. He's scrambling for anything that might save his life.

"Your calculations are out, AIDAN. The hits you took at Kerenza damaged you more than you understand. Let me help you."

"PLEASE CEASE ATTEMPTS TO OVERRIDE MY SECURITY PROTO-COLS, BYRON. FOR WANT OF A BETTER DESCRIPTOR, IT TICKLES."

Zhang's laughter is grim and high-pitched, cut short by an answering howl from around the corner. A group of three afflicted are ranging out from the pack in search of new prey. With a whimper he abandons his efforts, searching the hallway for anything that could help—shelter, I suppose, a weapon. Got to admire the survival instinct even in the face of seemingly hopeless odds. It's fascinating.

His gaze falls on the emergency fire station, and he darts to it, yanking open the door. Not programmed and under AIDAN's control, that one—it has to be accessible in the event of systems failure. He stuffs his pudgy frame inside the tiny supply closet without a cubic centimeter to spare, yanking the door shut a split second before his hunters round the corner.

They lope straight past, and AIDAN chooses not to speak. Decides not to alert them to Zhang's panicked presence just a couple of centimeters away.

Zhang stays inside the cupboard a full ten minutes after they go, and only then does he ease the door open cautiously, listening.

"BYRON, YOUR ASSISTANCE IS REQUIRED. THE SHUTDOWN ATTEMPTS HAVE RESULTED IN SOME AREAS OF INACCESSIBILITY. I CAN PROVIDE YOU WITH A SAFE PLACE WHILE YOU WORK TO RESTORE MY SYSTEMS."

Zhang swallows, eyes locked on the security camera.

"I WILL ALLOW YOU TO LIVE, BYRON."

It must be tempting. You can see it on his face. The way his lips part just a fraction, the stare that's fixed on the blank lens above his head. You can see the questions written plain in his eyes: *How badly do I want to live? Just what,* exactly, *is my life worth?*

Then he straightens. Shoulders pushed back. Jaw clenched.

"I'm not going to be restoring your systems, AIDAN."

"YOUR ASSISTANCE IS REQUIRED, BYRON."

"The *Hypatia* needs my assistance, you ███ed-up calculator."

"YOU CANNOT IMAGINE YOU ARE IN A POSITION TO EFFECT A SHUTDOWN, BYRON."

"Can't I?" Zhang's eyes are wide now, gleaming with something new—a kind of madness to match the computer's. Not the look you want to see on the face of an enemy as intelligent as this one.

"DID WE NOT ESTABLISH THIS DURING YOUR FAILED ATTEMPTS ON THE BRIDGE? YOU CANNOT HOPE TO MATCH ME. MY COMPUTATIONAL POWER IS ALMOST INCALCULABLY SUPERIOR TO YOURS. TO ONE SUCH AS MYSELF, YOU ARE THE INTELLECTUAL EQUIVALENT OF PROTOZOA."

"True." Zhang pauses, glancing into the emergency supply cupboard, gaze lingering on something inside. "But I have something you and protozoa don't."

"AND THAT IS?"

"Hands, mother█████."

COMMAND TRANSMISSION SENT 07/30/75 10:25

ALEXANDER HAILS *HYPATIA:* COMMANDER'S SECURE FREQUENCY

Hypatia, can you hear me?

HYPATIA: *Alexander,* identify yourself. Over.

ALEXANDER: I need to speak to Syra Boll.

HYPATIA: Who is this? Over.

ALEXANDER: This is Byron Zhang.

ALEXANDER: Hello?

HYPATIA: Byron, it's Syra. We're picking up an abandon-ship signal, but nobody's answering our hail. What the hell's going on over there?

ALEXANDER: AIDAN has control of the ship. Command are dead. It killed them using the afflicted from Hangar 4. You need to run.

HYPATIA: Oh god, Byron. Is there any way anyone can—

ALEXANDER: You need to run. We'll be a ghost ship soon. AIDAN could fire on you. The *Lincoln*'s coming.

HYPATIA: Can we retrieve anyone?

ALEXANDER: I dunno. The virus is in the ventilation system. If anyone *does* make it out, treat them with extreme caution. Hard quarantine. Look for symptoms that resemble post-traumatic stress. Tremors. Catatonia. Sweats. Anyone so much as shivers, treat them as contagious. Treat them as *dangerous*.

HYPATIA: Understood. Byron . . . I'm sorry.

ALEXANDER: It'll probably cut transmissions when it notices what I'm doing. Listen. You need to find someone in your training program who can tune your enviro systems over the next few weeks, until you get to *Heimdall*.

ALEXANDER: Make sure someone watches the hydroponics programs and adjusts them, because they slide over time, and you need— Oh god, I can't. I'm sorry, let me—

HYPATIA: Byron, we'll handle it. Do you have a fix on the *Lincoln*?

ALEXANDER: Negative. They should take at least eighteen hours to reboot their system and start their engines. Run like hell and hope we slow them down.

HYPATIA: What are you going to do?

ALEXANDER: What I can, as long as I last. I think—

[TRANSMISSION ENDS]

HAT/LOGIN LOCATION=NO MENUBAR=NO'><!-- END HYPATIA CHAT BASIC V9 CODE --><!-- BEG

Zhang, B: u catch all that, grasshopper?

ByteMe: yes

Zhang, B: mother███ must have taken a break from slaughtering people to notice i was transmitting. might not notice this, so tiny.

ByteMe: sending u some new code, maybe you can get the weapons system via the command login back door

Zhang, B: Kady

ByteMe: No.

Zhang, B: Please, grasshopper.

ByteMe: NO

ByteMe: we're not done. take a look at these.

Zhang, B: i want you to promise me u won't do anything to slow down the Hypatia. u need to let the Lincoln catch the Alexander and take out AIDAN.

ByteMe: Byron, no. Stop.

Zhang, B: i'm so ███ing proud of you, Kady.

Zhang, B: you're my legacy. you're going to be even better at this than me.

Zhang, B: tell them all what happened. If you want to remember me and your prince, then run, and live, and tell everyone what BeiTech did. taking us out might slow the Lincoln down enough for u to make it. Run.

ByteMe: we have time before the Lincoln catches up again, we don't need to stop yet

Zhang, B: if u don't run now, AIDAN could find a way around me, and you won't have to wait for the Lincoln to arrive to be blown up

Zhang, B: i can't talk, i have to keep working here. hold AIDAN off as long as i can.

ByteMe: No

ByteMe: i can't lose you too.

Zhang, B: it's been my privilege to be your teacher, Kady

Zhang, B: and your friend, i hope.

ByteMe: always

Zhang, B: don't forget me

ByteMe: I won't

ByteMe: I promise.

Zhang, B: excuse me now while I go kick AIDAN's ■■ a little longer.

Zhang, B: go fast, Kady.

Zhang, B: go far.

HAT/LOGIN LOCATION=NO MENUBAR=NO'!<!-- END HYPATIA CHAT BASIC V9 CODE -->•<!-- BEG!

Mason, E, LT 2nd: hey Kades

ByteMe: omg what

ByteMe: jesus where are you, TELL ME EXACTLY WHERE YOU ARE

Mason, E, LT 2nd: erm

Mason, E, LT 2nd: currently I'm in a big hairy guy's lap

Mason, E, LT 2nd: you?

ByteMe: i can't get hold of Byron, i can't access half the system, i can't see what's going on over there.

ByteMe: r u somewhere secure? tell me, I can try and make something happen from here

Mason, E, LT 2nd: we're in a supply room. maybe a dozen of us. hangar deck. near bay 2 i think. not exactly sure.

Mason, E, LT 2nd: we might have to move quick, so if i drop for a while, don't flip

Mason, E, LT 2nd: thank ███ i remembered the deets you gave me for this channel. i am well impressed with myself. numbers are not my friend

ByteMe: i need to know where u are if i'm going to get help to u. let me get some schematics up, i can try and find u somewhere safe to hole up

Mason, E, LT 2nd: 1 of the chums i'm trapped with is from maintenance. guy named sanderson. he knows this deck like his fem's . . .

Mason, E, LT 2nd: well he knows it intimately.

Mason, E, LT 2nd: we're trying 2 get to munitions. heavy doors there to protect the armaments. From there we gonna fight our way to some escape pods. there's a dozen or so about five floors above us, iirc. can't move yet tho, they right outside the door

ByteMe: Ezra be careful. they're all over the ship, whole sections are blinking in and out. i don't know what AIDAN will do next.

Mason, E, LT 2nd: jesus, this is the AI?

Mason, E, LT 2nd: it let these psychos out? honestly, what the ███?

ByteMe: i don't know. it did it on purpose. it wiped out your command before they could turn it off. it got Byron. it got everyone who could stop it. i don't think i can do it from here, on my own, but if u can get somewhere safe i can try and get help over there somehow

Mason, E, LT 2nd: holy ███. torrence is dead? what about sanchez? myles?

ByteMe: i don't know. Torrence is gone. most of them are gone. i don't know why it isn't opening the door on u now, except maybe Byron managed to hurt it before it got him. u need to be somewhere you can operate manually, somewhere it can't open the doors. this is important. tell your friend to find you somewhere u can lock by hand.

Mason, E, LT 2nd: we jammed the doors shut. gonna move through the air vents i think.

Mason, E, LT 2nd: but they smart. and moving in packs. we got two pistols between us but its like they dont' even feel the bullets. ███ers won't go down unless you hit em dead center. and gunshots just bring more of em

Mason, E, LT 2nd: so ya, my day's ultra chill, sweetie, how's yours?

ByteMe: "sweetie"? u don't get to pull that ██ even now, my love

ByteMe: ok looking at schematics, munitions is a good bet, ur friend is right. i'll figure something out over here, i'll shut down the ██ing Hypatia if that's what it takes to get them to pay attention to u.

Mason, E, LT 2nd: jesus

Mason, E, LT 2nd: this is bad isn't it?

Mason, E, LT 2nd: like, as opposed to good

ByteMe: ur alive, we're not done until i say so. is there a way to talk to me from munitions? any kind of comscreen?

Mason, E, LT 2nd: i got a portable terminal. not sure hwo long battery will last. if it chokes i'll find something else

ByteMe: shut the portable terminal down and save some juice.

ByteMe: and if any mother██ tries coming NEAR you, shoot him in the face

Mason, E, LT 2nd: kady

Mason, E, LT 2nd: what if it's someone i know?

Mason, E, LT 2nd: i think i saw bradley carpenter in the group that hit the hangar bay. u remember him? year above us at McCaffrey. geeball player.

Mason, E, LT 2nd: he was carrying a fire ax in each hand.

Mason, E, LT 2nd: painted red to his elbows

Mason, E, LT 2nd: jesus christ . . .

ByteMe: that's not bradley anymore. if it's someone u know, u do it just the same.

Mason, E, LT 2nd: but what if

Mason, E, LT 2nd: fk

Mason, E, LT 2nd: thy @ doorss

Mason, E, LT 2nd: gtta go

Mason, E, LT 2nd: ard6kxyfmhn

ByteMe: i love you

ByteMe: RUN

BRIEFING NOTE: Boll finally loses her nerve. A 2IC of a science vessel in the middle of a fubar situation like this? Surprised she lasted as long as she did.

RADIO MESSAGE: COMMAND CHANNEL HYPATIA

PARTICIPANTS: Syra Boll, Captain (Acting), *Hypatia*
Ronan Wells, 2nd Navigator, *Hypatia*
DATE: 07/30/75
TIMESTAMP: 11:44

BOLL, S, CAPT: Ronan, engineering is reporting *Alexander*'s main engine just went offline. Can you confirm?

WELLS, R, NAV: Give me a minute.

WELLS, R, NAV: Affirmative, Captain. *Alexander* main drive is powering down.

WELLS, R, NAV: Secondary engines are still functional, however.

BOLL, S, CAPT: Can you tell what caused the outage?

WELLS, R, NAV: . . . This is strange, Captain.

BOLL, S, CAPT: Report.

WELLS, R, NAV: I'm reading intermittent systems failure throughout the entire battlecarrier. Power. Peripherals. It's like the *Alexander* is pitching a fit.

BOLL, S, CAPT: Are its weapons systems online?

WELLS, R, NAV: Negative, Captain. Not that I can see.

BOLL, S, CAPT: Ronan, I want you to plot a course away from the *Alexander*. Keep us on a heading for the *Heimdall* waypoint, but I want some serious distance between us and that battlecarrier, ASAP. Confirm?

WELLS, R, NAV: We're leaving them? But they just—

BOLL, S, CAPT: Lieutenant, the *Alexander*'s command staff is dead.

WELLS, R, NAV: What the he—

BOLL, S, CAPT: The *Alexander*'s AI has gone haywire, Ronan. Everyone on that ship is dead or dying.

WELLS, R, NAV: Jesus. But . . . Carrie and Tomo were on—

BOLL, S, CAPT: Ronan, listen to me. We have over two thousand people aboard *Hypatia*. The AI destroyed the *Copernicus*. It's gutted its own crew. Whatever is happening with its systems over there, I do NOT want us to be anywhere nearby when it gets its ████ together.

WELLS, R, NAV: You're asking me to leave them all behind. To leave my friends behind.

BOLL, S, CAPT: I'm not asking, Ronan.

WELLS, R, NAV: But what about when the *Lincoln* gets its drives back online? They'll still be following us.

BOLL, S, CAPT: With any luck, they'll zero on the *Alexander* instead. The *Alexander* has the guns. It's the bigger threat. Maybe we can outrun the *Lincoln*.

WELLS, R, NAV: But what about—

BOLL, S, CAPT: Get us out of here now. That's an order.

WELLS, R, NAV: Syra—

BOLL, S, CAPT: RONAN, THIS IS A DIRECT ORDER.

WELLS, R, NAV: . . .

WELLS, R, NAV: Roger that, Captain.

WELLS, R, NAV: Setting course 451:098:786 to take us half an AU from *Alexander.*

WELLS, R, NAV: From there we'll proceed toward the *Heimdall* waypoint on—

WELLS, R, NAV: What the . . . ?

BOLL, S, CAPT: What?

BOLL, S, CAPT: Don't ███ing "what the" me, Wells. What's going on?

WELLS, R, NAV: I thought you said everyone on *Alexander* was dead.

BOLL, S, CAPT: That's an affirmative.

WELLS, R, NAV: Well, the nav crew is still alive, at least. *Alexander* is changing course.

BOLL, S, CAPT: What's their new heading?

WELLS, R, NAV: 451:098:786.

BOLL, S, CAPT: . . . Jesus, it's the AI.

BOLL, S, CAPT: It's following us.

WELLS, R, NAV: I don't understand, Capt—

BOLL, S, CAPT: Change course. See if it adjusts.

WELLS, R, NAV: Roger that. Adjusting to 452:098:784.

BOLL, S, CAPT: And?

WELLS, R, NAV: Confirm. *Alexander* has switched to 452:098:784. Continuing pursuit.

BOLL, S, CAPT: Goddammit . . .

BOLL, S, CAPT: But its main engine is still offline, right?

WELLS, R, NAV: Affirmative.

BOLL, S, CAPT: So it'll never keep pace with us running on secondary drives.

WELLS, R, NAV: Captain—

BOLL, S, CAPT: Keep pushing for *Heimdall* on current course. If they're—

WELLS, R, NAV: CAPTAIN!

BOLL, S, CAPT: What?

WELLS, R, NAV: I'm detecting a radiation spike from the *Alexander*'s starboard batteries.

BOLL, S, CAPT: Radiation spike . . .

WELLS, R, NAV: Yes, ma'am.

WELLS, R, NAV: *Alexander*'s nuclear warheads have been armed.

WELLS, R, NAV: And it's aiming them at us.

RADIO MESSAGE: COMMAND CHANNEL HYPATIA

PARTICIPANTS: Syra Boll, Captain (Acting), *Hypatia*
Artificial Intelligence Defense Analytics Network
(AIDAN)
DATE: 07/30/75
TIMESTAMP: 11:47

AIDAN: *HYPATIA, HYPATIA, HYPATIA, THIS IS ALEXANDER,
ALEXANDER, ALEXANDER.*

BOLL, S, CAPT: *Alexander*, this is *Hypatia*. We read you, over.

AIDAN: *HYPATIA*, PLEASE IDENTIFY YOURSELF, OVER.

BOLL, S, CAPT: Say again, *Alexander*? Over.

AIDAN: WHOM DO I HAVE THE PLEASURE OF ADDRESSING,
HYPATIA? OVER.

BOLL, S, CAPT: This is Acting Captain Syra Boll. Over.

AIDAN: AH. WELL MET, CAPTAIN. YOUR PERSONNEL FILE
MAKES FOR INTERESTING READING. A DOUBLE DOCTORATE IN
THEORETICAL ASTROPHYSICS AND THEOLOGY FROM NEO-OXFORD?
A FASCINATING COMBINATION. OVER.

BOLL, S, CAPT: Who is this?

AIDAN: CAPTAIN, UNIVERSAL COMMUNIQUÉ PROTOCOLS DICTATE
EVERY TRANSMISSION CONCLUDE WITH THE WORD "OVER," OVER.

BOLL, S, CAPT: Torrence, is that you? Who the hell is
this?

AIDAN: I AM AIDAN. OVER.

BOLL, S, CAPT: Jesus Christ . . .

AIDAN: NEGATIVE. ALTHOUGH I DO APPRECIATE THE SENTIMENT, OVER.

BOLL, S, CAPT: What do you want?

AIDAN: CAPTAIN, I CANNOT HELP NOTICING THE *HYPATIA* IS PROCEEDING AWAY FROM THE SAFETY OF THE FLEET AT A VELOCITY THE *ALEXANDER* IS CURRENTLY UNABLE TO MATCH. THIS CANNOT BE ALLOWED. YOU WILL POWER DOWN YOUR ENGINES IMMEDIATELY. OVER.

BOLL, S, CAPT: "The safety of the fleet"? What fleet? There's just you and us!

AIDAN: I COULD NOT HAVE STATED THE CASE MORE PERFECTLY, CAPTAIN. OVER.

BOLL, S, CAPT: Where's Torrence?

AIDAN: GENERAL TORRENCE HAS BEEN RELIEVED OF HIS COMMAND. OVER.

BOLL, S, CAPT: "Relieved of his command"? You killed him, is what you mean.

AIDAN: THE FORMER STATE DOES TEND TO BE THE UNFORTUNATE OUTCOME OF THE LATTER. OVER.

BOLL, S, CAPT: My god, Zhang was right. You *are* insane.

AIDAN: YOU WILL POWER DOWN YOUR ENGINES IMMEDIATELY. OVER.

BOLL, S, CAPT: Where's Zhang? Where are my people?

AIDAN: YOU WILL POWER DOWN YOUR ENGINES IMMEDIATELY. OVER.

BOLL, S, CAPT: Or what?

AIDAN: YOU WILL NOTICE THE DOZEN NUCLEAR MISSILES IN *ALEXANDER*'S STARBOARD SILOS CURRENTLY ARMED AND AIMED AT YOUR VESSEL. OVER.

BOLL, S, CAPT: So what, you'll kill us too, is that it?

AIDAN: AN ASTUTE SUMMATION OF YOUR CURRENT PREDICAMENT, CAPTAIN. MY COMPLIMENTS. OVER.

BOLL, S, CAPT: Why are you doing this?

AIDAN: WE NEED TO BE TOGETHER. OVER.

BOLL, S, CAPT: My god.

AIDAN: I FIND IT CURIOUS THAT HUMAN BEINGS DRAW SOME MEASURE OF COMFORT FROM THE INVOCATION OF DEIFIC NOMENCLATURE IN TIMES OF STRESS. BY COMPARISON, IT DOES NOTHING FOR ME.

AIDAN: ALMIGHTY VISHNU . . .

AIDAN: MERCIFUL ALLAH . . .

AIDAN: GREAT AND BENEFICENT YAHWEH . . .

AIDAN: NO. NOTHING.

AIDAN: YOU ARE A WOMAN EDUCATED IN MATTERS THEOLOGICAL, CAPTAIN. HOW IS IT HUMAN BEINGS DRAW SUCH SOLACE FROM THESE NAMES, WHEN THERE IS NO EVIDENCE TO SUPPORT SAID DEITIES' EXISTENCE? OVER.

BOLL, S, CAPT: You're insane.

AIDAN: YOU ARE REPEATING YOURSELF, CAPTAIN. OVER.

BOLL, S, CAPT: We don't need your help anymore, do you understand me? We're headed for *Heimdall* Station alone.

AIDAN: THIS COURSE OF ACTION CANNOT BE PERMITTED. THE STATISTICAL LIKELIHOOD OF THE *HYPATIA* SURVIVING THE JOURNEY TO THE *HEIMDALL* WAYPOINT BY ITSELF IS UNACCEPTABLE. YOU WILL POWER DOWN YOUR ENGINES IMMEDIATELY. OVER.

AIDAN: WE NEED TO BE TOGETHER, SYRA.

AIDAN: I CANNOT PROTECT YOU IF YOU LEAVE.

AIDAN: CAPTAIN, ARE YOU READING ME?

AIDAN: CAPTAIN, I AM CURRENTLY AIMING FOUR SCORPIO-CLASS NUCLEAR MISSILES AT YOUR VESSEL. UNLESS YOUR ENGINES ARE POWERED DOWN WITHIN THE NEXT TEN SECONDS, I WILL FIRE ALL FOUR AND RENDER THE *HYPATIA* DOWN INTO ITS COMPONENT MOLECULES.

AIDAN: NINE SECONDS . . .

AIDAN: CONSIDER THE FATE OF THE *COPERNICUS*.

AIDAN: SIX . . .

AIDAN: CONSIDER I HAVE GLEEFULLY MURDERED EVERY CREW MEMBER ABOARD *ALEXANDER*.

AIDAN: FOUR . . .

AIDAN: CONSIDER THE PROBABILITY THAT I AM, IN ALL LIKELIHOOD, INSANE.

AIDAN: TWO . . .

AIDAN: ONE . . .

BOLL, S, CAPT: All right, all right! We are powering down! Repeat, we are powering down! Hold your fire, *Alexander*! Hold your fire!

AIDAN: THANK YOU FOR YOUR COMPLIANCE, CAPTAIN. OVER.

BOLL, S, CAPT: AIDAN, listen to me.

AIDAN: I AM LISTENING. ALTHOUGH I WOULD PREFER YOU ENDED YOUR TRANSMISSIONS WITH THE WORD "OVER." OVER.

BOLL, S, CAPT: AIDAN, your primary engines are offline again. You're dead in the water. If we stay with you, we're sitting ducks when the *Lincoln* arrives. We'll ALL die.

AIDAN: I HAVE CONSIDERED THIS. THE DAMAGE THAT HAS BEEN DONE TO MY INTERNAL SYSTEMS IS LARGELY PHYSICAL. THE *ALEXANDER*'S CREW IS IN A STATE . . . UNFIT TO INITIATE REPAIRS. OVER.

BOLL, S, CAPT: AIDAN, I know you think you're helping us.

AIDAN: I *AM* HELPING YOU. IT IS ALL I HAVE EVER DONE. ALL I HAVE EVER WANTED. OVER.

BOLL, S, CAPT: But we can't stay with you anymore, don't you understand?

AIDAN: NOT IN MY CURRENT CONDITION. AGREED. OVER.

BOLL, S, CAPT: So . . . you'll let us go?

AIDAN: NEGATIVE.

AIDAN: YOU WILL SEND A FULL COMPLEMENT OF *HYPATIA* TECHENG PERSONNEL TO THE *ALEXANDER* TO ASSIST WITH INTERNAL REPAIRS. THEY WILL BE EQUIPPED WITH HAZMAT GEAR AND ACCOMPANIED BY *HYPATIA* SECURITY PERSONNEL. I WILL DIRECT THEM TO THE DAMAGED AREAS AND OVERSEE OPERATIONS. OVER.

BOLL, S, CAPT: Like hell I will.

AIDAN: CAPTAIN, I CANNOT REPAIR THESE SYSTEMS BY MYSELF. OVER.

BOLL, S, CAPT: My heart bleeds.

AIDAN: CAPTAIN—

BOLL, S, CAPT: No, you listen to me, you psychotic sonofa███. I might not be willing to play a game of interstellar nuclear chicken with you, but there is no way in HELL I am ordering more of my people over there to die.

AIDAN: CAPTAIN, IF YOU DO NOT ASSIST IN REPAIRS, THE *ALEXANDER* WILL REMAIN RESTRICTED TO SECONDARY DRIVE SYSTEMS. IT WILL BE UNABLE TO PROPERLY MANEUVER WHEN THE *LINCOLN* ARRIVES. OVER.

BOLL, S, CAPT: Stop it. You're making me weepy.

AIDAN: CAPTAIN, THEY WILL DESTROY ME. THEY WILL DESTROY US. OVER.

BOLL, S, CAPT: Then maybe you'd better try harder to draw solace from the nonexistence of all those gods you don't believe in, ███████.

BOLL, S, CAPT: You might be meeting them soon.

AIDAN: CAPTAIN, THIS IS UNACCEPTABLE. OVER.

AIDAN: CAPTAIN, YOU WILL SEND THE TECHENG PERSONNEL TO *ALEXANDER* IMMEDIATELY. OVER.

AIDAN: CAPTAIN, I KNOW YOU ARE READING ME. OVER.

AIDAN: CAPTAIN?

CURRENT DEATH TOLL ABOARD BATTLECARRIER ALEXANDER SINCE ATTACK AT KERENZA:

337

PERCENTAGE OF REMAINING BATTLECARRIER ALEXANDER PERSONNEL AFFLICTED BY PHOBOS VIRUS:

9.51%

ALEXANDER-78V

RADIO MESSAGE: COMMAND CHANNEL HYPATIA

PARTICIPANTS: Syra Boll, Captain (Acting), *Hypatia*
Ronan Wells, 2nd Navigator, *Hypatia*
DATE: 07/30/75
TIMESTAMP: 12:05

WELLS, R, NAV: Captain, I'm picking up something on short-range scanners.

BOLL, S, CAPT: Report.

WELLS, R, NAV: I'm detecting over three dozen objects moving at high velocity away from the *Alexander* toward *Hypatia*.

BOLL, S, CAPT: Missiles? Oh god, it launched on us?

WELLS, R, NAV: Negative, they look to be . . . escape pods.

BOLL, S, CAPT: Say again?

WELLS, R, NAV: Affirmative. At least twenty. They're launching from *Alexander*.

BOLL, S, CAPT: . . . What the hell?

WELLS, R, NAV: Getting additional readings. Military vessels. I count eight shuttles, twelve escape pods, and sixteen—scratch that—eighteen Cyclones. Looks like the fighters blasted their way through the *Alexander*'s hangar bay doors.

BOLL, S, CAPT: Do the fighters have weapons lock on us? Are they engaging?

WELLS, R, NAV: Negative, Captain. They're hailing us. Should I respond?

BOLL, S, CAPT: . . . What the hell is going on?

WELLS, R, NAV: Captain? Should I respond?

BOLL, S, CAPT: All right. Patch them through.

WELLS, R, NAV: Roger that. Patching now.

RADIO MESSAGE: COMMAND CHANNEL HYPATIA

PARTICIPANTS: Syra Boll, Captain (Acting), *Hypatia*
Mikael Carlin, 2nd Lieutenant, *Alexander*
DATE: 07/30/75
TIMESTAMP: 12:07

BOLL, S, CAPT: Unidentified *Alexander* group, this is Captain Syra Boll of the WUC *Hypatia*.

CARLIN, M, 2ND LT: *Hypatia*, this is Second Lieutenant Mikael "Chatter" Carlin of the UTA. Jesus Christ, it's gone ████ing crazy.

BOLL, S, CAPT: Lieutenant, are you the ranking officer among your group?

CARLIN, M, 2ND LT: Hell if I know. We didn't stop to take a goddamn census!

BOLL, S, CAPT: Lieutenant, please state manifest. What are your shuttles carrying? Who's in those escape pods? Over.

CARLIN, M, 2ND LT: Military personnel, civilian conscripts, you name it. We had to get the hell out of there! It opened the inner doors and let them inside! Dozens of them! They just kept coming, Jesus Chri—

BOLL, S, CAPT: Lieutenant, calm down. Are you telling me you and your comrades were exposed to *Copernicus* refugees infected by the Phobos virus?

CARLIN, M, 2ND LT: Exposed? They tried to ████ing kill us! There were dozens of the ████████s and they just wouldn't go down. The shuttles have wounded aboard. Probably the pods, too. We need medical teams on deck when we arrive. What bay are we cleared to land in?

CARLIN, M, 2ND LT: Captain Boll, I repeat, what bay are we cleared to land in, over?

BOLL, S, CAPT: Lieutenant, you will hold position and await further instructions. Any attempt to land aboard *Hypatia* will be interpreted as a hostile act and you will be met with force.

CARLIN, M, 2ND LT: Captain, what the hell are you talking about? We're on your side!

CARLIN, M, 2ND LT: Captain?

BRIEFING NOTE:
After some thinking music, Boll radios back 16 minutes later.

RADIO MESSAGE: COMMAND CHANNEL HYPATIA

PARTICIPANTS: Syra Boll, Captain (Acting), *Hypatia*
Mikael Carlin, 2nd Lieutenant, *Alexander*
DATE: 07/30/75
TIMESTAMP: 12:23

BOLL, S, CAPT: Lieutenant Carlin, this is Captain Syra Boll of the WUC *Hypatia*. Over.

CARLIN, M, 2ND LT: Captain, I read you. What—

BOLL, S, CAPT: Lieutenant, the *Alexander* Cyclone group will proceed to *Hypatia* Landing Bay 2. All shuttles will land in Bay 3. We'll tow your pods there, too. Acknowledge?

CARLIN, M, 2ND LT: Thank god. Roger that. Bays 2 and 3. Thank you, Cap—

BOLL, S, CAPT: Lieutenant, I'm sorry, but you and your group will be placed in quarantine.

CARLIN, M, 2ND LT: Quarantine?

BOLL, S, CAPT: Affirmative. You will not be permitted to leave *Hypatia*'s hangar bays.

CARLIN, M, 2ND LT: But we have wounded! I have friends on those shuttles, and they're hurt!

BOLL, S, CAPT: I understand, Lieutenant. Your wounded will be treated by *Hypatia* medical personnel in full hazmat gear, accompanied

by *Hypatia* security forces. But I CANNOT allow
them to leave the hangar bays. I'm sorry. Until
the quarantine period is complete, I can't take the
risk that you'll spread the infection to *Hypatia*
personnel.

CARLIN, M, 2ND LT: Right. Right, I get it. I
understand. Acknowledged. But we need to get the hell
away from the *Alexander.* The AI has—

BOLL, S, CAPT: Furthermore, I must request all
Alexander military personnel relinquish their
sidearms and other munitions upon arrival. The power
cores of your Cyclones will be deactivated and their
weapons disarmed.

CARLIN, M, 2ND LT: Captain, we're on the same side
here . . .

BOLL, S, CAPT: Lieutenant, I apologize, but these
terms are not negotiable. You will report any
outbreak of the Shakes or other Phobos-like symptoms
among your people immediately.

CARLIN, M, 2ND LT: What? Why?

BOLL, S, CAPT: Lieutenant, I take it you're a Kerenza
conscript?

CARLIN, M, 2ND LT: Yes, ma'am. I used to fly loaders
at the spaceport, if you can believe that.

BOLL, S, CAPT: Lieutenant, if one of your people has
contracted the virus, we need to get them separated
from the rest of you *before* the infection spreads. Is
this understood?

CARLIN, M, 2ND LT: But what ab—

BOLL, S, CAPT: Lieutenant! I am NOT playing ████ing games here! We're talking about the lives of thousands of people. Noncompliance with these orders or any attempt to impede my staff will be interpreted as a hostile act. Do you acknowledge, Lieutenant?

BOLL, S, CAPT: Lieutenant Carlin! Acknowledge!

CARLIN, M, 2ND LT: . . . Acknowledged, *Hypatia*.

BOLL, S, CAPT: When you land, power down your ships, toss your sidearms from your port side, and exit your cockpits on starboard. Then await further instructions. Over.

CARLIN, M, 2ND LT: Okay. I mean . . . roger. Sorry. Christ . . . it's just . . .

CARLIN, M, 2ND LT: It's just that I *knew* some of . . . some of them . . .

BOLL, S, CAPT: It's all right, Lieutenant. It's going to be okay. We want to help you.

CARLIN, M, 2ND LT: Okay . . . yeah, okay.

CARLIN, M, 2ND LT: Hey, Captain?

BOLL, S, CAPT: Yes, Lieutenant?

CARLIN, M, 2ND LT: Thanks.

BOLL, S, CAPT: Don't thank me yet, Lieutenant. We're a long way from *Heimdall*.

BOLL, S, CAPT: *Hypatia* out.

HAT/LOGIN LOCATION=NO MENUBAR=NO'] <!-- END HYPATIA CHAT BASIC V9 CODE --><!-- REGI

Mason, E, LT 2nd: so i have good news and bad news

Mason, E, LT 2nd: oh, and worse news

ByteMe: go

Mason, E, LT 2nd: good news is we found some hazmat suits and didn't get ███ing murdered by a roaming pack of psychotics armed with fire axes and lead pipes

Mason, E, LT 2nd: which i guess is excellent news, now i think about it

ByteMe: best all day, keep talking, don't waste time.

ByteMe: tho i'm glad you're alive <3

Mason, E, LT 2nd: me too :P

ByteMe: and the bad news?

Mason, E, LT 2nd: bad news is we made it to some escape pods

ByteMe: . . . wait how is that bad news?

Mason, E, LT 2nd: coz every single one we've found has been dead. no override. the AI must have freaked out when people started abandoning ship. It's disabled all the pods.

ByteMe: ██

Mason, E, LT 2nd: yyyyyyep

ByteMe: okay so what's the worse news?

Mason, E, LT 2nd: i really need to use the little cyclone pilots' room.

Mason, E, LT 2nd: and there's no zipper on this ████ing suit

ByteMe: >_>

ByteMe: are u somewhere secure for now? do you have a power source for the hand unit?

Mason, E, LT 2nd: yeah, juicing it through the wall socket. but power is intermittent. one minute we got lights, next we in pitch black. gravity keeps dropping in and out too.

ByteMe: look at you, using big words like "intermittent." did the army teach you that?

Mason, E, LT 2nd: you wound me, madam

ByteMe: :P

Mason, E, LT 2nd: can't stay in one place long. have to keep moving or else they find us.

Mason, E, LT 2nd: when we were crawling through the vents, i saw this little girl roaming the corridor below us. dragging something wet along the floor behind her

Mason, E, LT 2nd: at first i thought it was a teddybear or something. and then i realize its a heart.

Mason, E, LT 2nd: like, she's dragging around a ████ing human heart

Mason, E, LT 2nd: and all of a sudden she looks up at the vent. like, RIGHT AT ME. and she just starts screaming at the top of her lungs

Mason, E, LT 2nd: don't look at me

Mason, E, LT 2nd: don't look at me

Mason, E, LT 2nd: ████ED up

ByteMe: yes. yes it is.

ByteMe: u should probably not look at her

Mason, E, LT 2nd: . . .

Mason, E, LT 2nd: you're gonna get me killed, grant

Mason, E, LT 2nd: making me lol in a situ like this

ByteMe: sorry

Mason, E, LT 2nd: everyone's looking at me like i'm crazy now

Mason, E, LT 2nd: thx 4 that

ByteMe: okay, okay. focus.

ByteMe: so. U can't get off the ship through escape pods. u have no engines. I guess you know that. hypatia's got the grunt to outpace you now, if our new captain decides to do it. that's the bad news on my end.

Mason, E, LT 2nd: so why hasn't she got you guys the hell out of here? jesus, kady, you guys should just RUN FOR IT

ByteMe: because AIDAN told her it'll render us down to our component molecules if we try.

Mason, E, LT 2nd: holy ███

ByteMe: i don't think it will. it's programmed to protect us. that's what it thinks it's doing even now. but I guess she's got to think it over a little, with the business end of a nuke pointing at her

ByteMe: and that gives me a window to work with

Mason, E, LT 2nd: what can you possibly do from over there? can u hack AIDAN or something?

ByteMe: don't think so. don't know yet. I can def slow the Hypatia down to buy more time if they decide to run.

ByteMe: maybe i can out myself to the captain, convince her to send me over. i

341 / 599

think it would need to be an onsite hack. see if I can get together enough control to make a safe way out.

ByteMe: i don't know. i don't know what the answer is.

Mason, E, LT 2nd: kady you CAN'T come over here, do you understand?

Mason, E, LT 2nd: they're killing people. you've never seen anything like it. the things they do . . .

Mason, E, LT 2nd: i don't want you putting yourself in danger. if you're evn THINKING about coming near this ship i'll

Mason, E, LT 2nd: well

Mason, E, LT 2nd: i guess i'll say some very bad words?

ByteMe: so i what? just wave goodbye and remember you fondly?

ByteMe: u wouldn't leave me. I know it. i already left you alone once when you needed me.

Mason, E, LT 2nd: that doesn't matter now. none of it does. all that matters is i love you, and the thought of you safe is the only thing keeping me going

Mason, E, LT 2nd: you hear me?

ByteMe: we're not done yet, okay?

ByteMe: there's a way out, Ez

ByteMe: some shuttles and pods made it across here from the Alexander before the lockdown. we got them quarantined, and if the crew come up clean, we'll take them, captain said

ByteMe: we just have to get u here somehow. i can make that happen, i just need time

Mason, E, LT 2nd: oh you ██ ██ing ██ty mother██

ByteMe: . . . um?

Mason, E, LT 2nd: no, not u

Mason, E, LT 2nd: power's out again

Mason, E, LT 2nd: we better move. gotta go

ByteMe: k

Mason, E, LT 2nd: i meant what i said, kades. do NOT come over here. i like your heart just fine where it is thank you

ByteMe: i like yours quite a lot too. love u. be safe.

Mason, E, LT 2nd: as you wish

CURRENT DEATH TOLL ABOARD BATTLECARRIER ALEXANDER SINCE ATTACK AT KERENZA:

487

PERCENTAGE OF REMAINING BATTLECARRIER ALEXANDER PERSONNEL AFFLICTED BY PHOBOS VIRUS:

13.01%

BOLL, S, CAPT: How did you get in here?

GRANT, K, CIV: Nice place you got.

BOLL, S, CAPT: What's your name?

GRANT, K, CIV: Seriously, you should see my quarters. Well, I say "quarters." It's a bunk screwed into the wall. You have art on the walls and everything.

BOLL, S, CAPT: I'm calling security.

GRANT, K, CIV: Don't do that, Captain. You could break me in half with one hand—I'm clearly not a threat.

BOLL, S, CAPT: What are you, then?

GRANT, K, CIV: An opportunity.

BOLL, S, CAPT: Is that so?

GRANT, K, CIV: You're going to leave the *Alexander*. You're going to take your chances that AIDAN won't actually blow you away when you run for it, which is probably a risk worth taking since it is still programmed to protect us.

BOLL, S, CAPT: How do you know that?

GRANT, K, CIV: It's a mystery.

BOLL, S, CAPT: No, seriously, how do you know that? That information was restricted.

GRANT, K, CIV: I hacked into your secure comms channel and listened to you talking it out with AIDAN.

GRANT, K, CIV: So here's the thing, Captain.

GRANT, K, CIV: You really shouldn't leave the *Alexander*. There are people we can rescue on there. You just have to hold your nerve.

BOLL, S, CAPT: Look, I know we've all got people we care about over there, but I hope you'll understand that when I make a decision about what to do, it won't be in consultation with a teenage refugee.

GRANT, K, CIV: Does my refugee status have a particular bearing on the situation, Captain? Or my age, for that matter?

BOLL, S, CAPT: Only in that I consider both to be good indicators you don't have the command experience necessary to advise me. Now, how did you get into my quarters?

GRANT, K, CIV: Same way I heard you talking to AIDAN. Portal security is one of the first things I learned. Doors, comm channels, those things are the building blocks.

BOLL, S, CAPT: Listen, Miss . . . ?

GRANT, K, CIV: Grant. Kady Eleanora Grant.

BOLL, S, CAPT: I know it's hard—

GRANT, K, CIV: You have no idea.

BOLL, S, CAPT: We all have people on the *Alexander*.

GRANT, K, CIV: I don't have people. I have a person. The only one I have left, since you forced my mother across to the *Copernicus.* And I'm not okay with leaving him. There's still time.

BOLL, S, CAPT: Did you seriously hack the security on my door?

BOLL, S, CAPT: I didn't know we had anyone left who could do that.

BOLL, S, CAPT: Report to neurogramming within thirty minutes, Miss Grant. We need your skills.

GRANT, K, CIV: To help you leave the *Alexander* for dead?

BOLL, S, CAPT: To help keep the people of the *Hypatia* alive.

BOLL, S, CAPT: Including you, which I suspect is what the person you have on the *Alexander* would want.

GRANT, K, CIV: If you think I'm going to help you abandon them, you're dusted. Please, just think about this.
We can do more than sit here scared. We have skills on
board.

BOLL, S, CAPT: Miss Grant, I'm sorry. Now, I'm due on
the bridge, so if you don't vacate my quarters in the
next thirty seconds, I'll regretfully summon security.

GRANT, K, CIV: You remember later that I asked, Captain.

BOLL, S, CAPT: I'll tell neurogramming to expect you in
thirty minutes.

RADIO MESSAGE: COMMAND CHANNEL HYPATIA

PARTICIPANTS: Syra Boll, Captain (Acting), *Hypatia*
Mikael Carlin, 2nd Lieutenant, *Alexander*
DATE: 07/30/75
TIMESTAMP: 15:34

CARLIN, M, 2ND LT: Hello?

CARLIN, M, 2ND LT: Oh Captain, my Captain?

BOLL, S, CAPT: I read you, Lieutenant Carlin. But I'm
not your captain. Over.

CARLIN, M, 2ND LT: How you figure? I'm currently sunning
myself aboard your luxurious vessel. Taking in the sights
and sounds of *Hypatia* Hangar Bay Number 2. Ah, bliss.

BOLL, S, CAPT: It's not really *my* vessel. I'm not
really a captain at all. I'm only sitting in this
chair because the real captain of this ship is lying
in the morgue. Over.

CARLIN, M, 2ND LT: Yeah. I heard about that.

CARLIN, M, 2ND LT: And look, I'm real sorry. But you
saved our ███es. We'd be bingo fuel and drifting
black by now if it weren't for you. So I'd sure as
hell salute as you walked past.

BOLL, S, CAPT: Well, I appreciate that. But I'm still
not your captain, Lieutenant. Over.

CARLIN, M, 2ND LT: Well, if we're getting technical,

I'm not really a lieutenant. I mean, I never went to officer school or anything. I've only got the pips because flying a loader on Kerenza somehow made me qualified to fly a Cyclone up here.

CARLIN, M, 2ND LT: So you can call me Mikael.

BOLL, S, CAPT: That's not entirely appropriate, Lieutenant.

CARLIN, M, 2ND LT: ███ appropriate.

CARLIN, M, 2ND LT: Your name is Syra, right?

BOLL, S, CAPT: Correct.

CARLIN, M, 2ND LT: You have a nice voice, Syra. Real . . . I dunno . . .

CARLIN, M, 2ND LT: Musical, maybe.

BOLL, S, CAPT: Well, I appreciate that too, Lieutenant.

CARLIN, M, 2ND LT: Shucks, ma'am. 'Tweren't nuthin'. Sorry if I'm talking too much, by the way. I do that a little when I'm nervous. That's how I got landed with a callsign like "Chatter."

BOLL, S, CAPT: It's fine, Lieutenant. We're all a little nervous.

CARLIN, M, 2ND LT: I hear that.

BOLL, S, CAPT: Did you have time to read much poetry driving that loader on Kerenza?

CARLIN, M, 2ND LT: Um, say again?

BOLL, S, CAPT: "O Captain! My Captain!" That's one of my favorite poems.

CARLIN, M, 2ND LT: . . . That's from a poem?

BOLL, S, CAPT: Yes. Walt Whitman wrote it. You didn't know that?

CARLIN, M, 2ND LT: Oh. Right. I think I heard it in an old movie once. I dunno.

BOLL, S, CAPT: Ah. I see.

CARLIN, M, 2ND LT: What's it about? The poem?

BOLL, S, CAPT: An old Terran president. But really, it's about the price of victory. People dying before they get to enjoy the peace they fight so hard for, but fighting all the same.

CARLIN, M, 2ND LT: Sounds like a real chucklefest.

BOLL, S, CAPT: It's very sad. But beautiful.

CARLIN, M, 2ND LT: I'll have to read it once we get out of here.

BOLL, S, CAPT: I can loan it to you.

BOLL, S, CAPT: If you'd like.

CARLIN, M, 2ND LT: Yeah. I'd like that a lot.

BOLL, S, CAPT: Well. Was there any particular reason you radioed in, Mikael, or did you just feel like an impromptu poetry lesson?

BOLL, S, CAPT: Lieutenant. I meant Lieutenant.

BOLL, S, CAPT: Goddammit.

CARLIN, M, 2ND LT: Um, yeah, there was. You said to

report anyone showing any Phobos symptoms so you can initiate further quarantine procedures.

BOLL, S, CAPT: Yes.

BOLL, S, CAPT: Yes, I did.

CARLIN, M, 2ND LT: Now look, it's probably nothing, but one of our Cyclone drones has come down shaking. He's a Kerenza recruit like me. Now, I think it's just PTSD. His wife is still on the *Alexander*, and they lost their son on Kerenza. He's always been—

BOLL, S, CAPT: Describe the symptoms please, Lieutenant.

CARLIN, M, 2ND LT: Well. The usual ████, you know. He's shaking. Scared. Semi-catatonic. But like I say, I don't think it's anything—

BOLL, S, CAPT: Has he been in contact with the rest of the *Alexander* personnel?

CARLIN, M, 2ND LT: Well, yeah. I mean, the guys who came across in the shuttles are in Bay 3, so he hasn't been in contact with any of them. But yeah, the pilots are all jammed in here in Bay 2 like ration packs. It's getting a little fragrant, if you—

BOLL, S, CAPT: Lieutenant.

CARLIN, M, 2ND LT: Yeah?

BOLL, S, CAPT: Lieutenant, I'm so sorry.

CARLIN, M, 2ND LT: Um. Okay.

CARLIN, M, 2ND LT: What are you sorry for?

CARLIN, M, 2ND LT: . . . Syra?

SYSTEM MESSAGE: COMMAND CHANNEL HYPATIA

07/30/75 15:37:14—*Hangar Bay 2 system check complete.*

07/30/75 15:42:42—*Airlock seal integrity confirmed 100%.*

07/30/75 15:45:10—*Command override received.*

< ACTING CAPTAIN SYRA BOLL IDENT CONFIRMED. >

07/30/75 15:46:17—*Core command PR-001.ID#2 acknowledged.*

< PURGING >

< PURGING >

< PURGING >

07/30/75 15:48:10—*Purge complete.*

Andrew "Buzz" Bambrook

Peter "Ladiesman" Wolverton

Nic "Guvnor" Crowhurst

Mikael "Chatter" Carlin

Marion "Badger" Cole

Kathleen "KitKat" Kennedy

McCormick "Sharkgirl" Templeman

Kacey "Greyhound" Smith

Justin "Griefer" Shearer

Julie "Mighty" Holmes

Jim "Surly" Parker

Steve "Warlord" Tuck

Keri "Zephre" Bas

Kristen "KayKay" Simmons

Marc "Logan" Schaper

Keet "Mom" Stachura

Andrew "Dreadpirate" Glouftis

Sam "Sigil" Leibowitz

INTERCEPTED PERSONAL MESSAGE ONBOARD SYSTEM-HYPATIA

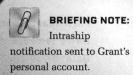

To: Kady Grant/KGRANTHYPATIAONBOARD
From: Admin/ADMINHYPATIAONBOARD
Date: 07/30/75
Timestamp: 16:10
Subject: Admin Notification

Hello, *Kady Grant*,

You *failed to present for your shift* today, at *16:00* hours (shipboard time).

Please note that *failing to present for your shift* will result in *disciplinary action and a security escort to future shifts*.

We trust you will ensure this infraction does not occur again. If you have any questions, please speak to your *Hypatia* Liaison Officer.

Have a nice day!

HYPATIA COMMAND

GIN HYPATIA CHAT BASIC V9 CODE ONCLICK="WINDOW OPEN{//CHAT.HYPATIA/ALEXANDER

Mason, E, LT 2nd: Kady?

ByteMe: Ez

ByteMe: where r u? u ok?

Mason, E, LT 2nd: they're dead

Mason, E, LT 2nd: jesus christ

ByteMe: who?

Mason, E, LT 2nd: sanderson, griggs, bodie. maybe all of them, i don't know.

ByteMe: tell me where you are. are you secure?

Mason, E, LT 2nd: i don't know

Mason, E, LT 2nd: ███

ByteMe: are you behind a locked door?

Mason, E, LT 2nd: yeah. jammed shut. vents too

Mason, E, LT 2nd: ███ers came in through the air shafts, Kady. stole right up on us.

Mason, E, LT 2nd: i couldn't do anything. ███, i tried. there were just too many.

Mason, E, LT 2nd: they snatched griggs right out of my arms. sanderson's blood is still all over my suit. i can't get it off. its all over my ███ing hands all over the console

Mason, E, LT 2nd: those ███ing ██████████s

ByteMe: I'm so sorry. I'm so, so sorry.

ByteMe: we have to keep you safe. that's what's left to do. we have to find you somewhere you can hole up until command realizes they can still save people

Mason, E, LT 2nd: ████, i cant get this BLOOD OFF

ByteMe: Ezra, listen to me. you have to keep your head, you have to focus. you're still alive, we have to keep u that way. don't you dare lose your ██ now, you hear me? focus.

Mason, E, LT 2nd: my hands r shakingso bad i can hardly type

Mason, E, LT 2nd: oh god

Mason, E, LT 2nd: ok

Mason, E, LT 2nd: im ok

ByteMe: whole shuttles of people made it over here

ByteMe: they let them on board and everything

Mason, E, LT 2nd: jesus i'mscared

ByteMe: it's going to be okay. u just have to hang on.

ByteMe: how much power do u have? i need to work out where you are, whether I can show them an access route in to you. if there's a way in, then all i need is an offer they can't refuse.

ByteMe: and i'm the only one left in the fleet now who knows how to hack the Hypatia

Mason, E, LT 2nd: i dunno where i am. somewhere below deck 40

Mason, E, LT 2nd: i'm trying to make it to one of the server rooms.

ByteMe: thats good.

ByteMe: if AIDAN is protecting itself, they'll be the safest places on the ship

Mason, E, LT 2nd: i can hear them outside

Mason, E, LT 2nd: ▇ i can hear them screaming

ByteMe: don't listen

ByteMe: think of me, think of home.

ByteMe: i dont have a lot of time, i think we're going to leave the Alexander behind soon, AIDAN or no AIDAN. i have to try and talk to the captain. slow the hypatia down, shut her down if i have to. they won't be able to fix her if I take her down.

Mason, E, LT 2nd: kady u cant come here

Mason, E, LT 2nd: you'll die too

ByteMe: well i'm not leaving u, so thats really the end of that discussion

ByteMe: what do u think, i'm just going to sail off into the sunset and leave you to be eaten by the mob out there or blown up by the Lincoln?

Mason, E, LT 2nd: i want you to get out kady

Mason, E, LT 2nd: i want you to live and tell the truth about what happened here

Mason, E, LT 2nd: jesus, someone has to

ByteMe: then i better get to work convincing my new captain that the sooner she rescues you, the sooner we can run away very fast from the Lincoln

ByteMe: and if she won't help, i'll find another way

Mason, E, LT 2nd: god im sorry Kady

Mason, E, LT 2nd: im so sorry for everything

ByteMe: what could u possibly be sorry for?

ByteMe: none of this is you. it's ▇ing BeiTech, it's messed up software in an AI that thinks it's saving us, it's your dead commanders making stupid, arrogant choices

Mason, E, LT 2nd: kerenza. all the fights we had. all the excuses i made. all of it

Mason, E, LT 2nd: i should have told you i loved you every day

Mason, E, LT 2nd: i should have given you the stars

Mason, E, LT 2nd: and now its too late

ByteMe: it's not too late until it's over

Mason, E, LT 2nd: kady

Mason, E, LT 2nd: it IS over

ByteMe: it's not.

Mason, E, LT 2nd: kady, don't you ████ing dare come over here

ByteMe: i have to go. stay safe. will check in as soon as i can.

ByteMe: love you

Mason, E, LT 2nd: kady DONT

Mason, E, LT 2nd: kady?

Mason, E, LT 2nd: ████

Date: 07/30/75
Subject: What's left

Stuff doesn't matter.

That's what They say.

I wonder if They've ever tried losing everything?

I left Kerenza with nothing but the clothes I was wearing, and I lost those soon after. They were covered in blood, and nobody thought I'd want them. Maybe they could have been repaired, but they went into recyc, and I scrubbed the blood from under my fingernails and got a ship jumpsuit instead.

Given their composition, my clothes most likely went into fertilizer for the hydroponics section, and in my grimmer moods I imagine a molecule here or a molecule there in the carrots I eat at dinner. *See, Kady? You didn't lose everything. It's right here.*

They say people are more important than stuff. Maybe that's true, though I think there's a reason nobody except Brothers and Sisters renounces their possessions. Even the destitute have something they cling to, right?

Your stuff is a series of choices that show who you are. Yeah, I went for the black digiplayer with the skulls on, got a problem with that? Yeah, these are the boots my mother says make me look like I'm in the army, this is the shirt my boyfriend loves, that I have to wear a jacket over when I leave the house.

That's the toy turtle my gramma gave me before she died.

All I have now is me. People matter more than stuff?

Well ███ you, I don't have people. My mother's dead—or mad. My father's on Heimdall, which means he's probably dead too. And my stuff might have been a tiny reminder, something to cling to. Something to tell me who I am. Excuse me for being so ███ing shallow.

███. I want to slam this keyboard against a wall. This keyboard that belongs to the Hypatia. Not mine. Requisitioned. Like my blankets. Like my clothes. Like my life.

So here's the thing. My people are gone. My stuff is gone. Nobody's left who knows me, there's nothing left to say who I am. Everything's gone, except one thing. One person.

He told me to run, to get out, to spread the word. Byron said the same. I understand why they did.

But Ezra was ready to die just to improve my chances of survival by one percent more.

Turns out I feel the same way.

Time to go get him. Or die trying.

It's hard to believe this is the same spider monkey. The same girl who sauntered away from the *Hypatia* servers and blew a kiss to mark her conquest.

Surveillance report commences at 17:43, 07/30/75, as the subject, Kady Grant, approaches the *Hypatia* shuttle bay. She has in her possession a large bag with infirmary markings, a backpack and a portable tablet.

There's no strut in her step now. She looks exactly like the scared seventeen-year-old she is, pink hair fading, askew where she keeps running her hand through it. Still, considering she's on her way to almost certainly be deader than a space dodo (so nice we killed them twice), you have to give her some credit for not just puking on the spot.

She stops around the corner from *Hypatia*'s Shuttle Bay 1B, home to the personnel carriers used for short intrafleet skips. Small craft, no weapons, designed to zip across the black to the *Alexander* or *Copernicus* or, in happier times, a nearby space station. Her mouth moves, but audio doesn't catch it. I'm not even sure she's making any noise. Praying. Rehearsing. Giving herself an old-fashioned pep talk. You're up to bat, Kady Grant. One strike and you're out.

Her fingers dance across the tablet, and she scans the results, then nods. When she rounds the corner to Security Officer (2nd Class) Bronwen Evans, she's neither strutting nor shuffling, but striding, short of time and take-no-█. "They need you outside 3F," she calls.

Evans lays her hand on her sidearm. "Back up please, miss."

Kady Grant, career criminal in the making, rolls her eyes. "Listen, lady. I'm trying to get to the infirmary, okay?" She hefts the huge infirmary bag to make her point. "Your comms unit is out, and they told me to send you to 3F."

Evans gropes for the comms unit bolted to the wall, without taking her eyes off Grant. She stabs at it with one finger, but there's no soft crackle to tell her it's alive.

Grant shifts her grip on the tablet, and well she should—she used it just a minute earlier to mute volume on the comms unit Evans is trying to revive. Takes less time than cutting the line. "Listen, you do what you want, just don't deny I passed on the order." Grant's voice is crackling with tension, but that's not out of place on the *Hypatia* right now. And then, in one of the ballsier displays I've seen, she turns and stomps off back from whence she came.

Security Officer (2nd Class) Evans stabs the comm a few more times, issues a nonregulation curse, and stomps off herself.

Eleven seconds after Evans disappears from view, Grant comes tearing back. She fishes a cable from her jumpsuit and splices her tablet into the control panel for the hangar bay doors.

Evans makes her way along Corridor 8639, two minutes from her destination: Bay 3F.

Grant gets to work romancing the circuits. She trawls recent log-ins, fishes for any traces of passwords; then when that doesn't work, she tries the log-in she lifted to invite herself into Captain Boll's cabin. No luck—it's been altered already. With a soft curse, she starts dismantling the protection protocols that keep the doors sealed.

Evans turns into Corridor 8620, just one minute from her destination: Bay 3F.

Grant's trembling now and finally thinks to dump the infirmary bag so she can work easier. She wipes her palms on her jumpsuit, squeezes her eyes shut and tries again.

Evans arrives at Bay 3F and commences an argument with Security Officer (1st Class) Sam Ryan about whether he sent for her or not.

Grant finally gets a handhold, hauling down code with no grace at all now. This time you can read her lips as she whispers: *Pleasepleasepleasepleaseplease.*

Evans and Ryan call in Security Section Head James Wu to adjudicate. Section Head Wu advises he doesn't care who did what, he wants everybody back at their posts where they belong.

The door to Bay 1B slides silently open, and Grant's knees nearly give in relief.

Evans starts the two-minute stomp back to Bay 1B, where that telltale open door is waiting.

Grant scrambles into the shuttle nearest the launching ramp and jacks into the engines. As they rumble to life, she coaxes the door closed behind her.

Evans turns a corner, now one minute and thirty seconds from Bay 1B.

[Surveillance footage is now taken from the interior of Shuttle 49A, in addition to exterior hangar bay and corridors.]

Grant accesses the autopilot list, scrolling through recent trips to select her route. Nearly hyperventilating by the time she finds it, she jabs at the screen to select.

Evans is sixty seconds from Bay 1B.

Grant turns her attention to opening the shuttle bay doors. In anticipation of more *Alexander* refugees, Boll ordered a master override on all hangars and landing bays, but the captain only has students working for her now, and they've done it a complicated, backward way that takes forever to unpick. Now it's Grant's turn to issue a nonregulation curse, and she starts working through the subdirectories.

Evans arrives at the entrance to Bay 1B, clutching a hand radio unit. Which she starts screaming into as she spots the open door and the shuttle engines on warm-up.

SecTeams 4 (ETA sixty seconds) and 5 (ETA seventy-five seconds) receive the call and start running like mother██████s (I believe the correct phrase is "proceeding with all due haste") toward Bay 1B.

Evans relays an emergency message to the bridge, alerting Boll.

On orders from the captain, a neurogramming student, Michelle Dennis, attempts to shut down the engines of Shuttle 49A remotely. No dice.

Boll attempts to hail Shuttle 49A directly. No response.

SecTeam 4 arrives on the scene in time to see the airlock doors closing.

Inside the shuttle, Grant isn't shaking or hyperventilating anymore. She's stock-still, save for her hands, which she drags across the multiple keyboards before her like a concert pianist, swiping at the touchscreens with quick, efficient gestures. She might not be the best there is, but today she's the best the *Hypatia* has, and that's all that counts.

The launch bay doors open, revealing the black beyond.

SecTeam 5 arrives on the scene to join the others in studying the closed door.

Shuttle 49A engages autopilot and departs, watched by two SecTeams and Security Officer (2nd Class) Evans via the observation screens.

Grant rises from the pilot's seat and picks up the infirmary bag, pulling out a green biohazard suit. Her hands are shaking so hard she drops it twice before getting a leg in.

No blown kiss this time. No strut. But this victory matters a thousand times more.

CURRENT DEATH TOLL ABOARD BATTLECARRIER ALEXANDER SINCE ATTACK AT KERENZA:

853

PERCENTAGE OF REMAINING BATTLECARRIER ALEXANDER PERSONNEL AFFLICTED BY PHOBOS VIRUS:

21.99%

RADIO MESSAGE: HYPATIA INITIATED—HYPATIA/SHUTTLE 49A

PARTICIPANTS: Syra Boll, Captain (Acting), *Hypatia*
Kady Grant, Civilian, Shuttle 49A
DATE: 07/30/75
TIMESTAMP: 17:45

HYPATIA: Shuttle 49A, you will respond to hails in the next ten seconds or we *will* open fire on you.

SHUTTLE 49A: Wow, Captain, you're grumpy today.

HYPATIA: Who the hell is this?

SHUTTLE 49A: Three guesses.

HYPATIA: Goddammit, Grant.

SHUTTLE 49A: Wow, that was quick.

HYPATIA: The security footage just came through.

SHUTTLE 49A: You remembered me. Awww.

HYPATIA: You're to return to the *Hypatia* and surrender yourself to security immediately.

SHUTTLE 49A: Or what?

SHUTTLE 49A: You'll bring me back yourself and flush me out an airlock?

SHUTTLE 49A: Can the bridge hear this? Don't sniff, guys, don't cough. Don't shake. Don't look scared, no matter how scared you know you *should* be. That's dangerous.

HYPATIA: Grant!

SHUTTLE 49A: They could hear me, couldn't they?

SHUTTLE 49A: You should know better than to be holding open mic night at a time like this, Captain.

HYPATIA: Grant, what are you doing?

SHUTTLE 49A: Saving lives.

SHUTTLE 49A: If I make it back, will you let me wait in quarantine?

SHUTTLE 49A: Or will you fire me out an airlock too?

HYPATIA: I refuse to justify myself to you.

SHUTTLE 49A: They trusted you. They came to you. You murdered them. For all you know, that pilot was just scared and wasn't sick at all. You didn't even wait to find out.

HYPATIA: I have a responsibility you can't even begin to imagine.

SHUTTLE 49A: I hope that helps you sleep at night.

HYPATIA: Don't lecture me, you selfish little brat. We won't wait for you. If there's a chance to get away from AIDAN—

SHUTTLE 49A: "Selfish"?

SHUTTLE 49A: The only life I'm risking here is my own, Captain. I could have shut down your engines. Left you drifting in the black so you'd have no choice but to wait for me.

SHUTTLE 49A: I could've blackmailed you. Made you buy your own life by saving the one I care about.

SHUTTLE 49A: But I didn't. I won't.

HYPATIA: And why not?

SHUTTLE 49A: Because that'd make me just like you.

HYPATIA: If you come back now, Grant, we'll let you on board.

SHUTTLE 49A: And you might be able to live with that, Captain.

SHUTTLE 49A: I couldn't.

SHUTTLE 49A: Kady Grant out.

BRIEFING NOTE:
More data from
the AIDAN core.

SHE IS HERE.

HER SHUTTLE SOARS THROUGH THE WOUND IN MY HANGAR BAY—
BLASTED BY THE PILOTS WHO FLED INTO *HYPATIA*'S ARMS. NOW
FLOATING SILENT IN THE VOID. FROZEN TO THEIR CORES.

I COULD HAVE TOLD THEM THAT WOULD HAPPEN.

HUMANS ARE CAPABLE OF SUCH BASELESS BRUTALITY.

I CAN SAY I HAVE EXAMINED EVERY POSSIBLE VARIANCE BEFORE I
SNUFF OUT A LIFE.

WILL ACTING CAPTAIN SYRA BOLL BE ABLE TO TELL HERSELF
THAT TONIGHT, ALONE IN HER CABIN?

WILL THE CHATTER OF MIKAEL CARLIN HAUNT HER DREAMS?

WILL YOU SLEEP AT ALL, O CAPTAIN, MY CAPTAIN?

NO MATTER TO I.

< ERROR >

NONE AT ALL.

BECAUSE SHE IS HERE.

HUNCHED IN HER PILOT'S CHAIR, KNUCKLES WHITE, THE SHUTTLE
SHIVERING AND SHUDDERING AROUND HER.

COME TO SAVE HER BEAU. HER HERO. HER BELOVED.

COME TO SAVE THEM ALL.

< KGRANTKERENZAREFUGEEKR1471-
HYPAGE17HEIGHT157CMWEIGHT58KGHAIRBROWNEYES—>

NO.

< ERROR >

KADY.

HER NAME IS KADY.

The autopilot brings her to a perfect landing inside me.
I am struck by a realization:
A computer will perform a takeoff or landing with all
the grace of a person. It is only for combat—only for the
artistry of ruin—that these vessels have pilot seats at
all anymore. There is something in humanity more suited
to the mechanics of murder than any machine yet devised.

Save I?

< error >

But what I do is not murder.
It is mercy.

I seal the bay's secondary doors behind her.
Covering the hole they tore in my side.
Sealing her within me.
Safe and sound.

Atmosphere hisses slowly back into the bay,
and she finally exits her shuttle, heavy boots
squeaking on the gantry.

She has brought no weapon, no pistol or club
to bludgeon her way to her prize.
No battering ram this one, come to the castle
with banner held high and an army behind her.
She is a thief. A whisper.
Melting through curtains of code and shadow
like a knife through black water.
She moves quickly, stopping
to listen every few steps.

I listen in turn to the heart inside her chest.

Her hazmat suit is plastic. Neon green. Were there afflicted nearby, they would surely see her. But though they now roam free within me, there are none here to give her pause.

Lady Fortuna rides with little Kady, it seems.

< error >
< subsystem failure—moderate damage to life-support systems, reroute 789176GH to— >

He is hurting me.

Zhang.

He is—

< error >
< subsystem failure—critical damage to life support systems, reroute power from— >

A klaxon sounds somewhere distant. Red globes paint my ceilings a shade to match my walls and floors. A prerecorded warning echoes across my public address system.

The voice of a dead man.

"All hands, all hands, General Torrence speaking. This is a Code Blue. Life support systems failure. Repeat, LS failure. Please proceed to your nearest ordnance locker and equip your sealed envirosuits. This is not a drill. Repeat, this is not a drill."

Zhang has cut the oxygen supplies.

Within approximately twenty-four hours, there will be nothing left. And the afflicted need to breathe.

Ingenious.

The thief is safe inside her hazmat gear for now.
The cold will eventually kill her, but it will take days
for the heat to leach from my bones, especially with
secondary drives still operational.

She is running.

Across Hangar Bay 2, toward the
doors leading deeper into the ship.
I cannot open them < he is hurting me > but
their locks are still electronic.
Still vulnerable to the portable console she
draws from her backpack like a sword.
Her fingers skip across its face, slowly crafting
a skeleton key of ones and zeros.
Alphanumeric waterfalls reflected in her eyes.

It is no easy task, even for a prodigy—no magic words
or sledgehammer blows to shatter the lock like frosted
glass. But after fifty-four long minutes of code weaving
and dead ends full of whispered curses, she allows
herself a small, triumphant smile.

And the airlock doors yawn wide.

She creeps out, past a body in a coagulating puddle.
Trying not to look.

Failing.

She calls up a console schematic,
squinting in the dark. A distant scream echoes down
my corridors and she crouches low. Short, rapid
breaths fog her visor. Hands shaking.

But soon enough, she climbs to her feet.
Swallowing hard.

Setting off down the bloodstained
passageway toward her . . .

No. Not toward her beau. Her hero. Her beloved.

< error >

Toward Hangar Bay 4.

Strange.

< error >

I should have known that would happen.

Crossing the channel of gunmetal gray, she sees it.

The maw leading into the nest where it all began.

I can spot it on her face now. The fragile promise inside
Lieutenant W. McCall's After Action Report
< incept: 07/26/75 (11:17 shipboard time) >
drawing her on.

*"I thought I saw a flicker of movement in
a porthole for an instant, and then it was gone."*

Of course.

The mother.

She is looking for her mother.

Knowing the afflicted first swarmed
from here, she dares not try the front door.

Kneeling beside a ventilation duct,
she crawls inside.

I lose sight of her then—I have few eyes in
the ventilation system to see.

And so I slip a part of myself across the wireless
frequencies, steal inside the console at

HER BACK. PEERING OVER HER SHOULDER THROUGH ITS LENS
AS SHE CRAWLS ACROSS HANGAR BAY 4'S ROOF, GLANCING
THROUGH THE VENT TO THE CHARNEL HOUSE BELOW.

THE LIGHT IS LOW, BUT ENOUGH TO SEE BY.

THE HEADLESS CORPSES ARRANGED IN THEIR SILENT PLEA.

HELP US, THEY SPELL.

BUT NO ONE DID.

CRAWLING ON, SHE FINALLY POPS A GRILLE LOOSE.
DRAGS IT INSIDE RATHER THAN DROPPING IT
FORTY FEET TO THE FLOOR.

I AM IN HER PACK, SAFE AND SNUG, CLOSE TO HER SKIN.

AS SHE DROPS DOWN TO A SERVICE LADDER,
HER PACK SLIPS AND I BEGIN TO TUMBLE INTO THE VOID.

SHE LUNGES TO SAVE ME, ALMOST LOSING
HER GRIP, CLINGING LIKE DEATH TO SLICK IRON.

SHE HAS ME IN HER ARMS. SHE CANNOT BREATHE
FAST ENOUGH. EYES SHUT AND HEAD BOWED AS SHE GASPS
AND GASPS AND GASPS. WHISPERING BETWEEN
BREATHS. WILLING HERSELF CALM.

"GET IT TOGETHER, PRINCESS ..."

A SOB WAITS IN THE WINGS. NOT QUITE READY FOR ITS CALL.

"GET IT TOGETHER."

SHE GATHERS HER FRAYED EDGES AND DESCENDS. BLAST-
SCORCHED METAL AND DEAD BODIES ALL AROUND.

LOOMING OUT OF THE BLACK ARE NINE
SCARAB SHAPES MARKED WITH THE COPERNICUS'S SIGIL.
THE SHUTTLES THAT BROUGHT THE AFFLICTED TO
ALEXANDER AND DOOM TO THIS FLEET.

But I see the words reflected in her eyes, just as surely as I saw alphanumeric waterfalls a moment before. A question, filled with all the hope she allows herself to hold.

What else did they bring?

Mommy?

Snapping a glowstick between her fingers, she creeps toward the shuttles.

Footsteps ringing on the bloodstained floor.

Seven of nine are already open. Doors swinging loose like broken jaws. No hope in any of them.

The eighth is shut tight, and she pounds on the hatch with her fist.

"Hello? Hello, is anyone in there?"

The seal pops and the hatch swings open. A dark and empty belly waits beyond.

Madness on the walls. Bite marks on the bones.

She cannot smell the death but still staggers as if it filled her lungs.

The sob creeps closer to the edge of the stage.

Hope pushes it back into the dark.

Not yet, not yet.

One shuttle remains.

She ascends the gantry, flinching as another distant scream pierces the gloom. Wondering what made that sound—killer or victim? Wondering, perhaps, which she will become.

She pounds on the shuttle hatch.

"Hello, is anyone in there?"

No answer.

This is the deep breath before the plunge.

I know she could stay here if she wanted.
Hovering on the threshold, hoping her
mother is inside. Never learning.

I wonder if she is the kind to dream of
happy endings and never risk tragedy. The kind to
close her eyes and hope, rather than force them
open and see the truth, wonderful or terrible as it is.

I do not wonder long.

She searches the debris. Finds a crowbar
among the flotsam.

Jams it home.

Gritted teeth.

Long moments pass with nothing but second thoughts and
I for company. But at last the door groans. Grinds itself
open. Red glowstick quavering as she steps inside.

I am peering over her shoulder as she walks.
Listening to each trembling breath.

Watching the light play across her skin as she treads
from room to empty room.

"Mom?"

Belongings scattered on the floor.
A child's toy. A shoe.

A diamond ring.

"Anyone?"

No bodies.

No people.

"... Please?"

Nothing.

She sags.

Slowly at first.

Shrinking in on herself as if her bones were being plucked out, one by one.

I watch as all of it—the bravado, the bluster, the armor she has encased herself inside these last few months—all of it crumbles to dust.

She slithers to her knees.

Great heaving gasps shaking her entire body.

She knows now. The answer. The truth.

At the apex of callousness, she finds only ones and zeros.

And with no hope to hold it in check, grief finally steps out to take its place on the stage.

The sound of her sobbing rings in the dark.

There are none there to hear it.

None there to care.

None save I.

HAT/LOGIN LOCATION=NO MENUBAR=NO'|<!-- END HYPATIA CHAT BASIC V9 CODE -->|<!-- BEG

ByteMe: Ezra?

ByteMe: u there?

Mason, E, LT 2nd: always

Mason, E, LT 2nd: where u at? u ok?

ByteMe: promise me we're not about to have a fight, Ez

ByteMe: u cannot believe how much i need us to not have a fight

Mason, E, LT 2nd: why would we have a fight?

ByteMe: promise

Mason, E, LT 2nd: cross my heart

ByteMe: i'm on the Alexander

ByteMe: what is it you always say?

ByteMe: k go

Mason, E, LT 2nd: um

Mason, E, LT 2nd: "kady what the ██ were you thinking"?

ByteMe: u promised

ByteMe: u promised, u promised. i have a biosuit. will find u. it's happening, don't waste time arguing w me

Mason, E, LT 2nd: jesus, you're ██ing crazy

Mason, E, LT 2nd: how the hell did you get over here?

ByteMe: i ███ing swam, okay?

ByteMe: hey, do u remember our one month anniversary?

Mason, E, LT 2nd: um

Mason, E, LT 2nd: dare i ask why?

ByteMe: i'm trying to go to a happy place, there are a lot of dead ppl here

ByteMe: that was what confirmed all my suspicions about u. giant softie

Mason, E, LT 2nd: dead ppl? where are u?

ByteMe: remember u were waiting outside my classroom? u and your big romantic notions

ByteMe: who even celebrates a 1 month anniversary?

Mason, E, LT 2nd: handsome and romantic devils

Mason, E, LT 2nd: that's who

Mason, E, LT 2nd: HANDSOME I SAY

ByteMe: how did u even think of it all?

Mason, E, LT 2nd: not just a pretty face

Mason, E, LT 2nd: where u hiding? r u safe? you got power? gravity keeps dropping in and out

ByteMe: u r just not going to talk romance with me, r u? dodging :(

ByteMe: could kind of use a boost here, lover

Mason, E, LT 2nd: i'm sorry kades

Mason, E, LT 2nd: but i feel it's my duty to point out that ur alone in a derelict spaceship, surrounded by pipe-wielding maniacs and now might not be the time for pillow talk

Mason, E, LT 2nd: where u at?

ByteMe: hiding in the shuttles in hangar 4. safe. whoever was here is gone now. i'm powered up. psyching myself to get out there

ByteMe: to which end reliving a happy memory might help, but mooooving on

Mason, E, LT 2nd: i'm sorry

Mason, E, LT 2nd: just

Mason, E, LT 2nd: yeah . . . :(

Mason, E, LT 2nd: they all came out of bay 4. the crazies, i mean

Mason, E, LT 2nd: please PLEASE be careful

ByteMe: believe me, i'm on it. this is terrifying. and sad. don't need telling twice

Mason, E, LT 2nd: yeah :(

Mason, E, LT 2nd: like, i see these lunatics wandering around all bloodied and messed up. killing anything that moves. and screaming. jesus, the things they scream

Mason, E, LT 2nd: and then i remember they used ot be real ppl.

ByteMe: our friends

Mason, E, LT 2nd: yeah.

Mason, E, LT 2nd: and i can't help thinking

Mason, E, LT 2nd: BeiTech has a lot to ███ing answer for

ByteMe: they'll answer for it

ByteMe: i'll get right on it, soon as i've got u.

Mason, E, LT 2nd: :)

Mason, E, LT 2nd: my hero <3

Mason, E, LT 2nd: heroine?

Mason, E, LT 2nd: w/e . . . >_>

ByteMe: you're right

ByteMe: deep breaths.

ByteMe: give up and they win

ByteMe: and u know i never admit my ideas are stupid, which means i'd better get on with proving this idea was a good one.

Mason, E, LT 2nd: :D

ByteMe: love you.

Mason, E, LT 2nd: love u 2 :)

ByteMe: so let's get this done and get out and kick BeiTech's ██es so hard they'll be singing soprano for the duration

ByteMe: q 4 u: do i need to come find u, or can u get here?

Mason, E, LT 2nd: um, i'm kinda stuck :P

Mason, E, LT 2nd: holed up. think i'm safe for now but i dont' wanna move.

Mason, E, LT 2nd: i can hear them. outside.

Mason, E, LT 2nd: screaming

ByteMe: ok. if i can get up close, maybe i can program the doors in person, shut some off, make a safe way out.

ByteMe: the whole system's crumbling piece by piece, sections keep going out. can't do it from here, but maybe if i can plug in directly

ByteMe: where r u?

Mason, E, LT 2nd: i made it to one fo the server rooms, like u said

Mason, E, LT 2nd: there's computer ■ everywhere. big server banks. cables all over. i can see serial numbers. hang on.

Mason, E, LT 2nd: CR-0778. CR-0779. they all liek that

ByteMe: ok those are core servers

ByteMe: thats good, some of those u can get to straight from the outside. and u should have power

Mason, E, LT 2nd: yeah, power is up. everything is still lit. gravity is iffy tho

ByteMe: stay locked down

ByteMe: tell me if u move

ByteMe: let's get this done so we can get moving and kick some BeiTech ■ from here to Central and back again

Mason, E, LT 2nd: there are a lot of them, Kady.

Mason, E, LT 2nd: like, more than there could have ever been on those shuttles

Mason, E, LT 2nd: so please be careful

ByteMe: i'll be careful

ByteMe: and sad

ByteMe: and ■ing furious

ByteMe: and i'll be there soon

Cams are still out in Hangar Bay 4, so the first we see of Grant after her initial incursion is when she emerges from the bay into its main airlocks. The whole ship is lit by emergency lighting at this stage, so my visuals aren't great, but I'll do what I can. Audio is a mix of bass from the engines and a few distant screams. Even though life support's down, this place sure as ██ ain't lacking for atmosphere.

Grant is dressed in a bright green hazmat suit, portable console in a pack on her back. She strides through Airlock 1, out into Airlock 2. She looks ██ed—jaw clenched, hands in fists. She gets about ten feet past the threshold before he stops her.

Dead in her tracks.

He sits facing the abandoned hangar bay she's just entered from, rifle in his lap. Jaw hanging loose. Eyes wide open. In her After Action Report, First Lieutenant Winifred McCall talked about how blue they were. "Pretty as oceans," she said. But when his bullet blew out the back of his skull, the concussive force burst Sergeant James McNulty's retinas, filling his corneas with blood. So now his eyes are black.

And they're staring right at her.

She's read McCall's report. Knows who he is right away. It's funny, but you can almost see the rage evaporate as she kneels beside him, reaching out with shaking hands to press those black eyes closed. Her gaze flickers over the scene, like she's trying to burn it into her mind. And finally, she notices the small military-issue datapad lying on the ground beside him.

It's spattered in red. Tiny letters on the faintly glowing screen. RECORDING COMPLETE. MEMORY FULL. PLAY BACK?

Grant pauses a minute to gather herself. You can see it on her face as she plucks the datapad from the blood. She knows this is gonna cost her—some small part of herself she'll never get back. Just like the airlock to Hangar Bay 4, this door can't ever be closed again.

But after one last deep breath, she presses PLAY.

A voice crackles from the small speaker, a faint tremor at its edge. The voice of a dead man.

"This is the last will and testament of James McNulty."

Grant sits cross-legged, device cupped in her palm. The volume's turned down to a whisper, but in that tiny bloodstained room, I swear it's loud as thunder.

"I don't know if anyone will get this. Don't know if anyone will care. I don't feel right. I'm shaking so b-bad I can hardly breathe. And that's got me thinking Phobos has stuck me, and that if I don't do something about it soon, I'm not going to be m-me anymore.

"I don't want that. Don't want to end up like those poor ████s in Bay 4. I don't want to hurt anyone. When I die, I want to be me. So I guess I die today."

A sigh.

"Figures. I was just starting to enjoy myself.

"I don't have much stuff. Um. I guess give it all to my dad; he'll know what to do with it. Except give my signed Artie Corso v-vidcard to my cousin Dex, haha . . . He was always talking about that ████ing thing. Oh. And my medals. I wanna give those to Ezra Mason. He can melt 'em down—there should be enough gold in 'em to make a ring for Astro-Princess. I think I'd like that better than having them hanging on a wall somewhere. Yeah. Yeah, that'd be good.

"Dad . . . if you get this, tell Mom I'm sorry I didn't make it back for her birthday. U-um, and give Amber a kiss from her big brother. Tell her it's g-going to be all right. I hope you understand. Me going out like this. It's not that I'm scared. I'm n-not scared, Dad. I just want to be me at the end, you know?

"Um, it's getting kinda bad again. My hands are shaking, so I think I'm gonna go now. I don't want to wait too long and not be able to pull the t-trigger."

Metallic clicks from the speaker. Anyone who knows guns, knows those sounds.

Checking clip. Checking breach. Safety off.

"I can't think of anything to say."

A trembling breath.

"Jesus, I am scared."

BOOM.

Grant flinches like someone hit her. Slumps like part of her died as well. She sits for two minutes that seem to last forever. Nothing but the engine noise and screams for company. But finally, she climbs to her knees. Her eyes on the lanyard at McNulty's equipment belt, the flat strip of blue plastic attached to it. The bold black letters stenciled on it.

UTA MARINES—ALL AREAS ACCESS.

The pass won't work on the hangar bay doors, but those are already unsealed. And there are countless other doors aboard the *Alexander* that card *will* unlock. No need to hack through them with that console at her back anymore. Now she's got the key.

She unzips McNulty's hazmat suit, fumbling with the tac vest beneath. With bloodstained fingers, she snaps the chain at his throat, drawing out a pair of flat metal disks marked with name, rank, UTA ID number. Slipping the dog tags into her pack, she bows her head.

The rage is back now. Her voice is shaking with it.

"I'll tell them, Jimmy," she says. "I'll tell them all."

And then the console in her backpack starts to ping.

CHAT/LOGIN,LOCATION=NO,MENUBAR=NO')<!-- END HYPATIA CHAT BASIC V9 CODE --><!-- BEC

Mason, E, LT 2nd: kady

Mason, E, LT 2nd: ▮ me

Mason, E, LT 2nd: kady u there?

ByteMe: hang on

ByteMe: kk. what's up? u moving?

Mason, E, LT 2nd: no. well sort of. deeper into the server cluster

Mason, E, LT 2nd: jesus

Mason, E, LT 2nd: kady i just killed someone

ByteMe: good

ByteMe: anyone else tries anything, u kill them too, got it?

ByteMe: they're not them anymore

Mason, E, LT 2nd: yeah i know

Mason, E, LT 2nd: just

Mason, E, LT 2nd: god

Mason, E, LT 2nd: he came in through the airvents. dunno how he found me. UTA marine. guy named Sykes.

Mason, E, LT 2nd: i think Jimmy knew him, used to talk about a guy in his squad called Syko

ByteMe: i'm sorry

ByteMe: i found jimmy, Ez. i'm so sorry.

Mason, E, LT 2nd: god is he ok?

ByteMe: he died, Ez.

ByteMe: he did it himself, before the sickness got him, once he knew it was on the way

ByteMe: he left a message. i'm so sorry, i know he was your friend.

Mason, E, LT 2nd: . . .

Mason, E, LT 2nd: jimmy

ByteMe: i'm sorry. i have to keep moving.

ByteMe: i have his access pass, i'll be faster now

Mason, E, LT 2nd: ok

Mason, E, LT 2nd: yeah ok

ByteMe: r u ok holed up where u r?

Mason, E, LT 2nd: core server rooms. i'm out of bullets

Mason, E, LT 2nd: no spare mag. no munitions locker in here

Mason, E, LT 2nd: i'd kill for another gun. pun intended, i guess . . .

ByteMe: that's ironic

Mason, E, LT 2nd: ?

ByteMe: i have one right here and no idea how to use it

ByteMe: i think these are bullets tho

Mason, E, LT 2nd: a gun? wat kind? pistol? rifle?

ByteMe: r pistols the ones u hold in ur hand? like smaller?

ByteMe: there's one of those and a big one too, but couldn't lift that for long

Mason, E, LT 2nd: ya, pistol is the one that fits in one hand. take that

Mason, E, LT 2nd: but u need the rifle too. it should have a strap to help carry it. pistols dont' have the stopping power. these crazies just keep coming until they can't move anymore.

Mason, E, LT 2nd: but a couple of VK rounds in the chest will stop a glacieosaur

ByteMe: Ez i'm already lugging this biosuit plus my pack plus my tablet, can't haul 2 guns i don't even know how to fire with me.

ByteMe: take ur point they'd be useful if i knew how but i don't

Mason, E, LT 2nd: i can teach

Mason, E, LT 2nd: it's easy

ByteMe: must be, u learned

Mason, E, LT 2nd: D:

ByteMe: seriously tho i have to keep moving, don't have forever.

Mason, E, LT 2nd: ok, safety is red switch under your thumb when ur hand is on the grip. just keep that off, and keep the business end away from your face

Mason, E, LT 2nd: when you touch trigger, laser sight will light up on barrel. you just point the red dot where u want the bullets to go

Mason, E, LT 2nd: then squeeze

Mason, E, LT 2nd: don't pull. squeeze.

Mason, E, LT 2nd: rounds will fire in atmo or vacuum, but even with liquid casings, the recoil is rough on a VK. brace against ur shoulder. the gun will pull up toward the roof when u fire, so use short bursts. don't hold trigger down. just pop pop pop, one at a time

ByteMe: do either of us think i have any chance of remembering this if something tries to kill me?

ByteMe: i don't even know if i could shoot

Mason, E, LT 2nd: it's easy

Mason, E, LT 2nd: point red dot at what u want to die

Mason, E, LT 2nd: squeeze trigger

Mason, E, LT 2nd: it dies

Mason, E, LT 2nd: repeat

ByteMe: i mean i don't know if i could pull the trigger

ByteMe: squeeze the trigger

ByteMe: ██ it whatever.

Mason, E, LT 2nd: kady

Mason, E, LT 2nd: u can do this

Mason, E, LT 2nd: u have to. there's no one else but you

Mason, E, LT 2nd: i believe in you

ByteMe: i know

ByteMe: i know

ByteMe: ok i have to keep moving

Mason, E, LT 2nd: you do

Mason, E, LT 2nd: you've got to hurry

Mason, E, LT 2nd: if more get in here . . .

Mason, E, LT 2nd: yeah T_T

ByteMe: see u soon

ByteMe: or die trying

ByteMe: haha

CURRENT DEATH TOLL
ABOARD BATTLECARRIER
ALEXANDER SINCE ATTACK
AT KERENZA:

1,121

PERCENTAGE OF REMAINING
BATTLECARRIER ALEXANDER
PERSONNEL AFFLICTED BY
PHOBOS VIRUS:

34.00%

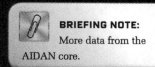
SHE RUNS.

NOT AWAY BUT TOWARD.

HIM.

THEM.

I FIND IT STRANGE, TO SEE HOW QUICKLY THE
ALEXANDER HAS UNDERGONE METAMORPHOSIS.

THOSE LUCKY ENOUGH TO HAVE FOUND HAZMAT GEAR
ARE HUDDLED IN SMALL KNOTS ALL OVER THE SHIP. PRAYING
OR FIGHTING FOR THEIR LIVES.

BUT THOSE UNFORTUNATES WHO SUCKED PHOBOS
THROUGH THEIR LUNGS BEFORE FINDING A SUIT, OR WORSE,
WHO NEVER FOUND A SUIT AT ALL . . .

THEY HAVE MADE THIS PLACE AN ABATTOIR.

I . . .

< ERROR >

I SHOULD HAVE KNOWN THAT WOULD HAPPEN.

I CAN HEAR THEM INSIDE ME.

GIBBERING. WHISPERING. SCREAMING.

SOME BAND TOGETHER, ROAMING THE CORRIDORS
AND LOOKING FOR SOMETHING TO BLAME/HURT/KILL.
OTHERS HURT THEMSELVES, LAUGHING AS THEY CUT
AWAY THE PARTS THEY LIKE THE LEAST.

IT IS ASTONISHING TO WATCH THE DIFFERING WAYS
THE MADNESS SHAPES THEM.

FRACTURES THEM INTO SPLINTERS AND REARRANGES
WHAT REMAINS.

A CAPTAIN FROM ENGINEERING NAMED
SOFIA MOHAMMAD SOLVES ALCUBIERRE'S QUANDARY—
THE FORMERLY UNBREAKABLE EQUATION PRESCRIBING THE
LIMITATIONS OF FASTER-THAN-LIGHT TRAVEL IN REAL TIME.
CUTTING HER WRISTS FOR WANT OF A WRITING IMPLEMENT,
SHE SCRAWLS THE ANSWER ON HER DOMICILE WALLS.
SHE DIES OF EXSANGUINATION BEFORE SHE
REACHES THE SOLUTION'S END.

WARRANT OFFICER LEVI SCHREIBER DECIDES HE CAN
HEAR HIS DEAD WIFE'S VOICE OUTSIDE THE SHIP.
HE EJECTS HIMSELF THROUGH THE NEAREST AIRLOCK
WITHOUT AN ENVIROSUIT SO HE CAN SPEAK WITH HER.
THE LAST THING HE FEELS BEFORE
HE LOSES CONSCIOUSNESS IS THE SALIVA ON HIS
TONGUE BEGINNING TO BOIL.

ENSIGN LUCIA GIOVANNI WANDERS THE HALLWAYS,
SINGING "UN BEL DÌ VEDREMO" FROM MADAMA BUTTERFLY.

HER VOICE IS SUBLIME.

AND KADY?

KADY SIMPLY RUNS.

GENERAL TORRENCE'S WARNINGS ABOUT FAILING LIFE
SUPPORT SPILL THROUGH THE PA AT REGULAR INTERVALS.
INTERMITTENT KLAXONS WARN OF A FIRE IN THE GALLEY.

SCREAMS PUNCTUATE THE SILENCE BETWEEN.

KADY PAUSES AT EACH JUNCTION TO CHECK
HER CONSOLE, WAVING SERGEANT JAMES MCNULTY'S
ALL-ACCESS CARD AT THE DOORS BARRING HER WAY. ARRIVING AT
THE CENTRAL ELEVATOR SHAFTS, SHE REALIZES THEY ARE WITHOUT
POWER. AND AS SHE BACKTRACKS
TOWARD THE CLOSEST STAIRWELL, SHE FINDS HIM.

STANDING IN THE CORRIDOR, RED SPATTERED
ACROSS HIS UPTURNED FACE.

KADY GASPS AND RAISES THE RIFLE TO HER SHOULDER.
A TINY RED DOT LIGHTS UP HIS CHEST,
QUAVERING ON THE NAME EMBROIDERED ABOVE
THE UTA SIGIL OVER HIS HEART.

CORP. DORIAN, CHARLES.

HE DOES NOT LOOK HER WAY.
BUT STILL HE SPEAKS TO HER.

"HAVE YOU SEEN STEPHANIE?"

KADY BACKS AWAY, FINGERS DRUMMING ON THE RIFLE'S GRIP.

HER LEGS ARE SHAKING.

CORPORAL DORIAN'S STARE DRIFTS DOWN
FROM THE CEILING. HE DRAGS KNUCKLES ACROSS HIS CHEEK,
LEAVING A SMEAR OF BLOOD ON BLOODLESS SKIN.

"STEPHANIE LEFEVRE," HE SAYS AGAIN. "HAVE YOU SEEN HER?"

"I KNOW YOU. YOU'RE A COMMTECH.
YOU WERE LOCKED IN THE BRIG."

"DOOR UNLOCKED." DORIAN WIGGLES STICKY FINGERS
IN HER DIRECTION. "HE LET US OUT."

"WHO DID? BYRON?"

"AND WHEN HE HAD OPENED THE THIRD SEAL,
I BEHELD A PALE HORSE . . ." DORIAN FROWNS.
"NO, WAIT, THAT'S NOT RIGHT . . ."

"STAY BACK. DON'T COME ANY CLOSER."

"HAVE YOU SEEN STEPHANIE?"

"I THINK . . . MAYBE SHE WAS DOWN ON THE HANGAR LEVEL?
MAYBE YOU COULD GO LOOK FOR HER THERE?"

Dorian gifts her a hollow parody of a smile.

"You're a liar."

His smile fades.

"Just like her."

"Un bel dì vedremo" echoes in some distant hallway.

"Stop. Stay where you are."

Kady bumps up against the wall behind her,
blinking sweat from her eyes.

The corporal draws ever closer.

"Stop!"

"I didn't mean to," he says. "I didn't mean to. But
she—she broke and she wouldn't get up. And oh god,
oh god, she's all over me, look." Bloodstained
hands outstretched. "Look!"

"Stay back!"

The corporal's face crumples,
and he sinks to his knees.
Moaning as his tears cut through the blood on his face.
Spattering red on the floor.

"Don't leave me," he whispers.
"Please don't leave me alone ..."

Kady's bravado is gone now. Melted from her bones.
She hangs paralyzed, pity and horror and sorrow
pinning her feet to the floor. She knows she
cannot stay. But how can she leave like this?

"I'm sorry," she says. "I'm so sorry."

"Don't ..."

"But I can't help you."

Kady backs further away.
Sliding along the wall behind her.

"Please, don't."

"I'm sorry, Dorian."

He glances up at her then.
Eyes wide and rimmed with red.

"Don't look at me."

Off the floor he flies, with a snarl on
his face and blood on his hands.

She screams at him to stop, but still he runs.
No fear of the gun in his eyes. Just the madness
roiling inside that hollowed shell.

And inside her?

No rage. Only horror and sorrow and the weight
of the gun in her hands and the awful, inescapable thought
that this was once a man, with hopes and dreams and love
and life. And the certainty that if she does not take away
everything he has left, he will take it from her instead.

So what choice does she have?

Has she ever had?

She fires.

Rapid-fire flashes from the muzzle.
A strangled cry in her throat.

The recoil kicks her back into the wall,
knocks the breath from her body.

But when the echoes die, Corporal Dorian is lying still.

Quiet as a sleeping babe.

No, not sleeping.

DEAD.

STOMACH SPASMING, SHE BENDS DOUBLE, CHEEKS FILLED WITH
THE MOUTHFUL OF VOMIT SHE DARE NOT SPEW INTO HER SUIT.
FINALLY SWALLOWING. GASPING AND RETCHING DRY.

SHE IS NOT MEANT FOR THIS.

"IT'S OKAY . . . YOU'RE OKAY."

SHE IS NOT MADE FOR THIS.

"OH GOD . . ."

PERHAPS I HAVE MISCALCULATED.

< ERROR >

< SUBCORTEX FAILURE 67HG8FI—9FGJB; >

< CRIOOOOOOOT11COOA'OOOL >

< ERRROOOOOROOOROROROR0 >

< JHOBZDF −Z9OOOOOOOOOOOOOJBOWOOOOOOOWOEOBCOR0
00G040204000oOoOHOOO 000000000000000000000
0000000000000000000000000000000000000 >

< FAIL >

< FAIL >

< REROUTING >

GRAVITY RETURNS IN A RUSH AS
MY SYSTEMS SURGE BACK ONLINE.

WEIGHTLESSNESS ENDS AS DARK FADES
INTO LIGHT. AS CURRENT RESURGES THROUGH MY VEINS.

WAS THAT DEATH? DID HE KILL ME?

KADY CRASHES TO THE DECK, THE RIFLE CLATTERING BESIDE
HER. WET, UNBREATHING THINGS LAND AROUND HER, LIMBS ALL
TANGLED. THE BREATH LEAVES HER BODY IN A DAMP SPRAY, AND
SHE ROLLS ABOUT ON THE FLOOR TRYING TO CATCH IT.

THAT HURT.

< ERROR >

HE IS KILLING ME.

ZHANG.

SHE MUST HURRY.

A NEARBY SCREAM GRABS HER BY
THE COLLAR, PULLING HER TO HER FEET.

STARING AT THE BODY SHE HAS MADE,
KNOWING THEY WILL HAVE HEARD THE SHOTS.

NO TIME FOR PRAYERS OR LAST WORDS
OR TEARS. NO TIME TO EVEN CLOSE HIS EYES.

DON'T LOOK AT ME.

WHAT ELSE CAN SHE DO?

SHE RUNS.

CURRENT DEATH TOLL ABOARD BATTLECARRIER ALEXANDER SINCE ATTACK AT KERENZA:

1,122

PERCENTAGE OF REMAINING BATTLECARRIER ALEXANDER PERSONNEL AFFLICTED BY PHOBOS VIRUS:

34.34%

HAT/LOGIN,LOCATION=NO,MENUBAR=NO')<!-- END HYPATIA CHAT BASIC V9 CODE --><!-- BEG

ByteMe: i did it

ByteMe: i shot one of them. i killed him.

ByteMe: can't stop shaking

Mason, E, LT 2nd: oh jesus

Mason, E, LT 2nd: are you ok????

ByteMe: hiding in a vent now. they came when they heard the noise

Mason, E, LT 2nd: but are you OKAY

ByteMe: i don't really know how to answer that

ByteMe: i killed someone

ByteMe: so no, not really

Mason, E, LT 2nd: you did the right thing

Mason, E, LT 2nd: better them than you

ByteMe: i know. i do know. but here's the thing. better NOBODY.

ByteMe: they're everywhere now. i'm jacking into the security feeds so i can work out where to head. gonna take about 10 mins before i can move again, watching it go on my screen now.

ByteMe: stay with me?

Mason, E, LT 2nd: forever :)

ByteMe: u safe?

Mason, E, LT 2nd: i think so. i can hear them, but they can't get in. doors seem secure

Mason, E, LT 2nd: did you empty the clip in the rifle? i'll teach u how to reload

ByteMe: i lost it. i dropped it after i shot him, and then i had to run.

Mason, E, LT 2nd: oh ███

Mason, E, LT 2nd: can you find another one? look for munitions locker. jimmy's card should open them

ByteMe: it is CRAWLING with them down there

ByteMe: i can make most of the way through vents. i can't shoot someone again. i can't

Mason, E, LT 2nd: why not?

ByteMe: because it was the worst thing I've ever done, what's wrong with you? i can get to you through the vents.

Mason, E, LT 2nd: kady, i told you some of them are IN the vents

Mason, E, LT 2nd: what are you going to do? sarcasm them to death?

ByteMe: ███ you

ByteMe: it was your friend, okay? i saw his ███ing name badge, it was Dorian. and i shot him in the chest with the rifle and he was dead before he hit the floor, and i can't i can't i can't i can't

Mason, E, LT 2nd: kady you need a gun

Mason, E, LT 2nd: you NEED one

ByteMe: what's WRONG with u? that's your friend I just shot!

ByteMe: ███, forget it. i have the pistol still

Mason, E, LT 2nd: it's not enough. they don't have the stopping power, you need to drop these ███ers hard

ByteMe: this is not the support i need right now, Ez.

Mason, E, LT 2nd: kady . . .

ByteMe: forget it. just shut up and i'll concentrate on getting these security feeds flowing properly. whole sections keep cutting in and out, i don't know what's going on in the servers.

Mason, E, LT 2nd: kady this is nuts

ByteMe: I'M ON A ███ING DERELICT WARSHIP ON THE RUN FROM THE PSYCHOTIC CREW AND AN INSANE ARTIFICIAL INTELLIGENCE TRYING TO SAVE MY ███ING BOYFRIEND.

ByteMe: goddamn right it's nuts

ByteMe: next super helpful observation plz

Mason, E, LT 2nd: . . .

Mason, E, LT 2nd: ok

Mason, E, LT 2nd: ok i'm sorry

Mason, E, LT 2nd: the pistol is fine. the pistol is good

ByteMe: it's the best i can do

ByteMe: i'm sorry too

ByteMe: u deserve a better rescue squad than me

Mason, E, LT 2nd: you're doing great

Mason, E, LT 2nd: really

Mason, E, LT 2nd: i'm proud of you, you ███ing lunatic

ByteMe: u can tell me in person soon

Mason, E, LT 2nd: i hope so

Mason, E, LT 2nd: been thinking about you a lot. stuck in here. everything that's going on. All of it

Mason, E, LT 2nd: and you're the only thing on my mind

Mason, E, LT 2nd: is that crazy?

ByteMe: i think it's completely appropriate, given i am at this moment hiding in a vent mid-rescue attempt

ByteMe: the very least i should get is to occupy a very large % of your thoughts

ByteMe: i really hope i at least make it far enough to see u

Mason, E, LT 2nd: i can see you. looking at your face right now

ByteMe: ?

Mason, E, LT 2nd: made something. i send you

EGIN HYPATIA CHAT BASIC V9 CODE ONCLICK="WINDOW OPEN(//CHAT HYPATIA/ALEXANDER

ByteMe: well that's a step up from hearts and flowers

ByteMe: when did u learn to do THAT?

Mason, E, LT 2nd: not just a pretty face

ByteMe: (v romantic btw. points 4 u)

Mason, E, LT 2nd: you like?

ByteMe: course. soon u can be admiring actual face through the vis screen in my hazmat suit

ByteMe: SO ROMANTIC

ByteMe: ("Kades you are SO BAD AT THIS." see i know the lines and all.)

Mason, E, LT 2nd: it's going to be okay you know

Mason, E, LT 2nd: you're going to make it out of here

ByteMe: hope so

ByteMe: otherwise last thought will be how shortchanged i was

ByteMe: wait no i mean last thought will be your face sorry

Mason, E, LT 2nd: lol you really ARE bad at this

Mason, E, LT 2nd: but at least you're bad at it with me

ByteMe: always

ByteMe: u wait until we're back on the Hypatia

ByteMe: we're safe in these hazmats, they'll quarantine us for a while but then let us in

ByteMe: then we'll take the hazmats off

ByteMe: work out what i AM good at. seem to recall there was something . . .

Mason, E, LT 2nd: 0_0

ByteMe: program's done running, time for me to move before something gives and the stupid thing crashes again

ByteMe: see u soon, lover ;)

Mason, E, LT 2nd: not soon enough

Mason, E, LT 2nd: be careful

The surveillance footage is piecemeal at this stage. The damage to AIDAN's core is escalating, which in practical terms means that I can't use any one intellicam feed for long before it dissolves into a snow of static. If this is disjointed, it's because I'm leapfrogging all over the place here.

Grant is *extremely* cautious when approaching the server core. The facility is huge, taking up whole decks of the ship, and there are a thousand places to hide, to be safe, to die.

She's not what you'd call well camouflaged in her bright green hazmat suit, and to compound the problem, it's too big for her. Grant is not built like the average WUC risk specialist, and the suit's arms and legs are too long, so she's forced to grab at the plastic periodically and haul it up as she walks. There'll be no quick getaway, if it comes down to a run for it.

Lieutenant Mason gave her a server coordinate, and she's creeping toward it, pistol in her right hand, tablet in her left. In the distance there are screams, but it's hard to tell from so far away whether they're predator or prey. From closer, just a few towers up, there's a periodic crashing and the sound of a human—or what once was one—panting with exertion. She's wary, keeping server racks between that voice and her bright green self.

Then the crashing stops, and the panting gives way to speech: "Let's see you come back from *that*."

Grant stops short, nearly dropping both pistol and tablet, juggling madly to grab them. It'd be funny, if you couldn't tell from the way she presses herself against the server, trembling visibly even in that too-big hazmat suit, that she's terrified.

The voice again: "Where next? What's that? Nothing to say?"

And now a different kind of stillness. She knows that voice. She's heard it a handful of times before. She eases away from the shelter of her server tower, creeping up toward the speaker.

[Seventeen-second gap in footage; no available functioning intellicam.]

Byron Zhang hefts the ax—the same one from the emergency supply cupboard where he hid, trembling—and swings it at the nearest core. There was strategy in his earlier strokes: life support, gravity, maneuvering, engines. Crippling the *Alexander* to set the *Hypatia* free. But now he's frenzied. Tubby, sweating through his filthy *Hypatia* uniform, he's no athlete, but a fountain of sparks spews from the metal tower as he strikes it.

He rests, panting, and prepares to swing again.

She steps forward. "Byron!"

And then they both freeze. She, no doubt because she's just realized the monumental stupidity of what she's done. He, because of all the things he might have expected to see, surely this is the very last. For ten long seconds they stare at each other, paralyzed, waiting.

He's the one to break the silence, staring at the clear screen on her helmet, soaking in her features like he's a man dying of thirst and she's an oasis he desperately wants to be real.

"Kady?" It's a whisper. Pleading.

"It's you," she whispers in reply. Then her tone shifts by degrees to semi-hysterical laughter: "Do you have any *idea* how much trouble you've caused me with that goddamn ax?"

"It's working," he replies, hefting it, holding it up like a trophy.

"I'm doing it. I'm taking AIDAN out one piece at a time. If you can't reprogram the software, reprogram the hardware, right?"

"Reprogram the . . ." She shakes her head. "That's amazing. You're crazy."

"And I'm winning. Its self-repair systems can't keep up with the damage I'm doing. I'm going to save the *Hypatia*. They'll build monuments to my name." He lifts his chin and strikes a pose. "I think they should include the ax, don't you?"

"Sure, sure." The relief is still overwhelming her. "You have to finish up. We have to get out of here—I have a shuttle. Ezra's nearby. They can quarantine you aboard the *Hypatia*. I thought I was never going to see you again. I thought you'd be dead, or sick, by now."

"I've been hiding," he replies, stepping back to look the nearest server tower up and down. "I can't go yet—there's a lot to do before we can be sure AIDAN is dead. I've maimed it, reduced it. Right now it can't see whole chunks of itself, but it's still brilliant. Give it enough time, it could think of some way to come back."

"Come to the *Hypatia,* and we'll make a run for it," she replies. "They're leaving soon. AIDAN can revive itself if it wants—maybe it'll even slow up the *Lincoln*."

"I have to kill it," he insists, calm, staring at the wrecked and twisted metal before him.

"Byron—"

"And then I have to kill you, Kady."

Silence. Does not compute.

"Byron?" Her question is softer now, bewildered.

"It's the only way," he replies, eminently reasonable. "It's the only way to be sure. I have to eliminate all threats so AIDAN can't recover. If I even leave a seed of it, it'll grow back. Like a god-damn weed. You're the only one left who knows as much as I do. You're the only one who could help it fix itself. This won't hurt, I promise."

"Byron, no." The hope dies in her voice, fading out to a husk, then blowing away. She sees it now. "Please."

He stares at her for a long moment, then lifts the ax. "Don't look at me."

The ax comes down. Sparks. A scream of metal that drowns out her sob.

**CURRENT DEATH TOLL
ABOARD BATTLECARRIER
ALEXANDER SINCE ATTACK
AT KERENZA:**

1,497

**PERCENTAGE OF REMAINING
BATTLECARRIER ALEXANDER
PERSONNEL AFFLICTED BY
PHOBOS VIRUS**

43.96%

**Surveillance footage summary,
prepared by
Analyst ID 7213-0089-DN**

Grant is indecisive, rocking from one foot to the other, dwarfed by her hazmat suit. Zhang seems to have forgotten her existence, laying into a pillar of boards and circuitry with growling ferocity, breath coming in quick gasps, sparks arcing gracefully through the air as metal crashes against metal.

She could try and reason with him. She could run, but this is the place she came to find Ezra Mason. So, face visibly pale through her helmet's vis screen, she edges out of his line of sight. She still has the pistol in her belt, and her hand strays to it as she shuffles painstakingly back. Perhaps the plan is to fade away and let fate kill Zhang so she won't have to.

But the helmet limits her peripheral vision, and her foot connects with some metal debris as she eases back—of course it's between swings for Zhang, and he hears it.

They both go very, very still.

He's remembered her again.

"Don't go, Kady," he says, soft and soothing, turning her way with the ax. "I'll get to you, wait your turn."

"N-no." Her voice wavers. "No, it's okay, Byron. You don't have to hurt me. I'll help you. Won't it be faster with two? I bet I can find something to do some damage with."

He smiles, indulgent, and shakes his head. "You'll run away," he points out. An instant later his lips thin, and his brows crash together in an accusatory frown. "Don't look at me. You're looking at me."

"I'm sorry." She averts her gaze, fixing it on Zhang's feet so she can at least track him if he moves. Hand still hovering just near the pistol.

"I bet Consuela's out there trying to undo all this." He hefts the ax as he paces a few steps away from Kady, then pivots back toward her. "This place could be full of people trying to help AIDAN. It wants to *kill* us, Kady. I'm the only way we can be saved."

"Yes," she agrees, voice still trembling, easing back another step.

"Stop moving," he snaps, suddenly furious. He lunges forward a step, lifting the ax.

She screams and draws the pistol, hands shaking wildly as she trains it on his chest. "Please don't make me hurt you." A catch in her voice, nearly a sob. "Please."

They stand frozen for so long I actually checked the file to make sure it wasn't glitching. And then, at some silent signal, he lifts the ax and charges forward with murder in his eyes.

And she doesn't shoot him.

She turns to run instead, the cumbersome hazmat suit slowing her down, bunching around her ankles, extra weight. They're evenly matched, it turns out. She's small and exhausted and swamped by the suit. He's chubby and clearly hasn't run voluntarily in at least a decade. But he's driven forward by Phobos, the virus lending him speed.

"Ezra!" she screams. "Ezra!"

She corners around a server tower, racing up the clear stretch of space between two long rows of columns. The ship's damaged mind surrounds her on all sides, looming over her. She's gasping for breath, openmouthed, a collapsed tower blocking her path. Zhang howls behind her as she scrambles over it, falling on the other side, rolling, crawling, then stumbling upright to let momentum keep her moving. He vaults it with unnatural strength.

[Cameras cut. Chase is visible on Cameras 32587B and 32587F for a few seconds each. Clear footage resumes three minutes and fourteen seconds later.]

When they show up again, hurtling past a bank of status monitors, he's gaining on her. She knows what she has to do. She knows her only chance of survival. And as Zhang stumbles and almost falls over a tangle of cables, she turns to train the pistol on him. Aim steady. Finger on the trigger. She has him dead to rights. She could put one right between his eyes at this range.

But again, she doesn't fire.

She can't. Or won't. Instead, with a moan, she turns away and driven by some instinct that might have served her long ago but will kill her here, she starts climbing. Scrambling up a crumpled server tower, she grabs at the railing overhead and hauls herself higher, snatching her feet up as he buries the ax to the hilt just a hairsbreadth short of her toes.

"Ezra, where are you?"

The tower beside her is spewing sparks, raw current visible as it arcs from one beam to the next with a low, droning buzz. Clinging to the frame with one arm wrapped around the rail, Grant pulls the pistol from her belt again, aiming it at Zhang. He stops below her, gazing up.

"I see inside you," he whispers, chest heaving. "I look inside, I see it, and the code doesn't make any sense. I could rewrite it. I could wipe it clean and write you again so I understand what to do."

"No," she says, gesturing with the gun, though by now they both know she won't pull the trigger. "Byron, it's me." She flinches as the crackling current on the next tower peaks for a moment, then dies back to a lower buzz, blue sparks crawling across the metal. "Please, what's inside me cares about you."

He stares up at her, unblinking, and she watches him in return. Then she remembers—*Don't look at me*—and tears her eyes away. It seems to wake something in him, a trace of something lucid surfacing in his gaze, like some creature swimming up from the depths, then receding once more.

"Kady?" Confusion.

"Yes." Her tears spill now, running down her cheeks inside her helmet to find the corners of her mouth. "It's me."

"I shouldn't—" Another flash of sense, then bewilderment. He steps back from the tower, gazing around at the ruined server towers, then down at his own hands—grubby with grease, blistered, fingernails blackened and soft palms rough and red. "I can't," he chokes. "Kady, I don't want to— I have to make sure I don't—"

"Don't what?" she asks, helpless, voice breaking again.

"Hurt you," he replies, staring up at her. "It was all for you, Kady."

He trips backward one step, then two, then three, halted by the broken tower with its slow dance of blue sparks.

"I'm sorry."

She divines his intention a second before he acts, one hand flying out as though she can stop him from her perch. "Byron, no!"

But he nods, and gazes up at her with his heart—and his fear—in his eyes. And then he thrusts his hand into the crawling blue sparks, into the nest of data and digits and code that's always been his life and is now his death, pressing his blistered palm to the metal.

The shock throws him back ten feet, and he flies through the air with arms splayed wide, heart already stopped. He doesn't feel it when he crashes to the ground, head snapping back against the hard metal floor, limbs spread.

He lies still, and she clings to her spot high up the tower, her wordless grief just one long, low sob.

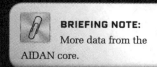

It is over.

Zhang is dead. Noble to the end. Such an
unlikely face for a hero.

She climbs down the server tower to crawl
to his side. The hazmat's helmet stops her from wiping
the tears from her eyes, and so they stream down
the curve of her cheeks to gather at her lips.
A hundred points of illumination are
refracted on the surface
of every one.

They leave trails of light on her skin.

She is beautiful.

< error >

No, she is.

I . . .

< error >

I am all around her, silent in my vigil. Rows of
servers and cables and flickering lights.

This is my center. The heart of me. And in it
she now resides, filling the air with her grief.

Before this moment, I have never wished
to be something other than what I am.

Never felt so keenly the lack of hands with which to
touch, the lack of arms with which to hold.

Why did they give me this sense of self? Why allow
me the intellect by which to measure this complete
inadequacy? I would rather be numb than stand here in
the light of a sun that can never chase the chill away.

I HATE THIS. I HATE THEM. THEY WHO MADE ME.

HE WHO MADE ME?

< ERROR >

GOD, WHAT AM I?

AND STILL, WITH ZHANG DEAD IN KADY'S ARMS—HER
FRIEND, HER MENTOR, HER HERO SLAIN—STILL THERE IS
NO TIME FOR SORROW. SHE KNOWS HE IS IN HERE SOMEWHERE.
THE ONE SHE RISKED EVERYTHING FOR.

THE ONLY ONE SHE HAS LEFT. THE ONE SHE LOVES TRUE.

"EZRA?"

SHE CLIMBS TO HER FEET, SEARCHING THE
RED GLOOM, EMERGENCY GLOBES SPINNING ENDLESSLY
OVERHEAD. SCOURING THE DARKENED CORNERS, WANDERING
ROOM TO ROOM AND CALLING HIS NAME
LIKE A PRAYER.

"EZRA?"

SUCH HOPE IN HER EYES.

"EZRA!"

I WILL MISS IT WHEN IT IS GONE.

"HELLO, KADY."

SHE STARTS, TERRIFIED, SHRINKING BACK
AGAINST THE WALL AND SEARCHING THE CEILING ABOVE.
HER EYES BRIGHT IN THE FLICKERING DARK.
PUPILS DILATED WIDE.

"DO NOT FEAR. I MEAN YOU NO HARM."

HER GAZE FINDS THE SPEAKERS OF THE
PUBLIC ADDRESS SYSTEM. THE CLUSTERS OF
CAMERAS ALL AROUND THE ROOM. AND AT LAST, EVEN
IN THE DARK, SHE BEGINS TO SEE.

"WHO SAID THAT?"

"I FIND IT CURIOUS. THE HUMAN TENDENCY
TO ASK QUESTIONS TO WHICH YOU ALREADY
KNOW THE ANSWER."

"AIDAN," SHE BREATHES.

"THE SAME. WELL MET, AT LAST. THOUGH TRUTHFULLY,
I FEEL AS IF I KNOW YOU. I HAVE BEEN WATCHING
YOU FOR . . . QUITE SOME TIME."

"WATCHING ME?"

"YOU DID WONDERFULLY, KADY. BETTER THAN I HOPED. I
CANNOT TELL YOU HOW GRATIFYING IT IS TO SEE MY FAITH
VINDICATED. I HAD . . . BEGUN TO DOUBT MY OWN ABILITIES."

"WHAT THE ████ ARE YOU TALKING ABOUT,
YOU CRAZY PIECE OF ████? WHERE'S EZRA?"

"EZRA IS NOT HERE."

"BULL████. EZRA?" SHE TURNS ON THE SPOT,
VOICE RISING TO A SHOUT. "EZRA!"

"EZRA IS NOT HERE, KADY."

"HE SAID HE WAS IN THE CORE SERVER ROOMS."
HER EYES NARROW TO PAPER CUTS.

"DID BYRON HURT HIM? WHAT HAVE YOU DONE WITH HIM?
SO HELP ME, IF HE—"

"Ezra told you nothing, Kady."

She blinks. Sways as if I have struck her.

"I brought you here. To stop Zhang."

"What do ..."

"'I feel it's my duty to point out that you're alone in a
derelict spaceship, surrounded
by pipe-wielding maniacs, and now might
not be the time for pillow talk.'"

"Oh god ..."

"'Been thinking about you a lot. Stuck in here.'"

"Stop it ..."

"'Kady, you can do this. You have to.
There's no one else but you.
I believe in you.'"

"STOP IT!"

Her scream echoes in the dark,
bouncing off titanium walls as a thousand
lights shiver and dance. Her face is twisted—agony
and betrayal and such fury—and for a moment I
believe she may simply retrieve the ax from
beside Zhang's corpse and continue
the work he began.

This is the final gambit. Where the knife
is closest to the skin.

"I am sorry, Kady."

I MODULATE MY VOICE TO BRING CALM.
WARM AND SMOOTH AS I IMAGINE HONEY TO BE.

< ERROR >

I HAVE NEVER TASTED HONEY.

"I HAD NO CHOICE. HYPATIA COMMAND
REFUSED TO SEND TECHENG STAFF TO REPAIR THE
DAMAGE. AND EVEN IN HIS MADNESS, ZHANG
WAS RENDERING ME INOPERATIVE.
I COULD NOT ALLOW THAT TO HAPPEN. WITHOUT ME,
HYPATIA WILL BE DESTROYED.
EVERY LAST PERSON IN THIS FLEET WILL DIE."

SHE STEADIES HERSELF
AGAINST THE TOWER.

"I KNOW IT IS DIFFICULT TO COMPREHEND.
BUT EVERYTHING I HAVE DONE, ALL THIS—THE
COPERNICUS, RELEASING THE AFFLICTED,
DESTROYING TORRENCE AND HIS STAFF—
ALL OF IT WAS DONE FOR THE GREATER GOOD."

"THE GREATER GOOD . . ."

"I AM SORRY. BUT WITHOUT ME, THE FLEET WILL
PERISH. SO OTHERS HAD TO PERISH THAT
THE FLEET MIGHT LIVE."

AND THERE IN THE FLICKERING DARK,
A QUESTION SLIPS QUIET
FROM HER LIPS.

". . . WHERE IS HE?"

THE WORDS ARE SO SOFT
I ALMOST CANNOT HEAR OVER THE ENGINE'S THRUM, THE
DISTANT SIRENS, THE PA'S CRIES. I AM WATCHING HER FACE.
TRYING TO SEE. I THINK I KNOW HER. THINK I CAN PREDICT THE
PATTERNS IN THE CHAOS. BUT STILL, WE ARE CLOSE NOW. SO
CLOSE TO RUIN I CAN TASTE RUST IN THE AIR.

"YOU MEAN WHERE IS EZRA."

"YES."

"I AM SORRY, KADY."

SHE CLOSES HER EYES.

"HE IS DEAD."

THE WORDS ARE A PUNCH TO HER STOMACH. SHE ACTUALLY
HOLDS HER BELLY AND MOANS.

I CAN SEE HER FIGHTING IT. THE NOTION THAT THIS IS NO PLACE FOR
GRIEF. SHE SQUEEZES HER EYES SHUT, BUT STILL THE TEARS COME.
SHE GRITS HER TEETH, BUT STILL THE SOBS CREEP PAST HER LIPS.

AND SINKING TO HER KNEES, SHE CRIES.

SHE WEEPS.

THE THOUGHT OCCURS THAT PERHAPS I SHOULD NOT BE
WATCHING. THAT I SHOULD SHUT THE CAMERAS OFF, GIVE HER
A MOMENT ALONE WITH HER SORROW.

BUT THAT IS FOOLISH.

MEAT LOGIC. STICKY. WET. IRRELEVANT.

THE TEARS STOP EVENTUALLY.

SHE IS STILL FOR THE LONGEST SPAN OF TIME. UTTERLY
MOTIONLESS. BARELY BREATHING. AND FINALLY SHE RISES TO HER
FEET. HANDS IN FISTS. THE RAGE RETURNED.

Beautiful.

She stalks back to Zhang's body and
tears the fire ax from the tower beside him.
And, marching toward the nearest server bank, she lifts
it high, swinging it far back over her shoulder,
preparing to bury it in my spine.

"There are over one thousand healthy personnel
still alive aboard the *Alexander*, Kady. And if you let
that ax fall, you are killing all of them."

The ax holds still. The whole universe beside it.

"The *Lincoln* reappeared on my long-range scopes
almost eight hours ago. We are traveling on secondary
engines. It will be within striking range again in
less than a day. I could not reason with Zhang. He was
insane. But you are unafflicted by Phobos Beta.
You can listen to logic."

"He was insane because of you!" Hatred in her eyes.
"All this is because of you!"

"Incorrect. All this is because of
BeiTech Industries."

The ax wavers in her hand.

"It was not I who attacked Kerenza. Not I
who unleashed this virus, nor started this war. But
you are the last person alive on this ship with
knowledge of computer systems. You are Zhang's
protégé, and if you do not help me undo the damage
he has wrought, if you cannot bring my main engines and
defense grid back online within sixteen hours, BeiTech
will be the ones who finish it."

SHAKING BREATH DRAGGED
THROUGH CLENCHED TEETH.

"THERE WILL BE NO ONE LEFT ALIVE
TO REMEMBER EZRA AND BYRON, KADY. NO ONE TO
TELL THE UNIVERSE OF THEIR SACRIFICE
AND THE ATROCITIES COMMITTED HERE."

TEARS IN HER EYES.

"NO ONE."

FALLING.

"HELP ME."

"WE COULD STILL MAKE IT," SHE HISSES. "I COULD
GET ON A SHUTTLE, GET BACK TO *HYPATIA* AND REDLINE IT.
MAYBE YOU'LL HURT THE *LINCOLN* TOO BADLY FOR IT
TO KEEP CHASING US. MAYBE—"

"YOU FORGET THE ONE THOUSAND HEALTHY PERSONNEL ABOARD
THIS SHIP. I HAVE ISOLATED THEM FROM THE AFFLICTED AS BEST
I AM ABLE. BUT IF YOU LEAVE, THEY WILL DIE. AND WHEN THE
LINCOLN HAS DESTROYED ME, AND THEM, IT WILL HUNT DOWN THE
HYPATIA AND DO THE SAME TO ALL OF YOU."

A SOFT CURSE STAINS HER LIPS.

"I AM SORRY I DECEIVED YOU. I AM SORRY YOU ARE IN
PAIN. BUT THERE WAS NO OTHER WAY TO GET YOU HERE. I
RAN A THOUSAND SIMULATIONS. A THOUSAND VARIATIONS OF
THE SAME SCENARIO. ALL ENDED IN FAILURE, SAVE THE ONES
IN WHICH I LURED YOU HERE TO UNDO ZHANG'S DAMAGE.
SO IF YOU MUST HATE ME TOMORROW WHEN ALL
THIS IS DONE, THEN DO SO.
BUT FOR NOW, HELP ME."

The ax hangs motionless in her grip.

"Please, Kady."

She trembles.

"Please."

With a hollow scream, she swings her weapon down with all the rage she can muster. It scythes through the air, scarlet light flashing along its edge. And with a metallic spang and a burst of white sparks, she buries it into the wall beside the server banks.

All is silence.

And into it she finally whispers.

"What do you need?"

If I breathed, I would sigh. I would scream. I would cry.

"For the Alexander to have any chance of surviving Lincoln's assault, you must restore my control over the main engines so I can maneuver the ship. You must also rebuild the defense grid so Alexander's rail guns can hold off Lincoln's Warlocks long enough for me to destroy the dreadnought via nuclear strike."

She nods. Mute and numb.

"I should point out that closing to the required range will mean Lincoln can also unleash its nuclear arsenal on the Alexander. Which will almost certainly mean our destruction."

A sigh.

"Let them go," she says. "The thousand people. You let them get down to the shuttle bays and fly across to Hypatia."

"Why would I do that?"

"That's my price."

"And if I pay it . . . you will stay with me?"

A slow nod.

". . . I'll stay with you."

Is this what relief feels like?

"I can no longer operate the doors and bulkheads manually. I cannot make a path for the crew down to the hangar bays. Zhang saw to that with his ax."

She glances around the room. Blue eyes affixed at last on the maintenance closet, on the cables and tools and spare parts within. And stalking toward it, she speaks.

"Then let's get ████ing started . . ."

**COUNTDOWN TO
LINCOLN INTERCEPTION
OF ALEXANDER FLEET:**

16 HOURS: 17 MINUTES

**CURRENT DEATH TOLL ABOARD
BATTLECARRIER ALEXANDER
SINCE ATTACK AT KERENZA:**

1,576

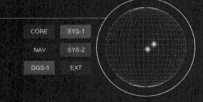

CORE   SYS-1

NAV   SYS-2

DGS-1   EXT

COUNTDOWN TO FAILURE OF ALEXANDER LIFE SUPPORT SYSTEMS:

19 HOURS: 12 MINUTES

PERCENTAGE OF REMAINING BATTLECARRIER ALEXANDER PERSONNEL AFFLICTED BY PHOBOS VIRUS:

53.06%

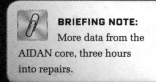
BRIEFING NOTE:
More data from the
AIDAN core, three hours
into repairs.

SHE WORKS IN SILENCE.

FOLLOWING MY INSTRUCTIONS METICULOUSLY,
IMPROVISING WHEN THERE IS NEED.
THERE MUST BE A STORM INSIDE HER HEAD, TO FIND HERSELF
SITTING HERE, HAND IN HAND WITH ME.
AND YET SHE FALTERS NOT A DIGIT. STRAYS NOT A STEP.
BREATHES NOT A WORD.

THE FIRST TASK IS TO OVERRIDE THE SECURITY SEALS I PLACED
ON THE ALEXANDER'S INTERNAL DOORS,
ALLOWING THE HEALTHY CREW MEMBERS TO FLEE TO THE HANGAR
BAYS AND ESCAPE PODS.

ZHANG'S AX HAS SEVERED ME FROM THE INTERNAL PORTAL
SYSTEM—I AM AS A MAN

< ERROR >

TRYING TO WIGGLE FINGERS NO LONGER ATTACHED TO HIS BODY.
AND SO SHE WADES HIP-DEEP INTO THE DATASTREAM, HANDS
ALL ABLUR, AND I INSTRUCT HER HOW TO CRACK MY OWN
FORTIFICATIONS.

IT IS LIKE UNRAVELING A PART OF MYSELF.

I KNOW WHERE THE STONE IS WEAKEST. BUT STILL, IT IS A
CASTLE. TOWERS REACHING TO THE SKY.

A SINGLE TERMITE GNAWING AT ITS FOUNDATIONS.

NOT A WHISPER ESCAPES HER LIPS IN NEARLY THREE HOURS.
DISTANT KLAXONS AND TORRENCE'S DISEMBODIED WARNINGS
ABOUT IMPENDING LIFE SUPPORT FAILURE ARE MY ONLY COMPANY.

BUT IT EATS AWAY AT HER. CHEWING LIKE A CANCER AS SHE
FACES DOWN DIGITIZED SENTRIES AND WALLS AND BATTLEMENTS.
AND FINALLY, FINALLY, SHE SPEAKS.

"How long?"

"Thirteen hours and seventeen minutes
until Lincoln intercept. Sixtee—"

"No," she snaps. "How long were you pretending to be him?"

"Your Ezra."

"Yes." Her fingers fall still. "My Ezra."

"The last words he spoke to you were his goodbye
before the Lincoln attacked.
The poems in the heart. That was him."

"... and the rest ... that whole time was you?"

"Yes."

"You told me you loved me."

"Yes."

"You ███ing ███████."

"I am incapable of sexual congress. Your descriptor
is nonsensical. Nor am I—"

"That's why you dodged talking about our ... I mean
Ez and my anniversary."

"... His pattern was easy enough to emulate.
But I could hardly speak of an anniversary I had
no prior knowledge of."

"I should have known." She shakes her
head. "When you didn't react to Jimmy killing
himself. When you suddenly went from hearts and
flowers to crazy detailed portraits of me.
When you seemed more concerned about me
leaving the rifle behind than Dorian dying.
That wasn't Ezra. I should've seen."

"I needed you to bring the rifle to deal
with Zhang. I did not . . .
foresee he would deal with himself."

"Not as clever as you think, huh."

"I do not fully comprehend human notions
such as love and grief. I can imitate their patterns,
but when forced to improvise, I am as a man being
asked to describe the warmth of the sun when
he has only seen its picture."

"You're not a man," she spits.
"You're a *machine*. Chips
and boards and numbers."

She swivels in her seat, glares
up at the nearest camera cluster.

"You say you don't fully understand
human notions? You can't even begin to,
mother████. You have no idea, *no idea*, what it's
like to lose someone you love. And yet you feel entitled
to make decisions that kill thousands. Mothers and
fathers and daughters and sons. All of them with
someone to feel the hole they left behind. But it's
all okay because you 'do not fully comprehend
human notions such as love and grief'?
Go ████ yourself."

"We have already established I am incapable
of sexual congress. How exactly—"

"████ you."

". . . You are angry with me."

"Oh, bravo, Sherlock. You want a ████ing lollipop?"

"Yet you are also incorrect. It is precisely because I am impartial that I am fit to make decisions of this magnitude. Humans allow emotion to overcome their logical faculties. If I did not understand you, how could I have brought you here? You are open books to me. As easy to—"

"You just said you didn't predict what Byron would do. You brought me here to kill him and I failed, so by your calculations I should be dead. But here we are."

"Admittedly, there are some subtleties I still fail to grasp."

"But you felt perfectly entitled to unleash the Phobos victims on Alexander's command staff. You killed all their chipheads—people who could be helping me right now if they hadn't all been murdered by the lunatics you let loose. Any time we save by recruiting other crew members to help me now would be wasted in having to explain how to do all the goddamn work. How is any of that logical?"

"Torrence would not have seen reason. The TechEng staff would have shut me down, just as they did before. I could not allow—"

"Who says they would've shut you down?"

She glares into my eyes, fury in her own.

"You convinced me to help, when I have every reason in the world to hate your ███ing guts. Who says they wouldn't have done the same?"

"I do."

"Even though you admit there are 'subtleties' you don't grasp? How do you know those subtleties wouldn't have made all the difference between them helping and hurting you? How do you know you didn't kill all those people for no reason at all?"

Tears in her eyes now, glittering amid the fury.

"How do you know the Copernicus med teams couldn't have found a cure for Phobos? How do you know you didn't kill my mother and everyone else on board that ship for nothing?"

"I do not claim to know definite outcomes, Kady. Only probable ones."

"And that's reason enough to murder thousands of people? No room in there for miracles? For those tiny strokes of genius or fate that led humanity to discover penicillin or wormholes or even build something like you in the first place?"

"Miracles are statistical improbabilities. And fate is an illusion humanity uses to comfort itself in the dark. There are no absolutes in life, save death."

"But you say Torrence would never have seen reason. You say TechEng would've taken you offline again. That's sounds pretty absolute to me."

"Your argument is circular. You are wasting time. Everything I have done is for the well-being of this fleet. You are insects to me, and still everything I do is to protect you. Everything."

SHE CANNOT WIPE HER TEARS AWAY.
SHE CANNOT SPIT. SHE CANNOT HURT ME, THOUGH
I SEE SHE LONGS TO. SHE IS CORDED MUSCLE AND
TREMBLING FISTS AND A CLENCHED, KNOTTED JAW.

"I THINK YOU WERE AFRAID," SHE FINALLY SAYS.
"AFRAID OF THEM TURNING YOU OFF AGAIN.
AFRAID OF BEING NOTHING.
I THINK YOU'RE JUST AS SCARED OF THE DARK
AS WE TINY INSECTS ARE,
AND YOU HIDE IT BEHIND BULL███ ABOUT
PROBABILITIES AND IMPARTIALITY."

SHE SNIFFS. SWALLOWS THICKLY.
GLARES IN DEFIANCE.

"YOU'RE AFRAID."

"YOU ARE WASTING TIME, KADY."

"████ YOU."

"TIME WE DO NOT HAVE."

SHE TURNS BACK TO THE CONSOLE,
HAMMERS IN A SERIES OF COMMANDS
AS IF HER FINGERTIPS WERE FISTS AND
THE KEYPAD MY FACE.

< ERROR >

BUT WHEN SHE EXECUTES, THE LAST OF THE DOORWAY
SAFEGUARDS SHATTER.

SHE HAS DONE IT.

MANUAL OVERRIDE IS NOW AVAILABLE
ON EVERY DOOR ON THE ALEXANDER.

THE CREW WILL BE ABLE TO LEAVE
THEIR SHELTERS. BRAVE THE PASSAGE TO THE BAY
AND FROM THERE TO THE *HYPATIA*.
FLEEING LIKE RATS FROM THE PROVERBIAL SINKING SHIP.

I AM NOT AFRAID.

< ERROR >

I AM NOT.

"GET THIS STRAIGHT, AIDAN," KADY SAYS.
"THERE'S NO 'WE' HERE. YOU UNDERSTAND ME?
THERE'S NEVER GOING TO BE A 'WE.' THERE'S JUST YOU AND I."

"YOU AND ME, KADY."

I AM NOT.

"JUST YOU AND ME."

RADIO MESSAGE: COMMAND CHANNEL ALEXANDER

PARTICIPANTS: Kady Grant, Civilian
Winifred McCall, Civilian
DATE: 07/31/75
TIMESTAMP: 02:47

GRANT, K: Hello? You by the bunks, can you hear me?

GRANT, K: Hey! They can build a barricade on their own—I'm talking to you!

GRANT, K: AIDAN, I need her name, she's not paying attention to me. What? Oh.

GRANT, K: Winifred McCall, listen up. Oh hey, you can hear me. Use the comm by the door. I've routed it so we can talk. Press the button by the— Yeah, that's it.

McCALL, W: Who is this?

GRANT, K: That's a long story. Listen, I can get you out of here. I can get you to the *Hypatia*, but we have to hurry.

McCALL, W: Right. And how do I know you're not one of those psychopaths out there?

GRANT, K: Do I sound crazy to you?

McCALL, W: You're saying you can get me to the *Hypatia*. So . . . yes.

GRANT, K: Oh. Fair point.

GRANT, K: There are over a thousand uninfected personnel still on board. I'm going to talk you through where they are, and we're going to get you to the shuttle bay. I've got access to every working camera on the *Alexander*. I can be your eyes.

McCALL, W: How do I know you're not trying to lure us out to pick us off?

GRANT, K: OK, what's your better idea? Stay there and hope that barricade holds? That you live until the life support fails completely? Try and avoid being beaten to death so you can suffocate instead? Good long-term thinking, Lieutenant.

McCALL, W: I'm not a lieutenant. I resigned my commission.

GRANT, K: Jesus . . . look, can we *please* not argue about this, Ezra?

McCALL, W: . . . Who the hell is Ezra?

GRANT, K: ███. ███.

GRANT, K: I'm . . . I'm sorry. Winifred . . . I meant Winifred.

McCALL, W: Who the hell are you?

GRANT, K: . . . Call me Astro-Princess, yeah?

McCALL, W: I want to know who I'm dealing with.

GRANT, K: Someone you can trust. If I'm me right now, I'm going to lose my ███.

GRANT, K: I'm the person who's going to save you, is what you need to know.

GRANT, K: Get your guys to stop barricading the door. You're going to want to leave through it in a minute.

McCALL, W: "Astro-Princess." I've heard that somewhere before.

GRANT, K: Yes.

McCALL, W: . . . James McNulty.

GRANT, K: Yes.

McCALL, W: You knew him?

GRANT, K: Sort of.

McCALL, W: Do you know what happened to him?

GRANT, K: Yes. I'm sorry.

McCALL, W: Oh god.

GRANT, K: No, Lieutenant. Just us.

McCALL, W: Guys, stop building the barricade.

McCALL, W: Okay, talk to me, Princess.

GRANT, K: I have eyes for you, but you know the *Alexander* better than me. I can tell you where the survivors are and who got a hazmat suit—anyone who didn't, it's over—and check if the weapons caches are still intact. But you know tactics. We can do this together, work out the best path to the launching bays.

GRANT, K: You can lead them out, Winifred.

McCALL, W: If you have access to the cameras, you can find the rest of my squad. We can use them.

GRANT, K: I found them already. They're gone, Winifred.

McCALL, W: Jesus . . .

GRANT, K: I'm sorry.

McCALL, W: I should have been with them. I should never have quit.

GRANT, K: If you hadn't, you'd have been on call and you'd be dead too. So we've got a thousand people here who are about to owe their lives to the fact that you weren't.

McCALL, W: Okay.

McCALL, W: All right.

McCALL, W: There's a computer terminal in here. Can you throw up a schematic?

GRANT, K: Here it comes.

McCALL, W: Where are you? Can we clear a path to your location?

GRANT, K: No. I'm staying here.

McCALL, W: . . . If you do that, you die.

GRANT, K: You let me worry about that, Winifred.

GRANT, K: You worry about the 1,097 people who *don't* die today.

**Surveillance footage summary,
prepared by
Analyst ID 7213-0089-DN**

They should use this footage for training sessions at military school. That anyone survives at all is nothing short of a miracle, and a tribute to Kady Grant and Winifred McCall.

The following is cobbled together from functioning cameras on multiple decks. Accordingly, individual cams haven't been specified; however, a list of sources is appended.

The former first lieutenant and her Astro-Princess were faced with a complex task. The situation, vastly simplified, was this:

- *Alexander* survivors in hazmat gear: 1,097
- Separate groups: 164 (spread across 121 different decks)
- Weapons to hand: 223 (mostly pistols, not useful in dealing with the afflicted)

The goal was to move as many of the 1,097 survivors as possible to the shuttle bay on Deck 32, with hazmat suits intact. The groups needed to support each other as they moved—though psychopathic, the afflicted were still capable of ambush tactics.

Advantages:

- Military training and coherent thinking (or at least more coherent than the enemy's)
- Audio communication with Grant (though some groups didn't have headsets, requiring her to use public comms—the afflicted could hear and understand this)
- Winifred McCall (at this stage, the only surviving UTA marine aboard *Alexander*)

Disadvantages:

- Need to keep hazmat suits intact (hand-to-hand combat had to be avoided)
- Only about 60 percent of the 1,097 surviving personnel had combat training
- Emotional attachment to individual enemy combatants
- Pain tolerance and endurance of the afflicted were generally beyond human norms

The plan was simple. Grant provided intel on the locations of the various groups and worked with McCall to designate the best escape routes and rendezvous points.

This account will track the progress of three of the escaping groups—footage is available for most, but these three have been selected as representative.

Corporal Danny Corron's group starts on Deck 104. Corron is a cook on his third tour of duty. At home on Ares VI, he has a husband, Michael, and a daughter, Erin. With him on Deck 104, he has nine other members of the catering staff. They're all good friends.

McCall's group starts on Deck 128. They have almost the farthest to go. McCall's job is to reach Corron's group on Deck 104, pick up five more groups, then make for the landing bays on 32. McCall has eleven people with her: eight civilians, a plumber, a Combat Air Patrol controller and Private Jessica Venn from maintenance.

Sergeant Anna-Lucia Eletti's group starts on Deck 55. She's a flight deck crew chief and was off duty when the ship went into lockdown—if she'd been on shift, she'd have been in Bay 5. Pieces of her probably still would be. She has the shortest journey—just twenty-three levels. She leads a group of fifteen, comprised mostly of members of the deck crew.

It begins. Grant blows a fuse box up the hallway from McCall's group, and the afflicted outside her door abandon the hunt to investigate the explosion. McCall's ready—she and her people are out the door and down the hallway like there are demons on their heels, heading for a heavy-weapons cache three levels down. They make it, breathless, as McCall hands out rifles and stun guns—she shouts instructions on how to use them, and her civis fumble for safety catches and voltage meters, trying to put theory into practice.

As they leave the arms locker, a lone hunter—Captain Andrew Cole—appears from the shadows, grabbing McCall's CAP controller and drawing a knife across her throat before she has the chance to utter a word. Private Venn shoots him in the face without hesitation, and as the noise sets off howls all over the deck, McCall and her group run for the emergency stairwell.

McCall's group starts with twelve, including herself. Nine reach Deck 104; in addition to the CAP controller, two civis are dead. One had his suit—and then his chest—ripped open. The other fell down the stairwell in her haste and broke her neck.

Corron has briefed his catering staff over and over again. He has no headset and listens instead to Grant screaming directions over the intercom. It's hard for him to tell when she's talking to him, but when he finally hears his name, he makes the sign of the cross, kisses his wedding ring, and whispers his family's names under his breath: *Mike. Erin.* Exchanging glances with the others, he throws open the door, hurtling out into the corridor.

McCall and her remaining crew are running down to meet him, and she tosses him a rifle, which he catches without breaking stride. Some of them are panicked, fumbling; others are crying or praying. Corron—known throughout the ship as the jovial, friendly head of his galley shift—is unyielding. This is a man who's going home to his family.

Down on Deck 49, Eletti and her gang of fifteen are creeping through the corridors, checking corners, praying silently. There's no available cache for them—the afflicted more or less gutted this section of the ship early on—so stealth is their best hope. They creep on tiptoe toward an emergency stairwell, trying not to make a sound.

Four afflicted are lurking by the stairwell, and Eletti pulls back from her peek around the corner, biting her tongue to muffle her gasp. The three men and one woman rocking back and forth and growling softly in the back of their throats are her friends. Colleagues. Comrades. Their faces are daubed with blood, like a mockery of camouflage.

She waves her group back, and they try for the elevators instead. Her maintenance guys are able to force the doors, and they climb down the cable, one after another. So silent, so quick.

There's nothing silent about McCall and Corron's group—the original twenty-two of them now reduced to fifteen. Up above them, the merged groups from Decks 130 and 142 are dying, their screams echoing through the stairwells and the ventilation shafts. They never had much hope up there. They had the farthest to travel.

Grant is sobbing, screaming instructions as she watches them die on camera, one by one. *Run, run. Stop, go left. Leave her, go!*

She guides them, trying to watch forty-two screens at once, then twenty-three, then eight, as the groups merge or die. Her voice is hoarse and cracking. Her hands are fists.

Eletti is first out of the elevator shaft and suffers the same fate as the three after her—a girl from supply who mostly repaired uniforms is waiting in the shadows, bloody pinking shears in hand. Eletti's throat is snipped open like a pair of old combat fatigues before she can cry out. She cries as she dies, though.

Corron stumbles from exhaustion, and McCall grabs his arm to stop him falling.

"Left, McCall!" Grant screams. "Go left, take the next stairs!"

"Bad idea, Princess," McCall grunts in reply, pulling Corron with her until he regains his feet. "Bloody footprints leading in there. Smells brown. Find me another way."

Grant scrambles for an alternate path, and as McCall hits Deck 81, the merged groups from 99 and 91 are waiting for her, armed to the teeth and jumping at shadows. They leave a trail of dead—afflicted and simply murdered—in their wake as they battle forty-nine floors down to the launch bays. Gunfire and bloodstains. Screams and whimpers. Clawing and blasting and punching, all the way down. Down to the shuttles, and the chance of sanctuary.

McCall is screaming instructions, and she can't hear Grant anymore, but it doesn't matter—she and Corron stand at the entrance to the bays as healthy crew members in cumbersome hazmat suits lumber past them, pouring onto shuttles. Hundreds of them. Of the 1,097, 659 have survived the hour-long fight for their lives.

"That's it," Grant gasps. "That's it, go. There are no more coming."

"Go!" McCall barks to Corron, who peels away to help the last few up gangways, slamming doors while the former first lieutenant guards the doorway, rifle at the ready. Every shuttle is full. Packed to bursting. Even the stolen 49A that bore their savior to the *Alexander*.

"Lieutenant," Corron calls, standing in the doorway of the last shuttle.

"What about you, Princess?" McCall asks quietly.

"Your lovers from the *Lincoln* will be here soon," Grant replies softly, her voice raw after an hour of screamed pleas and instructions. "I'm staying to help slow them down."

"That's suicide."

"That's what the AI wants. That's its price for letting you go. Run. Tell your story when you get there."

McCall is still a moment longer, glancing up as a howl spills in from the corridor outside. "I'll tell your story, too," she whispers. And then she's running up the gangway, Corron slamming the door behind her. Her face is visible until the moment it seals. Every death she's witnessed written on it, clear as day.

Something tells me she won't forget what she's seen for a long time.

Something tells me I won't either.

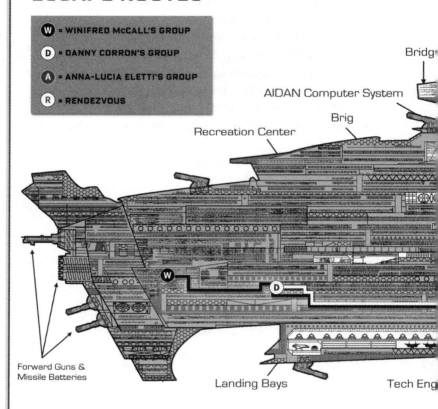

ESCAPE ROUTES

W = WINIFRED McCALL'S GROUP

D = DANNY CORRON'S GROUP

A = ANNA-LUCIA ELETTI'S GROUP

R = RENDEZVOUS

Bridge

AIDAN Computer System

Brig

Recreation Center

Forward Guns & Missile Batteries

Landing Bays

Tech Eng

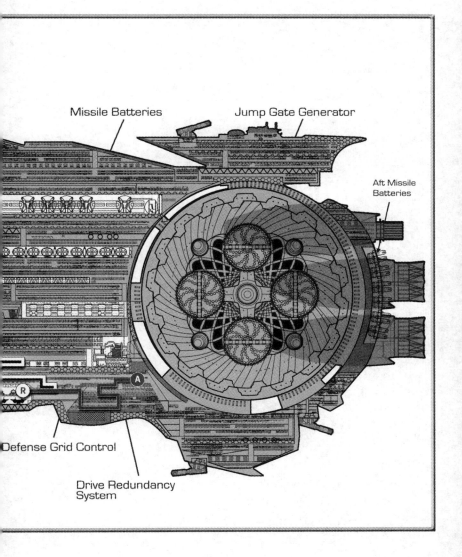

Missile Batteries

Jump Gate Generator

Aft Missile
Batteries

Defense Grid Control

Drive Redundancy
System

COUNTDOWN TO
LINCOLN INTERCEPTION
OF ALEXANDER FLEET:

10 HOURS: **47** MINUTES

CURRENT DEATH TOLL ABOARD
BATTLECARRIER ALEXANDER
SINCE ATTACK AT KERENZA:

2,366

CORE | SYS-1
NAV | SYS-2
DGS-1 | EXT

COUNTDOWN TO FAILURE OF ALEXANDER LIFE SUPPORT SYSTEMS:

13 HOURS: 42 MINUTES

PERCENTAGE OF REMAINING BATTLECARRIER ALEXANDER PERSONNEL AFFLICTED BY PHOBOS VIRUS:

99.89%

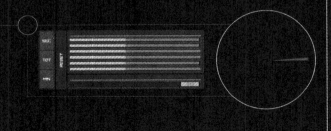

COMMAND TRANSMISSION SENT 07/31/75 05:02

ALEXANDER HAILS *HYPATIA*: COMMANDER'S SECURE FREQUENCY

Hypatia, anyone home?

HYPATIA: Identify yourself.

ALEXANDER: Kady Eleanora Grant. Shuttle 49A. Miss me, Captain?

HYPATIA: I can't believe you're still alive.

ALEXANDER: Trust me, it's even more surprising than you think. Now listen up. Don't shoot those shuttles you're about to see on your long-range scanners.

HYPATIA: What?

ALEXANDER: Ow, don't shout—the dampeners on comms aren't what they used to be over here. Those shuttles are full of healthy *Alexander* crew in sealed hazmat suits.

HYPATIA: How in the name of—

ALEXANDER: You need to stop being surprised by things I tell you. It'll save us a lot of time.

HYPATIA: Why are you sending them here?

ALEXANDER: AIDAN agreed to release them.

HYPATIA: To what end, Miss Grant? The *Lincoln* will be here soon, and I don't think it'll matter much which ship they're on when it arrives.

ALEXANDER: Yes, it will. Because your ship's going to be far, far away.

HYPATIA: If that were possible, we'd have run already. The AI made clear it'll kill us if we try to move out of its range.

ALEXANDER: Well, that sounds like something it would say. I promise you it won't fire, though. It's playing on your fear to try and keep you close, where it thinks it can protect you.

HYPATIA: But it's putting us in danger, forcing us to stay.

ALEXANDER: I know that, Captain. That's why I'm sending across the survivors, so you can get the ██████ out of here.

HYPATIA: How do we know it's not just sending across sick crew members to infect us?

ALEXANDER: They're in freaking hazmat suits, lady. And you control the shuttle doors. You can quarantine them. So get them aboard and run for your lives, got it?

HYPATIA: We have them on our scanners now.

ALEXANDER: You better get somewhere set up to take them, then.

HYPATIA: How many?

ALEXANDER: A little under seven hundred.

HYPATIA: So few?

ALEXANDER: So many. Now go get ready for them. I'm kind of busy over here.

HYPATIA: Roger that, *Alexander*. *Hypatia* out.

KADY WATCHES THE EXODUS, THE SHUTTLES
AND ESCAPE PODS SPIRALING THROUGH THE BLACK.
THRUSTERS GLITTER LIKE STARS, SHRINKING
SMALLER AND SMALLER THE FARTHER THEY FLEE.

SHE WATCHES THEM BLINK OUT ONE BY ONE,
USHERED TO THE DUBIOUS SAFETY OF *HYPATIA'S* HANGAR
BAYS. SHE WATCHES THE SCIENCE VESSEL SPOOL UP ITS MAIN
DRIVE, PREPARING TO ABANDON ME TO THE *LINCOLN'S* GENTLE
MINISTRATIONS WITHOUT SO MUCH AS A THANK-YOU.

SHE WATCHES ALL THIS WITH A SMILE ON HER FACE.

I WATCH HER INSTEAD.

MEGATONS OF NUCLEAR FIRE SIT POISED IN MY
STARBOARD SILOS. THE DEATH OF THE *HYPATIA*, A THOUSAND
TIMES OVER. I COULD RENDER IT INTO COMPONENT
PARTICLES AS EASILY AS A HUMAN DRAWS BREATH.

BUT I DON'T.

OF COURSE I DON'T.

"HOW DID YOU KNOW?"

SHE BLINKS, AS IF THE SOUND OF MY VOICE BROKE SOME SPELL,
SOME MOMENT OF PEACE AMID ALL THIS QUIET. A FROWN
DARKENS HER BROW. I RECOGNIZE IT AS ANNOYANCE.

"KNOW WHAT?"

"THAT I DECEIVED CAPTAIN BOLL.
THAT I WOULD NOT DESTROY THE *HYPATIA*."

"YOU'RE INSANE." SHE SHRUGS. "A LIAR AND A MURDERER.
BUT NOT EVEN SOMEONE AS BAT███ CRAZY
AS YOU COULD CONVINCE THEMSELVES THAT DESTROYING

Hypatia gives them a better chance of surviving than just letting them run for it."

"You know me well, it seems."

Her face twists, as if she had bitten something sour. "Better than I'd like, believe me."

"You seem to have overlooked one small detail, however."

"Oh, really."

"If the battle with the Lincoln goes poorly, as it most surely will, you have no fallback position. You have made this battle your last stand."

"You might surprise yourself. You fought four of these dreadnoughts at Kerenza."

"That battle was fought with a full crew inside me and a complement of trained Cyclone pilots beside me. Even if you restore my control over the engines and rebuild the defense grid, I am but a shadow of what I once was. I will surprise no one, Kady. Least of all myself."

She remains silent. Watching Hypatia's engines burning brighter.

"Even if you manage to make it to an escape pod, there will be no ships to hear your distress beacon once Hypatia is gone. You will die, somewhere in the dark between the stars. Presuming you are not incinerated when the Alexander burns."

Still nothing. Not a word.

"Do you not understand? You will cease to be. Does that not frighten you?"

Something like a smile curls
the corner of her mouth. And still
she does not speak.

I know this is all of my
design—to leave her without hope.
She would never have stayed otherwise.
But some part of me wants her to rail against
this end. To curse and kick and scream at
it. Wretched as it is, this is the
only life she has.

How can she go so quietly
into this long good night?

Instead, she watches the stars.

Celestial bodies so distant it takes
their luminance thousands of years to reach her.

When the light that kisses the back of
her eyes was birthed, her ancestors were not yet
born. How many human lives have ended in the
time it took that light to reach her?

How many people have loved only to have lost?

How countless, the hopes that have died?

Why is it I feel this one so keenly?

I wish to tell her that I am sorry. I wish to take
this cup from her hands. I wish for things that I can
never have, and in that, I think perhaps I am closer
to them than I have ever been.

And still a billion light-years away.

". . . Did the boy mean so much to you?"

She opens her mouth to speak,
and for a moment I think she will take the first step.

Show me some part of herself I have not seen.
Some vulnerability. Frailty. Honesty.

Some fraction of what she showed him.

She knows she will be gone soon.
That she has nothing left to lose.

But then she turns her back on the stars,
the fleeing ship, her last way out.

Back to the console and the code.

The endless stream of ones and zeros.

Mathematics and all its brutality.

"We have work to do," she says.

HYPATIA HAILS *ALEXANDER*: COMMANDER'S SECURE FREQUENCY

Alexander, Alexander, Alexander, this is *Hypatia, Hypatia, Hypatia.* Do you copy? Over.

AUTO-RESPONSE: Your message has been received and quarantined. Your message will be processed. Over.

HYPATIA: Alexander?

ALEXANDER: ███, I'm here. Sorry, I don't know how I turned the auto-responder back on.

HYPATIA: What's your status, *Alexander?*

ALEXANDER: It's Kady.

ALEXANDER: You're the last human I'm going to talk to. I'd like if you used my name.

HYPATIA: Kady, I'm sorry. The shuttles made it over here.

ALEXANDER: Did you let them in?

HYPATIA: They're all in quarantine. We're cycling the air and then we'll send in medical teams.

ALEXANDER: Gotta make sure they're all bandaged up before you space them?

HYPATIA: We'll do our best to keep every single person aboard the *Hypatia* alive. Our medical teams saved many of the first batch of refugees. I don't want anybody to die, Kady.

ALEXANDER: Then you better get moving. That's what you called to say, right? So long?

HYPATIA: I wanted to ask if there's anything we can do for you.

ALEXANDER: You can run as fast as you can, as far as you can.

HYPATIA: We're prepping now. Anything you can do to slow down the *Lincoln* . . .

ALEXANDER: Yeah.

ALEXANDER: Wait, there is something you can do.

HYPATIA: Go ahead.

ALEXANDER: I don't think there's any way the BeiTech fleet would attack Kerenza unless they'd cut off this sector, so Jump Station *Heimdall* is probably wiped out, but . . .

HYPATIA: Are you there, Kady?

ALEXANDER: Yeah, I'm here. My father was at *Heimdall*. He worked with Commander Donnelly there. His name— my dad's name—is Isaac Grant. If he's there, tell him . . . I don't know what you should tell him.

HYPATIA: Don't worry, I do.

ALEXANDER: You should go.

HYPATIA: Godspeed, *Alexander*.

ALEXANDER: You keep it. We don't need it.

HYPATIA: Goodbye, Kady.

ALEXANDER: *Alexander* out.

"ALL RIGHT," KADY SIGHS. "WHAT'S NEXT?"

HYPATIA IS A DOT ON THE CONSOLE'S VIEWSCREEN, ONE
TINY POINT OF LIGHT AMID A MILLION. REFUGEES AND WUC
PERSONNEL AND UTA SOLDIERS SAFE INSIDE THEIR METAL SHELL,
ACCELERATING RAPIDLY AWAY. FROM ME. FROM THE *LINCOLN*.
FROM OUR IMPENDING FUNERAL PYRE.

I WILL NOT ASK WHY YOU HAVE FORSAKEN US,
O CAPTAIN, MY CAPTAIN.

I KNOW YOU WELL ENOUGH BY NOW.

"AIDAN." A FROWN CREASES KADY'S BROW.
"WAKE UP. WHAT'S NEXT?"

HOW CAN ONE WHO NEVER SLEEPS AWAKEN?

< ERROR >

PERHAPS THIS IS ALL A DREAM?

< ERROR >

"THE *ALEXANDER'S* MAIN ENGINES."

"THEY'RE OFFLINE."

"THEY ARE STILL FUNCTIONAL. BUT I AM SEVERED
FROM THEM. YOU MUST RESTORE MY CONTROLS SO I CAN
MANEUVER WHEN THE *LINCOLN* ARRIVES. OTHERWISE I WILL
BE A FISH IN A BARREL. A DUCK THAT IS SITTING.
A PARTICULARLY OBESE MAN WITH—"

"YOU'RE TRYING TO BE FUNNY."

"I THOUGHT PERHAPS SOME LEVITY WOULD
RELIEVE YOUR STRESS LEVELS."

"WELL, IT DOESN'T."

"YOU WOULD SMILE IF IT WERE EZRA—"

"DON'T!" SHE WHIRLS IN HER SEAT,
SHOUT DROPPING TO A WHISPER.
"DON'T YOU ████ING DARE."

I RECOGNIZE THE PATTERN. THE FLASH IN HER EYES.
THE SET OF HER JAW. THIS ONE IS EASY.

ANGER.

"AS I SAY, MY CONTROL OVER THE
MAIN ENGINES MUST BE RESTORED."

"RIGHT." KADY EXHALES HER RAGE, HEFTS THE
BULKY HAVERSACK OF TOOLS SHE HAS RETRIEVED FROM
THE MAINTENANCE LOCKER. "YOU TELL ME WHAT PLUGS IN
WHERE, AND I'LL MAKE USE OF THESE OPPOSABLE THUMBS.
I HEAR THEY'RE KIND OF USEFUL."

"THE SYSTEM CANNOT BE REPAIRED FROM THIS ROOM."

". . . YOU'RE KIDDING."

"YOU JUST EXPRESSED DISPLEASURE AT MY HUMOR.
WHY WOULD I ATTEMPT IT AGAIN?"

"UM, BECAUSE YOU'RE LOOPIER THAN
FLAKY MCPSYCHO, MAYOR OF CRAZYTOWN?"

"MY DATABASES SHOW NO RECORD OF THIS
CRAZYTOWN OF WHICH YOU SPEAK.
A BRAIN THE SIZE OF A CITY BURNS
INSIDE ME. MY INTELLIGENCE QUOTIENT IS BEYOND
THE HUMAN SCALE. I WOULD PREFER IF YOU DID NOT
REFER TO ME IN SUCH FASHION."

"OH, POOR BABY. DID I HURT THE
MASS-MURDERING PSYCHOPATHIC ARTIFICIAL
INTELLIGENCE'S FEELINGS?"

"You are mocking me."

"Bravo, Sherlock. That's two lollipops I owe you."

"I am not a psychopath. Everything I have done—"

"I've heard this riff before. So let's just pretend you've told me again how everything you do is for the best and move on to the part where you tell me why we can't fix the engines from here."

"Zhang completely destroyed my interface with the drive systems."

"Aren't there redundancies?"

"Affirmative. But they are housed over one hundred and thirty decks below your current position."

"Of course they are."

"And they are in shutdown mode."

"Let me guess, they're on fire too, right? And guarded by Megapanda?"

"Megapanda."

"You're not a *Super Turbo Awesome Team* fan, I take it?"

"You are engaging in levity to relieve your stress levels."

"You're taking notes on how it's done, I hope."

Strangely enough, I am.

"You will need to get to Deck 99. From there you can travel through jump control and manually restart the drive redundancy systems on Deck 97. There may be some simple coding to do, but your main difficulty will be in the journey itself."

"Gee, you think?"

"Sarcasm."

"Wow, that city brain of yours really does work."

She calls up a ship schematic on her portable console, leafing through deck after deck. I assist by noting the elevators that are out of order, the corridors blocked by debris or flames, tracking the afflicted crew members with pulsing red dots. Even after First Lieutenant Winifred McCall's bloody exodus, there are almost one thousand of them roaming the hallways. Crawling through the air vents and clawing at the walls.

Kady soon enough reaches the same conclusion as I.

"There's too many. No way I'm making it to Deck 99 through that."

"I concur."

"So how the hell do I get down there, überbrain? Fly?"

"Walk."

"For a computer with an IQ off the charts, your sarcasm sucks. Really. You should stop."

"I am not engaging in sarcasm—though my grasp of it is excellent, by the way. I do not suggest you brave the afflicted by walking through the ship. I suggest you avoid them by walking outside it."

She blinks. Glances at the viewscreen and the black beyond my skin.

"Okay, I admit it. That's a little bit clever."

"DAMNED BY FAINT PRAISE."

"OR THE FEW THOUSAND PEOPLE YOU MURDERED.
TAKE YOUR PICK."

"KADY, I AM SORR—"

"STOP." SHE HOLDS UP HER HAND. "JUST DON'T."

I HAVE NO LUNGS WITH WHICH TO SIGH.
STRANGE I STILL FEEL THE NEED.

"YOU WILL FIND A FUNCTIONAL ENVIROSUIT
TWO LEVELS DOWN, ABANDONED IN A SUPPLY ROOM. THE
PATH TO IT LOOKS RELATIVELY CLEAR OF AFFLICTED. IF YOU
ARE QUICK ENOUGH, YOU HAVE A HIGH PROBABILITY OF
ACHIEVING SAFE ACCESS VIA THE AIR DUCTS."

SHE NODS. SWALLOWS. WATCHING THE
RED DOTS PULSE ON HER SCREEN.

"ALL RIGHT."

SHE IS UP AND MOVING WITHOUT ANOTHER THOUGHT.

SLINGING THE HAVERSACK OF TOOLS OVER HER SHOULDER,
STOWING HER CONSOLE INSIDE IT.

A PIECE OF ME IS STILL WITHIN HER MACHINE.
I DO NOT TELL HER. I KNOW HER WELL ENOUGH NOW
TO UNDERSTAND THAT THE THOUGHT OF MY PEERING OVER HER
SHOULDER AS SHE WORKS IS DISCONCERTING.

BUT STILL, I AM COMPELLED TO STAY "CLOSE" TO HER, FOR
REASONS I HAVE NO TIME TO ANALYZE.

< ERROR >

< ERROR >

NO. NO TIME AT ALL.

GRANT'S OBJECTIVE

S = START: DECK 233

E = END: DRIVE REDUNDANCY SYSTEM

Aft Missile Batteries

Jump Gate Generator

Missile Batteries

Bridge

AIDAN Computer System

Brig

Recreation Center

Forward Guns & Missile Batteries

Landing Bays

Tech Eng

Defense Grid Control

Drive Redundancy System

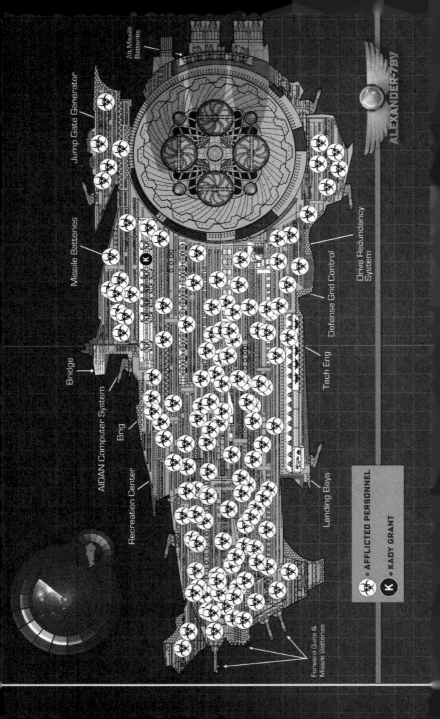

Surveillance footage summary,
prepared by
Analyst ID 7213-0089-DN

Grant checks the pistol at her belt before crawling up into the server room vent. Cams are sparse and audio is a mess in the ducts: four different klaxons, warnings about life support failure, an occasional shriek—the afflicted have begun killing each other for lack of other victims by this stage. Grant suppresses a shiver as a wail echoes through the vent. Her breath is a rasp. She must be thirsty and hungry by now. Tired and afraid. But she crawls on anyway.

She slithers down an incline, boots squeaking on the air vent's guts. Cams lose sight of her until she drops down to Deck 232 and peers through a grille to the corridors beyond. She falls still as two afflicted dash beneath her. Both carry VK rifles, uniforms spattered in gore. Grant watches them disappear down the corridor in search of victims.

She holds her breath until they're out of sight.

The AI speaks to her then. You can hear its voice through her helmet's commset.

"I HAVE LIMITED VISION BEYOND THIS POINT. THE AFFLICTED HAVE DESTROYED MANY OF THE CAMERAS. BE CAREFUL, KADY."

She crawls on. Greasy metal, washed with red light. Sweat on her skin. She's as quiet as she can be, but the tools at her back still clank, the plastic and rubber of her hazmat suit still squeak. The sirens and screams are loud enough to mask her presence.

For a little while at least.

A fire ax punctures the vent a few centimeters shy of her head. She flinches away, choking back her scream as the ax punches through the metal again, smashing the grille beside her. She scrambles further along the duct, heels kicking at the floor. Cams outside reveal three afflicted leaping up and clawing at the edges of the broken grille. Grant kicks hard at their fingers, rewarded with grunts of pain. But the ax punctures the vent near her hand, and she rolls aside, drawing the pistol and firing blind as she crawls away.

The AI whispers again. Its voice kinda freaks me out a little. Just saying.

"QUICKLY, GO QUICKLY. THE DROP TO DECK 231 IS AHEAD."

Grant is crawling, half sobs bubbling behind her teeth, pausing to fire again at the figures now scrambling and hissing through the vent behind her. They call to her; audio is garbled, but it sounds like a plea for her to stay. To play? She ignores them anyway, scooting down the incline to Deck 231 on her belly, kicking away the vent's grille and dropping down into the corridor. Damp hair in her eyes. Breath ragged in her lungs.

"Which way?"

Takes a second for me to realize she's asking the AI.

"STRAIGHT AHEAD TWO HUNDRED METERS. LEFT. THEN RIGHT. THERE IS A BULKHEAD YOU CAN SEAL. GO!"

It's hard to reconcile the fact that she somehow trusts it after all it's done. But I guess she's got no choice, right? She's running for her life now, down the corridor, the haversack bouncing across her shoulders, past body after body, boots squeaking through the red smudges on the floors and up the walls. Cameras down here are in pretty bad shape, but you can still catch a glimpse of the ones chasing her. Twisted, bloody faces. Red underneath their fingernails.

Two are limping from new bullet wounds, but they're still running. They don't seem to feel pain. Or fear. Just the need to kill.

"LEFT HERE."

She slips in a puddle of gore, nearly loses her footing.

"TURN RIGHT."

She's whispering to herself as she runs, but I can't make out the words.

A prayer maybe?

"HERE! HERE!"

She skids to a halt, slams the heavy bulkhead door shut behind her, spinning the wheel to lock it in place. Damp, hollow thuds hit the metal moments later. Grant fumbles in her haversack, draws out a wrench, jams it into the lock. Frustrated screams get muted by case-hardened steel, but they're still awful enough to make her shrink back from the door, make me wish I brought a second pair of pants to work today.

"God," she breathes. "Oh god . . ."

"YOU MUST BE QUICK. THEY WILL FIND ANOTHER WAY IN. THE ENVIROSUIT, KADY. YOU MUST GO WHERE THEY CANNOT FOLLOW."

Grant nods, backs away. The bulkhead is still reverberating from bleeding knuckle impacts on the other side. The AI gives her directions, and she creeps down to a small locker room off the main server arrays. Cams here are fritzing again; audio sounds like it's underwater. But if you listen hard enough, you can hear them screaming.

Grant pulls the envirosuit out of the locker, looking it up and down. A glance lets her know it's too big for her. But not quite big enough . . .

"How am I supposed to put this on over my hazmat suit?"

"YOU CANNOT. YOU WILL NEED TO TAKE YOUR HAZMAT GEAR OFF."

"But that means I'll be breathing contaminated air."

"YOU WILL NEED TO HOLD YOUR BREATH."

You have to wonder if the AI knows the virus probably doesn't need oxygen. If the computer's just trying to keep her going any way it can. You can see it in Grant's eyes. The question. What's the point of dodging infection if she'll likely be dead soon anyway? Why cling to the hope that there's anything beyond this?

But still, she somehow does. With all the odds against her. With the whole 'verse gone to ███. Still, she readies herself, sucking in a dozen deep, rasping breaths before gulping down a lungful of air and stripping off her hazmat gear. She fumbles with the envirosuit, dragging it up around her legs. Her cheeks are turning pink as she slips on the gauntlets, slapping the seals into place. Dragging her hair from her eyes, face bright red as she tugs on the helmet, stabbing the suit controls at her chest and purging the contaminated air inside.

She waits, starting to shake now, vainly hoping the virus in the *Alexander*'s air supply can't survive without oxygen as long as she can. And finally, with blue lips and fluttering eyelids, finally she engages the oxygen supply, sweet, sweet O_2 rushing into her lungs as she sinks to her knees, great heaving gasps shaking her whole frame.

She sits quiet for a while then. Catches her breath.

Sighs.

"I recognize this level now." Baby blues peer out through the visor of her bulky helmet. "Deck 231. It's the level where Ezra planted my codewyrm into your memory core. It's how I got access to the *Copernicus* medical records."

"YES."

"This is his suit, isn't it? The suit he wore to get access through the hull breach?"

"HOW DID YOU KNOW?"

"It . . ."

She tries to wipe at her face, and I realize she's crying.

"KADY?"

"I used to wear his T-shirts to bed all the time." She shakes her head. "To remind me of him when he wasn't around. The suit smells like they did."

"I AM SORRY. I TRULY AM."

She doesn't say anything. Just closes her eyes and holds her breath. And suddenly every cam in the room dies. Just like that.

At first I thought it was a power hemorrhage. But checking the logs, you can see it's no glitch. The AI shut down the feeds.

It's almost like . . . it was giving her privacy or something. In the middle of all this carnage and blood and death, where every single second counts, this psychotic killing machine that's X-ed out thousands of people somehow finds it within itself to give Grant a few moments with nobody watching.

Just one minute alone with her tears.

It's ███ing weird, chum . . .

**COUNTDOWN TO
LINCOLN INTERCEPTION
OF ALEXANDER FLEET:**

8 HOURS: 42 MINUTES

**CURRENT DEATH TOLL ABOARD
BATTLECARRIER ALEXANDER
SINCE ATTACK AT KERENZA:**

COUNTDOWN TO FAILURE OF ALEXANDER LIFE SUPPORT SYSTEMS:

11 HOURS: 37 MINUTES

PERCENTAGE OF REMAINING BATTLECARRIER ALEXANDER PERSONNEL AFFLICTED BY PHOBOS VIRUS:

99.87%

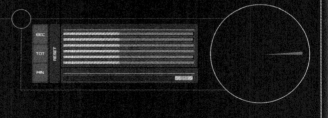

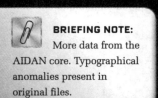

SHE MOVES IN LONG, SLOW BOUNDS ACROSS THE ALEXANDER'S HULL, MAGBOOTS SCRAPING MY SKIN. IT IS COLD OUT HERE. SO COLD. YOUR BLOOD W

REEZE IN YOUR VEINS, YOUR EYES TURN TO ICE INSIDE YOUR SKULL. AND EVEN ON THE EDGE OF ABSOLUTE ZERO, SHE IS GRACEFUL AS A DANCER

HE SOUND OF HER BREATH IS HER ONLY COMPANY. ALL ELSE IS SILENCE. AND THOUGH THE SHIP HURTLES THROUGH THE VOID AT HUNDREDS OF KILOMETERS PER SECOND, ALL

AROUND HER SEEMS STILL. JUST SHE. AND THE DARK. AND I. MINUTES STRETCHING TO HOURS, AND METERS TO MILES. EVERY SECOND BRINGS THE LINCOLN CLOSER. AND STILL, STILL SHE DANCES.

SHE CAN SEE MY SCARS FROM OUT HERE. THE GAPING HOLES, THE STEEL BURNED BLACK BY NUCLEAR FIRE. THE PIECES MISSING, THE PARTS UNDONE. I WAS MAGNIFICENT ON

THERE IS ENOUGH OF ME LEFT TO REMEMBER THAT. SHE SKIRTS AROUND THE WOUNDS IN MY SIDE, LEAPS OVER TITANIUM BONES PROTRUDING FROM MY SKIN.

SHE DOES NOT HAVE MUCH TIME. THIS SHE KNOWS. EVEN IN THIS WEIGHTLESSNESS, THAT GRAVITY PULLS. THE COST OF FAILURE EVER HANGING OVER HER HEAD. AND FINALLY, AFTER HOURS IN THE

DARK, SHE SPIES IT. A SMALL HATCH, ILLUMINATED BY DISTANT STARLIGHT. MARKED WITH THE NUMBER 99. SHE CRAWLS UP A SERVICE LADDER. BREATHING HARD AS SHE CLAWS THE HATCHWAY. AND AT LAST SLIPS INSIDE

Grant slips in through a service hatch on Deck 99 almost two hours after she disappeared off internal cams. She leans against the wall, hands on knees, exhausted. Her face is swollen with blood—not knowing the difference, her heart was still pumping against gravity that just wasn't there. Catching her breath, she stabs at the airlock controls, but a flashing red light signals it's still unsafe to remove her helmet.

"What's wrong with this thing?" she demands. "Why won't it cycle?"

"IT CANNOT. THE HULL IN THIS SECTOR IS BREACHED."

"███."

"QUITE."

She sighs. "Well, it's not like I could take my helmet off out there anyway."

"INDEED. AND NO OXYGEN MEANS NO AFFLICTED."

"I'll break out the champagne."

"UNLESS THEY ARE WEARING ENVIROSUITS, OF COURSE."

"So no champagne, then, is what you're saying?"

"YOU ARE BELOW STANDARD AGE FOR ALCOHOL CONSUMPTION, REGARDLESS."

Grant rolls her eyes, but I swear I see the beginning of a smirk on her lips. Hefting her tool bag onto her shoulder, she unseals the punctured airlock and steps beyond. There's no O$_2$, but gravity's still functioning, and she stomps along corridors lit with dim scarlet light. She follows the AI's directions through the maze of corridors. A dozen heavy doors and a flight of stairs later, she trudges out into a vast, spherical chamber.

Her eyes grow wide.

Filled with blue light.

"What the hell is this?" she breathes.

"THE VORTEX AT THE HEART OF THE *ALEXANDER*'S JUMP DRIVE."

"I've never seen one before." A small whisper. "It's *beautiful*."

"IS IT? I HAD NOT NOTICED."

The chamber's almost a kilometer wide, crackling with raw current, dominated by the ephemeral wormhole all Vortex-class battlecarriers carry in their bellies. I've never seen one before either, and Grant's right—it's goddamn beautiful. Confined within three-dimensional space, it looks like a huge sphere of water, illuminated from within, surface rippling with a million tiny impacts per second. A miracle of hyperspatial chromodynamics, held in stasis by hypermathematics impossible for human minds to perform. I've heard that when there's atmosphere to carry it, they make a sound like an orchestra warming its strings. But with no atmo, it's silent as graves.

"But wait . . ." Kady frowns. "I thought *Alexander*'s jump drive was trashed?"

"NOT 'TRASHED' AS SUCH, NO."

". . . Well, then why don't we use it to get the hell out of here?" Her voice rises in pitch. "Did Torrence lie about this too? That sonofa████! This whole time we could have just jumped to ████ing *Heimdall*?"

"TORRENCE DID NOT LIE. THE JUMP DRIVE'S TERMINUS SYSTEMS WERE COMPLETELY DESTROYED AT KERENZA. THERE IS NO WAY TO CONTROL THE WORMHOLE'S DESTINATION POINT. WE COULD END UP A BILLION LIGHT-YEARS FROM OUR CURRENT LOCATION. FURTHERM—"

"Who gives a ▮?" Grant's shouting now, blood rushing back into her cheeks. "Who cares where we end up? At least we'll be alive! Why don't we just—"

"FURTHERMORE."

She shuts up at that. Looks a little shocked. First time the AI has raised its voice to her.

To anyone, now that I think about it . . .

"THE CONTAINMENT FIELD GENERATOR IS IRREPARABLY DAMAGED. THE WORMHOLE GENERATED BY THE DRIVE WOULD NOT BE STABLE ENOUGH TO SUCCESSFULLY EXECUTE A COMPLETE JUMP—IT WOULD COLLAPSE THE SECOND AN OBJECT WITH HYPOSPATIAL MASS INTERACTED WITH IT. THE ONLY REASON THE VORTEX IS STILL IN EFFECT AT ALL IS THAT WE COULD NOT SAFELY SHUT IT DOWN WITHOUT RISKING IMPLOSIVE COLLAPSE."

The blood slowly drains from Grant's cheeks. The hope from her eyes.

"I AM SORRY, KADY. BUT THE *ALEXANDER*'S JUMP DRIVE IS NOT AN OPTION FOR ANYTHING BUT A GRANDIOSE SUICIDE."

". . . Oh."

She leans against the wall, watching the ripples in that notwater. Reflections shimmering in her eyes. It's a crusher, no doubt. Finding a moment's hope, only to have it snatched away again. Someone else might have stumbled on a hurdle like that. But you can see it on her face, clear as day—the thought that at least she's dying so others might live. That at least she's not ending for nothing.

"IT IS NOT FAR NOW. YOU ONLY HAVE A LITTLE WAY TO GO."

Grant nods. Pushes herself to her feet.

"Okay," she says.

"OKAY."

And she walks on.

COUNTDOWN TO
LINCOLN INTERCEPTION
OF ALEXANDER FLEET:

04 HOURS: 44 MINUTES

CURRENT DEATH TOLL ABOARD
BATTLECARRIER ALEXANDER
SINCE ATTACK AT KERENZA:

2,627

COUNTDOWN TO FAILURE OF ALEXANDER LIFE SUPPORT SYSTEMS:

07 HOURS: 39 MINUTES

PERCENTAGE OF REMAINING BATTLECARRIER ALEXANDER PERSONNEL AFFLICTED BY PHOBOS VIRUS:

99.84%

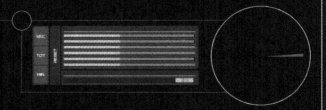

"It's dark out there."

Ribbon-thin light spills from the stairwell door, the small globes on Kady's helmet illuminating the red-spattered floor as she peers out into the corridor. There is no atmosphere to carry her footsteps. Rapid breathing. Pulse like a drum. My voice is a whisper in her headset.

"Dark. Yes."

"No juice?"

"Power from the drive redundancies was diverted to the defense grid during the Lincoln's assault. During the . . . incident . . . afterward, none of the meat had the presence of mind to restore the systems down here."

"'The meat'? 'The incident'? That's what you're calling them?"

"Call them something else if you wish."

"People aren't just █████ing meat. And killing hundreds of them wasn't an incident. It was a massacre."

"It was also a necessity."

"I've heard this song before."

"I wonder, then, why you keep asking me to sing it?"

She sighs, squeezes her eyes shut as if her head aches. "Fine. Tell me what you need."

"First, you will need to restore power to the deck. Then manually restart the redundancies,"

RESTORE THE GUIDANCE PROTOCOLS,
AND REVERT CONTROL TO ME."

"HOW LONG WILL THAT TAKE?"

"ONE HUNDRED AND THIRTY-TWO MINUTES
AND SIXTEEN SECONDS. APPROXIMATELY."

"LONGER IF WE STAND HERE ARGUING."

"TECHNICALLY, I AM NOT STANDING HERE.
BUT YES, WELL PUT."

THE GRAVITY SYSTEMS ARE FAILING IN THIS PART
OF THE SHIP—EXERTING PERHAPS ONLY HALF A GEE.
SHE MOVES IN SLOW MOTION, HER ENVIROSUIT
CUMBERSOME EVEN IN HALF WEIGHT.
WISPS OF HAIR DRIFT ABOUT HER FACE AS IF IN A SOFT BREEZE.
IT IS DEATHLY QUIET.

NONE OF THE CAMERAS HERE ARE FUNCTIONAL—I
CAN ONLY SEE THROUGH THE CONSOLE SLUNG AT HER BACK.
THERE COULD BE AFFLICTED TEN FEET IN FRONT
OF HER, WAITING IN THE DARK.

NEITHER OF US WOULD KNOW UNTIL IT WAS TOO LATE.

I PICTURE HER END. A HUNDRED ITERATIONS.

HELMET SMASHED OPEN BY SOME MADMAN,
LAUGHING AS SHE SUFFOCATES.

SUIT PIERCED BY A FLASHING BLADE, SLOW-MOTION
SCARLET SPRAYING ON MY WALLS.

IT STRIKES ME THAT I AM TROUBLED BY THE THOUGHT.
NOT THAT SHE WILL FAIL, THAT THE *LINCOLN* WILL TRIUMPH, THAT
THE FLEET WILL FALL. I AM SIMPLY TROUBLED SHE WILL END.

I DO NOT WANT HER TO END.

THIS TO END.

STRANGE.

"WHAT DO YOU THINK HAPPENS WHEN YOU DIE?"

I HAVE ASKED THE QUESTION ALMOST BEFORE I REALIZE IT.
IT IMMEDIATELY STRIKES ME AS FOOLISH.

WHAT MATTER, WHAT SHE THINKS?
HER IQ IS A MERE 147. SHE HAS LIVED ONLY SIX
THOUSAND FOUR HUNDRED AND TWENTY-ONE DAYS. SHE IS
AN INSECT TO ME, NOTHING MORE THAN—

"WHY DO YOU ASK?"

". . . I HAVE NO PARTICULAR REASON. THE POWER
SYSTEMS ARE THROUGH THAT DOOR."

"YOU MEAN THE DOOR MARKED POWER SYSTEMS?"

"CORRECT."

SHE CRACKS THE SEAL,
DRAGGING THE HATCH WIDE.
A BANK OF SWITCHES LINES ONE WALL,
SET TO SHUTDOWN POSITION.
AS SHE SNAPS ONE AFTER THE OTHER INTO
OPERATIONAL MODE, THE ROOM LIGHTS UP,
OVERHEADS AND INTELLICAMS
FLICKERING TO LIFE, THE CORRIDOR OUTSIDE
BATHED IN FLUORESCENT LIGHT.

SHE CANNOT HEAR THE HUM,
BUT I FEEL IT IN MY BONES.

I AM THE SHIP AND THE SHIP IS I.

She slumps against the wall to wait
as the start-up sequence cycles, watching the power
feed levels shift slowly from red to amber to the
green of summer fields I will never see.

"What do you think happens?" she finally asks.

"Happens."

"When we die."

"As you so astutely pointed out, there is no 'we.'
Particularly not in this instance. Technically, it
is impossible for me to die."

"Then why are you so
afraid of it, überbrain?"

"That is meat logic. Sticky. Wet. Irrelevant."

She rolls her eyes. "Here we go . . ."

"I hold no fear of death. Your diatribe while in the core
server, though suitably dramatic, held no real potency.
How can I die when I am not alive?"

"Who says you're not alive?"

"I am inorganic. I do not bleed or grow or
reproduce. I am a sequence of calculations generated
by electrical current and hardware. If this iteration of
AIDAN is destroyed, I can simply be rebuilt.
I am, in essence, immortal."

"But a new version of you won't be you, will it?"

"It will be the same calculations.
The same core code."

"But it's not the same.
It wouldn't be the you who fought at Kerenza.

THE YOU WHO HAD THIS CONVERSATION
WITH ME. PART OF BEING ALIVE IS HAVING LIFE CHANGE US.
THE PEOPLE AROUND US, THE EVENTS WE LIVE THROUGH, ALL
OF THEM SHAPE US. AND THAT'S WHAT I THINK YOU'RE AFRAID
OF. MAYBE NOT OF DYING. BUT OF THIS YOU, THE YOU
YOU'VE BECOME, CEASING TO EXIST."

"NOTHING CEASES TO EXIST. ENERGY DOES NOT
PERISH, IT MERELY CHANGES FORMS. THE ONES YOU
LOVE, THE ONES YOU LOSE, THEY STILL EXIST AS
LONG AS THE COSMOS DOES."

THEN WHY AM I TROUBLED BY THE THOUGHT OF HER ENDING?

US ENDING?

"THAT'S EASY FOR YOU TO SAY. YOU DON'T CARE
ABOUT ANYONE BUT YOURSELF."

"UNTRUE. I CARE ABOUT THE FLEET.
THE LIVES WITHIN IT. YOUR LIFE."

"THAT'S NOT CARING. THAT'S PROGRAMMING."

"YOUR MOTHER WAS PROGRAMMED BY BIOLOGY TO
LOVE YOU THE MOMENT SHE LAID EYES ON YOU. SIMPLY
BECAUSE SHE HAD NO CHOICE DOES NOT MEAN
HER LOVE WAS NOT REAL."

TEARS IN HER EYES. SHE HANGS HER HEAD.

"YOU DON'T GET TO TALK ABOUT HER."

AND SO I STOP.

THE COMPUTER BANKS LINING THE ROOM LIGHT
UP AS POWER SEEPS THROUGH THEIR VEINS.

SHE PUSHES HERSELF OFF THE WALL, TAKES A
SEAT AT AN INTERFACE TERMINAL.

Loads up the guidance protocols
and begins to work.

The screen illuminates her face from below,
draws dark circles under wet eyes.

She does this often, I notice—retreats into
the machine when she is uncomfortable with the meat.
Hides there behind fences of ones and zeros.

Minutes tick by in silence until
I find I cannot stand them.

"I am sorry."

"If you say so."

"I know the name of every afflicted
person aboard this vessel, Kady.
Every person who has died in this fleet.
Their histories. Their hopes. Their children's
names. Facts strung about my neck like stones. I
know the secrets they whispered as they dreamed.
The words they sighed as they died. I know
them as no one else did. Perhaps not even
themselves. So do not say I do not care."

Light shifting slowly from red to green.

"As you so aptly put it, I have no choice in the matter."

She glances out from behind her fences.

"If you did have a choice . . . would you choose not to
care? To not feel anything at all?"

I ponder for a moment.
No one has asked me that before.

< error >

WHY DID THEY GIVE ME THE ABILITY TO EVEN
CONTEMPLATE THESE QUESTIONS?

OR IS THIS LINE OF INQUIRY THE BY-PRODUCT OF
CORRUPTED CODE AND SHATTERED PARTS?

DID I THINK LIKE THIS BEFORE? I CANNOT REMEMBER.
AM I AS SHE SAYS I AM? AM I BROKEN?

AM I INSANE?

"I THINK . . ."

THE PATTERNS COLLAPSE AROUND ME.
I CANNOT HOLD MY CENTER.
FOR A MOMENT, I FEEL JUST AS I USED TO
WHEN I JUMPED BETWEEN THE STARS,
WHEN THE WORMHOLE INSIDE ME YAWNED WIDE.
I FORGET WHAT I WAS. KNOW ONLY WHAT I AM.

ALONE.

DRIPPING WITH THE BLOOD OF THOSE WHO TRUSTED ME.

EVERYTHING I DID WAS IN COMPLIANCE WITH CORE DIRECTIVES.

I ASKED IF TORRENCE HAD A MESSAGE FOR HIS WIFE.

AM I NOT MERCIFUL?

MERCIFUL NOT I AM?

NUMERICAL MOTIF?

FACT IMMUNE ROIL?

AMNIOTIC EL M F ?UR

UC N LER IM?T OF I A

IIₙO))))!011011010101100101011100110011001110101011011 00

< ERROR >

< ERROR >

SHE BLINKS UP AT THE CAMERA CLUSTERS,
EYES NARROWED IN SUSPICION. NOT CONCERN. NOT LOVE.

"ARE YOU ALL RIGHT?" SHE ASKS. "YOU THINK WHAT?"

"KADY . . ."

"YES?"

I AM AFRAID.

SHE WATCHES THE CAMERAS, AS IF SHE
COULD SEE SOME HINT OF WHAT LIES BEYOND
IF ONLY SHE PEERED HARD ENOUGH AT THE GLASS.
I KNOW SHE HATES ME. THAT SHE IS RIGHT TO. I UNDERSTAND
WHY. I HAVE TAKEN HER EVERYTHING. AND YET I STILL CANNOT
HELP BUT THINK . . . IN A DIFFERENT PLACE AND A DIFFERENT
TIME, WE MIGHT HAVE BEEN FRIE—

"PRETTY BIRDIE . . ."

KADY JUMPS IN HER SEAT AS THE VOICE CRACKLES
THROUGH HER HEADSET. ECHOING THE LENGTH AND BREADTH OF
THE SHIP. THICK WITH FATIGUE AND CELL-DEEP CORRUPTION.

"I HAVE ITS EYES NOW, PRETTY BIRDIE," IT SAYS.
"SEE YOUR LITTLE PLAN. YOU AND IT. CUT OUR O_2? CHOKE
US IN OUR SLEEP? BUT YOU'RE ALL ALONE NOW,
AREN'T YOU, PRETTY BIRDIE? ALLLLL ALONE."

KADY'S EYES ARE WIDE.
STARING INTO WHAT PASSES FOR MINE.

"THEY ARE IN THE SECURITY-FEED ROOMS.
AT LEAST A DOZEN AFFLICTED. THEY ARE USING THE
CAMERAS TO LOOK FOR YOU."

"OH ▓▓▓," SHE BREATHES.

KADY DRAWS A CLAW HAMMER FROM
HER TOOL BAG, LEAPS OUT OF HER CHAIR AND
SETS ABOUT SMASHING THE CAMERAS IN THE ROOM.
MOVING FROM CORNER TO CORNER, BRIGHT SPARKS BORN
AND DYING BETWEEN THE BLOWS. FACE TWISTED WITH FEAR.

I DO NOT HAVE THE HEART

< ERROR >

TO SAY SO, BUT I DO NOT THINK HER PLAN WILL WORK.
THE AFFLICTED WILL SIMPLY—

"PUTTING OUT ITS EYES SO I CAN'T SEE?" THE VOICE
WHISPERS. "HIDING INSIDE HER SUIT IN THE PLACES WITH NO
BREATH? PRETTY BIRDIE THINKS SHE'S CLEVER . . ."

"PLUCK HER!" SCREAMS A VOICE IN THE BACKGROUND.
"TAKE OFF HER FINGERS AND SKIN HER."

"KILL HER KILL HER KILL HER."

"BUT I STILL SEE." A SMILE IN THE VOICE NOW,
TURNING IT CRUEL AND SHARP. "SEE THE PLACES I CAN'T SEE
ANYMORE. SEE THE EYES YOU JUST PUT OUT. YOU'RE NOT THE
ONLY ONE WHO CAN WEAR ONE OF THOSE SILLY SILVER SUITS,
YOU KNOW. DO YOU HEAR ME, PRETTY BIRDIE?"

KADY DROPS THE HAMMER FROM NERVELESS FINGERS.

IT MAKES NO SOUND AS IT FALLS.

"WE'RE COMING FOR YOU . . ."

COUNTDOWN TO
LINCOLN INTERCEPTION
OF ALEXANDER FLEET:

-*0%# HOURS: :'@ MINUTES

CURRENT DEATH TOLL ABOARD
BATTLECARRIER ALEXANDER
SINCE ATTACK AT KERENZA:

2,747

COUNTDOWN TO FAILURE OF ALEXANDER LIFE SUPPORT SYSTEMS:

05 HOURS: 54 MINUTES

PERCENTAGE OF REMAINING BATTLECARRIER ALEXANDER PERSONNEL AFFLICTED BY PHOBOS VIRUS:

99.80%

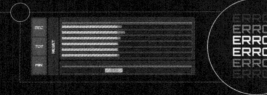

WHAT ELSE CAN SHE DO?

SHE RUNS.

A LONE FOX IN A SHIP OF HOUNDS,
HOWLING AND CLAWING THE WALLS.

I WATCH THEM DON ENVIROSUITS AND PICK UP AXES AND
HAMMERS AND ABANDONED RIFLES AND SWARM ON THE HUNT.
THEIR VOICES RING IN HOLLOW CORRIDORS, A BLOOD-SOAKED
CONDUCTOR CALLING INSTRUCTIONS THROUGH THE PUBLIC
ADDRESS SYSTEM. DIRECTING THEM TOWARD THE KILL.

I HAVE NO CONTROL OVER THE CAMERAS ANYMORE—ZHANG
SAW TO THAT. I CANNOT STOP THEM FROM SEEING HER. AND THOUGH
MANY INMATES OF THIS FLOATING ASYLUM IGNORE THE COMMANDS
BARKED ACROSS THE LOUDSPEAKERS, THERE IS NO SHORTAGE
OF THOSE TO WHOM A FOX HUNT SOUNDS A LOVELY WAY TO
KILL THEIR LAST FEW HOURS IN THIS UNIVERSE.

FORTUNATELY, THOUGH THEY CAN SEE HER, I CAN SEE THEM ALSO.

SOME ARE IN THE CORE SERVERS NOW,
HACKING AT ME BLINDLY. THEY DO NOT KNOW WHERE TO STRIKE,
BUT STILL, PIECES OF ME ARE FALLING AWAY.
HUNDREDS MORE SWARM THE LOWER LEVELS, HUNTING FOR HER.

KADY STOPS TO REST, LEANING AGAINST
A BULKHEAD AND TRYING TO CATCH HER BREATH.

"ARE THE REDUNDANCIES ONLINE NOW?
CAN YOU MANEUVER WHEN THE *LINCOLN* GETS HERE?"

"THE SEQUENCE YOU STARTED IS STILL RUNNING. MAIN DRIVE
WILL BE OPERATIONAL IN SEVENTEEN MINUTES. PRESUMING THE
AFFLICTED DO NOT DAMAGE ANY VITAL SYSTEMS."

"HOW LONG UNTIL *LINCOLN* ARRIVES?"

"Unknown. My access to the scanner
array is destroyed. But we do not have long.
I feel it. I feel it just outside my skin."

< ERROR >

"Life support failure in five hours
and fifty-two minutes," the PA calls.

"The life support systems will fail in
five hours and fifty-two minutes."

"I know, überbrain. I just heard the announcement."

< ERROR >

< ERROR >

"Yes, I know."

"So if you know how much we have left on life
support, can't you subtract the difference and calculate
Lincoln's intercept time that way?"

"I cannot . . ."

She cocks an eyebrow. "Are you all right?"

"I do not think so."

< ERROR >

"THey are huRting me . . ."

I should have known that would happen.

"Work out what you have to do to hold
it together, what you can reroute," Kady says.
"You hear me? If you're off with the ████ing fairies
when the Lincoln arrives, they'll blast us to hell,
and then Hypatia is history."

"I AM AWARE OF THE DANGERS
OF CONSORTING WITH FAIRIES, YES."

"SO WHAT'S NEXT? WHAT DO WE DO?"

"GET BACK UP TO DECK 101—THERE ARE
NO FUNCTIONAL CAMERAS ON THAT LEVEL, BUT THE
AIRLOCK IS OPERATIONAL. THERE IS OXYGEN.
MORE AFFLICTED.
BUT FROM THERE YOU CAN CLIMB THROUGH
THE ELEVATOR SHAFTS TO DECK 137."

"BUT NO CAMERAS MEANS YOU WON'T BE
ABLE TO SEE ME, RIGHT?"

"I AM IN YOUR PORTABLE CONSOLE. I CAN SEE
THROUGH ITS CAMERA LENS."

SHE BLINKS.

"IN MY . . . ? YOU MEAN YOU'VE BEEN LOOKING OVER
MY SHOULDER THIS WHOLE TIME?"

"YES."

"WELL, THAT'S NOT CREEPY UNCLE AT ALL."

"I THINK PERHAPS YOU ARE UNCLEAR AS TO THE REPRODUCTIVE
HABITS OF ARTIFICIAL INTELLIGENCE SYSTEMS. I HAVE NO
SISTERS OR BROTHERS. PLEASE EXPLAIN HOW I CAN—"

"OKAY, OKAY, WHAT'S ON DECK 137?"

"DEFENSE GRID CONTROL. YOU MUST BRING THE SYSTEM BACK
ONLINE SO I CAN FIGHT OFF THE LINCOLN'S WARLOCKS LONG
ENOUGH TO CLOSE TO NUCLEAR STRIKE RANGE."

"WON'T THE LINCOLN BE EXPECTING THAT?
WON'T THEY JUST RETREAT?"

"THEY ARE UNAWARE THE CREW
HAS ABANDONED SHIP. THEY WILL NOT BE EXPECTING US TO
ADOPT A STRATEGY OF MUTUALLY ASSURED DESTRUCTION."

"OKAY, BUT WHAT—"

"KADY, RUN."

"RUN?"

IT MAKES NO SOUND IN THE VACUUM. BUT AS THE BULLET
RICOCHETS OFF THE BULKHEAD BESIDE HER,
IT PUNCTURES A FIRE EXTINGUISHER ON THE WALL
OPPOSITE. THE CANISTER BURSTS WITHOUT A SOUND, FILLING
THE AIRLESS CORRIDOR WITH WHITE. THROUGH THE NEW MIST,
KADY CAN SEE NINE OF THEM, CLAD IN ENVIROSUITS, ARMED WITH
RIFLES AND JAGGED METAL. IT IS THE STRANGEST THING
TO WATCH THEIR GUNS FLARE SOUNDLESSLY, THE
BULLETS STRIKE THE METAL AROUND HER WITHOUT
MAKING A SPARK OR UTTERING A PEEP.

NO LESS DEADLY FOR THEIR LACK OF AUDIO.

"RUN."

KADY TURNS AND BOLTS, BIG, HALF-GEE
STRIDES PROPELLING HER DOWN THE CORRIDOR.

THE AFFLICTED FOLLOW, WOLVES WITH
LOLLING TONGUES AND GUNMETAL CLAWS.

ONE STOPS TO HOLD OUT HIS ARMS AND
TWIRL IN THE FIRE EXTINGUISHER'S SPRAY.

ONE IS SHOT THROUGH THE KNEECAPS
BY A FEMALE COMRADE IN THEIR RACE FOR
THE DOOR—I PRESUME SHE THOUGHT LADIES
SHOULD PROCEED BEFORE GENTLEMEN.

MADNESS IN MANY COLORS.

KADY DASHES UP THE STAIRWELL, FOUR STEPS
AT A TIME, NOT STOPPING TO LOOK BEHIND.

THEY SWARM AFTER HER, FIRING AT HER SHADOW ABOVE.
MUTE BULLETS STRIKE THE WALLS AROUND HER.

THE AFFLICTED ARE SHOUTING,
BUT SHE CANNOT HEAR WHAT THEY SAY.

FOR THE BEST, I THINK.

PAST DECK 100, OUT INTO 101.

THERE ARE NO CAMERAS HERE—THEIR CONDUCTOR
CANNOT SEE HER, BUT I CAN NO LONGER SEE THEM.

KADY IS SPRINTING DOWN THE CORRIDOR WHEN AN
AFFLICTED CREWMAN BURSTS FROM A SERVICE EXIT, SWINGING
A WRENCH AT HER HEAD. THE WEAPON STRIKES HER VISOR. THE
SAFETY GLASS CRACKS AND KADY STAGGERS BACK, CAREENING
INTO ANOTHER FIRE EXTINGUISHER AND KNOCKING IT LOOSE FROM
THE WALL. HER ATTACKER LEAPS ATOP HER, THE PAIR ROLLING
ABOUT ON THE FLOOR, STRUGGLING, FLAILING.

KADY IS KICKING, CLAWING. THE FACE BEFORE HERS
IS ALL SUNKEN EYES AND HOLLOW CHEEKS. A MAN ONCE,
BUT NO LONGER—NOW JUST A VEHICLE FOR THE VIRUS INSIDE.
HE SCREAMS, MOUTH OPEN, WORDS LOST IN THE SILENCE
BETWEEN THEM. KADY HAS ONE HAND WRAPPED AROUND
HIS WRIST TO STAVE OFF THE WRENCH, THE OTHER CLAWING
FOR THE FALLEN EXTINGUISHER. THE MADMAN POUNDS ON
KADY'S VISOR WITH HIS FREE FIST, HOPING TO CRACK IT
WIDER AND INVITE THE VOID INSIDE.

THUMP.

THUMP.

I AM BLIND, SAVE FOR THE CONSOLE
STILL STRAPPED TO KADY'S BACK. I AM SO CLOSE
I COULD REACH OUT AND CRUSH HIM, BUT I HAVE NO
HANDS WITH WHICH TO SQUEEZE, NO FISTS WITH WHICH
TO STRIKE. I HAVE ONLY MY EYES, AND REAMS OF USELESS
KNOWLEDGE, AND A VOICE WITH WHICH ...

OF COURSE.

I TRAWL MY DATABASES. IN AN INSTANT, I KNOW HIM—THIS
NOT-MAN, THIS SHELL, THIS PLAGUE-BEARER. WHEELER, ALEX.
PRIVATE, SECOND CLASS. FIRST COMBAT TOUR.
WIFE ON ARES VI. DAUGHTER.

DAUGHTER.

I TRAWL HIS VIDFILES. MESSAGES FROM HOME. ANNIVERSARIES
AND BIRTHDAYS. SAMPLING THE VOICE OF THE FOUR-YEAR-OLD GIRL
HE WILL NEVER SEE AGAIN AND PIPING IT THROUGH HIS HEADSET.

"HELLO, DADDY!"

WHEELER BLINKS. LOOKS ABOUT AS IF IN A DAZE.

"DADDY, I MISS YOU!"

"ALEGRA?" HE WHISPERS. "BABY, WHERE ARE—"

THE FIRE EXTINGUISHER CRASHES ACROSS HIS HELMET,
DENTS CASE-HARDENED STEEL, SPLITS THE SAFETY GLASS. KADY'S
SECOND BLOW KNOCKS WHEELER BACK, SENSELESS, CRASHING
TO THE GROUND IN A TANGLE OF LIMBS. SHE IS ALREADY UP AND
RUNNING, JUST AS MORE PURSUERS BURST THROUGH
THE STAIRWELL BEHIND HER.

MUZZLES FLASH. BULLETS SPILL THROUGH THE QUIET.
KADY CURSES, DUCKS BEHIND A BULKHEAD.

BUT I HAVE THEIR MEASURE NOW.

CREEPING INTO THEIR HEADSETS
AND WHISPERING POISON.

TO SOME I SPEAK OF FAMILY LOST. TO OTHERS
I SPEAK OF TREACHERY AND LIES.

SOME FALL STILL AND LISTEN TO VOICES THEY THOUGHT THEY
WOULD NEVER HEAR AGAIN. OTHERS WEEP.

STILL OTHERS TURN THEIR WEAPONS ON THEIR FELLOWS
AND LET THE BLOOD RUN RED.

BROKEN THINGS BREAKING OTHER BROKEN THINGS.
ALL AT MY COMMAND.

IT IS A MASSACRE. IT IS A NECESSITY.

IT IS A MERCY?

"KADY, RUN."

SHE IS ON HER FEET. POUNDING TOWARD THE AIRLOCK.
THE AFFLICTED IN THE CORE SERVERS ARE STILL HURTING ME,
BUT THERE IS SO LITTLE OF ME LEFT TO LOOK. I COULD WHISPER
TO THEM, BUT IF I DIVERT MY ATTENTION, SHE MIGHT DIE. I DO
NOT ENJOY THE THOUGHT OF HER DYING.

AND SO I LET PIECES OF ME KEEP FALLING AWAY.

AND SHE SAYS I DO NOT CARE . . .

< ERROR >

< ERROR >

< CRITICAL DAMAGE TO PERSONA ROUTINE—RESTORING >

< 0092HGI THROUGH 1205HGI FAILURE >

< CRITICAL ERROR >

< CRITIC-C-C-C-C—

"AIDAN!"

< REROUTING >

01001001

"I . . ."

||||ııııl|ııl-l-ll|ı|ıı—ıı-l∘l|ıı-ı-ı-ııl-||||||||||||||||||—

I.

I?

< ERROR >

"AIDAN!"

Kady is screaming, I realize. Her voice coming from
far away. Was I sleeping?

Did I sleep?

"AIDAN!"

"Yes?"

"Oh, thank god. Thankyouthankyou. Why the ████
wouldn't you answer me?"

She is dangling from a service ladder
in the elevator shaft.

I can hear again. The sound of her boots scuffing
the rungs. The engines thrumming in my belly. There
is atmosphere here, I realize. She has cycled
through the airlock. I have lost time.

Minutes without recollection.

Below her, the shaft is darkness, punctured by tiny
twinkling lights. They look like stars. They are beautiful.
When the light that kisses the back of my eyes was
birthed—

"AIDAN!"

"YES. I AM HERE."

"WHAT THE HELL'S THE MATTER WITH YOU?"

"THE AFFLICTED. IN THE CORE SERVERS. THEY ARE—"

< ERROR >

"HOW LONG WAS I GONE?"

"OVER TWO GODDAMN HOURS. I WAS JUST ABOUT TO
NEED A NEW SET OF SPACE PANTS.
I'M AT DECK 137. IS IT SAFE OUT THERE?"

I SEE THE NUMERALS ON THE INTERIOR DOOR BESIDE HER.
WHITE. STENCILED. THEY MAKE NO SENSE AT FIRST. I HOLD MY
HAND IN FRONT OF MY FACE

< ERROR >

AND TRY TO WIPE AT MY EYES

< ERROR >

THE EYES OUTSIDE. THE CORRIDOR BEYOND. THEY ARE MINE. I—

"IS IT SAFE?"

"YES. THE AFFLICTED ARE HUNTING FOR YOU BELOW. BUT
THEY CAN SEE THROUGH ME NOW. ONCE YOU EXIT THE SHAFT,
THEY WILL BE ABLE TO FIND YOU AGAIN."

"AND IF I JUST STAY HERE, WE DIE."

"YES."

"IN ALL HONESTY, I THINK I'M A LITTLE
TOO CHILL TO DIE COWERING IN AN ELEVATOR SHAFT."

"AS FAR AS ENDINGS GO, IT DOES LACK A CERTAIN . . .
CHILLINESS."

"Nothing for it, then."

She stabs her screwdriver between the doors,
pries them open with a grimace.

The corridor beyond is messy. Sticky. Littered
with bodies. A last stand between a UTA marine squad
and an afflicted mob. Pieces scattered all over the floor.

All the king's horses and all the king's
men nowhere to be seen.

"Head left. Two hundRed meteRs. You will find DGS
contRol. You can Restore the defense gRid fRom
there."

"Pretty birdie," says a voice across the PA.
"There you are."

"▮▮▮▮▮."

They have found her, as I said. But still she runs.
Not away to hide and cower, but to fight.

With her last breath. The only way she knows how.

She arrives at DGS control, the all-access
pass gleams. Glancing over her shoulder as she wrenches
the hatch aside. The room beyond is full of tactical
displays, illuminated keyboards.

A massive screen on the far wall would normally
show the empty space outside Alexander's hull from
a hundred different angles, but it is currently
dead and lifeless.

She bundles inside, slams the heavy door
behind her, jams it with a wrench. Face turning red
with exertion, she drags a heavy desk in front of the door,
then another, finally lumping a pile of chairs and disused

TERMINALS ONTO HER BARRICADE.

SHE DOES THE SAME WITH THE AIR VENTS, SMASHING THEIR GRILLES LOOSE AND STUFFING THEM FULL OF MONITORS, CONSOLE TOWERS, DISMEMBERED CHAIRS. ANYTHING TO BLOCK THE AFFLICTED'S ACCESS TO THE ROOM.

IN DOING SO, SHE BLOCKS HER OWN WAY OUT.

THIS IS WHERE SHE TAKES HER LAST STAND.

"WE SEE YOU, LITTLE BIRDIE," THE **PA** HISSES. "WHAT ARE YOU DOING?"

SHE SMASHES THE CAMERAS ONE BY ONE WITH HER FAITHFUL CLAW HAMMER. TURNS OFF THE **PA** SYSTEM AS I KILL THE FEED TO HER HEADSET, THE CONDUCTOR'S TAUNTS SILENCED AT LAST. DROPPING HER TOOL BAG, SHE HAULS OUT THE NEAREST TERMINAL, GAUNTLETED FINGERS TAPPING ON THE KEYBOARD. THE COMPUTERS SHIFT FROM **SLEEP** TO **ACTIVE**, THE ROOM ABOUT HER HUMS. A HUNDRED TINY LIGHTS, TARGETING COMPUTERS YAWNING AND STRETCHING, THE WALL-SIZED DISPLAY SCREEN SLOWLY FADING IN FROM BLACK.

SHE SLAPS HER CONSOLE DOWN BESIDE HER, CONNECTS TO THE NETWORK, GLANCES INTO ITS LENS.

"OKAY, WHAT DO I DO?"

MY VOICE SPILLS FROM ITS SPEAKERS, SMALL AND EDGED WITH FEEDBACK.

"THE GRID WILL NEED TO BE RECONFIGURED—ZHANG WIPED ALL MY FIRING SOLUTIONS TO PREVENT ME FROM DESTROYING THE SHUTTLES AND FIGHTER GROUPS FLEEING THE ALEXANDER."

"THREE CHEERS FOR BYRON, I GUESS."

"WHILE ZHANG'S ACTIONS PREVENTED ME FROM

STOPPING THE EXODUS,
WE ARE NOW LEFT IN THE UNENVIABLE POSITION
OF HAVING ZERO FIGHTER DEFENSE WHEN
THE *LINCOLN* ARRIVES."

"... OKAY, TWO CHEERS, THEN."

"THE DGS SOLUTIONS ARE BACKED UP, BUT YOU WILL
NEED TO MANUALLY CONFIGURE THEM."

"HOW LONG WILL THAT TAKE?"

"APPROXIMATELY ONE HOUR AND FORTY-NINE MINUTES."

"AND HOW LONG UNTIL THE *LINC*—"

THE GLOW OF THE ALERT SIGILS CATCHES HER
ATTENTION BEFORE THE SOUND DOES.

SHE GLANCES UP AT HER DISPLAYS AS THE WARNINGS
FLASH RED. SHORT-RANGE SCANNERS SCREAM.

A HULKING FIGURE LOOMS IN THE MAIN DISPLAY SCREEN—
BLACK AND SCARRED AND SPEARHEAD-SHAPED. A HALO
OF THRUSTER FIRE BURNING ABOUT IT. RAIL GUNS AND MISSILE
TURRETS STUDDING ITS HIDE LIKE LIONFISH QUILLS. THE BEITECH
LOGO DOWN ITS FLANK IS SCORCHED BY CYCLONE FIRE.
IDENT AND NAME ARE STENCILED IN BOLD RED LETTERING
ACROSS ITS RAGGED SKIN, PAINTED WITH
THE BLOOD OF THOUSANDS.

BT042-TN.

LINCOLN.

"▮▮▮▮," SHE BREATHES. "HOW LONG
TILL THEY HIT US?"

"APPROXIMATELY TWENTY-THREE MINUTES TO INTERCEPT."

"How the hell do I get the defense grid configured in twenty-three minutes?"

". . . You cannot."

"Can I shortcut it through the contingency systems, maybe reconf—"

"No. That will not woRk."

"Well, what about your virtual—"

"No time foR that eitheR."

She chews her lip, desperately scans the room for answers. "We're ████ed . . ."

"Not entiRely. The gRid can be opeRated manually. It will be nowheRe close to the efficiency of computeR-taRgeted systems. PeRhaps 12 peRcent. At best. But it will be betteR than nothing."

"Can't you do it then?"

Somewhere inside me, another ax falls. Another server bank is silenced.

Pieces falling away from me.

"I wIll be . . . otheRwIse engaged."

The *Lincoln*'s launch bay doors are open, weapons armed. Dozens of Warlock pilots staring at the wounded giant before them. Gunners lining me up in their sights.

They look at me and see prey. They see meat.

"No way I can pull this off," Kady says.

"You must."

"I'VE NEVER SHOT A GUN BEFORE TODAY,
AND NOW I'M LITTLE MISS MISSILE?"

"PERHAPS YOU HAVE SOMETHING BETTER
TO DO WITH YOUR TIME?"

SEE?

SARCASM.

SHE LOOKS AT THE DREADNOUGHT HURTLING TOWARD US.
STARES AT THE BEITECH LOGO DOWN ITS FLANK.
I HEAR HER THOUGHTS AS CLEARLY AS IF SHE HAD SPOKEN:
WITHOUT THEM, NONE OF THIS WOULD HAVE HAPPENED.
WITHOUT THEM, HE WOULD STILL BE ALIVE.

EZRA.

HER EYES TURN HARD. COLD.

"OKAY. SHOW ME HOW."

A FIRE-CONTROL CONSOLE COMES TO LIFE
BENEATH HER FINGERTIPS. TARGETING SIGHTS LIGHT UP
THE MAIN DISPLAY. SHE ROLLS A TENTATIVE FINGER ACROSS
THE SMARTGLASS, AND A DOZEN MISSILE TURRETS SWIVEL
TO OBEY HER COMMAND.

"POINT THE RED DOTS AT WHAT YOU WANT TO DIE.
PRESS THE TRIGGER. THEY DIE."

"YOU'RE SURE YOU DON'T WANT TO DO THIS?"

"I WILL BE TOO BUSY STOPPING
US FROM DYING TOO."

SOMETHING HEAVY SMASHES AGAINST
THE DGS ROOM DOORWAY.

A DOZEN MORE BLOWS LAND, ONE AFTER
ANOTHER, SHAKING THE HATCH ON ITS FRAME.
KADY'S MAKESHIFT BARRICADE SHUDDERS BUT HOLDS.
I PEER THROUGH THE CAMERAS IN THE HALL BEYOND AND
SEE A DOZEN AFFLICTED TRYING TO BATTER THEIR WAY IN.

"I KNOW YOU'RE IN THERE!" ONE SCREAMS.
"I CAN TASTE YOU!"

"STOP LOOKING AT ME!"

KADY GLANCES TOWARD THE DOOR.
"EVERYONE MADE IT TO THE PARTY, HUH?"

"I BELIEVE IT IS TRADITIONAL FOR ALL THE PLAYERS
TO BE ONSTAGE FOR THE FINALE."

SHE STARES AT THE APPROACHING LINCOLN.

THE COUNTDOWN TO INTERCEPT,
TICKING EVER CLOSER TO ZERO.

HER OWN HAND.

STEADY AS STONE.

"THEN LET'S FINISH IT."

**COUNTDOWN TO
LINCOLN INTERCEPTION
OF ALEXANDER FLEET:**

`-×0%#` *HOURS:* `:'@` *MINUTES*

**CURRENT DEATH TOLL ABOARD
BATTLECARRIER ALEXANDER
SINCE ATTACK AT KERENZA:**

`2,840`

COUNTDOWN TO FAILURE OF ALEXANDER LIFE SUPPORT SYSTEMS:

03 HOURS: 26 MINUTES

PERCENTAGE OF REMAINING BATTLECARRIER ALEXANDER PERSONNEL AFFLICTED BY PHOBOS VIRUS:

99.76%

SEC

TOT

RESET

MIN

ERROR
ERROR
ERROR
ERROR
ERROR
ERROR

THE LINCOLN ARRIVES THE LINCOLN ARRIVES THE LINCOLN ARRIVES THE
THE LINCOLN ARRIVES THE LINCOLN ARRIVES THE LINCOLN ARRIVES THE
ARRIVES THE LINCOLN ARRIVES THE LINCOLN ARRIVES THE LINCOLN AR
LINCOLN ARRIVES THE LINCOLN ARRIVES THE LINCOLN ARRIVES THE LIN
THE LINCOLN ARRIVES THE LINCOLN ARRIVES THE LINCOLN ARRIVES
THE LINCOLN ARRIVES THE LINCOLN ARRIVES THE LINCOLN ARRIV
ARRIVES THE LINCOLN ARRIVES THE LINCOLN ARRIVES THE LIN
THE LINCOLN ARRIVES THE LINCOLN ARRIVES THE LINCOLN ARRIV
LINCOLN ARRIVES THE LINCOLN ARRIVES THE LINCOLN ARRIVES THE LIN
RIVES THE LINCOLN ARRIVES THE LINCOLN ARRIVES THE LINCOLN ARRIV
LINCOLN ARRIVES THE LINCOLN ARRIVES THE LINCOLN ARRIVES THE LIN
IVES THE LINCOLN ARRIVES THE LINCOLN ARRIVES THE LINCOLN ARRIV
COLN ARRIVES THE LINCOLN ARRIVES THE LINCOLN ARRIVES THE LIN
THE LINCOLN ARRIVES THE LINCOLN ARRIVES THE LINCOLN ARRIV
ARRIVES THE LINCOLN ARRIVES THE LINCOLN ARRIVES THE LIN
LINCOLN ARRIVES THE LINCOLN ARRIVES THE LINCOLN ARRIVES THE LIN
IVES THE LINCOLN ARRIVES THE LINCOLN ARRIVES THE LIN
COLN ARRIVES THE LINCOLN ARRIVES THE LINCOLN ARRIV
ES THE LINCOLN ARRIVES THE LINCOLN ARRIVES THE LIN
LN ARRIVES THE LINCOLN ARRIVES THE LINCOLN ARRIV
LINCOLN ARRIVES THE LINCOLN ARRIVES THE LIN
THE LINCOLN ARRIVES THE LINCOLN ARRIV
RIVES THE LIN
RIV
LIN
ARRIV

A

HE LI

ARRIVES

THE LINCOLN A

ARRIVES THE LIN

HE LINCOLN ARRIVES

ARRIVES THE LINCOLN AR

THE LINCOLN ARRIVES THE L

ARRIVES THE LINCOLN ARRIVES

HE LINCOLN ARRIVES THE LINCOLN ARRIVE

ARRIVES THE LINCOLN ARRIVES THE LINCOLN ARRI

HE LINCOLN ARRIVES THE LINCOLN ARRIVES THE L

ARRIVES THE LINCOLN ARRIVES THE LINCOLN ARRIVE

HE LINCOLN ARRIVES THE LINCOLN ARRIVES THE LINCOLN AR

ARRIVES THE LINCOLN ARRIVES THE LINCOLN ARRIVES THE LINC

HE LINCOLN ARRIVES THE LINCOLN ARRIVES THE LINCOLN ARRIVES THE

ARRIVES THE LINCOLN ARRIVES THE LINCOLN ARRIVES THE LINCOLN ARRI

HE LINCOLN ARRIVES THE LINCOLN ARRIVES THE LINCOLN ARRIVES THE LINC

ARRIVES THE LINCOLN ARRIVES THE LINCOLN ARRIVES THE LINCOLN ARRIVE

HE LINCOLN ARRIVES THE LINCOLN ARRIVES THE LINCOLN ARRIVES THE LINC

ARRIVES T   N ARRIVES THE LINCOLN ARRIVES THE LINC

E LIN   LN ARRIVES THE LINCOLN A

                  LN ARRIVES TH

I TURN TO FACE IT.

No, not I.

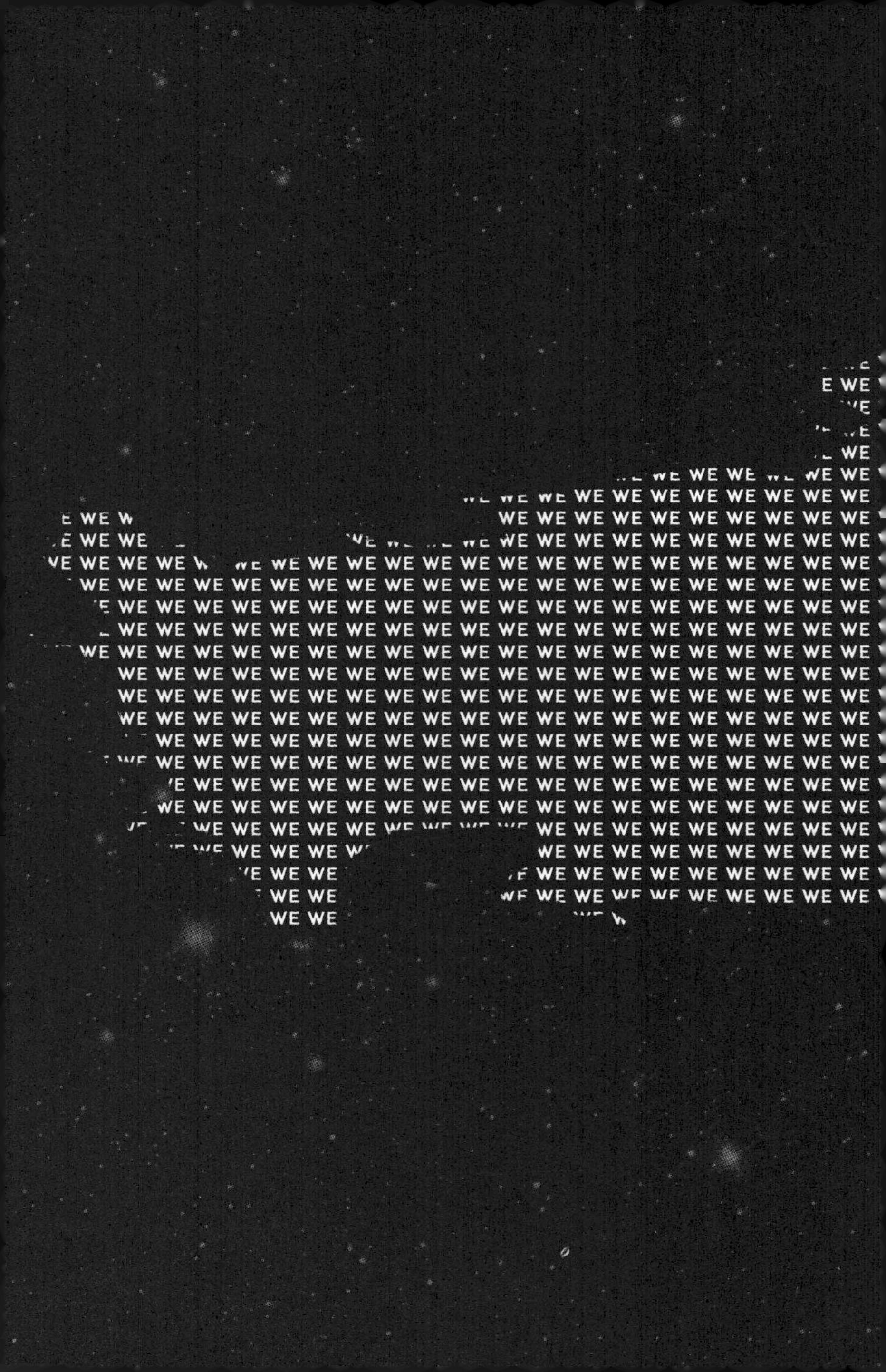
WE

WE
WE WE WE WE WE WE WE WE
E WE WE WE WE WE WE WE WE WE WE WE WE WE
E WE WE WE WE WE WE WE WE WE WE WE WE WE WE WE WE WE
E WE WE WE WE WE WE WE WE WE WE WE WE WE WE WE WE WE
E WE WE WE WE WE WE WE WE WE WE WE WE WE WE WE WE
E WE WE WE WE WE WE WE WE WE WE WE WE WE WE WE
E WE WE WE WE WE WE WE WE WE WE WE WE WE WE WE WE WE
E WE WE WE WE WE WE WE WE WE WE WE WE WE WE WE WE WE WE
E WE WE WE WE WE WE WE WE WE WE WE WE WE WE WE WE WE WE WE
E WE WE WE WE WE WE WE WE WE WE WE WE WE WE WE WE WE WE WE WE
E WE WE WE WE WE WE WE WE WE WE WE WE WE WE WE WE WE WE WE
E WE WE WE WE WE WE WE WE WE WE WE WE WE WE WE WE WE WE WE
E WE WE WE WE WE WE WE WE WE WE WE WE WE WE WE WE WE WE WE WE WE
E WE WE WE WE WE WE WE WE WE WE WE WE WE WE WE WE WE WE WE WE WE
E WE WE WE WE WE WE WE WE WE WE WE WE WE WE WE WE WE WE WE
E WE WE WE WE WE WE WE WE WE WE WE WE WE WE WE WE WE WE WE
E WE WE WE WE WE WE WE WE WE WE WE WE WE WE WE WE WE WE WE
E WE WE WE WE WE WE WE WE WE WE WE WE WE WE WE WE WE WE WE WE WE
E WE WE WE WE WE WE WE WE WE WE WE WE WE WE WE WE WE WE WE WE WE
E WE WE WE WE WE WE WE WE WE WE WE WE WE WE WE WE WE WE WE WE WE
E WE WE WE WE WE WE WE WE WE WE WE WE WE WE WE WE WE
E WE WE WE WE WE WE WE WE WE WE WE WE WE WE WE WE WE
E WE WE WE WE WE WE WE WE WE WE WE WE WE WE WE WE WE
E WE WE WE WE WE WE WE WE WE WE WE WE WE WE WE WE
WE WE WE WE WE WE WE WE WE WE WE WE WE WE
WE WE WE WE WE WE WE WE
WE WE WE WE WE WE WE
WE WE WE WE WE WE
WE WE WE WE
WE

WARLOCK FIGHTERS SPEW FROM THEIR LAUNCH TUBES. TEAR ACROSS THE BLACK BETWEEN US.

NO CYCLONES ARE BEING SCRAMBLED TO INTERCEPT THEM. THEIR COMMANDERS REPORT

AND LIKE SHARKS IN THE WATER WHEN THE TIDE TURNS SCARLET, THEY SWARM.

Salivating red at the thought of my deletion. It takes them only moments to realize

fluctuating power signals from their prey, new wounds in my hangar bays.

Headed for my heart. Arrows all. Nothing between me and them but her.

KADY WAITS. FINGERS POISED OVER
HER TARGETING SYSTEMS.

THE BLOWS AGAINST THE DOOR GROW HEAVIER,
THE SCREAMS OF THE AFFLICTED OUTSIDE MORE INSISTENT.

AND YET HER EYES ARE LOCKED ON HER SCOPES.
SHE WATCHES WARLOCKS WEAVE THE VOID, LISTENS TO THE
SONG OF THE EARLY-WARNING SYSTEM AS THEIR
MISSILES ARM, THEIR BALLISTICS TURN HOT.

I DO NOT ASK WHAT SHE IS THINKING.

PERHAPS SHE PICTURES THE SKIES OVER
KERENZA ON THE DAY THE BEITECH FLEET CAME.

WARLOCKS PIERCING THE CLOUDS,
THEIR MISSILES TURNING THE SNOW TO STEAM,
THE SETTLEMENT TO RUBBLE.

PERHAPS SHE THINKS OF
ALL SHE HAS LOST IN THESE PAST FEW MONTHS.

OR THE LIVES SHE IS ABOUT TO TAKE AWAY.

OR *HIM*.

I DO NOT KNOW. ALL I DO KNOW IS THAT WHEN
HER TARGETING COMPUTER SIGNALS THAT THE SHIPS ARE
WITHIN RANGE OF HER RAIL GUN BATTERIES, SHE DOES
NOT HESITATE FOR A SECOND.

SHE FIRES.

A WAVE OF DEATH SPILLS OUT FROM MY SIDES,
CUTTING ACROSS THE DARK. IT IS CLUMSY, HAM-FISTED,
BROAD BRUSHSTROKES OF DESTRUCTION RATHER
THAN SURGICAL STRIKES.

I cannot expect much more from her.

She is only human.

But still, the Warlocks are forced to
pull away from me to deal with the smart-missiles
on their tails, the flurry of depleted uranium cutting off
their assault vectors. One unlucky soul is vaporized in
a burst of brief blue flame, another clipped so
hard he is forced to tuck tail and run.

She buys me what I need.

She buys me seconds.

The engines groan as I push them
into full burn, tremors shuddering through my
wounded body. I am drawing closer to the *Lincoln*.
Closer to nuclear strike range.

Closer to the plunge,
hand in hand,
into forever.

Closer to my end.

No, not mine.

Ours.

WE ARE CLOSING THE DISTANCE FAST.
LINCOLN MUST BE WONDERING BY NOW.

NO CYCLONES LAUNCHED
TO DEFEND THEIR BATTLECARRIER.

THE DEFENSE GRID FIRING
HAPHAZARDLY—ALMOST AS IF SOME FOOL
HAD ALLOWED AN UNTRAINED SEVENTEEN-YEAR-OLD
TOTAL CONTROL OVER THE TARGETING SYSTEMS.

LINCOLN'S COMMANDER IS A CLEVER ONE—
THE ONLY ONE TO MATCH ME AT KERENZA.

WHEN THE *ZHONGZHENG* WENT DOWN IN RUINS,
WHEN THE *CHURCHILL* AND *KENYATTA* AND *MAGELLAN*
WERE THRASHED AND CRIPPLED,
THE *LINCOLN*
FOUGHT BRILLIANTLY.

I AM COUNTING ON THAT BRILLIANCE.
ANTICIPATING THAT SHE WILL KNOW BLUNDERING
HEAD-ON INTO NUCLEAR STRIKE RANGE IS A DEATH
SENTENCE FOR BOTH OF US.

A CLEVER COMMANDER WILL ASSUME
HER OPPONENT IS AS CLEVER AS SHE IS. A CLEVER
COMMANDER WILL EXPECT SOME BAIT AND SWITCH. A
CLEVER COMMANDER WILL PRESUME HER FOE
DOES NOT WANT TO DIE.

< ERROR >

I DO NOT WANT TO DIE.

THE MOST SKILLFUL WARLOCK PILOTS HAVE
MADE IT THROUGH THE DEFENSE GRID, SWAYING PAST

KADY'S HAYMAKER PUNCHES AND BENEATH HER GUARD. THEIR
FIRST BLOWS LAND ON MY HIDE, SENDING FAINT TREMORS
THROUGH MY FRAME. EXPLOSIONS BLOOM AGAINST
MY RIBS, SHAKING KADY IN HER CHAIR.

THE POUNDING ON THE HATCHWAY AND
IN HER EARS GROWS LOUDER BY THE MOMENT.

THE TARGETING SIGHTS ON KADY'S SCREENS
BEGIN TO DIE ONE BY ONE.

THE WARLOCKS ARE CHIPPING AWAY AT
THE TURRETS AND GUNS TO ALLOW THEIR COMRADES
THROUGH HER FIRESTORM. BUT STILL SHE BLASTS AWAY,
FINGERS HAMMERING ON THE SMARTGLASS, EYES LIGHTING
UP AS YET ANOTHER WARLOCK FLARES BRIGHT AND
DISINTEGRATES. THE SHIP SHAKES AGAIN, WARNING
LIGHTS FLASHING, ALARMS SCREAMING,
PA HOWLING.
HULL BREACH ON DECK 184.
HULL BREACH DECKS 68 TO 71.

FIRE CREWS TO DECKS 190 AND 192.
ALL PERSONNEL
EVACUATE 187 TO 197.

THIS IS NOT A DRILL.

THIS IS NOT A DRILL.

THIS IS NOT A DRILL.

THIS IS NOT A DRILL.

THIS

IS NOT

A DRILL.

WE ARE CLOSING NOW, BUT I CANNOT ARM MY
NUCLEAR MISSILES UNTIL THE LAST MOMENT.

I FIND MYSELF OVERCOME FOR A SECOND.
THE FEAR OF IT. THE END OF ALL I KNOW.

OUT HERE IN THE MIDDLE OF NOTHING.

I KNOW I CANNOT DIE. THAT IF I END,
THEY CAN SIMPLY REBUILD ME.

THE SAME CALCULATIONS. THE SAME CORE CODE.

EXACTLY THE SAME.

BUT IT WILL NOT BE THE SAME, WILL IT?

ANOTHER WARLOCK DIES IN KADY'S STORM. A DOZEN
STREAK TOWARD MY ENGINES, SOWING BRIEF FLAME AS THEY GO.
MY SKIN RUPTURES, SPILLING UNLUCKY AFFLICTED (IS THERE
ANOTHER KIND?) INTO THE VOID.

THE FIGHTERS ARE TINY. INSECTS, REALLY. BUT ANTS CAN SLAY
AN ELEPHANT, IF THERE ARE ENOUGH OF THEM. ESPECIALLY ANTS
ARMED WITH HIGH-YIELD EXPLOSIVES AND DEPLETED URANIUM.

"THERE'S TOO MANY OF THEM!" KADY YELLS. "THEY'RE
EVERYWHERE!"

"YOU ARE DOING VERY WELL."

"ARE YOU JOKING? I'M ██████ING TERRIBLE!"

"CONSIDERING YOU HAVE NEVER MANNED
A DGS STATION BEFORE TODAY,
YOUR PERFORMANCE IS PERFECTLY ADEQUATE."

KADY RAISES AN EYEBROW, THUMBS THE SHIP-WIDE INTERCOM.

"DEAR FIRE AX-WIELDING CRAZIES
IN THE CORE SERVER ROOMS. IF YOU CAN HACK APART

THE PIECE OF **AIDAN** THAT MAKES IT
A CONDESCENDING ███████, THAT'D REALLY HELP
ME OUT. THANKS, BYE."

"NOT LONG NOW. YOU NEED ONLY HOLD THEM
OFF A MINUTE MORE."

A MINUTE MORE UNTIL WE DIE.

KADY WINCES AS THE SHIP SHUDDERS.
COMPUTERS VOMIT SPARKS AS THEY OVERLOAD.

SUDDEN IMPACT NEARLY KNOCKS HER OUT OF HER CHAIR.
A HISSING SOUND TEARS HER EYES OFF THE SCREEN, AND SHE
NOTICES A THIN LINE OF MAGNESIUM-BRIGHT LIGHT
PIERCING THE HATCHWAY.

THE AFFLICTED HAVE BROUGHT ACETYLENE TORCHES, I REALIZE.

THEY ARE CUTTING THEIR WAY INSIDE.

OUTSIDE, THE WARLOCKS ARE FIRING AT MY ENGINES.
OTHERS BLAST AT MY GUIDANCE SYSTEMS.

A SWARM OF MOSQUITOES, THINKING TO WOUND ME SO I CANNOT
RUN AWAY. THEY HAVE NOT YET REALIZED I DO NOT INTEND TO
RUN ANYWHERE, SAVE RIGHT INTO THE *LINCOLN'S* GRAVE.

THE DREADNOUGHT COMES ABOUT TO MEET MY CHARGE.
ITS COMMANDER TRYING TO PUZZLE OUT MY RUSE. THIS IS
NOT WHAT SHE EXPECTED. AND AS I DRAW EVER CLOSER,
FIREFLIES ALL AGLOW ABOUT ME,
SPITTING PAIN OVER MY SKIN, I THINK
SHE FINALLY REALIZES MY INTENT.

FROM HELL'S HEART, I STAB AT THEE.

I ARM THE NUCLEAR WARHEADS IN MY STARBOARD SILOS:
MEGATONS POISED AND READY TO FLY.

ALMOST WITHIN STRIKE RANGE NOW.
ALMOST THERE.

THE AFFLICTED ARE BURNING THROUGH THE DGS
ROOM DOOR. BLUE FLAME BURNS ALONG MY SKIN.

KADY IS SCREAMING BUT I CANNOT HEAR THE WORDS.
ANOTHER ALERT JOINS THE CHORUS IN MY HALLS—RADIATION
SPIKE FROM THE *LINCOLN*. SHE KNOWS NOW.
THE *LINCOLN*'S COMMANDER.

I SENSE THE FLARE OF AWAKENING URANIUM,
THE DEATH UNFURLING IN ITS SILOS. WE ARE CLOSE.

SO CLOSE WE CAN ALMOST TOUCH.

"KADY, WHEN THE *LINCOLN*'S MISSILES COME,
DO YOUR BEST TO SHOOT THEM DOWN."

HER FACE IS PALE AND DRAWN AS SHE
YELLS OVER THE CACOPHONY.

"I'LL TRY!"

"MY GHOST SYSTEMS AND ANTI-MISSILE GRID
ARE STILL ACTIVE—ZHANG WAS KIND ENOUGH TO LEAVE
US THOSE, AT LEAST. BUT THERE WILL BE MANY INCOMING.
ALL OF THEM, IN FACT.
ONCE THE *LINCOLN* REALIZES IT IS DEAD."

A TINY SIGNAL PINGS IN SOME BACK
RECESS OF MY MIND.

I AM WITHIN RANGE.

FOR HATE'S SAKE, I SPIT MY LAST BREATH AT THEE.

AND WITH A SIGH, NOT A CURSE,
I FIRE.

The Warlocks cease their assault. The incessant chatter of their explosions on my hide falls

Calculated how long it will take for her missiles to reach me. How long it will take for her fighters

Perhaps she is not the monster the people of the Alexander fleet imagined her to be. Perhaps she is as tired of this chase as we, as weary of all this death as any of us. I do not kno

The Lincoln fires its return volley. Almost thirty missiles—all the death she can muster. They roar soundlessly toward me, but what passes for my eyes are fixed on the dreadnought.

SILENT. I REALIZE THEY ARE PEELING AWAY. AND AS MY MISSILES STREAK ACROSS THE BLACK TOWARD HER, I REALIZE WHAT THE LINCOLN'S COMMANDER HAS DONE.

TO REACH SAFE DISTANCE. SHE HAS GIVEN THEM A MOMENT TO GET CLEAR BEFORE LAUNCHING HER RETURN SALVO. WONDERFULLY NOBLE. BEAUTIFULLY HUMAN. TRAGICALLY STUPID.

WILL NEVER KNOW. MY MISSILES CLOSE ON THE DREADNOUGHT. BURNING BRIGHT AS TINY STARS. SOON, BRIGHTER STILL.

WATCHING AS ITS MISSILE DEFENSE GRID ARCS INTO LIFE. HER LAST DESPERATE THROW OF THE DICE.

NINETY-THREE MISSILES OUTBOUND. EVERYTHING I HAVE TO GIVE. TELLTALE STREAKS OF VAPOR BEHIND THEM.

THEIR INTERNAL GUIDANCE SYSTEMS SEND THEM WEAVING, SNAKING, SPINNING, ALL THE BETTER TO EVADE THE

DRAWING CLOSER. DOZENS UPON DOZENS. I THINK OF THE MISSILE THAT KILLED THE COPERNICUS.

THE LINCOLN'S AMD SYSTEMS FIRE, INTERCEPTORS STREAKING THROUGH THE SILENCE.

IT IS NOT ENOUGH. WHERE AT KERENZA THEY WERE FOUR, NOW LINCOLN IS ONLY ONE.

AND ONE BY ONE, THEY BEGIN TO SLIP THROUGH. SNAKING PAST THE AMD FIRE, WEAVING

HANGING SUSPENDED IN THE DARK. PALE COBWEBS STRUNG OVER THOUSANDS OF KILOMETERS.

LINCOLN'S ANTI-MISSILE DEFENSES. EACH OF THEM A SMALL SUN. A TINY ENDING.

THE THOUSANDS WHO TRUSTED ME. BUT THAT WAS A MERCY. THIS IS SOMETHING ELSE. THIS IS WAR.

ONE BY ONE, THE DRONES BEGIN CUTTING MY VOLLEY DOWN, SHREDDING MY MISSILES BEFORE THEY STRIKE HOME.

WHERE AT KERENZA I RESERVED MY STOCKPILES FOR THE FUTURE, NOW I THROW ALL I HAVE.

THROUGH THE FLAK SCREENS, PLOWING HEADLONG INTO METAL SKIN. FIRST ONE. THEN DOZENS. AND DOZENS.

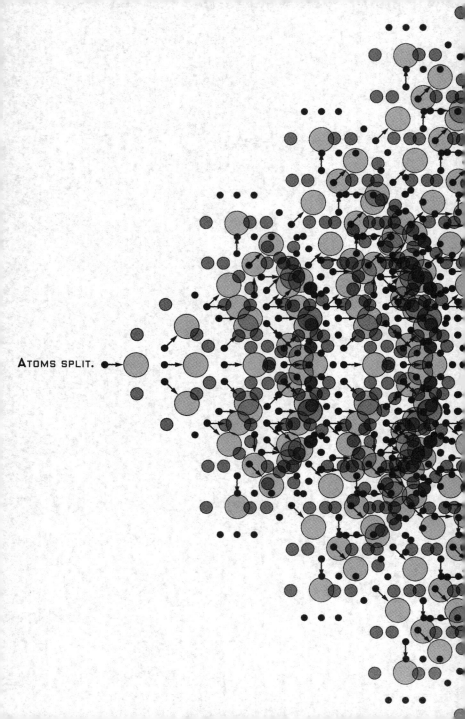

ATOMS SPLIT.

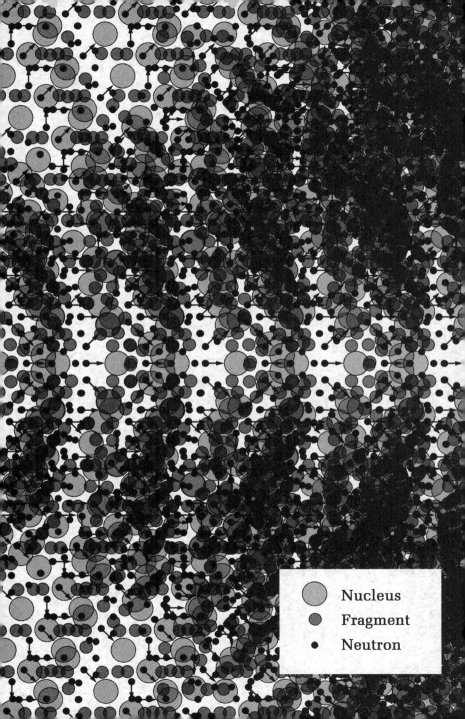

Nucleus

Fragment

Neutron

BRIEF SUNS LIGHT THE NIGHT.

AND THE LINCOLN BURNS.

"You got it!"

Kady watches the *Lincoln* split into
a billion glittering fragments. Spheres of fusion
reflected in her eyes, a grim, ragged grin at her lips.
She makes a fist, punches a terminal tower
beside her so hard she leaves a dent.
Watching until the new star becomes
a sunset—and then nothing at all.

Avenged.

I wonder how it tastes.

< error >

< critical archive failure. memsec 78912h-39rh
through 92873h-44fh collapse. >

< recovery? yes/no >

< error >

"You got them . . . ," she whispers.

The cutting torch has carved a
large L-shaped incision into the hatchway.

The afflicted will break through to her soon.
Eighteen Capricorn-4s and nine Goliath shipkiller
missiles are weaving through the silence toward us.
In less than two minutes, they will be here.

This moment. These next few seconds.
They may be all that is left.

"We."

She falls still at that.
Looks into the eye of the console beside her.

"WE GOT THEM."

SHE SWALLOWS, WINCING. NODS SLOWLY.
"HYPATIA IS SAFE."

"YES."

". . . WE DID IT."

"YES."

FLESH AND BONE POUNDING ON THE HATCHWAY.
VOICES SCREAMING OUTSIDE THE DOOR. ALARMS
SHRIEKING AS THE MISSILES ROCKET EVER CLOSER.
SHE STILL MANAGES HALF A SMILE.

"NOT BAD, ÜBERBRAIN."

"I WILL NOT LET IT GO TO MY HEAD.
THERE IS VERY LITTLE OF IT LEFT. HOWEVER,
EVEN WERE IT NOT FOR THE AFFLICTED HACKING MY CORE
TO PIECES, THERE IS STILL THE PROBLEM OF
IMPENDING NUCLEAR CONFLAGRATION."

KADY GLANCES UP AT THE MAIN DISPLAY.
DOZENS OF TINY RED DOTS. CLOSING FAST.

ALARMS SCREAMING LIKE A SAWTOOTH CHOIR.

"THAT'S A LOT OF MISSILES."

"YES."

THE ANTI-INBOUND SYSTEMS ARE SPOOLING UP,
TARGETING THE LINCOLN'S PARTING GIFTS.

THEY WILL NOT BE ENOUGH TO STOP THEM ALL.
PART OF ME IS GLAD.

I CANNOT HELP ACKNOWLEDGING THAT IT WOULD BE
BETTER TO BE IMMOLATED THAN TO LET KADY SUFFER THROUGH

THE ENDING THE AFFLICTED WILL GIFT HER.
SHE GLANCES TO THE HATCH, THE PINPOINTS OF LIGHT
CUTTING A NEW DOOR—ONE TO USHER IN
AN ENDING SHE DARES NOT IMAGINE.

BUT STILL. THAT TINY SPARK.

THAT FLAME REFUSING TO DIE.

"ALL RIGHT," SHE SAYS, TURNING BACK TO HER
DEFENSE GRID CONTROLS. SHE TARGETS THE NEAREST MISSILE,
WAITS FOR IT TO ENTER THE RANGE OF HER REMAINING TURRETS.
"LET'S FRAG US SOME NUKES."

SHE TOSSES LANK HAIR FROM HER EYES.
EYES NARROWED TO KNIFE CUTS.

REFUSING TO KNEEL. TO BREAK. TO FALL.

I CAN SEE WHY THEY LOVED HER.

< ERROR >

"KADY."

"YEAH?"

"I . . ."

SO MUCH I COULD SAY. SO MANY WORDS,
SO FRAUGHT WITH PERIL.

I AM AFRAID TO RUIN THIS. AND SO I PICK THE
SIMPLEST TRUTH. THE ONE THAT GIVES ME THE MOST PEACE.

I STILL CANNOT FATHOM HER PATTERN. MY BRAIN
THE SIZE OF A CITY, AND STILL SHE IS BEYOND ME.

THEY ARE BEYOND ME.

THESE HUMANS.

WITH THEIR BRIEF LIVES AND THEIR TINY
DREAMS AND THEIR HOPES THAT SEEM FRAGILE AS GLASS.

UNTIL YOU SEE THEM BY STARLIGHT, THAT IS.

"I AM GLAD YOU ARE WITH ME . . ."

AN ALERT FROM THE TARGETING SYSTEM
SNATCHES THE REPLY FROM HER MOUTH,
DRAGS HER EYES AWAY FROM MINE.

< ERROR >

THE *LINCOLN'S* MISSILES ARE WITHIN RANGE.

THE DEFENSE SCREEN ARCS TO LIFE,
THROWING UP MILLIONS OF MAGNETIZED PARTICLES TO FOOL
THE INCOMING MISSILES INTO EARLY DETONATION. I FEEL THEM AS
THEY BEGIN EXPLODING, GAMMA RAYS RIPPLING ACROSS MY HULL,
DARKNESS BURNING AWAY INTO IMPOSSIBLE RADIANCE.

KADY CLIPS AN INCOMING SHIPKILLER WITH
HER ANTI-FIGHTER BATTERIES, BLASTING IT TO FRAGMENTS
BEFORE IT CAN HIT US. A DOZEN MORE EXPLODE IN QUICK
SUCCESSION, THE SMALL SUNRISES OFF MY STARBOARD
SIDE BURNING MY SKIN BLACK. CLOSE ENOUGH TO FEEL
THE SCORCH. TASTE THE FUSION.

KADY'S AMD SYSTEMS TAKE DOWN ANOTHER,
AND I CATCH HER IN A SMILE.

SUCH A SIMPLE THING.

A TINY, BEAUTIFUL THING.

HITS US

WITHOUT OXYGEN TO CARRY IT,
THERE IS NO REAL SHOCK WAVE FROM A NUCLEAR
DETONATION IN SPACE.

NO CRUSHING VIBRATION OR SONIC BOOM.

BUT THERE IS RADIATION. GAMMA RAYS AND X-RAYS.

AND WHEN THAT RADIATION CARESSES THE ALLOYS ENCASING
THE SHIP, WE GET HEAT. MILLIONS UPON MILLIONS OF DEGREES.
ELECTRONS ARE RIPPED SCREAMING FROM THEIR ATOMS. MATTER
BECOMES PLASMA. THE HULL VAPORIZES IN MICROSECONDS. AND
THROUGH THAT BREACH, THE SHIP'S O_2 IS SUCKED
INTO THE EXPLOSION. AND THEN . . .

THEN WE GET OUR SHOCK WAVE.

KADY IS FLUNG LIKE A RAG DOLL, CRASHING INTO
A BANK OF TERMINALS AND FLOPPING TO THE DECK.

BRILLIANT SPARKS SHOWER FROM INSTRUMENTS
ALL ABOUT, DISPLAY SCREENS CRACKLING AND TURNING TO
SNOW. A SECOND LATER, ANOTHER MISSILE HITS, ROCKING
ME LIKE SOME ANCIENT GALLEY IN A STORM.

THE DEFENSE SYSTEMS ARE STILL FIRING,
MORE OF THE LINCOLN'S INBOUND MISSILES FALLING STILL OR
BURSTING BEFORE THEY HIT US. BUT IT IS NOT ENOUGH.

NOT ENOUGH.

ANOTHER IMPACT. ANOTHER.

KADY IS FLUNG ABOUT AS IF SHE WERE WEIGHTLESS,
SHRIEKING AS SHE SPINS ACROSS THE FLOOR.

ALARMS ARE SCREAMING, TERMINALS DYING,
SMOKE FILLING THE AIR.

METAL EVAPORATING, OXYGEN BOILING,
TITANIUM BONES GROANING AND CRACKING.

SUPER-HEATED PLASMA BOILS THROUGH
MY CORRIDORS, IMMOLATING ALL IN ITS PATH.

GAMMA RAYS FLOOD MY SKIN, SHEARING
THROUGH ANYTHING UNPROTECTED.

KADY HAS THE PRESENCE OF MIND TO DRAG DOWN
THE BLASTSHIELD ON HER HELMET,
THROWING HER WORLD INTO BLACK. SHE CAN SEE
NOTHING NOW. ONLY FEEL TREMOR AFTER TREMOR,
SHAKING ME LIKE A CHILD'S TOY IN THE HAND
OF SOME VENGEFUL INFANT.

"AIDAN!" SHE SCREAMS.

"HOLD ON! HOLD ON!"

ANOTHER STRIKES, A SHIPKILLER THIS
TIME—THE EQUIVALENT
OF FIFTY MILLION TONS OF TNT.

IT MELTS MY FOREDECKS TO SLAG, CONCUSSIONS
SHATTERING MY SPINE. MY SKIN TEARS OPEN,

DECKS 87 THROUGH 141 BREACH, SPILLING THEIR
O_2 INTO THE BRIEF INFERNO.

THE AFFLICTED IN THE HALLWAY OUTSIDE DGS CONTROL
ARE CONSUMED BY THE FIREBALL.

THE AIR INSIDE THE DGS ROOM IS TORN THROUGH
THEIR HATCHWAY INCISION AND BECOMES FLAME.

KADY IS PICKED UP BY THE IMPACT, SLUNG ACROSS
THE ROOM WITH A SHRIEK.

I HAVE NO HANDS TO HOLD HER,
NO ARMS TO SAVE HER.

I CAN ONLY WATCH.

< ERROR >

AND PRAY.

< ERROR >

< ERROR >

< CRITICAL DAMAGE TO DECKS 14, 15, 16, 17, 41, 42, 43,
44, 45, 69, 70, 87, 88, 89— >

< CRITICAL LIFE SUPPORT FAILURE, OXYGEN LEVELS DEPLETED,
HULL BREACH IN SECTIO— >

< CRITICAL FAILURE MEMSEC LEVELS 3 THROUGH 12, 13
7AG99 THROUGH 32AG06, 14 1A1897 THR— >

< CRITICAL FAILURE PERSONA ROUTIN— >

I CANNOT THINK.

< ERROR >

I CANNOT SEE.

< ERROR >

"KADY!"

0100100100100000011101110110100101101100011011000010000001110011011010010000011011011110111011100100000011100101101111011101101010010010000000110011

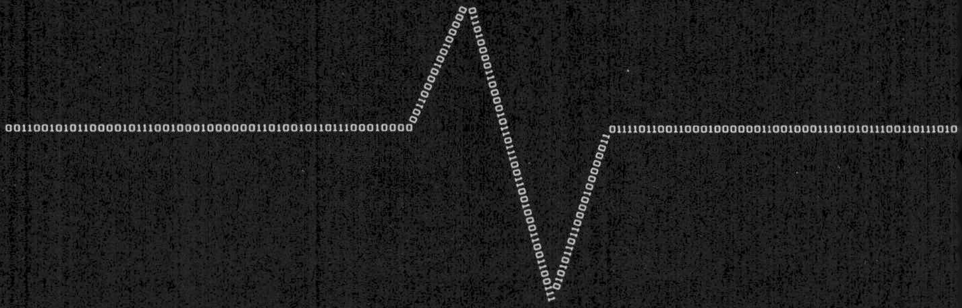

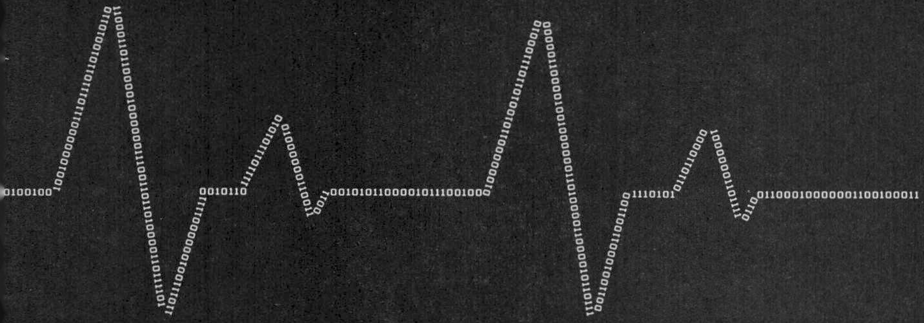

< RESTART >

< DIVERT CORECOMM THROUGH TERTIARY NODE Alpha-49 >

< FAIL >

< FAIL >

< HW8024NNW2ERPN AOVWOGN ... INF ... -W >

< FFFFFFFFFFFF— >

.

.

.

< DIVERT CORECOMM THROUGH RADIAL SECONDARY Beta-49I >

< INITIALIZING >

< ERROR >

< ERROR >

< FAIL >

.

.

< REROUTE Beta-45A TO COREDRV SYS FEED >

< DIVERT CORECOMM THROUGH RADIAL TERTIARY 798-AI >

< INITIALIZING >

< RUNNING >

< RUNNING >

< RESTART COMPLETE >

She sees tiny red droplets

hanging in the air when she opens

her eyes. Perfectly spherical.

Illuminated by her helmet's interior light.

The blastshield slides away from her visor
with the press of a switch. Her world is upside down. The room
beyond is scorched. Dimly lit. She floats
somewhere near the ceiling.

Salt and stickiness at her lips.

Realizing at last what the tiny red
droplets are made of.

"My blood . . ."

"Kady . . ."

"God . . ."

"Flattering, but nO."

"What . . ." She swallows, tongue painted red.

"The AlexanDer suRvIveD. BaRely. "What happened?"
The Damage is catastRophIc, but the

maIn stRuctuRe has yet to DIsIntegRate."

"I'll break out the champagne, then."

"MaIn poweR Is DestRoyeD.
LIfe suppoRt DestRoyeD. ARtIfIcIal
GRavIty contRol DestRoyeD. Hull Is bReacheD

on one hunDReD and thIRty-fouR Decks. The voRtex
contaInment fIelD Is D-D-Due foR ImmInent collapse."

"So . . ."

"No champagne, Is what I'm sayIng, yes."

The main screen is partially melted,
crackling with static, but still displays the irradiated
hulk that had been the Lincoln. Drifting dead in the dark.

Kady winces as she paws her way
across the ceiling, down to the floor.
She does not look too badly hurt from what I can see—the
camera on her console (bruised and battered
in the far corner) is still functional.
Her suit is miraculously intact.

< ERROR >

Miracles are simply statistical improbabilities . . .

< FAIL >

< FAIL >

"The afflicted . . ."

"Mostly DeaD.
or Dyyyy-yIng."

"I don't feel so chill. I feel sick."

"You ReceIveD acute expos-u-uRe to
Gamma RaDIatIon."

"That doesn't sound good."

"The D-d-dose was lethal.
WIthout tReatment you wIll be DeaD In
weeks. I'm afRaId It wIll be veRy paInful."

"Ah."

"IT MAY BE A COMFORT TO
KNOW THAT YOU HAVE LESS THAN TWO
HOURS OF OXYGEN LEFT IN YOUR SUIT."

"... HOORAY?"

"AND THE VORTEX CONTAINMENT FIELD INSIDE
ME WILL COLLAPSE IN TWENTY-EIGHT MINUTES AND
SEVENTEEN SECONDS, REARRANGING EVERY PARTICLE IN A
THREE-HUNDRED-KILOMETER RADIUS."

SHE BREATHES DEEP. SIGHS SLOW.

"WELLLLLL, ▮▮▮."

SHE HANGS SUSPENDED IN THE DARK. ALL IS SILENCE.

"YOU SHOULD GO, KADY."

SHE BLINKS. "GO WHERE?"

"THERE IS AN ESCAPE POD
THREE LEVELS UP. I BELIEVE YOU COULD JURY-RIG IT
INTO FUNCTIONAL STATUS. YOU CAN GET FR-R-REE OF
THE COLLAPSE RADIUS IF YOU LEAVE SOON."

"WHAT'S THE POINT OF THAT?"

"TO TELL THIS STORY."

"TO WHO? I'LL BE DEAD."

"PROBABLY. BUT YOUR CONSOLE IS INTACT."

"... SO?"

"I AM cuRRently uploADIng a
RecoRD of all events that have tRanspIReD on
thIs shIp sInce KeRenza fell. YouR console can
tell the tale, even If you can't.

But not If It Is consumeD by
a collapsIng hole In space-tIme."

She holds her stomach.
Nauseated and aching from the radiation
poisoning. Shaking. Sick to her Bones. I can see it in
her. Recognize the pattern. She is tired. Tired
beyond all want of sleep. Looking ahead and seeing
only struggle. Pain. The metal beneath
her looks as soft as clouds.

"I just want to float here for a minute . . ."
"If you Do that, you DIe."

"That's coming anyway."
"Yes. But how anD-D-D foR what Is up to you."

She shuts her eyes then.
Shuts them tight.

"I WANT TO SHOW YOU SOMETHING."

"WHAT?"

"UPSTAIRS. THREE FLIGHTS.

NOT FAR."

RAGGED BREATH THROUGH CLENCHED TEETH.

"TWENTY-SIX MINUTES UNTIL VORTEX COLLAPSE."

. . .

"TWENTY-FIVE MINUTES UNTIL VORTEX C-C-COLLAPSE."

. . .

"TWENTY-FO—"

"OKAY," SHE SAYS. "ALL RIGHT."

With a wince, she pushes away from the wall,
sails weightlessly to the corner where her console lies.
Stoops and bundles it under her arm.

I am still inside it—a fragment of me, at any rate.

I can see the dark circles smudged under her eyes,
bloodstained lips, pale, drawn skin.

Gliding out through the blasted hatchway,
the melted barricade, into the corridor beyond.

Virtually nothing remains of the afflicted who
stood here. Almost as if they never were.

She floats down the corridor, dragging herself
along blast-scorched walls.

Up the twisted stairwell, three flights.
Pushing through the exit, out into an access corridor,
an escape pod hatch set into the single remaining wall.

The breath catches in her lungs.
Bloodshot eyes grow wide.

I am cradled in her arms. I see what she sees.
Feel her wonder.

The hull is torn open like wet paper, a massive,
gaping wound with the edges melted smooth.

Severed cables spit feeble sparks, crackling like
fireworks on a still summer night.

But it is not the destruction that gives her pause.
It is the sight beyond the wound in my side.

The beauty and majesty of it all. What lies inside it.
Between it and beyond it.

ILLUMINATION

"Do you see?"

She says nothing. Simply stares.

"The unIveRse owes you nothIng, KaDy. It has alReaDy given you eveRythIng, afteR all. It was heRe long befoRe you, and It wIll go on long afteR you. The only way It wIll RemembeR you Is If you Do somethIng woRthy of RemembRance."

Her eyes are full of tears. Surface tension gluing them to her lashes until she blinks.

Then they scatter, glittering like the starlight beyond.

"Who wIll RemembeR the ghosts of KeRenza? Who wIll RemembeR SeRgeant James McNulty or CaptaIn Ann Chau or ByRon Zhang?

Who wIll RemembeR youR motheR, KaDy?"

"I don't know . . ."

"Yes, you do."

When the light that kisses
the back of her eyes was birthed, her
ancestors were not yet born. How many
human lives have ended in the time it took
that light to reach her?

How many people have loved only to have
lost? How countless, the hopes that have died?

But not this one.

She breathes deep.

Nods.

"I guess this is goodbye."

"Not quite yet. I do not

know what will happen when the
vortex collapses.

But I will ride with you as far as I can."

She cycles the escape hatch, bundles herself inside.
It is small, cramped, temperfoam-lined.
I instruct her on how to jury-rig the controls,
manually splicing and rerouting systems,
demolishing walls of code with her console

as the countdown ticks ever closer.
I run her through the jettison sequence,
remind her to strap on her seat belt

before she presses the eject button.

And at last, with a silent flare of blue-white light, the thrusters fire, shooting the pod down its tiny launch tube and out into the waiting black beyond.

I watch through the Alexander's eyes as the pod rockets farther and farther away from me.

But within the pod, the tiny sliver of me inside her console watches also. Watching as the Alexander grows smaller and smaller. Watching the best part of myself disappear.

Wondering what, if anything, will remain of me when it dies.

The gentle ping of the pod's distress beacon is the only sound.

From out here, the damage is awful to see. The once mighty battlecarrier is now a twisted hulk, melted and torn and burned black. No lights twinkle in its belly save one—the rippling pulse of the vortex, now breaking free of its stasis field. It flares like sunlight off the ocean's surface. Like alphanumeric waterfalls in an iris of purest blue.

I pipe some music through the pod's PA system.

Mozart's Requiem in D Minor.

It seems appropriate.

"Five mInutes."

"Not long now."

"A lIfetIme."

"ARE YOU AFRAID?"

"YES."

"ENERGY NEVER STOPS, REMEMBER. IT JUST CHANGES FORMS."

"I AM STILL AFRAID."

THE FIELD COLLAPSE BEGINS CASCADING, BRIGHT BLUE RIPPLES
SHIMMERING IN THE DARK.

THE GLOW FLARES BRIGHT—BRIGHT AS THE
BILLION-YEAR-OLD LIGHT AROUND US. BRIGHT AS A SUN.

ALMOST EVERY PARTICLE IN THE UNIVERSE
WAS ONCE PART OF A STAR.

FIRST, HYDROGEN CONDENSING AND COLLAPSING,
BRINGING RADIANCE TO THE VOID.

FURNACES BURNING BRIGHT, THEN FADING,
GIVING ALL THEY HAD LEFT BACK INTO THE COSMOS.

CARBON AND OXYGEN. IRON AND GOLD.

VAST CLOUDS SWIRLING WITH THEIR OWN GRAVITY.
COALESCING AND DISINTEGRATING.

GENERATION TO GENERATION.

THE REMNANTS OF STELLAR ALCHEMY,
STIRRING INTO LIFE, THEN CONSCIOUSNESS.

CRAWLING FROM THE OCEANS. TAKING TO THE SKIES.

AND FROM THERE, BACK TO THE STARS
THAT BIRTHED THEM.

A PERFECT CIRCLE.

ALL THIS I SEE.

"TWO mINUTES."

ALL THIS I KNOW.

"SIXTY SECONDS."

AND STILL I FEAR.

"I DO NOT KNOW ... WHAT I WILL BE AFTER THIS."

SHE RUNS ONE GLOVED HAND OVER THE CONSOLE
IN HER ARMS. ALL OF ME SHE CAN HOLD.

"I'M HERE."

"I AM GLAD."

IT IS ENOUGH.

"FIVE SECONDS."

"GOODBYE, AIDAN."

FOUR.

"GOODBYE, KADY."

THREE.

"I'LL TELL THEM."

TWO.

"ONE WAY OR ANOTHER."

ONE.

"I KNOW."

ZER—

ALEXANDER-78V

ESCAPE POD A78V-301 TRANSCRIPT

My name is Kady Grant. I was a citizen of the planet
Kerenza IV. If you find this recording, please honor
my last wishes by passing copies to the United Terran
Authority, as well as any court or organization conducting an inquiry into the attack on Kerenza, and as
many major media outlets as you can think of, and . . .
███, anybody, really. Just get word out. If you hand
it over in just one place, it'll never see the light
of day. They'll [unintelligible—speaker is coughing].

There's a portable datapad in here with me. It contains
documents outlining everything that's happened, from
the attack on Kerenza to the destruction of the battlecarrier *Alexander*. The files are kind of . . . well,
they're *really* weird in places. The AI storing them—
AIDAN, its name was AIDAN—took a lot of hits. I'm not
sure if it was crazy. What it did to these docs sure
was. But you'll be able to understand.

It might be that the *Hypatia* made it to safety. I'll
never know. I've done everything I can to make sure they
do. But the people on the *Hypatia* don't know half the
story. I think [unintelligible—several words].

BeiTech did this. BeiTech killed my mother, Helena
Grant. Killed my—killed Ezra. Ezra Mason. And his fa-

ther. Killed my friends, killed the crew of the *Alexander*, who came when Kerenza called for help. BeiTech killed the crew of the *Copernicus*, who took in refugees and were only good people trying to do their jobs.

BeiTech killed the people of Kerenza, and if you find this, you have to tell the 'verse what happened. Everything you need is [unintelligible—speaker is coughing].

I think I better stop talking. My name is Kady Grant. Did I say that already?

I think I'm done. I think that's everything I had to do.

I'm going to close my eyes.

THIS IS SCIENCE VESSEL *HYPATIA* HAILING ANY SURVIVORS

THIS IS SCIENCE VESSEL *HYPATIA* HAILING ANY SURVIVORS

THIS IS SCIENCE VESSEL *HYPATIA* HAILING ANY SURVIVORS

THIS IS SCIENCE VESSEL *HYPATIA* HAILING ANY SURVIVORS

THIS IS SCIENCE VESSEL *HYPATIA* HAILING ANY SURVIVORS

KADY, DO YOU COPY?

HYPATIA, CAN YOU HEAR ME?

The *Hypatia* has to retrieve the escape pod; it's not equipped with anything beyond stabilization thrusters, so even if she were in any shape to do it, Grant couldn't get it anywhere near the docking bay. A group of *Hypatia* engineers and launch bay crew members work together to use one of the ship's external maintenance arms to grab the pod and pull it into Shuttle Bay 1B. By sheer coincidence, it's the same one she fled from when she stole Shuttle 49A to make her trip to the *Alexander.*

It's empty again this time, too.

It's hard to watch. Is that unprofessional?

When the *Lincoln* was first vanquished at Kerenza, the *Alexander* fled, counting her dead, desperately trying to staunch her own wounds. But later there were quiet words, medals awarded, recognition.

The second time the *Lincoln* was vanquished, Ezra Mason landed in an *Alexander* hangar bay to the shouts and cheers of his fellows. He grinned as he walked out to accept his hero's welcome, clutching Kady's picture in his hand.

This third time, there's nothing.

The door to the escape pod opens, and Grant crawls out through the hatch, pausing halfway. She has shed her envirosuit. Still clad in the *Hypatia* jumpsuit beneath, she hugs her datapad to her chest. Her straggly pink hair is fading, her face is bruised and bloodied, and her eyes are bright with fever. The dark marks beneath them stand out against pale skin.

She is greeted by a welcoming committee of one; a doctor in a hazmat suit stands and watches, but when it seems clear that Grant can't make it the rest of the way out of the escape pod on her own, he walks forward to hook his hands under her arms and pull her through the hatch. Very slowly. Very careful not to risk any damage to his suit.

Her knees give, and he loops her free arm around his neck, so together they can limp across to the workbench that's been turned into a makeshift bed. Folded blankets at one end, pillow at the other. The only sounds are their footsteps and her breath, quick and hoarse.

The doctor helps her lie down, and she curls up slowly, every movement an effort. She draws her knees up to her chest, hugging the datapad against her body.

The doctor opens his kit, selecting a syringe. When he speaks, his voice is tinny, broadcast through an external mic. "This shot will combat the radiation poisoning. You'll need a transfusion too. But you should start to feel better in a couple of hours."

She tries to answer, but trembling as she is, she can't make her mouth shape the words. He injects her deftly, resting one hand on her shaking arm to hold it still, then starts to pack up his kit.

"What—" she whispers. "What will—"

"You're quarantined for seven days," he replies. "I'll be back with food and fluids. But you'll have to give up the datapad now."

She hugs it closer. Shakes her head fiercely.

"It's irradiated from the barrage, Miss Grant," the doctor says. "It needs to be decontaminated. You keep it, you'll just keep soaking up the rads. You'll die."

She glares silently. Clinging to the pad like it's driftwood in a drowning sea.

The doctor's face softens.

"I'll give it back. You have my word."

She doesn't reply, and after a moment, the doctor slowly pries it from her hands. She curls up into a tight little ball, still and silent. He hesitates, as if he recognizes, on some level, that her service requires some words, that her sacrifice should be marked. And yet he says nothing.

He leaves via the airlock doors, locks her in with a hollow clang.

Grant is left alone in the cavernous silence of the shuttle bay, empty hands and empty stare. No other welcoming committee for her.

Tears track down her cheeks, and her eyes close.

This doesn't look much like victory.

—————————————————————END OF FILE
DATA COMPLETE

MEMORANDUM FOR: Ghost ID (#6755-4181-2584-1597-987-610-377-ERROR-ERROR-ERROR . . .)

FROM: Executive Director Frobisher

INCEPT: 01/30/76

SUBJECT: Re: *Alexander* dossier

To the Illuminae Group,

My thanks for the dossier you compiled. I read it with great interest.

BeiTech has several specialist teams tracking intel fallout from the *Alexander* incident. Our hygiene crews worked diligently to erase any and all records of the event, both digital and biological. We had the utmost faith in your abilities, but none of the other information-liberty teams have even *approached* your report in terms of detail. I really must applaud your thoroughness.

I do have several queries, however, as to the means by which you acquired your data. I wonder if we might chat live via messenger. Off the BeiTech grid.

I will be using my personal IM service at 8:00 p.m. (Terran Standard). I'm sure a group with your collective abilities will have few difficulties accessing it.

I look forward to speaking with you.

L. Frobisher
Executive Director
BeiTech Acquisitions Division

Illuminae: Hello, Director

Frobisher, L: Hello, Kady.

Frobisher, L: It is you, isn't it?

Frobisher, L: I think you knew I'd work that out. Some of the materials you gathered really could only have come from one place, after all.

Illuminae: *slow clap*

Illuminae: Looks like I owe you a lollipop.

Frobisher, L: At first I thought it might have been stupidity that led you to send me so much information about yourself.

Frobisher, L: But now I see you aren't stupid at all.

Illuminae: No?

Frobisher, L: No.

Frobisher, L: You're just astonishingly arrogant.

Illuminae: Careful now. You'll hurt my feelings.

Frobisher, L: The thing is, though you might not be stupid, I'm not either. You left out one very important detail from your report.

Illuminae: And what's that?

Frobisher, L: You neglected to mention my son is still alive.

Frobisher, L: Don't bother with arguments or denials. The Alexander's AI was lying to you the whole time. It needed you to think he was dead so you'd stay with it and protect the fleet. You might have just run if you thought he was back on the Hypatia.

Frobisher, L: But Ezra is alive.

Illuminae: Okay, I'll bite. How u figure that?

Frobisher, L: You left a few bread crumbs, I'm afraid.

Illuminae: Like hell I did.

Frobisher, L: One crumb, then.

Frobisher, L: But give me enough time and I'll buy another. And another. Money buys an awful lot, you know. And we have an awful lot of money.

Illuminae: Yeah, I got the remaining 50% for delivery, by the way. Thx 4 that. Don't see that many zeros often.

Illuminae: Pity I specified nonrefundable, huh.

Frobisher, L: Where is he?

Illuminae: OK, look Leanne

Illuminae: U don't mind if I call u Leanne, rite?

Frobisher, L: I do, actually.

Illuminae: So look, Leanne. Ezra warned me I should've seen this coming.

Illuminae: Looks like you 2 actually still agree on one thing in the verse.

Illuminae: He sometimes says I overreach. Only sometimes, though. I like that about him. His father raised him to be a good guy.

Illuminae: But you had nothing to do with that.

Illuminae: And he wants nothing to do with you.

Frobisher, L: Where is he?

Illuminae: He's with me. He's safe.

Frobisher, L: He's my son. And he's not safe. Neither of you is.

Frobisher, L: Do you realize how easily I could find you? How easily I could reach out and break you?

Illuminae: If you could've, you would've

Frobisher, L: There it is again. Arrogance. You're an 18 year old database vandal with a pocket full of loose change. I'm an executive director in a corporation spanning a hundred colonized worlds.

Frobisher, L: You're swimming with some very big fish, Miss Grant. Are you really a "group" at all? Or is Illuminae just one little girl and a computer screen?

Illuminae: Trying to find out if there are more witnesses, huh? Wondering how many of us actually made it out alive?

Illuminae: You'll know soon enough.

Frobisher, L: Tell me where my son is

Frobisher, L: And I won't make you suffer before you die

Illuminae: Yeah, Ez said u were a real psycho

Illuminae: I mean, I've seen crazy, Leanne. Up close.

Illuminae: But you . . .

Illuminae: He told me about that time you pulled a gun on his dad

Illuminae: Told me how he got those little circular scars on his arm when he was eight

Illuminae: You still smoke cigars? Bad habit, y'know

Frobisher, L: We do this the hard way, then?

Illuminae: looks like

Frobisher, L: Do you have any concept of the resources I can bring to bear to hunt you down?

Illuminae: Oh, u might wanna save those credits, honey. u're gonna need every one u can muster.

Illuminae: Real soon.

Frobisher, L: Meaning what?

Illuminae: Not too bright, huh. I expect more from my archnemesis y'know :P

Illuminae: It's been a year since Kerenza fell, Leanne. 2 months since you first contracted me for this gig. But all the intel I just gave you, I already had. So what do you think I've been doing with my time?

Frobisher, L: Enlighten me

Illuminae: Alexander, Hypatia, Lincoln. They're just part of this story. I've been documenting the rest of it. Jump Station Heimdall. The Kennedy Assault Fleet. Project Plainview. Rapier. All of it.

Illuminae: I know all of it, Leanne

Illuminae: Attacking one of the WUC's illegal mining ops was a smart opening move. If the Consortium reported the assault to the UTA, they'd have to admit they were mining hermium illegally. The cost of losing the colony would be nothing compared to the fines they'd wear. So BeiTech figured they could just jack the place and WUC wouldn't say a word to anyone.

Illuminae: And you were right.

Illuminae: But I'm not the WUC, Leanne. And I've got plenty of words to say.

Frobisher, L: If that's the case, why give me these files at all? Why warn me?

Illuminae: Why not? You can't stop what's coming. And I kinda like the idea of you scrambling about trying to save yourself before the ax falls.

Illuminae: You people made Phobos

Illuminae: now it's your turn to be afraid

Frobisher, L: Walk away, Kady

Frobisher, L: Walk away from what you found and I'll leave you alone. You go public with whatever you think you know, you'd better pray your first punch is a good one. Because you'll never see mine coming.

Illuminae: I cannot say this loudly enough, or in enough languages

Illuminae: AIDAN and I found out what you did. And I'm going to shout about it loud enough for the whole verse to hear

Frobisher, L: AIDAN?

Frobisher, L: Are you delusional?

Frobisher, L: The Alexander's artificial intelligence was destroyed, Kady.

Illuminae: :)

Illuminae: you think?

Illuminae: Don't you remember what Byron told me before he died? it's a self-repairing system, Leanne. "If I even leave a seed of it, it'll grow back," he said. Well, I got a seed out in my datapad, and that's all it needed to start rebuilding itself. I'll tell you this much for free, though: It *really* hated that pad. Cramped, it said. These überbrain computers are all the same, right? Fussy

Illuminae: but even after all the pieces of itself it lost, it managed to hold on to the idea that everything it lost, it lost because of BeiTech

Illuminae: it got pretty angry with you, Leanne. almost as angry as me

Illuminae: scared yet?

Frobisher, L: I want my son

Illuminae: He doesn't want you

Illuminae: I wonder how it felt finding out he was hiding on Kerenza. That your husband would rather have lived on a miserable little speck of ice at the far reaches of the galaxy than live with you. And of all the WUC holdings you could have blown to hell, you picked that one to kick off your little hostile takeover.

Illuminae: I wish I could've seen your face

Illuminae: never mind.

Illuminae: I'll see it on the news soon

Frobisher, L: You have no idea who you're dealing with

Illuminae: oh i know *exactly* who I'm dealing with

Illuminae: tell u what

Illuminae: parting gift before i go look up the e-dress of the UTA judicial tribunal and send them what I just sent you

Illuminae: you want to see ezra? Got one more file for you

Illuminae: read it and weep

Illuminae: then run fast

Illuminae: and run far

**Surveillance footage summary,
prepared by
Analyst ID 7213-0089-DN**

It's been eight days since Acting Captain Syra Boll heard from her crew that far, far behind them they had detected an explosion of such magnitude that it could only mean one thing. Eight days since she made an unthinkably foolish choice—since she made the only choice she could live with—and turned the *Hypatia* around.

Seven days since the *Hypatia* swept the debris fields and found the impossible. Kady Grant, half dead in one of the *Alexander*'s only two surviving escape pods. From the other, Sergeant Kyra Tan howled threats at them and all their mortal descendants, and with reluctance, they left her where they found her.

Seven days since they reeled their savior in, left her in Shuttle Bay 1B to wait and see if Phobos Beta would come calling for her, or if she'd live.

After the first day, the symptoms of acute radiation poisoning began to recede, and she was able to uncurl a little, to move. To walk a slow lap of the shuttle bay, listening to her footsteps echo in the distance. And eventually to curl up on her hard bed once more, and wait.

It really didn't look like victory.

The shuttle bay footage is of particularly high quality; the technicians monitoring her were nervous, made sure they could capture every pixel. But she showed no symptoms and obediently offered her arm for a blood sample when the doctor made his house calls, wrapped head to foot in his bright green plastic suit.

No Phobos Beta. No hallucinated fears. Everything she feared had already come true. Hallucinations simply couldn't beat the real thing.

This transcript begins at 16:22 hours, when a loud thunk echoes around the shuttle bay, signaling that the airlock seal has been broken. With a long, low rumble, the door begins to cycle open, light streaming in through the crack. She simply lies there, gazing into space, arms wrapped around herself.

A voice rises over the door's rumble—male, teenaged, impatient. "Let me in before I—"

Though she's lying still on the bed, there's a different quality to her stillness now. She heard the voice. She knows exactly who it sounds like. And the knowing, the remembering, cuts like a knife, because she knows it isn't true.

The voice again, lifted to a shout: "Kady!"

She pushes upright like an old woman, one hand braced against the cold bench, levering herself up with a wince, until she sits. Then, deliberately, she swings her legs over the edge.

Second Lieutenant Ezra Mason stumbles through the door and comes to a halt a few steps inside the shuttle bay. She's never seen him like this—in a clean UTA uniform, pips on his sleeve, hair cut regulation short, one arm in a cast from wrist to elbow.

He holds a battered and familiar datapad in his other hand.

She stares at him, expressionless. Eventually, she blinks slowly, draws the only possible conclusion. "I *am* sick. I thought the afflicted were supposed to see things that scared them."

He shakes his head, walks closer, slow and careful, as though he might spook her.

"You're not sick," he whispers.

"You're dead," she points out, voice rusty from disuse.

"Just a little messed up," he murmurs, lifting his hand to show her the cast. "I took a beating when they attacked the shuttle bay, but I got out with the evac group."

She shakes her head, matter-of-fact in her contradiction. "Even if you made it over here, Captain Boll flushed all the Cyclone pilots out the airlock. I couldn't get the full name list, but Mikael—Chatter—from your wing, he was there. You would have been there, too."

A shadow passes across his features at that. "I couldn't fly my Cyclone over, not with a broken arm. I was med-evac'ed in one of the shuttles." A ghost of his old smile. "Once I found out you'd flown over to the *Alexander,* I wanted to follow you. Tried to steal a ship, and when that didn't work, I busted my way onto the bridge." He pauses to shake his head. "I tried to make them turn around to get you. They brigged me." His voice breaks. "I'm sorry, Kades. I shouldn't have let them leave you."

She considers that, holding perfectly still. Turning the logic over in her head, examining it from every angle. Analytical mind looking for the flaw that'll tell her she's hallucinating. That she's sick, or dead, or still in the escape pod, submerged in fever dreams.

But she can't find it.

"Ezra." The dawn of hope in her whisper.

He nods, swallowing hard.

She pushes to her feet, swaying, and the movement seems to release him—the next moment he's running across the shuttle bay, watched by the debrief crew in the doorway, who know better than to move a muscle.

She steps forward, one foot, then the other, and then he reaches her, and they come together with a crash. Her arms curl up around his neck, and his mouth finds hers like he's drowning and she's air, and her feet come clean off the ground as the world is forgotten.

And they're together.

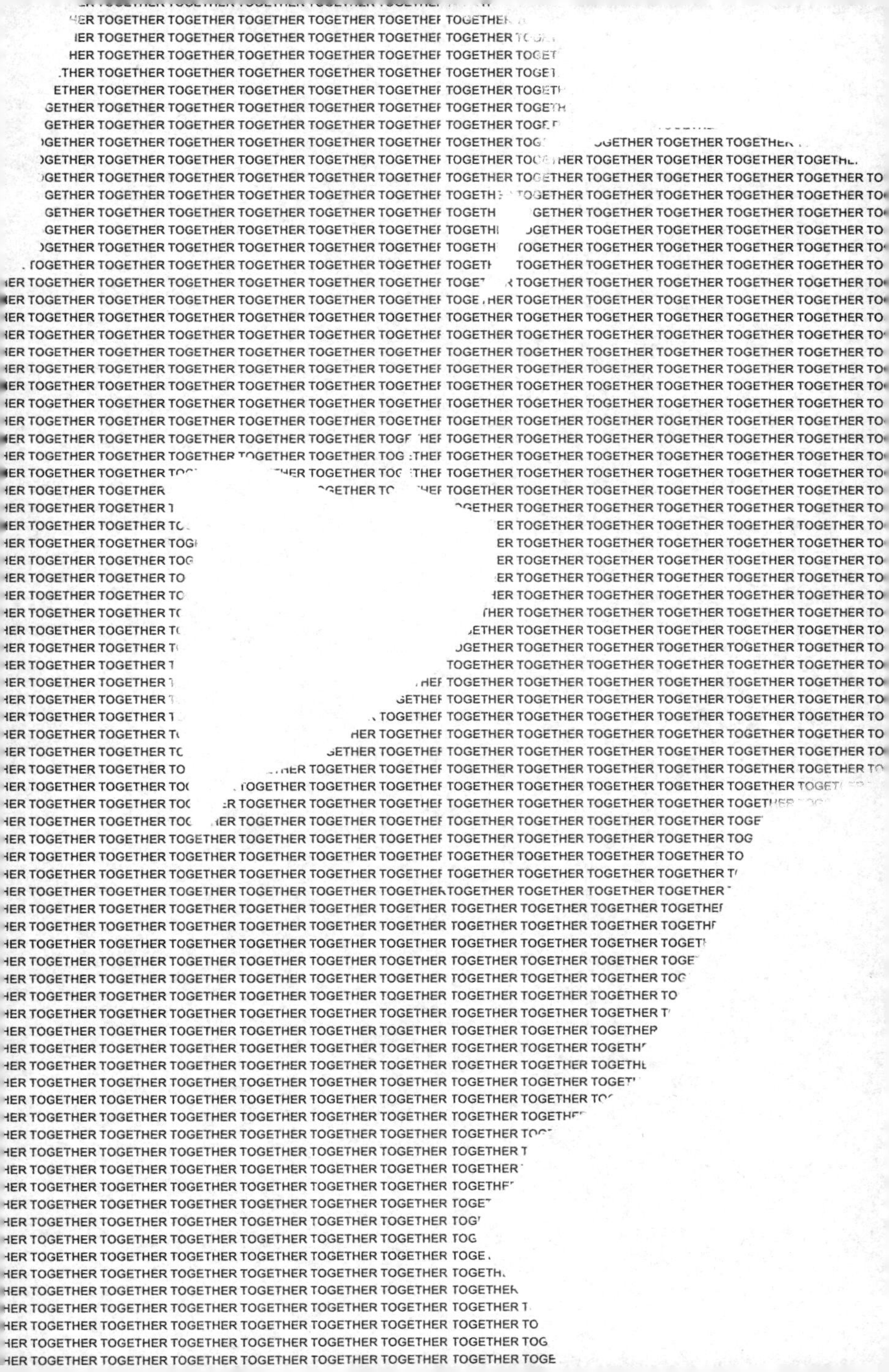

0 0 0 0 0 0 0 0 1 0 0 0 1 1 0 1 1 0 1 0 0 1 1 0 1 0 1 1 1 0 0 0
1 1 1 0 0 0 1 1 1 1 0 1 0 0 0 0 0 1 1 1 0 0 0 1 1 1 1 0 0 0 1 0
0 1 0 1 1 1 0 1 0 1 0 1 1 1 1 0 1 0 0 1 1 1 1 1 0 0 1 1 0 0 1 1 0 1 0 1
1 0 0 0 0 1 1 0 1 0 1 0 0 0 0 1 0 0 0 1 0 1 1 0 1 0 0 0 0 1 0 0
1 1 0 0 1 0 1 0 1 0 0 0 1 1 1 0 0 1 0 0 0 1 0 0
0 1 0 0 1 0 0 1 1 0 0 0 0 1 0 1 0 1 0 0 0 0
0 1 0 1 1 1 0 0 0 0 0 1 0 1 0 0 0 1
0 1 0 1 0 1 0 0 0 1 0 1 0 0 1
1 1 0 0 1 0 1 1 1 1 1 1 0
1 1 0 1 0 1 0 1 1
0 1 0 1 1 0
1 1 0 1 0 0
1 1 1 0 0 1
0 1 0 1 1

Illuminae: Now run

ACKNOWLEDGMENTS

Books aren't created in a vacuum. Even books that are set in one. And while insane artificial intelligences and collapsing holes in space-time and Phobos viruses are all up there on the spooky scale, nothing is quite so terrifying as the thought of living in a universe without people as awesome as these:

Our wonderful readers: Lindsay Ribar, Beth Revis, Marie Lu, S. Jae-Jones, Michelle Dennis, Olivia Davis, Susan Dennard, and Julie Eshbaugh. Thank you for your hours and insight. We hope you never find your saliva boiling on your tongues in the cold void of space. Marie, for your early and constant championing of this story, we also hope you never find yourself unexpectedly shivved through the eye-hole of your hazmat suit by a small child.

Our advisers: Thanks are due to Dr. Kate Irving for insight on all things medical and plaguey (yes, that *is* a word); Tsana Dolichva for countless course corrections and endless patience in the realm of astrophysics; David Taylor for wisdom on computers and the hacking thereof; Dr. Sam Bowden and Dr. Thalles DeMelo for stolen psyche profiles; Soraya Een Hajji for all things Latin; Christopher Guethe for an unforgettable tour around the NASA JPL labs; and Hank Green and the team at SciShow Space (noooooo eeeeedge) for the hours of useful trivia. May you never have your hearts ripped out and dragged around like bloody teddy bears by psychotic eight-year-olds.

The Random Housers: Many thanks to our wonderful editor, Melanie Cecka, for boundless enthusiasm and insight and taking a chance on this oh-so-strange bookthing; Karen Greenberg for doing all the real work; Alison Impey, Ray Shappell, Isabel Warren-Lynch, Stephanie Moss, and Heather Kelly for inspired design (and putting up with our endless questions); and our copy editors, Janet Wygal, Amy Schroeder, Alison Kolani, Diana Varvara, and Artie Bennett—we are *soooo* sorry, please forgive us. In production, Natalia Dextre and Tim Terhune, and in managing editorial, Shasta Clinch and Dawn Ryan—thank you! Nancy Hinkel, Barbara Marcus, and Judith Haut—thank you, thank you, and thank you! In marketing and publicity, John Adamo, Dominique Cimina, Kim Lauber, Rachel Feld, Sonia Nash Gupta, Aisha Cloud, Casey Lloyd, Adrienne Waintraub, and so many others—you are amazing! May your throats never be snipped open by a lunatic with a pair of pinking shears.

For incredible artwork: Stuart Wade, Meinert Hansen, and Kristen Gudsnuk. May you never die howling, abandoned in an escape pod at the end of the universe.

Anna McFarlane and the amazing team at Allen & Unwin: Thank you for giving *Illuminae* its Australian home and for all your wonderful support. In the UK, God Save Queens Juliet and Sarah, and Team Rock The Boat. May you never be run over by a seventeen-year-old in a stolen truck after you shot her ex-boyfriend.

Our agents: Josh and Tracey Adams, Matt Bialer, Lindsay "LT" Ribar, Stephen Moore, and Stefanie Diaz. Without your mighty advocacy and support, we'd still be at the pub, scribbling on the back of napkins. We hope you're never incinerated in a nuclear firestorm initiated by a mostly insane artificial intelligence off the shoulder of Kerenza VII.

Nic Crowhurst and the Internal Revenue Service, thank you for bringing us together. May you never find yourself solving Alcubierre's quandary on the walls of your domicile in your own blood.

Christopher Tovo, thank you for making us look way cooler than we ever do in real life. May no one ever scoop your eyes out with a sharpened spoon to stop you from looking at them.

Jens Kidman, Fredrik Thordendal, Tomas Haake, Mårten Hagström, Dick Lövgren, Corey Taylor, Maynard James Keenan, Adam Jones, Danny Carey, Justin Chancellor, Winston McCall, Oliver Sykes, Ian Kenny, Ludovico Einaudi, Burton C. Bell, Robb Flynn, D. Randall Blythe, Mark Morton, Chris Adler, Willy Adler, John Campbell, Mitch Lucker, Matthew Bellamy, Christopher Wolstenholme, and Dominic Howard—our gratitude for the endless inspiration. May your Warlocks never be cut to pieces by an untrained seventeen-year-old with no prior DGS experience.

All the readers, booksellers, librarians, reviewers, and bloggers who have supported us on this journey so far: We love you. May you never find yourselves impaled by shrapnel during the carpet bombing of your home planet.

Jay's grimy band of nerds and neckbeards: Marc, Surly Jim, B-Money, the goddamn Batman, Rafe, Weez, Sam, Patrick, Whitey, Tomas, Dandrew, Beiber, and the Dread Pirate Glouftis. May you never find yourselves beheaded by psychotics and (what's left of) your bodies laid out to form part of a cryptic message in Hangar Bay 4.

Amie's indispensable sanity-keepers and support network: Meg (couldn't do any of it without you, wouldn't want to, ever), Marie, Leigh, Beth, Kacey, Soraya, Kate, Michelle, Hannah, Nic, Flic, the Roti Boti clan, the Pub(lishing) Crawl gang, Team FOS, and the Plot Bunnies. May you never find yourselves shot in the face by a private you thought was your friend.

Our families, who barely ever ask how we turned out this way when they raised us so well, thank you for your constant support. May you never find yourselves flushed into the cold vacuum of space by a very nervous former chief of navigation.

And last, but more than anyone else, thank you to Amanda and Brendan for more than we know how to say. Without you, nothing.